STRANGERS

By the same author
Forest of Souls

CARLA BANKS

Strangers

HarperCollins*Publishers*

Harper
An Imprint of HarperCollins*Publishers*
77–85 Fulham Palace Road, London W6 8JB

www.harpercollins.co.uk

Published by HarperCollins 2007

1

A catalogue record for this book
is available from the British Library

ISBN-10: 0-00-719212-6
ISBN-13: 978-0-00-719212-0

Typeset in Meridien by Palimpsest Book Production Limited,
Grangemouth, Stirlingshire

Printed in Great Britain by
Clays Ltd, St Ives plc

Mixed Sources
Product group from well-managed
forests and other controlled sources
www.fsc.org Cert no. TT-COC-2139
© 1996 Forest Stewardship Council
FSC

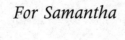

For Samantha

Acknowledgements

With many thanks to the people who helped me when I was researching this book, particularly the Saudis who offered me advice about and insight into a culture that is very different from my own. Riyadh is a complex and continually changing city. I hope the inhabitants will forgive me for the changes I have made to its geography. I'd also like to thank Teresa Chris for her support and encouragement, Eileen Fauset for reading the manuscript and my editors Julia Wisdom and Anne O'Brien.

And of course, as always, Ken.

PART ONE

1

Haroun is dead.

The desert kingdom has taken him away from me.

Riyadh, Saudi Arabia, April 2004

The message had come through earlier that morning:
It's today.

Joe Massey left his apartment in the northern suburbs and drove south towards the old city. The roads were busy. The traffic careered past him with blithe disregard for the law or for safety. Saudis lived with a different sense of their own mortality. The sky was almost white, and the sun glanced back from the surface of the road, stabbing into his eyes. He could feel the headache starting behind his temples.

He slowed as he approached the junction, ignoring the chorus of car horns that greeted his manoeuvre. He pulled in to the car park behind the al-Masmak fort, a relic of old Arabia standing in the centre of the modern city that had sprung from the desert only decades before. His car slid neatly into the last remaining gap between two SUVs. The city was thronging with weekend shoppers, with visitors – and today, with sightseers.

He pushed open his door, and the sun hit him with a force that made him reel. It burned into his uncovered face, trying to peel the flesh away from his cheekbones, to burn through his upper lip.

He checked his watch. It was half past eleven. He could feel the sweat starting on his scalp and the itch between his shoulder blades that told him he had been seen, he was observed. The coffee he had drunk earlier tasted sour in his mouth.

As he left the car park, the narrow streets beckoned him, the dark heart of the city; the souk, where the fragrance of spices filled the air and the brilliance of fabric and rugs and brass glowed in the shadowy recesses of the stalls.

He had walked through those narrow streets often enough. But not today. Today the crowds were heading in another direction. He could feel their suppressed excitement like a charge of electricity through him. Voices called, people jostled past him. The smell of meat cooking caught his throat and made him want to gag. In the intense heat, he felt cold and dizzy, and he made himself pause and wait until the darkness at the edge of his vision subsided.

Then it was noon and the call to prayer sounded from the minarets. The shops closed and the streets emptied. He sat quietly, waiting. The crowds would be back, soon enough. Once the people began to return to the street, he stood up and started walking. He didn't need directions. They were all going to the same place.

Progress was easy now. He just had to relax and let the crowd carry him. Once, when he was a child, he had gone swimming off the Cornish coast. The current had taken him. One moment he was floating in the cool sea, rocked by the ebb and flow, next he was being drawn out, away from the beach, away from the shore, away from his family and safety. He'd tried to swim against it, then he had stopped fighting. The current had carried him round the bay and then released him into the gentle waters near another beach where he had waded ashore, unhurt. He closed his eyes, and let his memories of the sea overtake him.

When he opened his eyes again, he had arrived at his destination. The last time he had been here, it had been evening. The spacious, blue-tiled square had been full of people who had gathered to meet, to talk and to drink tea. Children had raced across the open space, expending their energies in shouts and screams.

Now, it was empty. He could see the police standing on the corners, see their eyes searching the crowd as they positioned themselves, their batons swinging casually. He had dressed to blend in, wearing the ghutra, the ubiquitous red-and-white chequered scarf, and a thobe, the long white robe that served as a practical defence against the sun. Today, he had covered his eyes with dark glasses to conceal their tell-tale blue.

The air smelled of sweat and spices, and the staccato jab of Arabic attacked his ears. His mind escaped to another childhood memory, to the fair that came to the town every year with its crowds, the laughter, the shouts of the stallholders, the tinny music that meant freedom and summer. The smell of hotdogs and onions.

And now he could smell death. He had a sudden picture of Haroun sitting across the table from him as they talked over coffee, his dark eyes bright with laughter. *Joseph!* Haroun's voice spoke in his ear. Haroun was the only person who had ever called him by his full name. *It is good to see you.*

It's good to see you, too . . . But the voices in his head faltered and faded. *Joseph* . . .

The crowd pressed forward and he went with it until he found himself in the shadow of a palm tree which gave him some relief from the sun. The empty square opened up in front of him. His eyes were drawn to the stones, blue-grey in the hard light, with intricate, interlaid patterns. There was no mark, no stain.

The hands on his watch barely seemed to move, and yet he had a sense of time running past him, faster and faster, as if there was some way he could stop it, as if someone was saying, *Now! Do it now! Now!* But it was too late. It had always been too late. He could feel his heart beating fast, the breath catching in his throat. *Haroun!*

Then the police were there, pushing the crowd back, back. Just for a second, he wanted to let himself go with them, to be carried to the back where the deadly stones would be hidden. *Be careful!* he had warned Haroun, but his warning had been half-laughing, a warning against the minor carelessnesses with which Haroun met the vagaries of life. *Joseph, you worry! Don't worry!*

And now this was the last thing he could do.

He held his ground until there was nothing between him and the waiting square but the line of armed police. The crowd closed in behind him, and the possibility of choice was gone. He saw that a tarpaulin had been laid out on the ground, less than twenty yards away from him. In the heat, a wave of cold washed over him and once again the blackness threatened at the edge of his vision.

And then two vans approached the square. One was unmarked. The other, incongruously, was an ambulance. They drew up outside the mosque. Armed men climbed out. They turned and stood by as the doors were held open, and a man was led out. He was blindfolded and shackled, and he stumbled as he stepped down on to the ground. His head lifted towards the vast emptiness of the sky above him as if he were straining to have one last sight of it.

'Haroun.' In his mind he heard the familiar

laugh and he felt his arms move in involuntary expectation of an exuberant embrace. But the blindfold meant that he would never look into that dark gaze again.

It was no more than a whisper, but the shackled man stiffened, and his head turned, blindly searching the crowd. Then he was forced to his knees, facing the holy city, facing Mecca. A man read out loud from a sheet of paper – the charges against the condemned man. Another man, dark-skinned and powerful, stepped forward. He carried a long, flat sword. He stood behind the kneeling man. Everything froze between one second and the next.

Then time seemed to jump as the bowed man jerked upright and the sword swung round on the indrawn breath of the crowd. The blood was a red fountain from the neck and poured from the severed head on to the tarpaulin.

Allah Akbar! The roar from the crowd. God's will is done.

His stomach contracted. His legs could barely hold his weight. The square seemed to darken in front of him, and the edges of his vision faded to blackness. He couldn't pass out. Not here. Not now. He let his shoulders slump, breathed slowly and deeply until his head began to clear.

He knew, even though he had only seen the weapon and not the hand that wielded it, that he had just witnessed a murder.

2

Tuesday was a bad day. It started out quite promis-
ingly, but after that it was downhill all the way.
When Roisin's alarm clock went off at six thirty,
the sky was leaden and heavy with clouds. By the
time she had showered, the first spatters of rain
were already hitting the window.

She went through to the kitchen and tipped
some muesli into a bowl. The cramped kitchen
still contained the original fittings from when the
flat was built in the early sixties, a fact that would
probably add enormous value when the taste for
retro cycled through a few more years. The pots
of herbs she kept on the window sill contrasted
with the red of the formica tops to make it look
like an old-fashioned Italian restaurant, and her
eclectic collection of pans, the bottles of oil and
the usual half-full bottle of red wine added to the
effect. She didn't much like the flat – a box in an

ex-council block – but the kitchen always felt warm and homey.

A year before, she had been in Warsaw. She and her then partner, Michel, had been about to open their own language school. They planned to teach English and Spanish through the year, and offer summer schools to students from all over the world.

Roisin had provided the start-up costs, sinking her savings and a small legacy from her father into the venture. Michel was to provide the financial backing for the first year of running the business until they had got themselves established in what was a competitive market. But the whole enterprise had gone sour.

She made herself stop thinking about it – there was no point in wasting energy in futile anger. She dumped her bowl into the sink and ran some water over it. She blasted her hair with the drier, which turned it into a blonde tangle. She swore and attacked it with the comb then pulled on her jogging gear and hurried down the stairs of the apartment block, wanting to get out before the rain began in earnest, before traffic really got going and tainted the air with fumes and noise. She knocked on the door of the ground-floor flat directly below hers.

There was a flurry of barks, and she heard grumbling as someone shuffled to answer her knock. A warm fug drifted out, a mix of dust, mildew and unwashed dog. George, the old man who lived

in the flat, observed her without obvious enthusiasm.

'Rosie,' he said. He yawned and scratched his
chest. 'Thought I heard you banging about up
there. Suppose you want a cuppa, now you've got
me up?' His dog, Shadow, scratched at the wall
behind him and tried to push his muzzle past the
old man's legs, whimpering with excitement.
'Geddown,' he said.

'I'll make it.' George's tea was a bright orange
brew that he sweetened with condensed milk. She
went into his kitchen before his 'I can do that,
thank you, missy,' could stop her.

The kitchen was small – a mirror image of hers
– and spartanly neat. A loaf of Mother's Pride was
on the worktop next to a carton of margarine, a
bag of sugar and a tin of milk. She filled the blackened gas kettle – he refused to have anything to
do with the brand new electric one his niece had
bought him – and lit the hob. Then she waited
interminable minutes for the kettle to boil and
made them both tea.

He spooned in enough sugar to make her teeth
ache and retired to his chair. Shadow laid a
pleading chin on his knee. 'Geddown,' he said
again, carefully tipping some of his drink into the
empty dog dish by his chair. Shadow's plump sleek-
ness contrasted with his master's thin frame.
George, who was in his eighties, looked more frail
now than when she had first met him six months
ago when she had knocked on his door to sort

out a mail mix-up caused by the postman's inability to tell the difference between 13 and 31.

'I'm going for a run. I thought I'd borrow Shadow, if that's OK.'

He surveyed the day outside the heavily netted window. 'Running in this? You daft or what?' He shrugged. 'He may as well make himself useful.' Shadow's tail thumped on the ground. She and George kept up the pretence that he was doing her a favour by letting her take the dog when she went running. His knees were arthritic and their walks were sedate affairs. She waited as he finished his drink, listening as he gave her his take on the day. He probably wouldn't talk to another person before she came back from work and dropped in to say hello. Then she clipped on the dog's lead and left.

With the excited mongrel dragging her along, she went past the rows of front doors and stepped out into the chaos that was King's Cross. The rain had stopped for the moment, but its fall had left the air smelling fresh, even in this polluted corner of the city. The traffic was starting to build up, people were heading towards the bus stops and the stations, and she could hear the rumble of heavy machinery and the shouts of the workmen from the building site. She walked down St Pancras Road, restraining Shadow until she reached the canal, then she let the eager dog off the lead and followed him down the steps on to the tow path.

Silence closed round her. She could smell the

dankness of the water and the musty fragrance of leaves that had lain rotting since autumn as Shadow pushed through the undergrowth. He came bounding back with a stick in his mouth and deposited it at Roisin's feet, shaking the wet off his coat. Then he cast his eye in the direction of the canal, and began gathering his muscles for the leap. She issued a sharp instruction. He gave her a sideways glance, as if trying to decide whether to obey her, but maybe he, too, thought the water looked uninviting, and he danced away up the tow path.

The grey coldness of the water reminded her suddenly of the Tyne as it ran through her home city of Newcastle. The river had been the back-drop to her teens. When she was seventeen, she and her best friend Amy, high on pills, had climbed through the metal girders of the Tyne Bridge so Roisin could take a photograph of the mist on the water. She couldn't remember now why they had decided to do such a thing, but she could remember Amy gripping her arm and bracing herself against a stanchion as Roisin leant out over the dizzying drop so she could angle her camera to get the picture she wanted. The memory made her laugh and a man, passing the other way, gave her a worried sideways glance and quickened his pace.

Shadow was running ahead now, so she broke into a slow jog, letting her mind wander as the rhythm took over. The tow path in the early morning was like a club. The same joggers and dog walkers used it every day, and the London convention of avoiding eye contact and not acknowledging fellow human beings didn't operate down here. She nodded 'Good morning' to familiar faces as she passed them, calling to Shadow as he got involved in the rituals of dog greeting that her father in an uncharacteristic moment of crudity had dubbed 'ring-a-ring-a-arses'. She suppressed another laugh at the memory.

The tow path was wide and well paved here, overlooked by offices, expensive apartment blocks, and tall, red-brick buildings that rose an improbable height from the water. When she reached Camden Lock she stopped to catch her breath, leaning against the railings that surrounded it. There was a boat in, and she watched the boatman bracing himself against the foot grips to push the gates open. The water gushed in and his boat began its slow rise.

Another jogger was coming along the path towards her. As he came closer, she recognized him as a recently familiar face, a man who had joined the morning run a couple of weeks ago. He was tall with dark hair and an attractive smile. He had the tan of someone who had recently returned from a hot and sunny climate. She'd found herself wishing, once or twice, that their routes would coincide when they were going in the same direction.

She saw recognition on his face, and they exchanged smiles, then he was past her and moving away down the tow path with an easy lope that suggested he could run for miles yet. She watched him for a moment, then looked round for Shadow, who seemed to have vanished. She called sharply and he came bounding out from nowhere. As she watched in horror, he cannoned into the man's legs, and they teetered together at the edge of the deep, icy water. Then the man was sprawling on the ground warding off the frightened dog who was barking in his face.

'Christ!' She ran up to him. Her heart was hammering with delayed shock. 'I am *so* sorry. That was my fault. Shut up, Shadow. Are you OK?' She clipped on the dog's lead. Shadow barked again and bristled with hostility. 'Shut *up*! Here, let me help you.'

He was trying to get to his feet, his face clenching suddenly in pain as he put his weight on his foot. He took the arm she proffered to help him get his balance and tried his leg a couple of times. 'I think it's just twisted,' he said, after a moment. He looked pale under his tan, and she could see him trying to disguise the pain he was obviously feeling. 'Shit,' he said as he tried again. 'Sorry.'

'Don't apologize. It was my dog that knocked you over. I should have checked where he was before I called him.'

'Is he all right?' He reached out a hand to Shadow. 'Here. Good boy.' Shadow barked mistrustfully then fell silent as the man ruffled his fur. 'You didn't mean it, did you?' He balanced carefully, keeping the weight off his leg. He was looking down at her and as he smiled, she could see the laughter lines round his eyes. 'I may as well take the opportunity to introduce myself. I'm Joe.' He held out his hand.

'Roisin,' she said.

'Ro*sheen*. I like that. Where does it come from?'

'It's Irish.' She didn't want to go into the complexity of her background, so she said quickly, 'I've seen you here before.'

He nodded. 'I started work at the hospital a couple of weeks ago. I've been meaning to get acquainted, so it's an ill wind, right, dog?' He addressed this remark to Shadow, who hung back behind Roisin, observing the scene dubiously.

'This is Shadow,' Roisin said.

His smile broadened. 'I kind of thought it might be. Shit!' He stumbled again as he put more weight on his leg. 'Sorry.'

'You need to get that seen to. Come on, let me help you up to the road. We should be able to get a taxi.'

'No need. If I can just get up here, I can make it to the tube at Camden Town.'

She didn't think he would be able to manage even that short distance. 'I'll walk with you. Shouldn't you go to A & E?'

'And spend the morning waiting to be told I've twisted my ankle? I'll get it checked out at work.'

But he accepted her help up the steps, resting his arm on her shoulder to keep his balance. Once

16

they were at the top, he stopped, using the wall for support. 'Look, I'll be fine. You don't need to hang around. You must have things to do.'

'I feel responsible,' she said.

'Well, don't. I should have been looking where I was going. Tell you what, let me buy you a drink later on, and I can give you an update. Give me your number.'

'OK. I'd like that. But it'd better be me buying.' She indicated the subdued dog.

'Poor old lad.' He reached down and tugged Shadow's ear. He waited as she scribbled her number down, then glanced at the paper and put it in his pocket. 'I'll call you tonight,' he said. She watched him as he hobbled away down the road towards the tube station, then she turned back to the canal. If she didn't get a move on, she was going to be late.

That was the good bit.

When she got into the college where she taught English to overseas students, she was greeted by the news that one of her colleagues was off sick and she had to pick up two of his classes, groups of engineering students who combined a poor grasp of English with an insistence that they knew exactly how they should be taught, and who tested Roisin's not very enduring patience for the next five hours. It was a comedown for someone who had come close – very close – to owning her own language school.

But those plans had come to grief in the bitter

17

war that Michel was fighting with his ex-wife. Their joint venture had somehow become entangled in the proceedings, and they had had no option but to sell, and sell at a loss. Michel had taken half of the money that was left. That was the law – the business assets were in their joint names. The fact that this had been Roisin's money, and that very little of his money had yet been committed, was irrelevant. She had trusted him, and he had let her down.

So now she was in London with a mortgage that she could barely afford on a run-down flat in the middle of a building site, keeping her head above water with part-time contracts, and trying to decide what to do next. Teaching English to disruptive young engineers hadn't been part of her life plan, but just at the moment she had no choice.

She left work in a bad temper and with a headache that wasn't improved by long delays on the Northern Line. When she finally got home, she realized she'd missed the date for paying off her credit card and would incur a hefty interest payment.

And, of course, the canal-side man didn't phone.

3

Roisin wasn't surprised when the man she'd met on the tow path didn't call her. Nor was she surprised when she didn't see him the next time she went running with Shadow. She was no expert, but it had looked to her like a more serious injury than a sprain and she assumed he was probably housebound and had had more time to think over the matter of her culpability.

She mentioned the episode to friends over a drink at the weekend. They were intrigued, and then disappointed when the story fizzled out into 'And I never heard from him again.' Roisin hadn't been involved with anyone since the disastrous end of her relationship with Michel, and they thought it was time she tested the waters. 'Oh, come on,' she said when they began speculating about ways she could contact the elusive Joe, 'I tripped him up and probably broke his leg. No wonder he doesn't want to see me. I'm more likely to get a letter from his solicitor.' When pressed, she was prepared to admit that she found him attractive.

Old George was just as bad, but for different reasons. 'That bloke had the guts to call you yet?' he asked her every time she went to collect Shadow or to join him for a cup of poisonous tea. She had told him about the episode when she returned the dog, and he'd made adverse comments about her lack of care and foresight. 'Poor old lad,' he'd said under his breath as he'd checked his dog anxiously for cuts and bruises. The man on the tow path was now 'the man who kicked Shadow' and who should have the courage to face the music. But the mysterious Joe seemed to have vanished.

She put it out of her mind. She was busy at work, but the job was only temporary, a stop-gap that she had taken without too much thought under the pressing necessity of earning some money. She had to start making decisions about what to do next. Her career path had been leading up to the moment when she had the funds, the expertise and the credibility to start her own business, and the way the rug had been pulled from underneath her had left her floundering. She had to decide whether to start again, to see if she could get some more money together and raise some more loans, go through the web of bureaucracy that all the permissions required, or if she should resign herself to the admitted security but endless frustration of working for other people in large, unyielding institutions.

Some of the options were attractive. The European universities were always eager for experienced language teachers and offered a whole field of academic work she'd barely explored. Beijing University was actively recruiting, as were universities in Korea and Japan. She'd never been to the Far East and was curious to travel there, but she had a life in Europe she wasn't quite ready to give up. There was also the complication of her mother.

Roisin was adopted, and all her life she had been aware of her mother's fear that one day she would walk away and declare an allegiance to a different past. Since her father's death, this anxiety seemed to have grown and become a factor that Roisin had to weave into all her plans and considerations. 'Why don't you come back to Newcastle, pet?' had been the most recent theme. Roisin loved her mother and wanted to help her settle into a new life, but she wasn't prepared to go back home and live with her.

So she didn't really have time to brood about a phone call that had not been forthcoming.

Spring was late arriving. London pulled a grey blanket over its head and rained. The buildings seemed to grow darker and the streets were sodden and filthy. Her morning runs with Shadow became an ordeal rather than a pleasure – for her at least. For Shadow, there was no such thing as bad weather – there was just weather and it was all good.

She was back in her flat one Saturday morning, rubbing her hair dry and warming her frozen hands round a cup of coffee, when her phone buzzed in her pocket. She pulled it out and checked the number. No one she knew. 'Hello?'

'Roisin? You probably don't remember me. It's Joe. Joe Massey. I tripped over your dog and nearly ended up in the canal.'

'Of course I remember. How are you?' She felt ridiculously pleased.

'Look, I'm sorry I haven't been in touch before. I lost your number. I thought I must have dropped it when I was sorting out my money on the tube. I wasn't concentrating too much that day. I thought I was going to have to wait until I was fit enough to get back on the tow path, but I just found it.'

'That's OK. How's your ankle?'

'I tore a ligament – it's not too bad now. Look, I owe you a drink. I probably owe you dinner by now. Could we meet? I don't suppose you're free tonight?'

She was. She'd planned to spend the evening catching up with some of her outstanding work, but dinner with Joe Massey seemed a much more attractive option. They agreed to meet that evening.

Roisin dressed carefully for their date. Most of her clothes were things she'd bought for work and they all looked too sober and businesslike. In the end, she opted for trousers – hip-hugging with a

22

wide belt – and a green top that heightened the colour of her eyes. Her hair was blessed with being naturally curly and – with a bit of help – naturally blonde. She put on boots that added a couple of inches to her height. She could remember helping Joe up the steps by Camden Lock, her head barely reaching his shoulder.

They'd agreed to meet in Camden Town – the scene of the crime. She wondered if he would look the way she remembered him, or if her eyes would pass over him, seeing only some stranger, but as she walked towards the station, she recognized him at once. He was standing under the canopy, reading a folded newspaper. He was wearing glasses, and his dark hair was damp from the fine drizzle that had been falling. When he glanced up and saw her, his smile lit up his face.

'Roisin,' he said. She could see the approval in his eyes as he studied her, and felt an answering warmth. He'd dressed up for the occasion as well, wearing a light mac over a suit that looked well cut to fit his tall, rangy frame.

He was still moving with a slight limp, and she suggested that they go to a café bar she knew that was fairly close to the station, but he shook his head, putting his hand lightly on her arm. 'I booked us a table,' he said, flagging down a taxi. He directed the driver to Holborn and a small bistro that welcomed them with the yellow glow of lights and the buzz of conversation.

Afterwards, she couldn't remember much about

the food that they'd eaten. What she could remember was that they'd talked. He came from Liverpool, he told her. He'd grown up there, but he couldn't wait to get away. 'It's a good city now,' he said, 'but then . . . it was dying. I came south, to London, as soon as I could.'

She told him about her childhood in the North East, about the beauty and the wildness of the countryside, and the city where she had grown up. 'I still like to go back. My mother's there, and, I don't know, there's something . . .'

He was listening quietly, his eyes on her face. 'It's still home?' he suggested.

She laughed. 'I suppose it is.'

'I don't feel like that about Liverpool,' he said.

She took the opportunity to turn the conversation round to him. 'Does everyone call you Joe, or are you Joseph sometimes? I don't know any . . .' Her voice trailed away.

His face had changed, gone cold and distant. Then he seemed to remember where he was and gave a rather forced laugh. 'No. I've only ever been Joe.'

He was a pathologist, he told her, with a research interest in foetal medicine and neo-natal development. 'That's when it all happens,' he said. 'In a way, the path of your life is mapped out for you in those few months. After that, it's downhill all the way.' He didn't look too depressed about it. 'It's a bit like computer software. Leave a bug in there – most people have

24

one or two – and it will probably kill you in the end.'

'Like a predilection for tripping over dogs and falling in canals?'

'Don't knock it. Just because we haven't found it yet . . . It could be there. But no, in that case the dog stops you from dying of what you're programmed to die of.' He was marking time while he decided what he wanted to do next. He'd spent the last year in the Gulf, in the Kingdom of Saudi Arabia. As he said that, the same, rather cold look flickered across his face.

'Saudi Arabia,' she said. 'Tell me about it.' She'd had a chance to work there a few years ago. The money had been excellent, but she'd decided she couldn't face living under the restrictions the culture would impose on a single woman.

He hesitated, then said, 'It's not an easy place. They call it the magic kingdom. A whole modern world has just sprung up out of the desert, but the people haven't changed. It's like one of those optical illusions. You look and you see a modern country, and then you look again, and you're in the Middle Ages, and what you thought you were looking at, it isn't there any more. Which one is the real Saudi Arabia . . . ?' He shrugged. 'Maybe we don't have the equipment to see it. I have the option of going back, but . . .' He picked up a piece of bread and didn't finish the sentence.

'You don't want to stay here?'

He shook his head. 'The NHS – it's tied up in

red tape and bureaucracy. I want something with a bit more of a challenge.' He'd spent most of his working life overseas, and he planned to leave again as soon as he could. He'd applied for research posts in Canada and in Australia. 'Those are places I want to be.'

'That's something I've got to decide,' she said. 'Where I want to be.'

He raised an eyebrow in query, so she went on. 'I had plans to open a language school, but it went wrong. Money problems,' she said, to forestall any questions. 'So I need to decide – do I start again, or do I go and work for someone else? And where.'

'You don't want to stay in the UK either?'

She shook her head. She'd first started teaching English because it gave her an opportunity to travel. 'Not really.'

'So where?'

'China. I've never been there and there are some interesting jobs in Beijing. Or Tokyo, maybe. I'm not sure if I fancy Japan. Patagonia.'

'Patagonia?'

'I just like the sound of it. Mountains and condors and more space than you know what to do with.'

They arranged to meet again. He wanted to see her the next day, but she put him off. She had bruises from her relationship with Michel that could still hurt. She wasn't ready to go through that experience again. Joe wasn't going to be around for long. She wasn't going to be around for long. Whatever happened, their lives were going to cross only briefly. The parameters were already set. It would be crazy to get too involved.

Friends, she told herself. They could be friends.

He called her a couple of days later with a suggestion that they explore the Bow Back Rivers that Saturday.

'The what?' she said.

'I'll show you.'

He was waiting for her when she came out of Bromley-by-Bow station. He smiled when he saw her, and took her hand. The traffic roared by, heading for the Blackwall Tunnel. 'Half of Londoners don't know this exists,' he said. 'Come on.'

She thought she knew this part of London – a derelict area of industrial wasteland tracked by busy roads that was best escaped from, not explored. She followed him away from the roads, down some steps and found herself in a wilderness where waterways tangled together through overgrown footpaths and abandoned locks and bridges. They walked for an hour along the waterways without touching the city.

The rivers were choked with weed and the muddy banks were littered with rubbish, but there were swans on the water, and a heron rose lazily from the river ahead of them. He told her the names of the rivers as they walked – Pudding Mill, Bow Creek, Three Mills, Channelsea. The day was misty and cold.

They left the silence of the old waterways and came out into the roar of the traffic. It started to rain, and he opened his umbrella, putting his arm round her to pull her into its shelter. He had the thin frame of a runner, and she was aware of the hardness of his arm through the sleeve of his coat as they walked together.

They fell into a pattern of seeing each other a couple of times a week, often just walking, discovering parts of the city they didn't know, sometimes going for a drink. Their meetings were friendly and casual. She didn't know who he saw or what he did when he didn't see her. He didn't talk about himself much.

On an unseasonably cold day about six weeks after their first meeting they found themselves on the South Bank. They'd been to Tate Modern to see the Edward Hopper exhibition, and afterwards they'd wandered aimlessly back along the path. Joe had been quiet for most of the afternoon and Roisin was happy just to walk beside him and watch the river.

The water was translucent green except where the light glinting off the eddies and flows turned it silver. A tour boat went past, lines of seats visible inside the cabin where people sheltered from the brisk wind that blew up the river. The seats on the upper deck were empty apart from a couple who hung over the rail, pointing out the sights of the river as the boat passed. Briefly the voice of the guide boomed across the water: . . . *the Houses of Parliament, built in the* . . . A woman on the top deck leaned out dangerously to take a photograph as the boat rocked on an eddy.

'She's going to fall,' Roisin said.

She felt him stiffen beside her. 'She's dead if she does. In this water you've got maybe two minutes before the cold paralyses you.' They watched as the woman righted herself and the boat dwindled into the shadows under Waterloo Bridge. His voice was sombre when he spoke again. 'I used to get the river deaths when I worked here before – a lot of them ended up in our mortuary. It's a terrible way to die.'

She took his hand. This was the first time he'd talked about the darker side of his work. 'I don't remember reading about deaths in the river.'

He was still watching the water, his thoughts somewhere else. 'There are so many they hardly bother reporting it now.'

She thought about the dark waters closing above her, the cold eating into her until it drove all feeling away, knowing that her existence would be snuffed out and forgotten and when her body was pulled out of the river – if it ever was – no one would care. The sky was grey and the wind off the water had a cutting edge.

She was still holding his hand. He tucked it in his pocket, and they continued along the river-side. She had walked here last May, past the concrete maze of the South Bank, enjoying the early summer sun, watching the crowds sitting at the tables in front of the National Film Theatre. They were deserted now. The wind blew and an empty can rattled its way across the paving stones. Behind her, a boat sounded its horn.

She could feel the touch of Joe's fingers on her hand, the gentle pressure of his thumb as he circled it in her palm. Gulls were flying overhead, their calls echoing in the chill air. They didn't speak again as they walked up the steps at the end of the bridge and paused to watch the water again. 'What do you want to do now?' she said.

He leaned back against the parapet and drew her towards him. 'You're cold.'

'Everything's cold.'

He opened his coat and wrapped it round her. 'Not this,' he said. She could feel the wind buffeting her ears and blowing her hair around his face as he kissed her. His lips felt icy as they touched hers, and just for a moment, she thought about the dead lips of drowned women under the water.

It was time for a decision. She could step back and draw the line that would define the path of their relationship, but she didn't want to. She could feel the warmth of him pressing close to her, feel the slight roughness of his skin against her face. She had been standing in the shallows for too long, had been too frightened of stepping into the current, of getting her life back again. As Joe kissed her, she could feel the current start to lift her, start to carry her away. 'Joe?' she said.

He looked down at her. His face was warm and intent. 'Let's go back to your flat,' he said.

As they wended their way back through Bloomsbury, she reminded herself that he was leaving, that by the autumn he would probably be gone, but it didn't matter any more. What mattered was now.

4

It was a summer Roisin would never forget. In her memory, the sun always shone and the sky was cloudless. The forbidding river glittered as it flowed through the city, and the concrete of the South Bank warmed in the mellow light. She and Joe spent their lunch times wandering along the riverside, their evenings exploring the lanes and byways of London, and their nights at Roisin's flat. She barely saw her friends, spent as little time at work as she could get away with. After a few days, he moved his possessions in, and stayed. It was as if they knew that their time together was short, and they didn't want to lose a moment of it.

When she came home in the evenings, she'd pause for a moment with her key in the lock, wondering if he would be there, if the door would open to a waft of warmth and the smell of coffee brewing. 'Joe?' she'd call.

'Hey, babes.' He would come out of the small

box room that masqueraded as a second bedroom, now converted into a makeshift office, and scoop her off the floor to kiss her. They would go out to eat, or take Shadow for a walk along the tow path, or spend the evening in the flat. They lived quietly in their own personal bubble that was completely absorbing, but so fragile and impermanent.

They never talked about the future, because very soon they would have to go their separate ways. She knew she had a decision to make, and kept putting it off. Each week, she looked at the jobs available all over the world for someone with her skills, and each week, she found a reason to reject every one.

Joe worked long, irregular hours and sometimes vanished for days if he was sent out of town. She got used to hearing his key in the lock in the small hours, feeling the mattress give as he slipped into the bed beside her.

It was after one such return towards the end of the summer when she woke suddenly. The display on the radio told her it was almost four. She could tell by Joe's rigid stillness beside her that he was awake as well. 'Joe?' she whispered. 'Are you all right?'

He didn't reply. He just rolled over towards her, and pressed his face between her breasts. She could feel him shaking. 'Joe?' she said again.

'A bad dream,' he said. 'Go back to sleep, sweetheart. It was just a bad dream.'

33

The water gleamed in the moonlight, black and impenetrable where it surged between the standing stones of Tower Bridge, translucent brown where it washed against the banks. The office and apartment blocks were dark and silent.

The river was old here, close to the end of its journey to the sea. Now it carried the filth and detritus of the city, away from the slow meander through the fields of Wiltshire, past the bridges of Oxford and the gentle lawns of Henley.

The tide had turned. The river was in ebb, receding from the banks, leaving a waste of mud and shingle behind. Narrow steps led down to the river's edge where water washed against wooden piles. The moon was setting, and the first light of a grey dawn was gleaming through the clouds. The light caught the water, turning it to opaque steel, reflecting off the frameworks of glass that towered above the old city. The air carried the bite of frost.

The body of the woman had caught against the mooring and had been left on the bank as the water retreated. She was still wearing the remains of a black dress, sodden and skimpy. Her feet were bare. Her long hair lay in wet, dark lines across a face that the river had battered beyond recognition, the features almost gone.

She had been young. The men from the Marine Support Unit, the river police, could tell that much as they lifted the body, already pronounced dead by a doctor called from his bed in the small hours, short-tempered and abrupt. They had been expecting to find this body since the week before, when a witness had reported seeing a young woman jump from the riverside walk into the icy water.

Suicide, accident, foul play – bodies dragged from the Thames had different stories to tell. Some of them had families – grieving, frantic, knowing their loved ones had been lost. Others had no one, or no one who wanted to claim them. Drunks, the homeless, addicts, asylum seekers, the desperate with nowhere else to run. Some were old, some were, like this girl, young, and some were no more than children.

A clawed, blackened hand slipped from the body bag and hit the ground with a thud. Through the mud, a gleam of metal was visible from the ring on her finger. One of the men gently tipped some of the river water over it to clean away the dirt. It was etched with a distinctive pattern.

Maybe this girl would have a name.

Coroner's Court, London, September 2004
Post-Mortem Report, Dead Body 13
Body found in river, 7 September, at Stoners Quay

External examination	Female Age: est. 18–25 years (see Appendix ii),

	Height: 156 cm Weight: 38 kg General condition: Poorly nourished. Bruising in the deep tissue that had occurred over a period of time prior to her death. Post-mortem damage to the body was severe and limits the accuracy of these findings.
Time of death	1 September, 24.30 hours (see witness statement i)
Internal examination Liver and gall bladder Kidneys	Algae in liver Algae in kidneys
Final comments	. . . no evidence of drugs or alcohol in the body, no evidence of violence or sexual activity immediately prior to death . . .

The coroner's court of East London is all too familiar with river deaths. The curve in the river around the Isle of Dogs means that bodies are often left aground there as the water retreats with the tide.

Dead Body 13 was the stark designation of the

thirteenth body to be taken from the river in a year that was shaping up to be much as standard. The few people attending the inquest stood as the coroner entered. The court had little to do in this case. No one had been able to establish an identity for the dead woman, or trace the origins of the unusual ring she had been wearing on the middle finger of her right hand. The ring bore an inscription in Arabic, lines from a poem or other literary text: *take what is here now, let go of a promise. The drumbeat is best from far away.*

Her origins were in the Indian subcontinent. Whether she was a recent arrival, or a runaway from home, it was impossible to tell. No one had claimed her and no one seemed to be looking for her.

She had drowned. She had been alive when she went into the water – the presence of algae in her liver and kidneys confirmed that, and a witness had seen her fall. He was a man called Joe Massey who had been on the river walk near St Paul's. He gave his account, telling the court that he'd spent the evening in a bar and was on his way home when he had seen a woman standing on the wall looking down at the water. There had been a strong wind blowing and her balance had been precarious. He had called out a warning to her, but she hadn't heard, or hadn't listened. He couldn't say if she had deliberately jumped, or if she had fallen, but she had seemed heedless of the risk she was taking.

Someone or something had hurt her before she died. There was evidence of half-healed but extensive bruising on her back and legs, and at some time in her past her wrist had been broken and had healed poorly. But none of this had contributed to her death. Whether or not it had driven her to the dark waters of the Thames, no one could say. The damage that the river had done to her body had blackened her skin and obliterated her features. To the uninitiated eye, she looked as though she had been burned. Her body was battered and broken by tides, currents and river traffic.

The coroner gave the only verdict he could: an open one. 'It is not possible to say if this unfortunate young woman committed suicide, or if she fell into the water by accident.' Police enquiries as to her identity were ongoing.

Joe Massey attended the inquest as the only witness to the girl's last moments. Later, he went back to the riverside to the place where she had fallen in. He stood for a while, watching the water, then he swore, not quite under his breath. Two women walking along the path towards him stopped as they heard the obscenity, then walked quickly back the way they had come.

It was the end of September before the summer came to its inevitable end. Roisin was at work when Joe called her and suggested that they meet. He had seemed preoccupied for the past week and he was quiet as they followed their familiar route to the riverside. She could feel the slight tension in him. They walked past the bridge and the café tables outside the film theatre, crowded and cluttered with empty glasses, wrappers, and discarded food that the pigeons fought over.

They leaned against the parapet and watched the boats go by. The air was cooler, and she could feel the first touch of autumn. Summer was coming to an end. She looked across the water to the iron stanchions of the bridge. She could remember that grey day when they'd first walked along the river together.

After a moment, he spoke. 'I got a letter this morning. From McMaster . . .'

The Canadian university where he hoped to join a research team. This was it. Their timeless summer was over. She opened her eyes wide and stared across the river. She couldn't trust her voice. It was a moment before she could take in what he was saying.

'. . . wanted someone with more experience in the field.' He was watching the river as he spoke. 'If this had happened three months ago, I'd have been gutted. Now – it's almost a relief.' He looked at her. 'I just need to decide what to do next.'

'You aren't leaving . . .' Roisin blinked fast to clear her vision that had blurred and distorted and felt the tears spill out and run down her face.

'I'll go, if you feel that badly about it,' he said.

She tried to laugh, and wiped her face with the

back of her hand. 'I'm sorry. I just . . . I'm sorry you didn't get it.'

'Don't be. I'm not. I've had some more news. They want me to go back to the Gulf. They've been putting the pressure on for weeks and I've been giving it a lot of thought. The offer's too good to turn down. Roisin, I'll go, but only if you'll come with me.'

'Come with you?'

'To Riyadh. I've been looking into it. You could work – they need qualified women to teach English at the university. They've been short staffed for months. With all the troubles, they've been losing more people than they can recruit. I'm in a strong position. I can dictate some terms. Oh, hell. We can sort this out later. Roisin, I love you. Will you marry me?'

It was as simple as that. He produced a bottle of champagne from his bag and they sat on the parapet watching the river flow by, drinking champagne out of the bottle – he'd forgotten to bring glasses – planning their lives together.

Not everyone was as pleased with the news as Joe and Roisin were. Her friends were cautious in their response. They barely knew Joe, and the word 'rebound', unspoken, hung over the congratulations.

Her mother was more frank. 'Saudi Arabia? Rosie – that's so far away.'

The anxiety in her voice pricked Roisin's

conscience. Maggie Gardner had greeted her plans to go to Warsaw with a resigned acceptance, but Saudi was an alien environment in her mother's eyes, a veiled and dangerous place where Westerners could be – were – shot on the streets. 'It's only for a year,' Roisin said.

'And married. Rosie, you hardly know him.'

'I've known him for three months.' It didn't sound long – it felt like longer. 'I knew Michel for two years and it turned out I didn't know him at all.'

She heard her mother sigh. 'I suppose you know what you're doing,' she said, in a tone that suggested she thought the opposite.

Old George was the worst. 'Him?' Joe was still 'the man who kicked Shadow'. George had never warmed to him. When she told him she was leaving, moving to the other side of the world, he said, 'What you want to go out there for?' Then he turned away so that she wouldn't see his face, and shuffled back into his flat, Shadow looking back at her as the front door closed.

The day before the wedding, while Joe was at work, she took out her photograph album, her collection of pictures that marked, for her, the major events of her life. There was a dim, unfocused picture of two strangers holding a toddler – her birth parents, unknown to her and long gone. There was her mother and father holding her up to the camera on the day the adoption became official. There were photographs of

41

schoolfriends, youthful sporting triumphs, photos that marked private moments that meant something only to her. 'Why have you got a photo of that dreadful boy?' her mother had asked once when they looked at the album together. *Because he was the first man I ever had sex with* was what Roisin hadn't said.

And there were photos of her and Amy, one taken in the red-eye darkness of a rave, both of them high as kites on E's or some similar chemical, and another, more sober, of the two of them sitting on the steps outside college, smoking.

Amy. Her best friend through a large part of her adolescence. They had had an instant affinity that may have come from the fact that they both had disjunctures in their past. Amy's parents had died when she was thirteen, and she had grown up in care. Like Roisin, she had lost a sister in the events that had taken away their families, and they had found something in each other that came close to filling that – in Roisin's case – almost subliminal gap.

And then Amy had gone, years ago now. Roisin sighed and closed the book.

Snapshots.

A wedding: a bright gold autumn morning, Joe, looking at her in the pale green dress she had bought for the day, smiling that private smile he gave her when they were together in a crowd.

Her mother, half proud, half anxious as she

watched the daughter she had had to fight so hard for say the words that were going to take her away: *I do solemnly declare . . .*

Her friends, laughing and talking as they came out of the register office, falling silent before they shook hands with Joe and congratulated him.

And the moment when they threw petals, so that she and Joe were caught in a shower of brilliant colours.

And she remembered Joe, his face bright with laughter as he scooped her mother off the ground and kissed her. 'Hi, Mum,' he said. Her mother laughed with genuine delight, and the anxiety faded from her face for a moment.

Then, two days later, they flew to Riyadh.

PART TWO

5

Riyadh, October 2004

Embassy of the United States of America
Riyadh, Saudi Arabia
WARDEN MESSAGE
October 2004

The recent terrorist attacks on Westerners appear to have involved extensive planning and preparation and were likely preceded by pre-attack surveillance. Be aware of your surroundings. Take note of vehicles and individuals that do not appear to belong to the area and report them immediately . . .

The ad-Dirah market was in the heart of the old city, a covered souk with labyrinthine walkways, cool and shadowed after the relentless sun. The air smelled of sandalwood and spices and the stalls were piled high with goods that ranged from the commonplace to the exotic: translucent chunks of frankincense and reddish brown myrrh, brass coffee pots as tall as a child or small enough to fit in the palm of the hand, camel-hair shawls and scarves. Old men reclined on Persian carpets, smoking hookahs and drinking tea, enticing their customers in with gentle persuasion.

Roisin, dizzy with jet lag, wondered if she was dreaming a Hollywood incarnation of an Arabian street market. She felt as if she had closed her eyes in London on a grey October morning, and opened them again to the opulence and glitter of the souk.

She pulled her headscarf forward over the tell-tale blonde of her hair. She had never been in a country where she had to veil before. The abaya had felt odd and theatrical when she had put it on an hour ago, but here in the bustling market, she was glad of the anonymity. All the women she saw had covered their faces, and were dark shapes in abayas and veils. She could see nothing of them but their eyes, which gleamed in the shadows as they flickered in Roisin's direction. They looked oddly, exotically beautiful.

In the cool dimness of the walkways, the light reflected off the brilliant fabrics, the silver of the jewellery, and the white of the men's robes.

A man from the agency had met them in the hotel lobby at nine. 'Dr and Mrs Massey? I'm Damien O'Neill.' The name was familiar from the flurry of correspondence that Joe's sudden decision

– and their precipitate marriage – had engendered. Roisin had studied him as they shook hands. His appearance gave very little away. He was wearing a lightweight suit, and draped round his shoulders was one of the chequered scarves the local men wore. His hair was fair and he had a thin, long-jawed face. His eyes were concealed behind dark glasses. His manner was pleasant enough, but he seemed a bit distant and distracted. 'I'll take you to the house and get you settled in.'

She'd looked at Joe. 'Do we have to go there straight away? Do you have time to show us a bit of the city first? I've never been here before, and . . .' And the restrictions on women's freedom meant that it would be hard for her to explore Riyadh on her own.

'I have a bit of time. We could go to ad-Dirah. It's in the old city. The market's worth a visit.' He must get bored with acclimatizing new arrivals.

And now as she watched Joe bargaining with one of the market traders in a rapid exchange with hand gestures and laughter as his Arabic let him down, she was glad she had asked. She'd been told that the Saudis could be stand-offish and unfriendly, but these people seemed welcoming enough. She didn't try to join in. She wasn't sure what women were or were not allowed to do here. She could see local women, accompanied by men, haggling briskly at the stalls. She gave up trying to follow the bartering that was going on in front of her, and stepped back to join O'Neill.

'It's hot,' she said to him distractedly, fanning herself with a guidebook she'd picked up at the hotel. She gave herself the day's award for stating the blindingly obvious. 'Isn't that too warm?' She nodded at his scarf.

'The best way to deal with this sun is to cover up against it. Like they do.' He nodded towards the crowds who were thronging the market.

'Whereabouts is the university?' She would be working there, teaching English to the women students. She wondered if they would pass it today on their way to the house.

'It's on its own campus, to the west of the city in al-Nakhil.' He took off his glasses and slipped them into the pocket of his jacket. She saw that his eyes were grey. 'The ex-pats call it Camelot.'

'Camelot?' She would be living in the magic kingdom and working in Camelot. She wanted to say something about this, to try and make some contact with this man who was part of the community she was about to live and work among, but there was something about his face that discouraged any further comment. They stood in silence waiting for Joe.

He was moving away from the stall now, putting his money back into his belt, his eyes surveying the crowd. For a moment he hesitated as if he didn't know where he was, and she was about to wave and call when she remembered that women didn't do that here. He'd seen them, anyway, and came across. He caught Roisin's eye and smiled a quick query at her: *You OK?*

She smiled back and nodded. 'What did you buy?'

'Something for you.' He showed her a cluster of bangles made of delicate, thread-like silver. He liked to buy her small presents. She had a collection of scarves and earrings and beads that he had bought for her over the few months they had been together. O'Neill was glancing at his watch.

Joe slipped the bangles discreetly on her wrist. Men and women touching in public were likely to attract angry comment from the Mutawa'ah, the religious police. She felt the cold of the metal against her skin. 'They're beautiful. Thank you.' Their eyes met.

O'Neill hadn't been watching them. Roisin had noticed the way his eyes kept scanning the crowd, constantly checking their surroundings. 'We need to move on,' he said. He led them out into the narrow streets where the shops of the gold market lined the pavements, filled with necklaces, bracelets, pendants, earrings, coins, piled up in glittering brilliance. In London, these shops would have been protected by heavy glass, by metal grilles and shutters. Here, everything was out in the open.

As they threaded their way through the crowd, away from the covered market and back on to the street, Roisin's eyes were constantly drawn to new sights – a child watching her big-eyed from behind a stall, the glitter of gold in the thread of a fabric, ornamented shutters across an upper window, the hard lines of the shadows as the sun rose to its zenith.

The fragrance of cooking wafted over to her and she looked round. A man at a stall behind her was grilling kebabs on a clay oven, tearing open flat bread and slapping the meat inside it for the thronging customers. She could see salads of grain and chopped herbs, and dishes of hummus. Back home, it would be five in the evening, the time that she would be leaving work and heading to the small bistro on New Oxford Street where she and Joe customarily ate. Suddenly she was ravenous. She could almost taste the spices and feel the soft warmth of the bread in her mouth, but there was nothing she could do about it. Women didn't eat in public here.

She collided with Joe who had stopped abruptly in front of her. 'Which way are we going?' His voice, as he spoke to O'Neill, was sharp.

O'Neill looked surprised. 'To the al-Masmak fort,' he said.

'We need to get back. Roisin's tired.'

Roisin opened her mouth to object, then shut it again. She had no idea what had upset Joe, but his face had that bleak, distant look. 'It's a bit hot,' she said diplomatically.

O'Neill raised an eyebrow but didn't make any further comment. 'OK.' His shrug was in his tone. 'We can cut through this way to the car.'

She glanced quickly at Joe as O'Neill turned

away. 'I'm fine,' she said, but he didn't seem to hear. He was pushing ahead through the crowd and she couldn't see his face.

Just then, the crowd parted to let a man through. He was tall and his robes were dazzling in the light. Her eyes followed him instinctively. In the next instant a sudden surge caught her unawares, turning her around in a wave of bodies and almost knocking her off her feet. When she tried to turn back, O'Neill and Joe had vanished and she had no idea which way they'd gone.

They couldn't be far away, but she wasn't tall enough to see over the heads of the people and she was getting pushed back, further away from where she had been. The next surge carried her to the edge of the street, and then she was against the wall, trying to make herself inconspicuous as she oriented herself. The streets, narrow and shadowed, ran away from her in all directions. She had the sudden feeling – something she had never felt before – of hostile eyes searching for her, eyes that wouldn't be fooled for long by her disguise. She could feel the start of panic constricting her chest, and made herself breathe slowly and steadily. There was nothing to worry about. She'd got separated in the crowd. The worst that could happen was that the Mutawa'ah would shout at her.

Then she recognized the corner of a building. That was where they had left the souk. In that case, they had been heading towards . . . or was it this way? There was a straight lane ahead of her, free from the confusion of the market-place throng.

She followed it, and suddenly, to her relief, the crowd was gone. A square opened up in front of her, paved in patterned stone, surrounded by palm trees. At the far end was a low, flat building raised on pillars, and to her right a minaret reached up towards the sky. The shadows were solid and hard-edged. A white-robed figure stood in the shadow of the pillars, but otherwise the square was empty. It was shocking in its unexpected silence.

She stood still, frozen in a moment of déjà vu. She thought she knew this place. Then Joe was beside her, his face tense with anxiety. 'Christ, Roisin . . .'

'Joe!' She put her hand out to touch him, then drew it back, remembering where she was. 'I'm sorry. I got caught in the crowd.' She had been separated from them by a few yards.

Damien O'Neill was looking at her assessingly. 'Are you all right?'

'Yes. I'm fine. It was my fault. The crowd took me by surprise.'

'I'm sorry. I should have warned you about that.' He turned to Joe, who had fallen silent and was staring at the square in front of him. 'Come on. We can get back this way.'

Moving quickly, he led them away from the market and suddenly the old town and the crowds were behind them. Roisin's head was spinning in confusion. She was an adult woman in one of the major capitals of the world. She'd taken care of herself alone in a hundred cities and yet this place had rendered her helpless, had changed her status, just like that, to that of a child.

The sun was almost directly overhead. The Arab city had vanished. They were walking through a street that could be in Anycity, Anyplace, past high glass blocks of anonymous business space where the noise and smells of modern urban life surrounded her. By the time they reached the car park, she was glad to get back into the air-conditioned interior of the car.

She was starting to flag. She'd tried to push herself straight into local time, the only cure for jet lag that worked for her, but all she'd been able to do when the taxi driver had dropped them at the hotel shortly after five the evening before was fall on the bed and sleep.

She'd woken in the small hours. The green light of the clock said 3.10. She knew that she wasn't going to be able to sleep again and sat up carefully. The blinds weren't closed and the moonlight illuminated the room with a cold radiance.

Slipping out of bed, careful not to disturb Joe, she'd pulled on her robe and got herself some fruit juice from the mini bar. Then she went and sat by the window, looking out across Riyadh, her home for the next year.

The cityscape had blazed out in millions of lights. Skyscrapers, impossibly slender and fragile, thrust up towards the sky, and the highways bound them together with loops of light. It was as if someone had asked the designers and architects to build a stage set for a city of the future and they had created this edifice, a city that rested uncomfortably on the desert and on the customs of the people who inhabited it. She remembered what Joe had said when they first met. *It's like one of those optical illusions.* If she sat here watching for long enough, would the illusion fade? And if it did, what would she see?

Now, in the centre of the city, the broken night was catching up with her. The furnace blast of the air was sapping the vitality out of her, and she sank back into the car seat, enjoying the cool of the air-con. Her annoyance at Joe faded. He'd been right. She was tired. She could feel the sweat between her shoulder blades, and her hair felt damp. 'What was that place?' she asked, adjusting her scarf to stop it slipping off her head.

O'Neill steered the car into the stream of fast-moving traffic. He still looked cool and untouched by the heat. 'It's as-Sa'ah Square,' he said, his voice expressionless as he gave her the careful non-information. She wondered what he wasn't telling her. A car cut in from their right and he switched lanes smoothly to avoid a collision. 'You were based in one of the villages before?' he said to Joe. Joe didn't seem to hear. A truck careered towards them and swerved away at the last moment.

'Someone should tell them that they drive on the right here,' Roisin observed.

O'Neill glanced at her in the mirror. His mouth twitched in a sudden smile. 'It's optional,' he said.

Encouraged by the first sign of warmth, she tried again. 'Tell me about that square. It was so . . .' She searched for words. The cathedral-like silence had caught her imagination. Despite the hard glare of the light, she could imagine banks of candles lit for the souls of . . . who? She tried to catch Joe's eye, but he was staring out of the window, lost in his own thoughts.

O'Neill glanced at her again before he answered. 'It's known colloquially as Chop-Chop Square,' he said.

'Chop-Chop Square?' For a moment, she didn't understand what he was talking about, then she realized. The bright square with the blue patterned stones and the palm trees was the place where malefactors against the rigid laws of the Kingdom were dealt with. The place of punishment. The place of execution. All the impulse to laugh drained out of her. People had died on those sun-dazed stones, close to the place where she had been standing.

O'Neill had observed her reaction. 'It's part of what this place is,' he said. 'I give it a wide berth. Some Westerners go. For them it's the nearest thing we've got to a tourist attraction.'

Joe's voice cut into the exchange before she could respond. 'Have you seen that, Roisin?'

She leaned across the car to look out at the building they were passing. A tower of reflective glass rose hundreds of feet above them, ending in a parabolic curve beneath a fragile arch where the structure had been cut away forming a needle reaching up into the sky. She twisted round in amazement as the road swooped away.

'It's called the Kingdom Centre,' O'Neill said. 'Office space, conference centres, hotel, stuff like that. After 9/11, a bad joke went round Riyadh that they used it to train the hijackers. There's a mall.' He switched lanes and pulled away as a car drew level with them, almost boxing them in. 'With a floor for women. You don't need to wear a veil. A lot of the wives go there.'

No one spoke for a while. She watched the traffic as they sped along the six-lane highway. The cars were all moving at high speed, and the drivers wove recklessly from lane to lane with little apparent regard for the danger. She looked at O'Neill's profile, watched the way his hidden eyes observed the traffic, watched the way he anticipated the actions of the other drivers with the coolness of a chess player studying the board. He was a man who would fit in here. He was someone who knew how to become part of the background, who knew how to camouflage himself from the edginess and the tension that she could feel in the air around her.

He swung the car along the road that ran through the outskirts of the city, further away from the lights and the noise and the bustle. Roisin had seen maps of Saudi – a vast desert that would swallow up western Europe, with cities emerging from the wilderness almost at random, a country created in a brief space of time from disparate groups of nomadic people, a country where the beliefs and alliances were complex and alien to outsiders like her and Joe.

The road vanished into a hazy distance. It was lined with apartment blocks, stark and ugly after the beauty of the old city and the futuristic spires of the modern. They were on the outskirts now, with car parks, shacks and industrial complexes. Then a fence appeared on the horizon, dancing slightly in the heat haze. Roisin watched it as it emerged from the urban wasteland through which they were driving. It looked high and formidable, like a prison camp or a high-security installation. She found herself looking for the watch towers.

But she could see trees and buildings behind the fence, and O'Neill was turning the car towards a gate protected by chicanes, towards a kiosk where two uniformed men stood with their guns held ready. 'Security's heavy. Got your documents?'

O'Neill spoke to the guards, his Arabic sounding fluent and easy. There was a quick, unsmiling exchange. Roisin reminded herself that the promiscuous smiles of the West were not universal, that the severe faces did not denote hostility. O'Neill showed a security pass to the first guard, while the other one came round to the passenger side of the car and held his hand out for Joe to pass him their documents. The man didn't indicate by word or gesture that he was aware of Roisin's silent presence. She felt suddenly that she had ceased to exist.

Then the car was waved past. She read the notices that hung on the gates as O'Neill waited for the barrier to lift. They were written in Arabic and English: Checkpoint. Stop at the barrier. Have your documents ready.

Keep out. Sheer drop. Danger of death.

6

Damien O'Neill leaned back in the reclining chair and watched the sky. His house was in the old part of the city, a part that had been largely abandoned by the Saudis, who had moved out to the wealthy suburbs. When Damien had first arrived, more years ago than he cared to count, foreign workers were housed here, and he had never joined the exodus to what was seen as more luxurious, more suitable accommodation.

The house, old and shabby, was traditionally Arabic. There was little furniture. Cupboards were built into the walls, but otherwise the furniture was sparse and portable, designed to be moved to the shadier parts of the house as the seasons progressed. It was far too big for him, but he couldn't bring himself to abandon the cool, high-ceilinged rooms.

'You have no wife,' his friend Majid said, by way of excusing Damien's eccentricity. Majid chided him regularly about the lack of order in his life. He was concerned for his friend's welfare. 'You should marry,' he added with the zeal of the convert. Majid had recently married and he and his young wife were expecting their first child.

Damien knew too much about marriage. His own, embarked on with the careless optimism of his youth, had come to a catastrophic conclusion. If he let himself, he could still see Catherine's face twisted with misery and a love that had rotted into hatred. *You don't care about anyone! No one matters to you!* But no one could have filled the void that was Catherine's need, or that was what he told himself. 'One day,' he said to Majid, unwilling to explain the complexities of his past, complexities that Majid would not understand anyway.

'When you go home, maybe,' Majid had said.

But this was Damien's home. He had nowhere else he wanted to go.

He was feeling hungry. He stretched and headed down the stairs. The hallway was dim and cool, and the stone flags felt cold under his feet. It was shadowy down here. At street level, the house had no windows, just air holes to channel the breezes from the narrow streets. The kitchen smelled of coffee and spices.

There was a pot of stew simmering on the cooker, and bread under a net. His houseboy, Rai, must have been to market, because there was a dish full of fresh, sticky dates. Damien had planned to go to the market himself. He liked to spend

62

time drinking coffee in the cafés, talking to the men, catching up on the local news and gossip. This was part of his work: integrate, blend in, become part of the community.

He had come to the Kingdom as a civil servant, working for the British government, but realized soon enough that the rigid hierarchies, the red-tape and bureaucracy that tied up the diplomatic service were going to prevent him from doing anything he really wanted to do, and that, if the local people were to trust him, he would have to cut all visible ties with Western government organizations. As soon as he made it known he was available, an agency that recruited professionals to work in the Kingdom had snapped him up.

He worked at the interface between the ex-pat community and the Saudis, a precarious seesaw of mutual and often wilful miscomprehension. It was a difficult time just now. Ex-pat workers were leaving in droves as the insurgent campaign against them had been stepped up. Things were quieter after a clampdown by the security services, but Damien was still aware of the ediginess on the streets, something in the atmosphere that said trouble had not gone but simply changed its face, biding its time until it was ready to strike.

He'd spent the morning with two new recruits: Joe Massey, who had taken a post at the hospital, and his wife Roisin, who would be working at the university. He thought about the couple as he stood in the kitchen. Joe Massey had worked in the

Kingdom before, but he was the one who'd been anxious, who'd been tense and uncommunicative during their brief tour of the city.

Damien thought about it and corrected his impression. Massey had been tense and edgy from the time that his wife had got separated from them in the crowd. OK, that was fair enough, though Roisin Massey seemed well able to look after herself. She was a small, determined woman whose fair hair would have been a beacon on the streets of Riyadh if she hadn't had the sense to keep it tucked firmly away under her scarf. He suspected that she was going to have trouble accepting the restrictions of life for a woman in Saudi Arabia.

Riyadh could be a hard place for new arrivals. It was the centre of the lands known as the Nadj, the crucible of Wahhabi Islam. According to prophecy, the Nadj had been condemned by God as a place of earthquakes and sedition, the place where the devil's horn would rise up. It was the heart of the deepest and most rigid interpretation of the faith.

The day had faded, and he could see the city lights sparkling in the distance. He'd been invited to spend the evening with Majid's family and he'd need to set off soon if he wasn't going to be late. He had planned to phone and make his apologies – he had reports to complete that he'd left unfinished because of the Masseys, but now he made a snap decision. Work could wait. He wanted to get the feel of the city, take in its mood as he drove through the streets. The talk at Majid's, leisurely and convoluted though it would be, would tell him something about what was going on. And he would enjoy the hospitality.

Majid was an officer in the city police force – not the Mutawa'ah, the notorious protectors of virtue and opponents of vice, but the police who dealt with the more secular law breakers, and who were responsible for imposing one of the harshest and most rigid penal codes on the planet. He lived in the sprawling family compound in the suburbs to the west of the city, a cluster of houses that Majid's father had bought as his family expanded. Abu Abdulaziz Karim ibn Ahmad al-Amin was a traditional Saudi patriarch. He had two wives, five sons and three daughters. The daughters lived in their father's house, the brothers, all married, each had a house of their own.

In all the years Damien had known the family, he had never met the women, had only been aware sometimes of a veiled presence in the car, or waiting in the background. All he knew about Majid's mother, the second wife, was the name she had started using once she had given birth to a son: *Um Majid* – the mother of Majid.

The relationship between the brothers was complex and sometimes difficult but they never showed the internal rifts to him, the outsider. Family was all. Majid had once told him of a Saudi saying: 'Me and my brother against the cousin.'

Damien already knew the saying, and he knew what came next: *Me and my cousin against the stranger.*

Majid's marriage had caused some ripples in the family. In most ways it was a very suitable marriage; his wife, Yasmin, was the daughter of a wealthy businessman, but she was an only child and though she had been brought up in Riyadh, she had travelled in Europe and had been educated at a Parisian university. And she wasn't a true Saudi. Her mother was European and her father was the son of a Saudi mother and Armenian father. He was one of the few foreigners who had been allowed to take Saudi citizenship, but the insular Saudi culture still held him an outsider. He had brought his daughter back from Europe to marry Majid, no doubt hoping that his daughter's marriage into a Saudi family of the reputation and longevity of Majid's would help to integrate him more closely. Yasmin worked as a teaching assistant at Riyadh's King Saud University, and she was independent and opinionated by Saudi standards.

His phone rang as he was preparing to leave. He waited to see who was calling. 'Damien? It's Amy. Are you there?' He moved to answer it, then stopped. He was late, and conversations with Amy tended to lead into deeper water than he felt able to cope with at the moment. He let his hand drop as he heard her impatient sigh. 'Call me.'

Amy. The quick instruction was typical. *Call me.*

He would, but later. As he negotiated the car through the hazardous traffic, he couldn't stop himself thinking of her as he'd last seen her, her red hair springing up round her head, her towel slipping casually down as she leaned forward so he could light her cigarette, beautiful in the lamp-light. And then they'd had a pointless row about – what? He couldn't remember. It had been one of many that had been not so much reconciled as forgotten in his bed.

Twenty minutes later, he pulled up outside the gated compound where the family lived, and waited for the gates to swing open. Majid came to greet him and led him through the courtyard into the large room where the men customarily sat. Two of Majid's brothers were already there, talking to a third man, a man in Western dress who was sitting with his head turned away from the door. He looked round as Majid ushered Damien in.

Damien recognized him at once. This was Majid's father-in-law, Arshak Nazarian. Nazarian, an attractive, debonair man, described himself as a 'businessman'. The nature of his business – bringing cheap migrant labour into the Kingdom – made Damien wary of him. He avoided Nazarian's company as far as he could.

Faisal, the oldest of the brothers and head of the family in the father's absence, greeted Damien with a standard 'Peace be upon you.'

Damien returned the greeting politely, wondering

67

what he had interrupted as he took the seat that Majid urged him to. Over the years, Damien had become accustomed to the Arab style of sitting, usually cross-legged on floor cushions. It had felt awkward and uncomfortable at first, but now it felt natural.

He accepted a cup of coffee, light and spiced with cardamom, that the houseboy offered him, and made his enquiries about the family and their well-being. The houseboy stood vigilant, waiting to refill the cups. The conversation was desultory and wandered around the unusual nature of the recent heat and the pious hope that God would soon relieve the drought.

Damien realized quickly that there was something wrong, even though Majid's pleasure at seeing him had been sincere. But Nazarian's sudden silence on his entry, the oblique references to the inclemency of the weather, which was much the same as usual, the calling down of God's blessing that they might soon have rain, which was, in fact, unlikely, carried meaning beyond the mere facts that were being expressed. People who wanted to understand Arabic had to have an ear for metaphor, but Damien couldn't pick up the underlying message. He decided he wouldn't prolong the visit, but leave as soon as politeness permitted.

Nazarian said abruptly, 'We will discuss this later.' He stood up and held out his hand to Damien. 'O'Neill,' he said. 'Good to see you. There are things I need to talk to you about.' He spoke in English, though all the previous exchanges had been in Arabic.

'Call my office,' Damien said. He had no interest in a meeting with Nazarian if he could avoid it.

Nazarian gave him a long look, then made his farewells to the brothers. Damien waited until he had gone before he said, 'Your father-in-law is looking well.' He was curious about the conversation his arrival had clearly interrupted.

Majid's face darkened. 'He is concerned about his daughter.'

Damien never asked about the women in the family in the presence of the traditional Faisal, and with Majid, he always waited until the other man introduced the topic.

'Your wife is well?'

Majid looked frustrated. 'She wants a holiday, before the baby is born. She wants to go to Europe, but I have decided that we will stay in the Kingdom for now.'

So Nazarian probably represented the big guns to bring Yasmin into line. Majid wouldn't want to discuss his own inability to persuade his wife to do what he wanted, so Damien changed the subject. 'I met the new man today. Joe Massey. He's come to work at the hospital.' Majid was always interested in the ex-pats that came into the country.

Majid frowned. 'Joe Massey? A doctor? I have met him before.'

'He's a pathologist. He was here a few months ago. What's he like?'

'I did not know him at all.' Majid's voice was dismissive. 'He was employed at the hospital when there was a drugs theft. Now, my friend, what do you think about the election?'

The topic of Joe Massey was firmly cut off for one that Majid's brothers could contribute to. Damien made a mental note to ask Majid about Massey at a better time, and settled back to listen to a discussion he'd heard many times since the elections – the first ever to be held in the Kingdom – were announced. The powerful religious lobby was exercising its influence on the polls and there was tension between traditionalists and reformers. Dissent had surged through the Kingdom, casting its ripples and eddies in odd and disturbing places.

Damien murmured something anodyne and left the brothers to debate the issue while his own thoughts drifted to Amy. If he had picked up the phone, he could be with her now.

Her mouth had tasted of honey in the shaded room, and his tongue could still recapture the faint salt taste from her upper lip where the sweat had beaded. Her hair had been soft and springy under his fingers. She had had a fragrance like the sea. 'You aren't real,' he'd murmured. 'You're one of those creatures who lures men to disaster.'

She'd laughed. 'A siren? I don't think so.'

'Or a mermaid. Don't they call men to their doom?'

Her skin had been warm under his fingers, and her face was flushed. 'I'm no mermaid, Damien. See?' And in the shadowed room, he could see.

Majid was saying something, and he shook his head to clear his mind. 'I'm sorry?' he said.

'What is your opinion, Damien?'

Damien never commented on the politics of the Kingdom unless he was expressly invited to do so. The Saudis, like most people of the Middle East, were weary of criticism after years of outside interference. He ran the conversation quickly through his mind. The brothers had been discussing the movement among a minority of Saudi women for more rights. 'You know my views,' he said. 'Give women the vote – then you will know whether they want more rights.'

'My friend, Saudi women have their rights,' Majid protested. 'Women know that they are valued here, that they are cared for and protected.'

'Sometimes they don't know what is best for them,' Khalil said with a meaningful look.

Majid's mouth tightened. Accusations of leniency towards his untraditional wife stung. 'Rights can't be "given",' he said. 'If these rights existed, then women would have them.'

'Maybe rights can't be given,' Khalil said, 'but they can be taken away.'

'Not if they do not exist,' Majid said flatly.

Before Khalil could reply, Damien became aware of increased activity behind the closed doors that led into the main courtyard of the house, a bustle of movement and briefly, raised voices, women's voices, angry and animated. He saw Majid's quick glance of concern. It was time to go. 'Thank you for your hospitality,' he said, formally. 'Unfortunately, I have to work this evening, so I must leave you.'

Majid's attempts to persuade him to stay were sufficiently ritualized for Damien to understand he'd made the right decision. The two men embraced as he left. 'I hope your family will be well,' he said in oblique reference to the unnamed problem.

As Damien unlocked the door of his car, a movement caught his eye. He looked back at the house, at an upper window where the shutters were slightly open. A woman's face looked back at him, young, beautiful and startlingly unveiled. She stood at the window, looking down at Damien, and didn't draw back when she saw him watching her.

Her face stayed with him, hauntingly familiar as he drove back to his house. As he went in through the front door, the dark coolness surrounded him. He warmed up some bread and spread it thickly with hummus. He forked some tabbouleh on to a plate and poured himself some of the beer that Rai regularly brewed. He put the tray down on the table, which also served as his desk, and switched on a lamp. His mind was moving in directions he didn't want it to go, and he picked up a book to distract himself.

The pool of light made the shadows darker as he ate, forking the food absently as he read one of the stories from *The Book of One Thousand and One Nights*. This story, 'The Sleeper and the Waker', told of Aboulhusn and his life in the Khalif's palace. The story had echoes of biblical parable and of old European tales, but the image of the sleeper who lives a fantastic life in a dream world that is almost beyond imagining, and believes it gone when he wakes, carried uncomfortable resonances for Damien.

The shadows from the intricate wooden grilles sent the moonlight in dappled shadows that traversed the stone floor as the night progressed. The intrusions from the modern world faded and, as Damien read, it seemed as though the dreams of the thousand and one nights were in ascendance.

7

KING SAUD UNIVERSITY WEB SITE
English Department
Student discussion forums
Students may post articles or topics
for discussion.
All contributions must be appropriate
and must be in English.

Article from *New Societies* magazine, posted by Red
Rose, 1 Shawwal 1425

Veiled Knowledge

Ayesha Chamoun

*The Kingdom of Saudi Arabia is shortly to hold elec-
tions for the first time in forty years. Women have been
banned from the poll. What is the view of Saudi women
about this election?*
Times are a-changing for women in the Kingdom.

74

They are beginning to make their way in areas that have traditionally been closed to them – in academia, in the media and in industry. The role of women within the wider society is no longer a taboo subject. But does this debate – and a few minor reforms – mean that women can expect to make real progress in gaining significant rights?

The decision to exclude women from the poll has come as a blow to the fledgling movement for democratic reform. In the last year, leading male liberals have been imprisoned, and the news that prisoners would be allowed to vote whereas women would not, has angered many who hoped that Saudi Arabia was at last moving forward.

But these voices are in the minority. For the majority of Saudi women, the concept of 'rights' is not an issue they even think about. 'I see the way you live in the West, and it shows to me that women's lives are very hard if their society does not look after them,' says one student at Riyadh's King Saud University.

These attitudes, instilled in women by their education and by the way they live, are hard to uproot or challenge. All her life, a woman has a male guardian – her father, her husband, her brother or her son. She must have his permission before she can be educated, travel or go to hospital. It is difficult for a woman even to leave her home without a male escort . . .

At first, Roisin thought that their life in the Kingdom was going to work. They moved their stuff into the house they were renting – characterless, but comfortable enough, with more rooms

75

than they could possibly use – and tried to fight off the jet lag by exploring the compound where Roisin would spend all her time when she wasn't working.

It was small but adequate. The streets were an uneasy pastiche of small-town America, a residential suburb with the sunlight reflecting off the road and sidewalks, off the pale stucco of the houses. There was a library, a gym, and a commissary where Roisin could get supplies. Inside the compound, Western rules and customs prevailed. She was allowed to wear what she liked, to drive, and to wander freely. Outside, she was restricted by cultural taboos that were rigidly enforced.

On their first weekend, Joe organized a trip to the desert. 'I'm going to be busy after this,' he said. 'I don't know when we'll get another chance. If you only see one thing in Saudi, you should see the desert sky at night.' He borrowed an SUV, and they drove west of the city, out into the open wilderness. They pitched their tent where a sandstone canyon formed a jagged edge along the skyline and watched the sun set as the cold of the desert night began to close around them.

And the stars came out and blazed in their thousands. Roisin sat outside the tent, her hands wrapped round a mug of coffee, entranced by the icy, indifferent glory. Joe sat behind her and put his arms round her waist as they pointed out the constellations to each other. 'There's Orion,' she said, surprised that she could see the same constellations that shone in the night sky over the northern cities. 'The hunter.'

She felt rather than heard him laugh. 'Orion wasn't just a hunter. He was the most beautiful man in the world. The gods sent a scorpion to kill him, and Diana asked for him to be placed in the sky so she could remember him.'

They made love under the stars, and she lay awake for a long time afterwards, listening to the sounds as the desert, so dead during the day, came to life. And as she listened to Joe's quiet breathing, she wondered about the goddess huntress who had had to be content with her lover blazing in the night sky instead of in her arms.

They were going to be happy here.

She wasn't due to start work for a fortnight, so she threw herself into the task of getting the house organized, and of familiarizing herself with her new country. She wanted to see more of Riyadh than the brief tour that Damien O'Neill had given them on their first day. Usually, when she came to a new country, she spent time exploring. She liked to walk, to drive around and get the feel and measure of the place. Here, once she left the compound, she had to rely on taxis, and her ability to explore was severely limited. It wasn't wise for a woman to be on her own on the streets of Riyadh.

The city hid itself behind a veil. The centre was a sweep of concrete, ugly, dirty and crowded, where the past had been eradicated. She remembered Joe's fascination with finding the lost sectors of old cities – the hidden rivers and wild enclaves in the centre of London, the forgotten remnants of the past.

There was little of this here. The old city was fast disappearing but, despite the changes, the narrow streets of the old quarter still carried the remnants of the original labyrinthine pattern. Here and there she could still see the old buildings: houses made of clay, the doors and windows obscured by *mashrabiyaat*. These grilles allowed the people inside to look out on to the streets, but excluded all strangers. They were like the eyes of the women, dimly visible when the light caught the covering over their faces.

Other ex-pats told her that the city was changing so fast that landmarks could disappear overnight, whole blocks razed and replaced by newer, higher, more elaborate constructions. A culture built on sand has no sense of permanency.

By the end of the fortnight, she knew the compound from end to end. She knew the staff in the commissary, and she had attended coffee mornings at the houses of ex-pat wives who, having little prospect of work here, seemed to devote their lives to gossiping and complaining about their host country. The only thing she learned from them was how to make wine from fruit juice and bread yeast.

She got to know the gardeners – Filipinos,

mostly – who worked quietly and inconspicuously keeping the lawns green and immaculate and the gardens blooming. They were friendly and helpful to a newcomer who was trying to find her feet. She got into the habit of taking them fruit juice and biscuits while they were working, and sat on the step in the shade talking to them. They lived in poor conditions – mostly in segregated hostels. They weren't allowed to bring their wives and families with them, and they all seemed to be supporting extended families at home. They were cheerful and resourceful. She helped them with their English and, in exchange, they taught her a few words of Tagalog, including a useful obscenity or two.

She worked hard on the house. It was the first home of their marriage, and she wanted it to be comfortable and welcoming. Most of all, she wanted it to be theirs. They'd rented it furnished, so she tried to add some personal touches. She framed some of her Newcastle photographs and hung them on the wall. She bought a red glass vase on one of her trips into town and put it on a low table where it made a splash of colour against the neutral walls.

The kitchen alone was probably as big as her flat in London had been. Their pots, pans and crockery huddled in forlorn isolation in the cupboards, and Roisin's shopping from the commissary barely filled half the shelves of the massive ice box that dominated one corner of the room.

She spent a lot of time alone. Joe was working long hours. His department in the hospital had been without a senior pathologist for several weeks, and he had a massive backload of work to catch up on. He left the house at six each morning, and was rarely home before nine. By the end of her fortnight of enforced idleness, Roisin had had enough.

It was Wednesday afternoon. The weekends ran from Thursday to Saturday, and Roisin was due to start work the following week. Joe had promised to be home early, and they planned to spend the evening together. Roisin had hoped that they might be able to go into the city on Thursday or Friday and do some more exploring, but Joe said he would probably have to work.

'You haven't had a day off since you got here,' Roisin had protested.

'What do you think they pay these salaries for?' he'd said as he disappeared upstairs to shower. The subject hadn't come up again.

She looked at the clock: four thirty. The hands barely seemed to have shifted since she'd last looked. Joe should be back in half an hour. It would be their first proper evening together for a fortnight, and she'd planned a small celebration. She'd bought a chicken and it was simmering on the stove in coconut milk and spices, filling the house with its fragrance.

She went upstairs to shower – she was going to surprise Joe with the new dress she'd bought just before they'd left the UK and hadn't had a chance to wear. She'd lived in jeans for the past week. She was drying herself when the phone rang and she went into the study to answer it, catching her shin on the last unopened packing case. It was Joe's and it contained his medical books and notes. He'd said that he would unpack it himself, but it was still there, sitting uncompromisingly in the middle of the floor.

She swore and grabbed at her leg as she picked up the phone. 'Hello?'

'Sweetheart, it's me.'

Her heart sank. 'Joe.' She could hear the flatness in her voice – she knew what was coming.

'I've got to stay late again. I'm sorry. I can't do anything about it. You wouldn't believe the chaos here.'

He sounded tired. She swallowed her disappointment. 'OK. I'll be fine. The chicken will be a bit dried out.'

'Did you do something special? I'm sorry, sweetheart.'

She bit her tongue on a sharp comment. They'd discussed their plans before he'd left that morning. 'It's OK. I've got things to do.'

She finished drying her hair, and pulled on some jeans. The smell of spiced chicken that had been making her feel hungry seemed unpleasant now, rich and cloying. She went downstairs to switch off the stove, then stood in the vast empty kitchen wondering what to do with her evening.

Her leg was hurting where she'd caught it on the packing case. She rubbed it, wincing as her fingers touched the tender spot where a bruise was starting to form. It was OK for Joe to say, *I'll do it*, but he was never here. And it wasn't him hacking his shins on it every time he tried to get into the room. She went back up the stairs to the office and tried to push the box into the corner where it wouldn't be such an obstruction, but she couldn't get enough grip to get any traction. It was too heavy to lift. She decided to take all the stuff out, put it somewhere where Joe could sort through it, and get the box put away.

It was filled to the top with books. No wonder it was too heavy to move. She knelt on the floor and began taking them out, big medical tomes with dark covers and forbidding titles: *The Pathology of the Foetus and the Infant; Foetal and Neonatal Pathology* . . .

Underneath the books, Joe had stacked various papers and journals, which she moved carefully on to separate shelves, and right at the bottom of the case was a folder full of personal miscellany. She spent a happy ten minutes flicking through old magazines, looking at a postcard she'd had made of one of her photographs with a message she'd scrawled on the back in the early days of their relationship. And there was a photograph, slightly creased, of their wedding.

She sat on the floor, looking at it, remembering how, when they had come out of the register office, someone had thrown petals that came down in a shower and clung to her hair and to her dress. The photographer had caught them in that moment, laughing in a cloud of brilliant colours.

The phone rang. She made a long arm and picked it up, her eyes still on the photograph. 'Roisin Massey.'

'Oh, Mrs Massey. Could I speak to Dr Massey please?'

'He isn't here. Do you want to leave a message?'

'It's Mike Alport, his technician.'

'Hi, Mike.' She had talked to Mike on the phone but she hadn't met him yet.

'Sorry to disturb you. I thought he'd be back by now. Could you ask him to give me a ring when he gets in? Tell him it's about those results he wanted. They came in just after he left.'

Roisin stared at the phone.

'Mrs Massey?'

'Yes. I'm here. Sorry. *When* did you say he left?'

'About an hour ago.'

'Yes. Of course. He said he might stop at the shops.' Her voice sounded odd and artificial. 'I'll ask him to call you, OK?'

She sat looking at the phone after Mike had rung off. Joe must have . . . He was probably still in his office, dealing with a backlog of admin. He wouldn't necessarily have told Mike that. He'd want to be left alone to get on with it.

Her fingers reached for the phone, pulled back, then reached again. She dialled Joe's direct line, the one that went straight to his office, or to his pager if he was on duty and away from his desk. She listened to the phone ringing, then to the automated answering service that told her he wasn't available and invited her to leave a message.

He wasn't there.

She stacked his books carelessly on the shelves. One of them toppled off and fell open on to the floor with a heavy *thud* that resonated through the silent house. A dog barked in the distance. She picked up the book, trying to avert her eyes from the pictures, afraid she would see photographs of dead babies, babies with terrible diseases, but instead the infants looked normal: tiny, wrinkled, newborn, their minuscule fingers clenched, their eyes dark and curious.

One day . . . She and Joe had married in a hurry, but one thing they both knew was that they wanted children. Roisin, at thirty-two, didn't want to wait much longer and they had a tentative plan to try for a family after his contract in Riyadh ended. But, in the back of her mind, she could see his face, suddenly cold, turned away from her, and she could hear her mother's voice: *Rosie, you hardly know him!*

She made herself focus on the task in hand. The packing case was just about empty. She dug down to the bottom and found a page from a newspaper. It was tucked into a plastic pocket to preserve it, and it had been folded, leaving a photograph on display. It was a picture of a young man with a carefree smile. She unfolded the paper carefully, looking at the date. It was from April that year, and she wondered why Joe had kept it. Underneath the photograph, there was an article:

BRITISH STUDENT 'ABANDONED' IN SAUDI JUSTICE

Supporters of a man who was executed in Saudi Arabia last week, today accused the government of failing to intervene. Haroun Patel, a Pakistani national who was a student in the UK in 2003, was convicted of smuggling heroin in Riyadh. A spokesperson said, 'Her Majesty's government is unable to intervene in cases involving nationals from other countries.'

An execution. She remembered that first morning with Damien O'Neill, when she'd found her way to as-Sa'ah Square. *It's known colloquially as Chop-Chop Square . . .*

Early April. In early April, she and Joe hadn't even met. When that article was written, when people were reading it, she was running along the tow path with Shadow dancing ahead of her, and just a week or two later, Joe would be running along that path towards her, the course of their lives about to change for ever.

As she read on, the images of the Kingdom that she was starting to form in her mind melted and changed. They were confused and disparate images: the houses in the old city, tall with small, shuttered windows, houses built close together creating narrow, shadowed alleyways that protected the inhabitants from the relentless sun; the compound with its sharp-edged shadows cast by the buildings, the blinding reflections that enclosed the watcher in brightness, the dryness, like ashes, that the light left behind.

And she didn't know any more what she was seeing.

8

DESERT DEATHS

Riyadh: Thirteen workers – mostly Africans –
lost their way in the desert and died of thirst
in the Taef region of Saudi Arabia. They are
thought to have gone looking for work when
their residency permits ran out. (*Reuters*)

Damien O'Neill leaned back in his chair. It tilted,
and he stared at the ceiling, watching a lizard
making its way across the cracked plaster. He was
beginning to think that he might have a problem,
a problem that centred on Joe Massey. He'd been
concerned about Majid's rather dismissive hostility
when Massey's name had been mentioned.
Somehow, during his previous contract, Massey
had managed to bring himself to the attention of
the police.

And now there was something else. As he
walked home from work that evening, Damien

had passed one of the thriving internet cafés that had sprung up all over the city. And there, all his concentration focused on the screen in front of him, was Joe Massey. Damien had been sufficiently intrigued to stop and watch for a while, but Massey's intent gaze hadn't wavered as he keyed instructions into the machine, stared at whatever had appeared on the screen in response, scribbled down notes and keyed in more instructions.

All the ex-pat houses were set up for internet access, and Massey would also have had a computer in his office at the hospital. But internet traffic was closely monitored in the Kingdom. Though ostensibly for people without their own internet connection, in practice the cafés were often used by those who had particular reasons for keeping their activities anonymous.

These were troubled times. Westerners had been killed on the streets of the Kingdom, and Damien had an ex-pat community whose safety was his responsibility, as was their impact on the society they so imperfectly understood. If Massey was here with an agenda, then Damien wanted to know what it was. There was nothing he could do now though. He filed the problem for future consideration.

The call for *Maghrib*, sunset prayer, brought him back to the present. He scribbled down some notes for the report he intended writing next day, then went downstairs to see what Rai had left in the way of food. As he walked through the shadowed spaces, the doorbell jangled, an intrusion from another place and another time. He heard the sound of a car pulling away.

Damien paused. He didn't live behind the layers of security that protected most Westerners. He knew he was taking some risks, but he also knew that, if he hid behind those kinds of shields, he would effectively exclude himself from Saudi society, declare himself to be irretrievably *other*. Whoever was calling had chosen a time when Rai wasn't here, and when the streets outside were quiet. Risk? He spun the wheel in his head, then opened the door.

There, in the long shadows cast by the high walls and the walkways that linked the buildings, was a slender, black-swathed figure. Her eyes, behind the concealing niqaab veil, were luminous as she slipped through the half-open door into the twilight of the hallway.

'Amy!' He didn't know whether he was shocked or angry. Or just pleased. She shouldn't have come here alone.

'I wanted to see you,' she said simply.

'For Christ's . . .' His exasperation faded as she slipped off her abaya. She was wearing a simple blue dress. Her skin glowed in the shadows, and the brightness of her hair made the colours around her fade to monochrome. 'Do you know what could happen if anyone saw you coming here?'

'Of course I do. So I was careful. Please, Damien.

Don't let's get angry with each other, not now. It's been too long since I saw you.' She rested her hands lightly on his shoulders. Her eyes were almost level with his. He could smell her perfume, and see the way the delicate flush on her face was deepening as they looked at each other.

As he kissed her, he could feel the anger flowing through him and knew she could feel it as well. Suddenly, she was urgent, her nails digging into him as she pulled his shirt free. He could feel her fingers unbuckling his belt. He lifted her up and sat her on the edge of the table that stood by the wall, pushing up her skirt and impatiently pulling her clothes aside.

'Damien . . .' she said, then as he touched her, her breath caught and she stopped speaking as the shadows of the evening gathered around them.

By the time Joe got back, Roisin had finished unpacking the last case and had taken another shower to get rid of the sticky dust that seemed to settle over everything.

There was a bottle of wine in the fridge, some homebrew that a neighbour had given her. It was to have accompanied the chicken that was now cold and congealing in the pan. As the hands on the clock dragged from nine to ten, she got the bottle out and poured herself a glass.

She was lying on the settee, trying to concentrate on her book, when she heard his key in the door. It was almost twenty past ten, the latest he'd ever been. She sat up wearily and put her glass on the table.

He looked tired. He'd loosened his tie and his shirt collar was open. His face was pale under his tan and he had shadows of fatigue under his eyes. 'Roisin.'

'You look exhausted.' She kept her voice neutral. 'Have you eaten?'

'What? No. No, I didn't have time. I'm not hungry anyway.'

'You've got to have something.' She stood up. 'Joe, where have you been?'

He frowned slightly, studying her face. 'I've been working.'

'Mike phoned. He wanted you to call back.'

'When? I haven't seen him. I've been in the library.'

'The library?'

He shook his head. 'I know. I'm sorry. I should have come home like I said, but I'm getting behind with my own work. If I don't keep up with that, I'm not going to get a decent job when we leave.'

And he hadn't felt able to tell her. *You hardly know him, Rosie.* And he hardly knew her. 'You should have said.'

He was looking at her with half-amused doubt. 'What did you think? That I was out hitting the fleshpots of Riyadh? Because there aren't any.'

'Of course not. I just thought we'd agreed to spend this evening together.' She saw his face start to set in the cold, distant look. 'Mike said you'd left, and I was worried.'

He seemed to pull himself back from somewhere. 'I'm sorry,' he said. 'You've been on your own. I should have thought.' He put his arms round her. 'We could start the evening now. I didn't mean to make you worry. You look beautiful.' His smile was deliberately hangdog.

She knew what he was doing, but she couldn't resist smiling back. 'And you look shattered. Go and have a shower, and I'll get us something to eat. Here –' She gave him the glass of wine she'd barely touched.

He leaned forward and kissed her lightly.

He came downstairs in jeans and a T-shirt, looking more relaxed. She made a quick salad using some of the cold chicken. She poured them each a large glass of the homebrew and they sat on the settee and ate with fingers rather than forks.

When they'd finished, he lay down with his head in her lap. 'I thought today would never end. But it kept the best bit to the end.'

She played with his hair. 'Listen, next weekend it will be the end of my first week at work. Let's go into the desert again.'

'If I can.' He looked at her. 'I don't want to promise something and let you down again.'

She nodded, not completely happy. 'I unpacked that last case of stuff that was in the study.'

'You shouldn't have done that. I would have . . .'

'When? I nearly broke my leg on it twice today.'

'Right. Sorry, sweetheart. I didn't mean to leave it for you. It's just been . . .'

'It's OK. It didn't take long.' She trailed her fingers across his face. He hadn't shaved and she could feel the roughness of stubble. 'I found an article. About this place.'

She felt him stiffen. 'What article?'

'The one about the guy who was executed. I put it with your papers. Is it important?'

'No. I don't know why I kept it.'

'Was it someone you knew?'

'I said . . .' His voice was sharp, then he stopped himself. 'Sorry. I told you, I don't know why I kept it.' He pushed himself upright. 'I'm tired,' he said. 'I didn't sleep well last night. I'm still on UK time.'

Later, lying in bed, she was the one who couldn't sleep. She told herself it was because she was starting her classes soon, stepping out of the security of the compound and into the strangeness of the Saudi world.

As she floated somewhere between an uneasy sleep and wakefulness, words on a screen scrolled down in front of her eyes: . . . *died of thirst in the desert . . . executed . . . never to come back . . .* and she was in the square where they had stood the day they first arrived. It was empty and silent. Her feet were on the patterned stones that vanished into the distance. She was moving forward, reluctant step by reluctant step, to the ornate centre of the mosaic. The shadow from the minaret lay across it like a warning finger. *It's time.*

And under the pillars, in the shadows, someone was watching.

9

Damien watched the shadows playing through the closed shutters as he lay on the bed. Beside him, Amy was lying with her eyes closed, asleep, or lost in her own thoughts. The heat in the city this summer was extreme – he'd recorded forty-four degrees at noon. Even the Saudis were slowed down by it; the old men were absent from the street cafés and the souk had been somnolent in the blaze of the sun.

The temperature was dropping now and against the dampness of his skin the air felt cool. He pulled the sheet up to cover them, and Amy stirred. 'Damien,' she said.

He leaned over and kissed her lightly. 'Who else would it be? No, don't answer that.' Her body was outlined against the sheets, long slim arms and legs, a smooth, flat stomach. Her skin was a pale glimmer in the half-light and her mouth was the delicate pink of rosebuds. He could picture her face half an hour before, flushed and warm, her lips the colour of crushed raspberries, and he could still hear her gasps of pleasure as she'd dug her nails into his skin.

She laughed softly and rolled over towards him. 'Nobody else but you.' She reached across him to where a bottle of wine was cooling in a terracotta jar, and poured them each a glass.

'So tell me,' he said. 'Why are you here?' It was rare for them to meet spontaneously like this. The Saudi system made meetings between unmarried couples difficult. Damien preferred it that way. He had his own issues with commitment – his marriage had been enough to warn him away from those deep waters and Amy seemed happy enough with the status quo.

She ran her fingers lightly over him. He could feel himself responding to her and took hold of her wrist. 'Do you need to ask?' she said.

'Amy, I *know* I need to ask. What's wrong?' Amy always kept her own counsel, revealing only as much as she had to about herself. He had said to her once, 'Has it ever occurred to you that I might do what you want if you just told me what was going on?' She had given him a veiled look but hadn't answered.

She hesitated, then sighed. 'I don't know. That's the thing. I was talking to one of the new guys today – only he's not so new. He's on his second tour. He must be crazy.'

He knew at once who she was talking about. 'Joe Massey.'

'Yes.' She sounded surprised. 'You know him?'

'Not really. And . . . ?'

'He was here when that man got caught taking the drugs. Remember?'

Haroun Patel.

That was the connection that had been nagging at him. Joe Massey must have been in Riyadh at the time Haroun Patel had died. Majid had mentioned the drug theft the other night.

Damien had known and liked Haroun. He had been intelligent and energetic, a young man determined to do well in life, and not afraid to cut corners on the way. Only he'd chosen the wrong corner to cut and he was gone. The local police had landed every outstanding case of drug pilfering on his head, and then they had cut it off. His trial had been quick and secret, the evidence laid before the judges with no chance for Haroun to plead his case. By that time, anyway, he had confessed his guilt. As far as Damien knew, there had been no diplomatic fuss, no pressure to gain him a fair trial or a more proportionate sentence, just a small and quickly forgotten protest from people who had known him during his time in the UK. Haroun had been one more third-worlder, another immigrant worker trying his luck.

'I remember,' he said. 'Why are you asking?'

Amy sat up, and the sheet slipped away to lie in a pool round her hips. 'It was just . . . this Massey guy said something that got me thinking.

The case against Haroun never really made a lot of sense . . .'

'They caught him with the stuff. That's all the sense a case needs, here.'

'I know. But it wasn't the first theft, and I don't see how Haroun could have done the others . . .'

'You're right. He probably didn't. Amy, they caught him with enough stuff to land a trafficking charge on him. That was the crime that got him. The rest was just convenience. They needed a drugs trafficker, they got a drugs trafficker. They just cleared up anything outstanding. He was going anyway, he might as well take some extra baggage with him.' He was deliberately brutal. He didn't want her getting involved any further with this.

Amy ran her fingers through her hair. 'It's a lousy system. You know that?'

He shrugged. 'Have you only just found that out?'

'You seem happy enough with it.'

It was happening already. If they weren't having sex, it wasn't long before they were sniping at each other, looking for the weak points in each other's armour. He knew about the iniquities of the system – he didn't need Amy to point them out. This was one of the reasons he'd left the diplomatic service. 'You take their money, Amy. You know the score. It's just the way it is.'

'So no one's going to do anything about it?'

He pushed the sheet off in exasperation and got out of bed. 'Do what? What would be the point?'

She was silent, chewing her lip as she thought about it. 'He had a family. I thought it might be better for them if they knew he'd only stolen drugs once.'

'He got caught once. He might have done it loads of times – and then he got careless. Leave it.'

She stood up. Draped in the thin cotton sheet, she looked as though she had stepped out of an engraving for one of the stories of the thousand and one nights. 'Maybe.' Her tone didn't denote agreement, just that she wanted to close the subject.

She wouldn't leave it. He knew Amy.

10

Topic: Veiled Knowledge

Ibrahim: Red Rose, why did you post this article for us to read? If you think as a woman in Islam you have the right of leadership, you are totally wrong, because this kind of job is only valid for men.

For women to read and understand.

Allah Subhanahu Ta'âla (Az-Zukhruf: 18) says clearly that women are deficient in intellect and understanding. Women are physically weak and unable to fulfil the duties of leadership. It has thus been made the right of men only.

100

These are the rules that a Muslim woman should obey and these make her unfit for leadership should she be foolish enough to aspire to such a thing:

1. A woman should at all times remain in her home, but if due to any shar'ie necessity (eg Hajj, visiting her parents, visiting the ill, etc), then she should cover her entire body including the face.

2. She must not try to seduce strange men by making her voice low and attractive when speaking with them and she should not walk in such a manner that would attract the attention of men.

3. Intermingling of the sexes is prohibited in Islam.

Red Rose, I'll tell you a real story about an American Muslim woman who worked as a professor; she came to the King Saud University in Riyadh for a lecture. She said strong words to the girls that she saw with their bad behaviour and clothes. She said, 'I wish that I was born in a Muslim family so I could do as much as possible to bless the great one, unlike you who are wearing unsuitable clothes and behaving in an immodest and foolish way, like 'the women in my country do.' That was said by an American Muslim woman. How do you answer this?

Red Rose: Ibrahim, too many men in our country are thinking like you. I am good Muslim, but I have travelled. I have been to place where good Muslim women drive car, vote and travel without the permission of husband or father. I think it is time we see the difference between Islam and custom in this country too. Maybe you will be liking this article better. This one was written by a Saudi man:

Women and Islam – a new perspective

What is perceived as the rise of fundamentalism in the Islamic world has led to the criticism that women pay the price for the reestablishment of faith. Is it true that women are oppressed within Islam, or is this a distortion of what the Q'ran itself teaches?

When these accusations are made by the secularists, then the Islamists must turn again to the words of the prophet . . .

The university was on the main road to the north east of Riyadh. Roisin sat in the back of the car, enveloped in her abaya, and tried not to flinch too visibly as her driver carved a straight route through the weaving traffic. The inside of the car smelled faintly of leather and spices. The chill from the air-conditioning made a disorientating contrast to the hard glare of the sun outside.

The driver hadn't spoken apart from a response to her Arabic greeting, and a nod of assent when she told him her destination. He would be driving her three times a week, and she wondered if he would unbend with familiarity, or if they were condemned by custom and protocol to travel this route in silence for the next year.

They were leaving the city centre now, travelling fast along an eight-lane highway. She could see a haze of green in the distance, and as it drew closer the driver pulled across and took a turn-off, pulling up at a security gate.

Roisin remained mute and invisible in the back while the driver carried out the negotiations. Beyond the checkpoint she could see a landscaped park with packed red earth, green lawns, palm trees and low shrubs. As the car moved slowly past the barrier, she could see that the grass of the lawns was patchy as it fought to survive in the dry terrain, but otherwise, she was looking at a futuristic arcadia on the edge of the biggest desert in the world.

The buildings were high with curved, sweeping roofs, lifted off the ground on pillars or pointing, needle thin, to the sky. Even this early in the day, the campus was busy. Students wandered across the open spaces, young men in white thobes with red ghutra. There were no women visible, apart from her, and she was enclosed in the separate world of the car, hidden behind her abaya and headscarf. No one glanced her way.

The driver stopped at a second gate. 'Woman college,' he said. Only the second time he had spoken.

Roisin made sure her headscarf was in place and got out of the car. 'Thank you. Twelve thirty,' she said to the driver, who nodded abruptly and pulled away.

She stepped through the door into the building that housed the women's campus.

Cool twilight enclosed her. She was in a long corridor of high pillars, the ceiling punched with holes to admit the light that fell across the shadows in beams of gold where the dust motes danced. It was cloister-like in its silence. There were no groups of young women passing time chatting and laughing. The few women who were there moved purposefully, their footsteps quiet, their eyes cast down. Even though men did not come here – the male teachers taught their classes over video link – they wore the hijab and long skirts. Roisin hesitated then loosened her own headscarf and let it fall round her neck. Until someone told her otherwise, she was going to leave it off. She shook her hair free.

She followed the signs along the corridor, thankful that they were written in English as well as Arabic, until she found the office of the professor who would be her supervisor. Souad al-Munajjed was an internationally respected academic who taught and researched in the area of foreign language teaching. Roisin was curious to meet her. She knocked on the door, and when a voice responded, she went in.

Souad al-Munajjed made a lie of any preconceptions that Roisin had brought with her about Saudi women. She was in her late forties, married with children, and a professor of English at the prestigious university. She wrote books, attended academic conferences all over the world and enjoyed an international reputation for her work on translation.

She stood up from her chair as Roisin entered, moving forward to greet her. 'Good morning,' she said in heavily accented English, then switched to Arabic. 'Peace be upon you.' She was small and pretty. Like her students, she wore the hijab. Hers was folded in a style that made it drape elegantly over her hair and round her shoulders. Her dress was black and ankle-length, subtly ornamented with silver stitching.

'And upon you peace,' Roisin responded. *Wa-alay-kum as-salam.*

'*Salaam,*' Souad al-Munajjed corrected her pronunciation and nodded her approval of Roisin's courtesy. 'It is good that you speak Arabic,' she said, reverting to English.

'I speak very little.'

'But you try. This is good.' She studied Roisin in silence. 'The bangles you wear, they are very pretty.'

'Thank you. My husband bought them for me when we first arrived, from the market.'

Souad nodded as if this pleased her. 'We have good silversmiths here. Now, these first meetings are important, are they not? I would like to introduce to you one of our graduate students who will be your teaching assistant today.' She indicated a chair in the corner of the room where another woman was sitting, unnoticed until now.

As she stood up to greet Roisin, it was obvious she was pregnant. 'I am Yasmin,' she said.

She was beautiful. Her heart-shaped face was framed by a black hijab that emphasized the fairness of her skin. A curl of chestnut hair escaped the confines of the scarf. But she looked tired. Roisin could see dark circles of fatigue under her eyes, and lines around her mouth that denoted some kind of strain. 'I am most pleased to meet you,' she said. She spoke English with a slight French accent.

'And I'm pleased to meet you. I'm Roisin Gardner.' Roisin hadn't had time to get the name on her teaching papers changed to reflect her new status. 'Will we be working together?'

'Sometimes. I would like to learn better English.' Her smile to Roisin was cautious. 'I think I will be your student.'

'Yasmin will assist you in some classes,' Professor Souad explained. 'But I cannot spare her all the time. Some days, she teaches in the villages. We have a big programme, funded by our government, to bring education to the village women. Now, my dears, I think we should have tea.' She picked up the phone and spoke briefly, then sat down and gestured for Roisin to sit next to her. 'What is your impression of our university?'

'It's beautiful. But I was surprised there were so few students – in this part, I mean. I thought you had more women than men here.'

'Yes indeed. Our education policies are more enlightened than we are given credit for. But the girls don't arrive before classes start, unless they are here to see their tutors. Saudi girls don't waste their time in gossip and "hanging out".' She gave the phrase an ironic emphasis. 'Isn't that right?' she added to Yasmin, who smiled and nodded. 'Don't worry. Your class will be waiting for you. Now you must tell me about yourself.'

Over the next fifteen minutes, she subjected Roisin to a friendly but close interrogation, interrupted briefly by the arrival of tea and pastries. Her eyebrows lifted in surprise when Roisin told her she had no children. 'But, my dear, you are already thirty-two!'

'I only got married a few weeks ago,' Roisin said.

'I had four children when I was your age.' Souad patted Roisin's hand. 'Take my advice. Don't delay.'

'A lot of women in the West wait until their thirties.' Roisin noticed with some amusement the flash of slightly contemptuous pity in Souad al-Munajjed's eyes.

'The students,' the professor said briskly; 'you have seen their work online – what do you think of them? And you like our discussion forum? This was my idea.' She refilled Roisin's cup unasked, and put a sweet, crumbly pastry on her plate.

'There have been some interesting postings recently.' Roisin broke off a piece of the pastry and put it in her mouth, letting it melt on her tongue. Its intense sweetness was mellowed by the flavour of spices. 'I was surprised about the . . .' She hesitated for a moment, but these women were too intelligent not to be aware of what she was thinking. 'I was surprised at the openness of the discussion about women's rights. And about the vote.'

The professor nodded slowly. 'Truly we discourage openly political topics. There are some hotheads who do not understand about debate. Otherwise, why should the girls not discuss what they wish? You must be aware that sometimes they talk without thinking. They are very young, very inexperienced. There are a lot of wrong ideas about women in this country. I don't pretend for a moment that all is well, but women have their difficulties everywhere, and sometimes things can be made worse when they are brought into the open.'

Roisin noticed that Yasmin had withdrawn from the discussion and was sitting quietly studying her hands. 'You think they shouldn't discuss it?'

'I think that the – what is the word? The *status quo* – the status quo can be the best. For example, it has long been the rule in the Kingdom that women are not allowed to drive, but attitudes were perhaps starting to change. Then there was a protest here, and a group of women drove. All they achieved was to lose their jobs, anger the clerics and draw attention to a law that may have been quietly repealed in a year or two. Instead, their defiance made attitudes harden. So where was the value in the protest? All it did was to make life more difficult for everyone. Is that not so?' She turned to the silent Yasmin.

'It caused trouble, certainly,' Yasmin said after a moment.

'And now,' the professor continued, 'there are the elections. It can worry the students. They say things they do not understand.'

'Some women,' Yasmin said in her quiet voice, 'expected to be given the vote –'

'Ah, the vote.' Roisin got the impression that this was a topic the professor was used to dismissing. She turned to Roisin. 'Tell me, does your vote make any difference to who rules you, who makes the laws you must abide by?' She was smiling as she looked at Roisin, her head tilted like an interrogative bird.

Roisin evaded the question. 'I thought that Islamists believe laws come from God.'

'Ah, but you are not an Islamist, as that remark shows. Come now, what do *you* believe?'

Roisin shrugged. 'People make laws. Men make laws. One vote, no, it makes no difference. But . . .' She had a vague memory of an Arab proverb and she was trying to remember it: 'One small thing is . . . small. But a lot of small things together . . . The women could make a difference if they voted.'

'And you support the government that rules you?'

'Not entirely, no.'

'And did you vote for them?'

'No. I voted for someone else.'

The professor nodded slowly. 'So in this much-praised democracy, your vote counts for nothing and you are governed by someone you didn't choose? As these girls are governed by someone they didn't choose?'

'The government knows that not everyone supports them. That limits what they feel able to do. I was able to express my choice. I feel unhappy about a system that denies so many people that right.'

'When my children disagree with me, I let them tell me why. I let them have their say, I let them "express their choice", and then their father and I tell them what they must do. If I had a democratic family, it seems that the children would rule.' Her eyes gleamed as she watched Roisin's reaction.

'In a democracy, children don't have the vote.' Roisin saw the trap as soon as she had stepped into it.

'So you, like us, decide who can and who can't choose. I see we are not so different after all. At last I understand this democracy. Now, it's time to meet your students. Yasmin will take you to the seminar room.'

'Will you stay for the class?' Roisin asked as they left the room.

'If you are happy for me to,' Yasmin said.

As she followed the younger woman along the corridor, Roisin wasn't sure if she'd just participated in a good-natured debate, or if she had been given a warning. She had no doubt that everything she said to the students would reach the diligent ears of the professor.

11

Damien was sufficiently concerned by Amy's sudden interest in the Patel case – especially as it seemed to have been triggered by Joe Massey – to do a bit of digging on his own. He wasn't interested in the rights and wrongs of it – Patel had made a bad choice and had had the misfortune to fall foul of the Saudi legal system. Any crusade to get the case reopened would be a quixotic waste of time. The courts of the Kingdom didn't make mistakes and anyone who suggested they did was asking for a fast ticket out. He didn't like the system, but it wasn't his system. It was up to the Saudis themselves to clean it up.

He phoned Majid using his work number so that Majid would know this call was business rather than social. After the necessary exchange of courtesies – one of the things that had attracted Damien to Saudi culture when he first arrived was the voices calling the blessings of God upon their colleagues as a matter of routine – he introduced his topic: 'Majid, I came across an old case yesterday, one of yours, from earlier this year. A Pakistani man called Haroun Patel was . . .'

Uncharacteristically, Majid interrupted him. 'You, too, my friend? Why does everyone involve themselves with this man? He stole drugs. He paid the penalty.'

You, too. 'I think we're asking the same question. I'm asking you because someone asked me. I've forgotten the details. Remind me what happened.'

'My friend, there is no mystery and no secret. We did a check on the hospital drugs supply. All was in order except in the main pharmacy where two packets of morphine had gone.'

'They were stolen, not lost?'

'They were stolen. The hospital had done an inventory just the night before, because we had warned them we would be visiting. The drugs were there then.'

So the thief hadn't just taken a risk, he had been stupid.

'And then . . . ?'

'We searched the hospital and we found the missing drugs hidden in one of the lockers in the accommodation block where the technicians lived.'

'Haroun Patel's?'

'Haroun Patel's.'

'And it was Patel who had put them there?'

'The lockers have code numbers. No one but the user can access them.' Majid's voice was cooler.

No one but the user and the hospital authorities. But Damien kept that thought to himself. He chose his words carefully. He didn't want to offend Majid. 'I knew Haroun Patel. It seems to have been a very unintelligent crime, and Patel was not a stupid man. It puzzled me . . .'

'It wasn't so stupid,' Majid said. He sounded more relaxed now he understood Damien's concern. 'He did extra hours as a driver. He had been away the day before, delivering supplies round the villages. He didn't know there was going to be a check.'

'Thank you,' Damien said formally. After he hung up, he reflected that this conversation had removed some of the doubts he'd had himself about the case. He still didn't know why Patel had taken the risk of stealing the drugs, but if he thought he had time to get them away . . . Patel's confession to the other crimes, the ones he probably hadn't committed, had never surprised him. The Saudi police had interrogation methods that didn't bear close scrutiny. It was another sore in a system that was chronically diseased, and it distressed Damien that a man like Majid was touched by that contamination.

But someone was stirring things up. Majid, too, was aware of questions around the case. If the authorities were starting to pay attention, then that curiosity was dangerous and it was up to Damien to stop it. He needed to find out who was at the root of it, and why.

The *who* he had some ideas about. This had started after Joe Massey had arrived. Massey had actually been talking about the case to Amy. It was possible that someone else could have been asking questions that had prompted Massey to talk to Amy, but Occam's razor said that Massey was the *who*. The *why* eluded him completely. Why would anyone want to dig around the Haroun Patel case?

He went back over the conversation in his mind. Amy had queried Haroun's guilt, at least as far as some of the charges went. What was it she had said? *The case against him never made a lot of sense* . . . But sense was exactly what it had made. Patel had been a technician. He'd had access to the pharmacy. Means, motive, opportunity. Patel had the means and he had had the opportunity. The only thing Damien didn't know was the motive. But if Patel was putting in extra hours as a driver, then he clearly needed money and had taken a fatal gamble.

Damien shrugged off his doubts. People did stupid things when they panicked. It was academic. His concern now was to find out who was asking questions, who was about to cause some serious trouble in the ex-pat community, and put a stop to it.

The best way to find something out was to go straight to the source. He picked up the phone and found the name on his address list: Arshak Nazarian. Majid's father-in-law had cornered the lucrative Saudi market in migrant workers. By means of sweeteners, pay-offs, subtle pressure, and when all else failed, threats, Nazarian had gradually incorporated all the disparate groups who were recruiting third world migrants into his own agency. His organization would almost certainly have brokered Haroun Patel's presence in the Kingdom.

Nazarian was a powerful man with friends in high places. He was also, by Damien's definition, a crook, though in Saudi terms he had done nothing illegal. Through a network of agents in India, Pakistan, Bangladesh, the Philippines, Sri Lanka – countries where levels of poverty and unemployment were high – Nazarian recruited workers desperate to feed their families and to secure them some kind of future. He found them Saudi sponsors and offered them contracts that, by the standards of their own countries, were very well paid. But those contracts did not come cheap: the workers had to pay exorbitant sums for their sponsorship and visas. When they arrived in the Kingdom, they were made to sign contracts written in Arabic – the only contracts that were legally enforceable – only to find that their prom-ised salaries were much reduced and the length of time they were required to remain in the Kingdom much increased. If they broke their contracts and left early, the cost of their trans-portation would be added to the already substan-tial debts they had accrued. It was probably a debt of this nature that had driven Patel to take his fatal shortcut.

Once they were in the Kingdom, Nazarian took no further responsibility for the migrants. Their employers were free to act as they wished. In a country that had only abolished slavery in 1962, this form of labour exploitation raised few eyebrows. Nazarian's empire had never been challenged. He knew the game backwards, knew who had the power and who didn't, who to flatter, who to pay. Damien had tried several times to try and break the stranglehold he had on the unskilled labour market, but Nazarian was too well connected.

But maybe the 'good times' were finally nearing an end. The system was breaking down as the Islamists in Saudi recoiled from the exploitation of fellow Muslims, turning away from the corruption in the heart of their society and back to older, stricter ways. A few months earlier, an attempt had been made on Nazarian's life.

The Armenian was a difficult man to contact, but Damien's name got him through the barriers that he surrounded himself with. He left some messages and waited. After half an hour, his phone rang.

'O'Neill!' Nazarian's voice was deep and warm. Along with his other assets, he had a great deal of charm. 'Good to see you the other night. How are you? Well, I hope.'

They exchanged the usual courtesies, then

Nazarian said, 'I'm glad you called. I wanted to talk to you.'

'So you said.' Damien waited to see what Nazarian wanted.

There was silence on the other end of the line, as though Nazarian was choosing his words carefully. 'The hospital,' he said after a moment. 'You recruit many of the doctors, am I right?'

'Yes.' Hospital recruitment was high on Damien's list of responsibilities.

'Obstetricians,' Nazarian said abruptly. 'Do they get the best here, or . . . ?'

Damien suddenly understood what the problem was and, for the first time in his association with the man, he found himself feeling some sympathy towards Nazarian. Social restrictions made it close to impossible for male obstetricians and gynaecologists to work in the Kingdom. Nazarian was worried about the standard of care that would be offered to his daughter. 'They get the best,' he said. And it was true. Saudi trained its women to a high standard in women's medicine, and the Kingdom had always recruited and paid for the best when they couldn't fill posts from their own schools and universities.

Nazarian grunted, only half convinced. 'I keep thinking about taking her to Europe. That's where she . . .'

Majid would never permit that, but it was something that the two men would have to sort out between themselves. He felt a stab of sympathy for Yasmin who apparently was not allowed any say in this issue. 'She'll get excellent care here,' he said.

'OK.' Nazarian closed the subject abruptly. 'You wanted to talk to me.'

'Yes. Something's come up.' Damien saw no reason for subterfuge. Whatever had happened with Patel, Nazarian would have nothing he needed to hide. There was very little he could have done to the man that the authorities would have worried about. 'I've had a query about a man called Haroun Patel,' he said. He wanted to see if the name – one of thousands on Nazarian's books – would be recognized.

There was a moment of silence. 'A query about Patel? From whom?'

'That's what I'm not sure about.' Damien didn't want Amy in Nazarian's sights.

There was another beat of silence. 'Maybe we need to talk about this. Can you come to my office? Say . . . around two?'

After the call, Damien sat for a moment, his eyes unfocused as he thought. Nazarian hadn't even tried to feign ignorance. He'd recognized the name Patel as soon as Damien had spoken. Which was bad. The edginess that Damien had been feeling for the past few weeks intensified. There was something going on, and this something was associated with the long-dead Haroun Patel.

And now Amy had got herself involved.

12

Roisin had arranged to meet her students in a series of small seminars. She knew that Saudi teachers tended to prefer formal lectures in which discussion was kept to a minimum, but she couldn't teach unless her students felt able to talk to her and use the English they were trying to learn.

As she followed Yasmin into the classroom, she was aware of a faint whisper around the waiting group of young women. The teaching assistant greeted them in Arabic, then switched to English. 'This is Roisin Gardner who is your teacher for this semester.'

'Good morning,' Roisin greeted them, and received a collective murmur of *Good mornings* in return. The room was light and airy with tiled walls and floor. There were no desks or chairs. The students, a group of eight, sat cross-legged, or knelt with their legs tucked neatly underneath them on a crimson rug that covered most of the floor. Their hands rested in their laps.

She was struck first of all by their similarity – they all wore the hijab, and they were mostly dressed in sombre or neutral colours – browns, greys and blacks predominated. They were sitting with their heads bowed, studying their clasped hands. Roisin thought about the glittering brilliance of the souk and the opulence of the university where these women walked in their drab attire and wondered why they chose to drain the colour out of their lives – if it was a choice. She followed Yasmin's example and sat cross-legged on the carpet, relieved that years of yoga made her limber enough to do this without too much effort. The students were looking at her expectantly and she felt the slight adrenaline surge that always prefaced her first encounter with a new group.

They weren't beginners. They were studying for an advanced qualification in English, which made her task easier. She thought about the number of times she had found herself in front of groups like this when they had no common language in which to communicate.

She gathered her thoughts, then started speaking. 'Today, I'd like to introduce myself, and get to know you.' She could see one or two of the students glance quickly at her and then down again. 'My name's Roisin,' she said. 'I arrived in Riyadh two weeks ago. Before that, I worked in London. I've taught English in Europe and in South America, in Mexico. Now I'd like each of you to tell me about yourself.' She smiled at the girl sitting closest to her. 'Would you like to start?'

The girl glanced sideways at her companions, then said, 'My name is Mujada.' She giggled and glanced quickly at Roisin, who nodded her encouragement. 'I am student,' Mujada said. 'I study to be . . . teacher.' She ducked her head and Roisin smiled reassurance at her and moved on to the next student.

This girl was less shy. Instead of looking away with nervous giggles, she smiled when she met Roisin's gaze. She was a pretty girl with a round face and big eyes. Despite the uniform appearance, Roisin could already see the differences between them. The quiet girl, Mujada, was thinner, with black, wavy hair that escaped from her scarf. This girl's hijab was neatly draped, covering her head and framing her face. 'Hello, Roisin,' she said. 'My name is Fozia. I study design and I want to start my own business.'

The third student had been watching Roisin as these exchanges went round the group. 'I am Najia,' she said. Her scarf was lighter and pushed back from her hair, which was heavy and dark. Her full mouth curved into a warm smile. 'Roisin, where are you coming from?'

'Newcastle. Where do you come from?' Roisin added, carefully correcting Najia's construction.

She saw the student's lips move as she tried this out. 'I do come . . .' She caught Roisin's eye and smiled. 'I *come* from Jeddah. Roisin, where is being . . . where is Newcastle?'

'It's in the north of England.' She had a map of the British Isles, and she stood up to pin it on the wall. 'Here,' she said. Then she showed them London. 'That's where I was working before I came here,' she told them.

The students were a mixed group, studying a range of subjects, and all with their ambitions focused on different careers. It wasn't what she had expected. Some of them seemed rather young compared with UK students of the same age, shy and inclined to giggle, others seemed far more mature and serious. One woman, Haifa, studied Roisin with cool hostility. Her face, which had the fine-boned, slightly avian beauty that was very prevalent among Arab women, was tightly framed by her scarf. She said very little, except when Roisin addressed her directly. 'I study medicine. To be doctor,' she said, in response to Roisin's query. Then she resumed her silence.

As they talked, the students became more confident, joining in and adding to the discussion, even the shyer ones like Mujada. Towards the end of the session, the talk turned to the different customs of Western and Saudi culture. 'Tell me about the hijab,' Roisin said. She still hadn't grasped the rules governing its use. 'Is this . . .' she tried to think of an English word they would know '. . . custom?' They looked blank. '*Sunna*,' she tried – as far as she knew, this word expressed the concept of custom rather than compulsion. 'And what about . . . ?' She made a gesture of covering her

123

face. This elicited laughter round the group and the girls looked at each other as they tried to formulate a response.

'For us, it is required.' This was Haifa. 'You should wear the scarf, but you should not cover your face. You are not Muslim.'

'You are wrong,' Najia intervened. 'It is not required. It is custom. In many countries, good Muslima do not hide themselves like this.'

Haifa responded in Arabic, too fast for Roisin to understand. 'English, Haifa,' she said. 'That's the rule. In this class, you speak only English.' The student's mouth tightened, but she didn't say anything.

Yasmin, the teaching assistant who had been watching this exchange, stepped in suddenly. 'Haifa was explaining that she believes we Saudis must set the best examples as we are the guardians of the holy places.'

'This is the truth,' Haifa said, addressing Yasmin. 'Saudis are the guardians because our blood is pure. We carry no Christian blood,' she said, her eyes flicking contemptuously to Roisin. 'None at all.'

Saudi is another country, Roisin reminded herself. *They do things differently here.*

By the end of the morning, apart from the slight *frisson* with Haifa, she felt pleased with the way things had gone, and much more relaxed about the prospects for her work at the university. Yasmin, who had stayed with her, waited until the students had left, then said, 'I enjoyed that. You are a good teacher.'

Roisin felt her face flush with pleasure. 'Thank you.'

'I must apologize for Haifa. She was discourteous.'

'She has to say what she thinks.'

Yasmin studied her hands. 'She is . . . well thought of. Her family is very traditional.' Her gaze met Roisin's, but she didn't expand on her comment. 'I am glad to watch you teach,' she said. 'I need to learn to help my own teaching.'

'Here? In the university?'

Yasmin smiled. 'Here, I am just trainee, just *assistant*. No, I am teaching women in the villages – it's true what the professor says, we want to educate women here. But in the villages, it's hard for them to find a class they can attend, so we take it to them.'

'I'd like to see that,' Roisin said.

Yasmin studied her face. 'Maybe one day,' she said. 'Now, I have work to do.'

Roisin packed her bag and went along the corridor to the cloakroom to do battle with her scarf. The Saudi women were neatly, often elegantly hijabed, their scarves covering their hair and hanging in careful folds around their faces and shoulders. Souad's had been an accessory as well as a cultural requirement. Whatever views anyone might hold of the Islamic head covering, it was an attractive garment.

To Roisin, however, it was a pain. No matter how carefully she tied it, it was either too tight and gave her a headache, or it slipped back, uncovering her hair and she had to keep grabbing at it. She stood in front of the mirror and fixed the scarf carefully in place.

But as she turned away, it slipped again, and she sighed with exasperation. She grabbed the ends and tied them firmly under her chin. Framed tightly by black, her face looked deathly white and at least ten years older. She loosened the ends, and the scarf slipped off. She pulled it off her head and swore out loud. There was a suppressed laugh from behind her.

She looked round. A woman was standing there watching her. She was dressed to leave the campus, her hijab hanging in meticulous folds, her face carefully veiled. Her eyes watched Roisin in the cool light. Roisin coloured, wondering if the woman had understood the obscenity she'd used. 'Sorry,' she said. 'This thing is enough to make anyone swear.'

The woman lifted the veil away from her face, revealing herself as the student, Najia. Her eyes gleamed with laughter at Roisin's embarrassment. 'You do not do it right, Roisin,' she said. 'If you tie like this –' she held her own hijab tightly under her chin to demonstrate '– you look like someone's grandma.'

Roisin couldn't argue with that. 'So how do I do it?'

'Here, I show you.' Najia took the scarf from Roisin's hand and unknotted it, tutting slightly at the creases the tie had made. She shook the scarf out. 'You should get the proper hijab. This scarf is too small.' She folded it into an unequal triangle to make the back longer, and put it on Roisin's head, adjusting it to make the folds hang evenly. She tucked the sides behind Roisin's ears, pulling the front flat, then drew the folds forward. She pinned it under Roisin's chin, and pulled the ends round her shoulders. Then she pulled the scarf free from Roisin's ears and loosened the tight band across her forehead. 'With proper hijab, it hang down and you can pin,' she said. 'But now it is better, see?'

Roisin looked in the mirror and saw herself neatly hijabed, her face elegantly framed by the folds of the scarf. She moved her head cautiously. The scarf stayed secure. She moved her head again, starting to smile as the scarf remained in place.

'Thank you.'

Najia's eyes creased at the corners. 'You look nice now. Pretty. Not someone's grandma any more.'

Their laughter as they left the room echoed down the silent corridors where the light formed pools of gold among the shadows.

13

Arshak Nazarian's offices were in one of the older parts of the city, among decaying lots that were due for development and hastily erected blocks that were now empty and heading towards dereliction. He was hidden away from the thriving city, camouflaged among the detritus of urban fall-out.

He didn't stint himself in the other aspects of his life. The Kingdom had made him rich. He lived in a spacious house in the suburbs, with a mature garden that was maintained by teams of gardeners and irrigation systems available only to the water rich, in a land where that commodity was more valuable – though often less valued – than oil.

He lived his life in modern Riyadh and paid little attention to the desert city that underlay the world he knew, stepping carefully over the gaps where the mullahs prayed, the clerics wielded their swords and the poor scratched a living from the desert soil. His city contained malls, designer shops, fast cars and luxury – and a run-down office in a derelict block.

But sometimes, the desert intruded.

The offices might be run down, but the door was steel framed and fitted with the latest security locks. The windows were covered with shutters that were never opened. The man at the door and the men waiting inside the first office were Nazarian's own men. Since the assassination attempt, Nazarian took his security seriously.

He'd brushed it off at the time, dismissing it as the act of what he called 'local hotheads'. In his line of business, these things happened, and business he could handle, especially now that he had a son-in-law who was high up in the police force.

Damien, arriving on time for his appointment, waited as Nazarian's security men took their time checking his papers. They knew him, but they enjoyed the small exercise of power. It was an attempt, Damien always assumed, to unnerve him and reduce his status. But Damien had learned from the Arabs a long time ago and responded with cool politeness – discourtesy demeaned only the person using it. Such things could be dealt with later. Arabs were not a forgiving people. Many ex-pats thought the Saudis were ill-mannered and unfriendly, not recognizing that their own behaviour had doomed them to be forever pushed aside and ignored.

One of the men spoke into the intercom, which crackled in response. 'You go in now,' the man said. He passed through the door to the small office that was the centre of Nazarian's web of exploitation.

The Armenian was sitting at his desk when Damien came through the door, inspecting the screen of his computer. He flicked it off and stood up. He was tall and well built, and could use his muscular bulk to intimidate, but today he seemed out to charm. He held out his hand and smiled warmly. 'O'Neill. Good to see you. I'm sorry about all this –' He waved a hand at the door to indicate the security Damien had just been subjected to. 'Troubled times,' he said. 'Please, sit down.'

Damien took the proffered chair. 'Business good?'

Nazarian made a *so-so* face and tipped his hand from side to side. 'Business is business,' he said. 'Coffee?'

'Thank you, but I just had some.' People who ventured into the underworld should beware of accepting hospitality. 'I hope your family is well.' *Family*, for Nazarian, was his daughter Yasmin.

Nazarian smiled. 'I will soon be a grandfather.' For a moment, the human being was visible behind the mask of corporate hospitality, then Nazarian pulled the conversation back to business. 'You should come to see me more often, O'Neill – I go short of intelligent conversation in my days. But you're busy. I understand. What's this about Patel?'

'Just some talk on the streets – someone isn't happy about what happened.'

Nazarian allowed himself a smile. 'Including Patel, I presume.' He leaned back in his chair. 'It's over and done with. The man did something stupid. We try and warn them, but . . .' He shrugged. Easy come, easy go. 'Why concern yourself?'

Because Nazarian had asked him here as soon as Damien had mentioned the name. 'You brought Patel here?'

Nazarian's eyes narrowed. 'I hope you don't mean that I had a responsibility to protect him from the consequences of his own actions.'

'Not at all. But I wondered if someone else might think that. Maybe the person who's been asking questions . . .'

'Who says anyone has?'

Damien waited him out. Nazarian let the silence grow, then shrugged. 'Someone tried to pull his record off our system a few days ago. It wouldn't have mattered if he'd succeeded, but I don't like people breaking into my data.'

This explained why Nazarian had responded so quickly to Damien's original query. He wanted to know the identity of the hacker. Damien could probably help him, but he wasn't going to. Nazarian had some unpleasant ways of showing someone that they had made him unhappy.

He let the talk go on for a while, but he already had everything he needed. As he left the building, he had fixed in his mind the image of Joe Massey in the internet café, his eyes intent on the monitor in front of him.

14

Topic: Veiled Knowledge

Metaeb: Dear Red Rose, many people in the West criticize the Saudi system and Saudi men, and I am not saying that our system is perfect – we are human, and humans are flawed. But our faith does not allow men to oppress women – quite the contrary. I know that many men do not act as well as they should, and sometimes the laws protecting women are not enforced as rigorously as they ought to be. But, Red Rose, this is not exclusive to our country – I have travelled widely in Europe and in the US, and I can assure you that the same things happen to women there.

Red Rose: Dear Metaeb, if all Saudi men believe as you, then we do not need debate. But more men believe different interpretation that are not right. The words of the holy book do not say this, or in the life of the prophet (saaws).

Professor Souad al-Munajjed: Red Rose, from your writings I can see that you are not as experienced as you would like us to believe. After all, your opinions are not so confident that you put your real name to them!

Red Rose, elections and democracy are and have been the biggest political lies throughout the history of the modern world. Look at what is happening in the so-called democracies of the West. Do you really think that this is what the people chose when they voted?

Back to our main subject: women in Saudi Arabia. Why all this concentration on us? All over the world, the majority of women are oppressed, bullied, betrayed, abandoned, raped, and used as white slaves or prostitutes, so why isn't anybody mentioning this? Why enlarge our problems and minimize the major issues of others?

I want to ask you a question. How and why do you think women are oppressed in Saudi Arabia? Is it because we wear the hijab and don't mix with men? Why is this such a terrible thing? What would we gain if we changed it? And what would we lose? In the UK and the US, women have to fight to be allowed their own places where men cannot go.

As for the elections, my young friend – forget about it. This is just another big lie that the Western politicians use to reach their goals. If one man in the modern world had eliminated poverty and made fruitful education available for ALL his countrymen, I would believe in elections and democracy, but this has never happened and never will.

Now, I have to tell you something, Red Rose, Metaeb, Ibrahim, all of you. This site is not for political discussion, and if you continue to post unsuitable articles, I will ban you from the discussion boards.

Once she started work, Roisin was on familiar territory, and found the Kingdom less alien and alienating. Her work at the university occupied more of her time than she'd expected. She became friendly with Najia, the student who had helped her with the hijab on that first day, and also with Yasmin. The two women were clearly friends, and were eager to develop their advanced English skills. In addition, Yasmin was keen to pick up ideas about teaching from Roisin. She was happy to work with them. She enjoyed their company, and she had nothing better to do with her time.

Joe was still working long hours, so Roisin started spending an extra day on campus to work with them. When Professor Souad found she was

134

willingly putting in unpaid time, she started asking Roisin to work with the university archives to prepare teaching material that the English Language Department could use in the future.

'She's exploiting you,' Joe warned when she told him about the new arrangements. 'You know who'll get the credit for all that stuff.'

'I know.' They both knew how universities worked, senior staff taking credit for work done by junior members. Roisin didn't mind. It was hardly ground-breaking stuff she was producing. Souad al-Munajjed wasn't going to run away with a Nobel prize on the back of Roisin's work – she'd just have more resources for her section. 'Maybe I should sneak something un-Islamic in, then she won't dare to claim it as her own.'

'Right, and I'll come and visit you in the Riyadh slammer on alternate months.' He was suddenly serious. 'I know you're on your own here too much,' he said.

Now she had started work, she no longer felt overwhelmed with loneliness, but she missed Joe. The closeness they had developed in London was receding as the distance between them increased. It was almost like a bereavement, as if the companion she had depended on had left her without warning, leaving a void in her life.

She had no idea what she would do with all the spare time if she didn't spend it at the university. The alternatives were far from appealing: tedious coffee mornings with the stay-at-home wives, or devoting even more of her time to house-work – though the house was already more spot-less than any place she'd ever lived in. She'd heard the warning bells the day she found herself contemplating a pile of underwear, the iron in her hand.

It would be different if she could find another woman she could be friendly with, but most of the interesting women she had met were in full-time work – nurses, teachers, doctors, women who had established successful businesses when they had come here with their husbands – so instead she put in the extra hours at work, enjoying the familiar atmosphere of the academic world.

She was starting to get to know the students, though it was a slower process than she was used to. Instead of staying on campus after their classes were finished, they vanished, reappearing only at the start of classes the following day.

So she enjoyed the time she spent with Yasmin and Najia. They were intelligent and informed, and deeply engaged with the debate about the forthcoming election. They talked about the lives of Saudi women, their education, their experience of the world. Roisin, aware of her status as a teacher in this most rigid of societies, kept away from personal topics, but otherwise, the talk was unrestricted. She felt far more drawn to them than to the women she met in the compound and at the few ex-pat parties she and Joe had attended.

'Why do all the students disappear so quickly?'

Roisin asked them once when they were working in the library together. Yasmin was analysing a text, Najia was studying for her advanced English exam, and Roisin was reading a journal, trying to keep up to date with the latest theories on language learning. She had been taking a break, looking round the room, and had been struck by the absence of students. 'Is it true that the students aren't allowed to stay on campus once classes are finished?' This was one of the points that had been made in an article about women's rights that had been posted on the student web site.

'It's . . . discouraged,' Yasmin said.

Najia was more outspoken. 'The authorities are scared there might be an opportunity for vice. Look at us, sitting here, wasting time when we could be doing the same thing at home.'

Yasmin grimaced and fanned herself with a piece of paper. She still had some weeks to go, but she seemed overwhelmed by her pregnancy. She closed her eyes and leaned back in her chair, looking exhausted and uncomfortable.

'Are you well?' Najia's voice was anxious. 'Maybe you should go home.'

Yasmin shook her head. 'And listen to my mother-in-law tell me off for working? It's more restful here.'

'What do they say at the clinic?' Najia asked.

'I don't go to the clinic,' Yasmin said briskly. 'I wish to have my child at home.' Before Najia could respond, she turned to Roisin. 'Professor Souad did set up a library group a couple of years ago, for students to stay on campus and use the facilities, but that was stopped. The authorities decided that it was not a good idea.'

'You should go to the clinic,' Najia persisted. 'Shouldn't she, Roisin?'

Roisin met Yasmin's eyes. 'I'd go to the clinic, if it was me,' she said.

'Truly, Roisin, I am well cared for.' Her tone brooked no argument and she cast Najia a look that said clearly, *Not now.* 'The students here,' she said, returning to the subject they had been discussing, 'many of them are happy with what they have.'

'They have nothing,' Najia said abruptly. 'Everything they have, everything they do, it depends on some man. If their father, or their brother, or their husband says "No", then they are forbidden. They can't be educated, they can't travel, they can't even go to hospital if their guardian forbids it. Since my father died, I have to have my brother's permission to come here. He is younger than me, but it makes no difference. And if we break the rules, other students will report us.'

'But some women are talking about it, aren't they?' Roisin looked from one to the other. 'I've been watching the web site . . .'

'Some,' Yasmin agreed. 'But not many.' She frowned slightly and looked at Najia. 'When the elections were announced, some women were planning to run for office. We thought the government would support us.'

'But they didn't,' Najia said. 'We will not even be allowed to vote. Prisoners will, but women will not.'

'Are you going to do anything about it?' Back home, women would have been marching and protesting. Here, Roisin only knew about the women's views because of what Yasmin and Najia told her. The TV programmes and the newspapers were silent on the subject.

Najia and Yasmin exchanged a quick glance. 'We may have to make some hard choices. Political organizations are not legal here,' Yasmin said. 'Some of us . . . we have *cultural salons*. Other women, in other places, have these too. We can discuss things, talk about how we can work towards what we want.'

Najia studied the book that was open in front of her. 'We all have to make hard choices.' She glanced at Yasmin. 'As you did.'

Yasmin shook her head, frowning, and didn't respond. 'We have to be careful,' she explained to Roisin. 'There have been some arrests.'

'If there is anything . . .' Roisin was hesitant to make the offer. She didn't know what she could do, and she could imagine what Joe would say if she did get involved.

Yasmin smiled. 'Truly, Roisin, this is our problem, not yours.' There was silence for a while, then she said, 'Have you been to the al-Mamlaka mall yet?'

It was such an abrupt change of subject that it took Roisin a moment to respond. This must be the women's mall Damien O'Neill had mentioned that first day in Riyadh. Roisin could still remember the dismissive note in his voice. *A lot of the wives go there.* 'No,' she said. 'I haven't. Not yet.'

'One day,' Yasmin said, 'you must come with us. We can have coffee and talk.' Roisin waited, but the conversation seemed to be over, so she went back to her journal. Suddenly, Yasmin said, 'Do you have a maid?'

'No.' Roisin was surprised at the question. A lot of the ex-pats employed servants, usually houseboys, but she didn't.

'I wondered if you ever talked to them. The maids.'

'No. But I talk to the gardeners.'

Yasmin bit her lip. 'I have spent time in the West,' she said. 'My family – my husband's family – do not like this. But I have. We aren't good to our servants here, I think.'

'I've heard this,' Roisin said. She had heard stories of women being beaten and abused in London when they had travelled to the UK with the Saudi families who employed them, imprisoned because their employers held their passport, and because their permission to be in the country was dependent on their status as servants.

'I –' Yasmin stopped speaking abruptly.

'I see I am interrupting.' Professor Souad was standing in the doorway watching them. 'I thought

140

you were working, but I see you are discussing servants. It is an interesting problem.' She turned to Roisin. 'I believe that mostly in the UK you cannot afford servants.'

'Most people can't,' Roisin agreed. 'There's no need, anyway. People employ cleaners and child-minders. Mostly part-time.'

'I see. So there is no need to provide the food, the clothing and the accommodation. This is good. More and more I find myself admiring your democracy.'

Roisin, remembering her previous encounters with the professor, didn't comment. Souad waited, then said to Yasmin, 'There are student papers waiting for you in my office.' Then to Najia, 'Your family will not be pleased to find you wasting time when you are here to study.'

Najia gathered up her possessions and left quickly. Yasmin stayed where she was. 'I will collect the papers for grading when I have completed my work on this. Roisin and I have a class to plan.'

Souad raised her eyebrows. 'Roisin does not need help with planning her teaching.'

'No,' Yasmin agreed. 'But I need help in learning how to do this.'

Souad thought about this and gave an abrupt nod before she left the room. 'Papers. Today. For grading,' she said, leaving Roisin and Yasmin exchanging glances like unruly schoolgirls.

15

Damien's office was in one of the modern blocks in downtown Riyadh. From his high vantage point, he could look down on the drivers playing Russian roulette in the heavy traffic. In this part of the city, pedestrians were few, apart from people – always men – moving between office blocks or the small urban malls that lined the streets.

He was putting together a report about developments in recruitment and training strategy that might help to fill the skills gap that was developing. The economies of the developed world might not be healthy, but they could still pay their skilled workers good salaries. The Kingdom was haemorrhaging ex-pat workers. It was hardly surprising.

Earlier that year, a well-respected banker had been shot on the streets of al-Khobar, and his body had been dragged for miles behind a car followed by a mob howling their triumph – an event that would have brought down brutal reprisals if it had happened elsewhere in the Middle East. A group of ex-pats had been taken hostage in their housing compound, and several had their throats cut before the police drove the hostage-takers out. A TV journalist, a Middle East expert and sympathizer with the Arab cause, had been shot on the streets of Riyadh as he tried to film a report.

Damien knew he must be a target himself. He tried to be inconspicuous, but he moved in Arab circles, and to some people that would be provocation enough.

Will you walk into my parlour . . . ? The people who could afford to stayed away. The salaries they could command in the Kingdom were higher, but so were the chances of getting their throats cut. What he needed was a recession.

He was staring into space, letting his mind run through the problem again, when his phone rang. It wasn't the extension that would be routed through his secretary, it was his direct line.

'O'Neill.' The voice was abrupt. 'I want you to tell me what's going on.'

It was Arshak Nazarian.

Damien thought quickly, but he had no idea what was upsetting the man. 'Nothing out of the ordinary, as far as I know,' he said.

'I see. Someone tries to hack into my systems looking for stuff about Haroun Patel. Then you turn up in my offices asking questions about him. Maybe, just maybe that was coincidence. But now

143

someone's attacked my system again. What's this about?' Under the measured tones, Damien could hear real anger.

'All I know is that people are showing an interest in Haroun Patel.' There was no point in keeping that quiet. 'I've had one or two queries about his conviction.'

'His conviction . . .' Suddenly, Nazarian's voice was thoughtful. 'That's . . . odd. Who's been asking?'

Amy, for one. But Nazarian had actually echoed his own views. It didn't matter now whether Haroun Patel was innocent. The act of execution had sealed his guilt.

'What did the hacker go after?'

'Patel's records and . . .' He stopped. 'Whoever it was did a good job, but not good enough. I found his traces in my system this morning.'

Joe Massey was obviously spending a lot of time in the internet café.

Nazarian was speaking again. 'These people who've been asking you questions – I assume we aren't talking about anyone official.'

'No.'

'And are you going to tell me who they are?'

'They spoke to me in confidence.'

'I see.' Nazarian's voice was cold. He was right to be upset. His system contained information that might be sensitive – he had his business interests to protect. Damien might not like Nazarian's business, but it was all legal.

As far as he knew.

Maybe that was it. Maybe Nazarian had been cutting corners, and whoever was digging around in his systems was getting a bit too close. As he put the phone down, he was reminded of his own unfocused edginess, the feeling that there was something he had seen but had not noticed, something that had been tugging at his subconscious for the past few weeks. He let his mind drift to see if anything emerged, but there was nothing. Something had drawn Amy to the Patel case. Joe Massey had been asking questions. None of it meant anything. Maybe it was time to have a quiet word with Massey.

Nazarian's call had broken his concentration. He needed a break. He decided to go out to one of the street cafés for coffee. He picked up his hat and sunglasses, told his secretary he was going out, and left the air-conditioned cool of the building.

Outside, the street was brilliant in the high sun. The light reflected off the concrete walls and off the paving slabs. The sky was a deep, cloudless blue. He could feel the heat start to burn through his skin, even under the protective shadow of his hat.

But deep inside himself, he felt cold, as if he was aware of unfriendly eyes that were searching, tireless and indefatigable. For the first time, he felt as though he had attracted their attention, that they were studying him, hostile but uncertain, and if they looked at him, they might cast their gaze just a bit wider, and find . . . what?

16

Embassy of the United States of America
Riyadh, Saudi Arabia
WARDEN MESSAGE
December 2004

. . . Be aware of your surroundings. Take note
of vehicles or individuals that do not appear
to belong in the area and immediately report
them to authorities . . .

'I got an invitation to go to the mall the other
day.' Roisin was experimenting with her hair in
front of the mirror. She and Joe were getting ready
to go to a party – their first night out together in
weeks.

'Who from?' Joe was reluctantly getting
changed, making his lack of enthusiasm for the
evening clear.

'Yasmin – she's one of the teaching assistants.'

He was standing in front of the mirror, knotting

147

his tie. Dress standards in Saudi were more formal than in the UK. 'Better be careful. Saudi women wear Gucci to scrub the floor.'

'They don't scrub floors. Their maids do it. What do you think of this?' She turned from the mirror and showed him her hair swept up and clipped on top of her head.

'It's pretty.' He studied her for a minute. 'But . . .' He came across to her and ran his fingers through her hair, freeing it from the clips so that it fell loose round her face. 'That's prettier. I like it better like that. That's how you looked the first time I saw you.'

'The day I almost knocked you into the canal?'

'Oh, I saw you before that.' He was standing very close to her. 'Do we have to go to this thing?'

She looked up at him and sighed. 'I think we do – she phoned this morning to make sure we were still coming.'

He kept his eyes on hers. There was something in his gaze that disturbed her. Then he shrugged. 'OK.' He released her without further comment. Before she could say anything, he'd left the room, and she heard his feet on the stairs. She bit her lip. Just for a moment it had been like looking at a stranger.

You hardly know him . . .

She shook off her sudden doubt, and took her dress out of the closet. She slipped it on and looked in the mirror. Her hair hung round her shoulders in loose curls, brightened by the sun. All she needed in the way of make-up was a slick of colour on her lips and some sparkle round her eyes. Her green dress was softly draped, and cut with a deep V at the front.

When she went downstairs, Joe was waiting by the door, his eyes skimming the paper. He barely glanced at her. 'Ready?'

She touched his arm. 'Joe, what's wrong? You're wound up like a spring – I wish you'd talk to me.'

He shook her hand off. 'Christ, Roisin, what do I have to do to get it right with you? I'm coming to this party, aren't I?'

They left the house in silence.

The party was on the other side of the city. Roisin sat beside Joe as he negotiated the Riyadh traffic. They were both angry. He was driving faster than usual and she could see the tension in his jaw.

The sun had set – night came quickly here – but as they entered the city, Roisin could see that the young men behind the wheels wore glasses tinted to impenetrable black, they had their cell phones clamped to their ears, and drove with the recklessness of invincible youth. She was reminded of American teenagers driving their cars around town, cool and edgy, boys and girls eyeing each other up in a complex courtship ritual. But here the cars were bigger and more expensive, and a crucial part of the equation was missing.

She could feel the attention of the young men snagging on her as they stopped at a red light and was glad that she had tied her scarf tightly so that her blonde hair was concealed. There was something predatory in the air.

Joe turned off the highway on to a slip road, away from the centre out towards the suburbs. They followed the road for another twenty minutes then he pulled up outside the gate of a walled compound where the ubiquitous security guards waited, and presented his identification. The gate swung open and a guard waved them through.

The noise of the party spilled out as the houseboy opened the door to them. The first thing that struck her as she stepped into the house was the chill of the air-con and she was glad of her wrap. The hostess greeted them with a bright, social smile and a glass of homebrew. 'Roisin and Joe,' she said. 'I'm so pleased you could come.'

Roisin tasted her wine. It was sour and acidic. She glanced quickly at Joe, wanting to re-establish contact, but he didn't meet her eye. He was looking round the room and she could feel the tension in him. She heard him mutter 'Shit,' under his breath.

A woman waved to her from across the room, and beckoned her over. Roisin recognized her, and saw she was with a group of women she'd talked to before. She couldn't face another session of complaints about how terrible Saudi was, how awful the Saudis were, how inefficient and grasping the servants. She smiled brightly and looked quickly round the room. She spotted a fair-haired man standing on his own, looking rather bored. There was something familiar about his face – and then she recognized him. It was Damien O'Neill, the man who had shown them round the city on their first day.

She turned to Joe to point O'Neill out to him, but he'd moved across the room and was already incorporated into a group of people she didn't know, people from the hospital presumably.

She trod hard on her anger and made her way over to where O'Neill was standing. 'Hello,' she said. Her voice sounded abrupt and breathless in her ears. 'You probably don't remember me. Roisin Massey. You gave us a quick tour of the city when we arrived. I've been meaning to call you to say thanks.' She noticed he had orange juice rather than wine. Probably a wise choice.

His smile was carefully neutral. 'It was my pleasure. How are you?' It was the measured politeness of someone who didn't expect the exchange to last beyond social courtesy.

'I'm fine. Thank you.'

'Your husband?'

'Yes. He's fine.' For some reason, there seemed to be no other word in the English language apart from *fine*. 'Are you . . .' she floundered for a moment, trying to think of a question. 'Have there been many new arrivals recently?'

He looked distracted, as though he was running the conversation on auto-pilot, his mind elsewhere. 'No. Are you happy with your accommodation?'

She said quickly, ticking the items off on her fingers: 'The house is fine, thanks. Work's going well. We aren't planning a holiday, so we can't talk about that. I don't have a maid, but the gardener is doing a great job. And the weather's been good.' She looked at him. 'Fine, in fact. Like everything else.'

For a moment, his face was blank, then he laughed. 'Point taken,' he said. 'I'm sorry. There's a standard conversation you have at these parties. I can do it without thinking now.'

'So why do you come? You don't need to, do you?'

He looked round. 'Oh, I need to keep in touch. Actually, I'm supposed to be meeting someone, or I might have given this one a miss.' He was studying her more closely now, and she wondered what he saw, because he said, 'Are you really settling in OK? It's not an easy place, especially for a woman.'

'It's had its moments. But mostly, yes, it's been . . .'

'Fine?'

She laughed. 'Just about. I like the work. I'm getting to know my way around.'

'And your husband?'

'Yes, fi— He's OK, thanks, except he has to work long hours. I don't think he expected it to be quite so . . .'

A faint line appeared between his eyebrows. 'Was it so bad at the hospital? I know they've been short-staffed for a while.'

'It's getting better. Joe says he'll be on top of it soon.'

He nodded. She got the impression that he was still thinking about this as he started asking her about her impressions of the Kingdom, about how much of it she had seen. She told him about her trips into Riyadh – he nodded approvingly when she told him how much she liked the remains of the old architecture.

'There won't be anything left in a few years,' he said. 'Have you seen the al-Masmak fort?'

'Not apart from a glimpse on that first day. I thought it was all a tourist reconstruction.'

'They don't get tourists here, not to speak of. So it's the real thing. It's built of dried mud, and inside – on the upper floor – there are some carvings. You should go and see it if you want to understand this place.' He told her about the battle in 1902 when Abd al Aziz, with only fifteen warriors, scaled the walls of Riyadh, took the fort and was declared ruler by the populace. 'The history of the Kingdom – of the whole Middle East – was shaped by that one event.'

'I always thought it was shaped by the desert – the culture, the way the people live.'

'Have you been to the desert?'

'Yes, the first week we were here.' Her rising spirits deflated as she remembered how happy she'd been – how happy they'd both been that first weekend. She made an effort and smiled at O'Neill again.

She got the impression she hadn't fooled him, but all he said was, 'Well, the desert and Wahhabbism will tell you everything you need to know about the Kingdom.'

The desert and Wahhabbism – this was what Yasmin and Najia had to contend with. 'Is there a women's movement in Riyadh?' The question slipped out without thought. Until she spoke, she hadn't realized she was going to ask it.

He looked at her. The silence stretched out uncomfortably. 'Why do you want to know?' he said after a while.

'It was something one of my students said, that's all.'

'It depends what you mean by "women's movement". There are various radical Islamic groups. Women are members as well as men. If you want my advice, you'll stay well away from anything like that.'

'I meant a feminist movement.'

'It's illegal to set up political organizations.' He was choosing his words carefully. 'So the straight answer is no. There are various salon-type things – businesswomen, and women who want to be politically active, meet in their own homes sometimes. There was a well-orchestrated protest when they wouldn't let the women vote in the election – it was all done legally, but it got a lot of publicity. Someone knows what they're doing – and they're moving very carefully. It's a sensitive issue. I don't think it would help if a

154

Westerner was to take up the cause – they'd lose a lot of credibility.'

That was more or less what Yasmin had indicated. 'I realize that. I was just interested in what the students were saying.'

'It's a touchy issue at the moment. I'm surprised they talked about it at all.'

He was studying her face closely, and he looked worried, so she said, 'There was something posted on the university web site.'

'That won't have gone down well. But things are starting to change for women here. More of them work, these days. Some of them are very successful. A Saudi woman has just been appointed to lead the UN population fund. And there are women like Professor Souad al-Munajjed who are very successful in their own field. You know her, of course?'

'Yes, but I wonder how representative she is.'

He looked into the distance, considering. 'She stays where she is because she doesn't challenge the establishment. The traditionalists don't like her, but she's careful not to give them any ammunition. Her colleagues, the ones that did start challenging things, they're more marginalized now.' He told her about the time in 1990 when fifty women drove cars in protest against the ban. She remembered Souad talking about it. 'I worked for the consulate then,' he said.

'What happened?'

'The women lost their jobs and their families

were threatened,' he said. 'I thought a bit of solidarity from our government wouldn't go amiss, but . . .' He shrugged. 'We're selective about whose rights we support, and when.'

'Is that why you left the consulate?'

'Among other things.' He changed the subject. 'How are you getting on with the students?'

'Fi— Quite well. They're careful what they say to me.'

'Well, that's . . .' A man came across to O'Neill and spoke quickly to him. 'Would you excuse us?' he said to Roisin.

'Of course.' She found herself engaged in conversation by another man who told her he was an engineer on contract, then she talked to an Australian dentist, and then to a couple who could only talk about how much they despised the Saudis and how much they wanted to go home.

She shivered. The air-con was set too high and she could feel the deep chill of fatigue. She'd been up since six. She looked around the room, searching for Joe. She saw him, talking with someone she couldn't quite see – or rather listening to someone, she could recognize the slight tilt of his head that indicated he was paying close attention to the conversation. The crowd shifted, and she saw with some surprise that the person he was talking to was Damien O'Neill. Joe looked across at her. His mouth was set in a thin line. As soon as he caught her eye, his face relaxed. He said something to O'Neill then came across to her and put his arm round her. 'Are you OK?' His earlier coldness had vanished.

'I'm a bit tired. You?'

'I'm ready to go if you are. Roisin – I'm sorry about earlier. I behaved like a shit. It's been a bit tense at work – I shouldn't take it out on you.'

She felt the knot that had been in her stomach all evening start to unwind. 'You could talk to me about it.'

'I know. It's . . . when I get away from it, I just want to forget about it.'

'What kind of thing? I was talking to Damien O'Neill – he seemed a bit surprised you were still . . .'

'Oh, just – organization things. People being inefficient. Stuff like that. I saw you with O'Neill. What did he have to say?' There was a slight edge to his voice and she looked at him quickly.

'Not much. We talked about this place. I told him about our trip to the desert. Why?'

'Nothing. I don't like him. He's an officious bastard. It doesn't matter. Come on, let's go.'

'I'd better go and say our goodbyes.'

As she crossed the room, she became aware of someone watching her. A woman was standing by the French windows, a tall, slender woman with red hair. Roisin stopped, and the woman moved, the light catching her face. For a moment, they looked at each other blankly, then Roisin felt the jolt of recognition. She had a sudden vision of a figure leaning dangerously out of the window of a train, waving, calling something that was drowned by the noise of the engine and the echoes from the cavernous station, again and again as Roisin frantically shook her head and cupped her hand to her ear. *I can't hear you!*

Amy.

She saw the look of recognition on the woman's face. For a moment they stared at each other across a gap of almost sixteen years, then the woman moved away and was lost in the crowd.

17

'I think I just saw a ghost.' Roisin sank down into the reclining chair and kicked off her shoes. 'That's better.'

Joe stood at the other side of the room watching her. 'A ghost?' His face was in shadow.

'Just now, at the party. There was a woman there. I thought – at the time I could have sworn – that she was someone I used to know.'

'Why a ghost?'

'It must have been – what, sixteen years ago? Something like that. The woman at the party, did you see her? She was tall with red hair and she was wearing a black dress. For a moment, it was Amy to the life. But now . . . I don't know.'

His voice was quiet. 'Amy.'

'You know her?'

'Amy Seymour. Yes. She works at the hospital.'

'She was Amy Fenwick when I knew her.' So it *was* Amy. Amy, after all these years. She had been working with Joe. He knew her. 'That's so . . . How is she? What's she doing?'

'I don't know her well. She seems . . . OK, I suppose. She's in charge of the unit for premature babies, and she works for a women's health clinic. Roisin, why is she a ghost?'

'We were friends, years ago,' Roisin said slowly. 'I was seventeen. I was in the middle of the adolescent rebellion thing, you know? *You aren't my parents. You're keeping secrets* – all that sort of stuff.'

He was frowning as he looked at her. 'Were they?'

They'd never talked much about this before. She wasn't sure why, but she had always steered away from the topic of her adoption. 'They never talked to me about it. It was as if that part of my life, those first years, were some kind of mistake, a false start. They didn't want to acknowledge them. I told you my birth parents were dead, right? They died in a car crash.' She pushed the hair back from her face and showed him the small scar on her hairline. 'That's how I got that.

'I don't remember them, nothing about them at all. I have flashes sometimes – I can remember someone giving me a ride in a wheelbarrow. People are laughing, but I can't see their faces. It wasn't my family – my adoptive family. And I can remember another child. I can remember holding hands with another child for a photograph, and being frightened when the flash went off.' And a voice singing to her, a few remembered lines: . . . *between the salt water and the sea sand* . . .

'But that's about it. It's like I woke up when I was four, and I was living with my mum and dad in Newcastle. My parents wouldn't talk about it, but I knew I could remember another child. All the time I was growing up, what I wanted most was a sister. And then Amy . . .'

She looked away, trying to collect her thoughts. 'We met at college. We were both doing A-Levels. I was straight out of school and as dumb as they come. Amy was different. She was a year older – that's a lot, then – she was smart and she was cool. A lot of the students were a bit intimidated by her. But we really hit it off. We both had backgrounds that were . . . different, I suppose. She'd been in care, I was adopted. It was like I suddenly had the sister I'd always wanted, only without all the fights and the jealousy and the rest of it.'

She could picture Amy in her mind as clearly as if it had been yesterday; not the woman she had glimpsed at the party, but the adolescent Amy. Then, Amy had been a bit too tall, a bit too thin, not quite comfortable with her body. She was ebullient and extrovert, street-wise in a way Roisin couldn't then aspire to, giving the college lecturers a hard time, helping Roisin to plan the ways she could outwit her parents' strict curfew. She took pride in her lack of family – much the best way to live, she had insisted. She had no one trying to control *her* life, unlike Roisin.

She and Amy, sitting in Amy's flat smoking – Roisin's first experience of hash. She could remember looking out of the window to the estate laid out below her, the deep amphitheatre with its tiered blocks, the bright colours of the paint-work, the gardens and the hanging vines. Amy had been standing at the window, drawing the smoke into her lungs and watching the distant river. 'One day,' she'd said, 'one day . . .' And her gesture had encompassed the world that lay beyond the mouth of the river. That was when they'd started their plan to travel once they got their exams. Neither of them had left Britain's shores before. Roisin had never even left Northumberland. She'd lost Amy, but the desire to travel had remained.

'My parents didn't like her,' she remembered now. She could still see the way her mother's lips thinned every time Amy's name was mentioned. At the time, it had made Amy seem even more desirable.

'So what happened?'

'Well, I did a lot of things that would have horri-fied my parents if they'd known about it.' She smiled at the recollection of their Goth clothes and their determined cool. Some of their exploits came back to her, not all as harmless as climbing through the girders of the iron bridge to get the correct angle for a photograph of the Tyne. Whatever else had happened, she and Amy had had fun. 'But after a while, she told me a bit more of her story. She'd been taken into care after her parents had been killed. She said no one wanted to adopt her because she was too old and she was difficult. And she said she'd had a sister who she always used to look out for, but her sister was taken away from her and adopted.'

She looked across at Joe, who was listening quietly, a faint line appearing between his eyes.

'It got me thinking. There'd always been a gap, like I knew something should have been in my life and wasn't. I started telling myself that *I* was Amy's sister, I was the child who had been taken away and adopted, that my parents, my adoptive parents, had deliberately kept us apart because they wanted me all to themselves.' And there had been just enough of that kind of possessiveness in her mother's anxiety to make her fantasies possible. 'I knew deep down it couldn't be true, but I believed it anyway.'

And that was why she still thought about Amy, even after all these years. Their friendship hadn't been just the companionship of shared fun and risk as they spread their wings together. There had been no one she could talk to the way she could talk to Amy, and Amy had told her things she wouldn't tell other people.

Joe was watching her in silence. 'I wasn't happy at home then,' she said. 'I wanted to go to college and do an art qualification. I wanted to be a photographer.' She made a rueful face. 'I still think I could have made a go of it. But my parents wanted me to do teacher training. It was all rows and bad feeling. Amy and I decided we would go away together, take a gap year in Europe. We had it planned. And then when we got back we were going to share a flat in London while we were students – she wanted to be a designer and I was going to work at my photography.' She could so easily recapture those times with their excitement and their closeness. 'I don't think you ever make friends again the way you do when you're young.'

'Did Amy know that you thought you were her sister?'

'Not in so many words, but it was a kind of unspoken thing. She stopped talking about the family that she'd lost. And I felt as though there had been this gap in my life that I hadn't known about, and suddenly it wasn't there any more. Then something happened. I don't know what it was. Amy had been a bit edgy – she could be like that – and then she said out of the blue that she had to go to London for a while. She said she'd found something out she wanted to check. She didn't want to tell me then, but she said she'd tell me when she got back. It was like . . . she had this secret. She was really excited. She was . . . I can see her now. She was just glowing.

'I went to the station with her, and I waved her off. I can remember she was hanging out of the window calling something to me, and I

164

couldn't hear what she was saying. I was running along the platform shouting, "I can't hear you!" and she was calling, trying to make me understand.' The picture was as vivid in her mind now as it had been then. 'I never saw her again.'

Joe had drawn up a chair and was sitting in front of her, leaning forward, listening intently. 'She didn't come back? Didn't get in touch?'

'She never did. I had a big row with my parents – I blamed them. I told them they'd driven her away, that Amy was my sister, and they'd done something to keep us apart. My mum was devastated. She'd had no idea . . . They had a kind of album they'd never shown me, something they'd been given when they adopted me. I can still see my mother holding it out to me like some kind of offering, something dangerous. I spent hours that day just looking at the photographs.'

There had been photos of her birth parents, photos of her home, photos of her when she was small.

And photos of another child.

'That's the irony of it. I did have a sister. Nell. She was called Nell. She was a year younger than me. And she died in the crash.' . . . *between the salt water and the sea sand* . . .

There was silence once she'd finished, then Joe said, 'And it was her, it was your Amy, at the party tonight?'

Your Amy. Roisin nodded. She hadn't been hallucinating. She had seen Amy.

'Did she recognize you?'

'Yes. But she backed off at once. She was probably as shocked as I was.'

When Amy had gone – once she was able to admit to herself that her mother was right, that Amy was not coming back – she'd been devastated. She'd imagined terrible things: Amy lost, Amy sick, Amy dead. She'd gone to the police, but they hadn't been interested. A young girl, an adult, with a rootless past, choosing to disappear into the restless chaos of London, was hardly an emergency.

And now here was Amy – happy and prosperous, judging from the brief glance Roisin had had. 'I'll have to contact her. Can you get her number?'

Joe was looking at her, still concerned, but there was something in his expression that she couldn't quite read. 'You haven't had any contact with her for years,' he said. 'Why stir things up?'

It was as if she hadn't heard him properly. 'What?'

'With Amy. Why stir it up? If I were you, I'd leave it.'

A breeze blew across the room and Damien lay for a moment with his eyes closed, savouring its freshness. He had surfaced from a dream of veils that obscured his vision as he tried to find his way through a maze of stone and marble. The atonal piping that filled the air became the early-morning call to prayer, then he woke further and realized that what he was hearing was his phone. He swore and reached for it, his hand finding it instinctively before his eyes were open. The illuminated clock face said *04.09*, and he felt dread in the pit of his stomach. Phone calls in the dawn hours usually meant bad news.

'Damien? It's Amy.'

He sat up. 'What's wrong?'

'Wrong? Nothing. I needed to talk to you.'

A wash of exasperation flooded over him, followed by an unwelcome warmth. 'Amy, for God's sake – it's four a.m. If you wanted to talk, we had plenty of time this evening.' He'd only gone to the party because she'd asked him to, but she'd arrived late, and then been edgy and evasive, so he'd left.

'I didn't . . . I'm sorry. I'll call you tomorrow.'

It sounded almost as if she was crying. She never cried. 'Amy? What is it?'

There was silence at the other end of the phone, and when she spoke again, her voice sounded firmer. 'Nothing. It's just . . . I came across a part of my past last night. Damien, when did Roisin Gardner arrive? What's she doing here?'

His mind tangled as he tried to make sense of what she was saying. 'Roisin Gardner? I don't know of a Roisin Gardner.' Amy must be talking about Roisin Massey, but he wanted to know more about this before he gave her the information.

He heard the impatient catch in her breath.

'Roisin whatever she's called these days. I used to know her, years ago.'

'Amy, is four in the morning the right time to talk about this?'

Her laugh was edgy and he heard the sound of a lighter clicking. He could hear her sigh as she exhaled. 'I know. I'm sorry. I didn't realize what time it was. I was sitting up watching the moon. It's very bright tonight. Have you seen it?'

Pale light was streaming through the ornate window screens. 'Yes.'

'It made me think about that night in the desert. Do you remember?' Her voice didn't sound calculated or seductive, it just sounded sad.

'Of course I do.' He could hear her breathing on the other end of the line. 'Amy, why would I forget?'

He could still hear the sadness in her voice, hear the slight shake that told him she wasn't completely in control of her emotions. This wasn't the Amy he knew. 'Sometimes I hate this place,' she said. 'Sometimes I can't wait to go home. But the trouble is, I don't know where home is any more.'

'Where do you think of when you dream about home?' For Damien, that was Riyadh. The other dreams, he preferred to forget.

'England,' she said. 'The North East. I grew up in Newcastle.'

'Maybe that's where you need to go.'

'The place I dream about?' She laughed. 'It doesn't exist, not now.'

There was silence. When Amy spoke again, her voice was brisker. 'I was curious about Roisin – we used to be good friends, more years ago than I like to admit. I let her down badly. I've been sitting here thinking about her. And watching the moon. I want to contact her.'

He sighed. 'It could have waited until morning. She's out at al-Haidah, on the north side.'

'Miles away. And the number?'

'I don't have the number, but she'll be in the book. It's Massey, by the way. Roisin Massey.'

There was a beat of silence. 'She's married to Joe Massey?'

He waited.

'OK, I've got that. Thank you, Damien.'

'Goodnight, Amy.'

'Goodnight, my love.' She put the phone down.

. . . *My moment with you now is ending* . . . The words of the song ran through his mind. He wondered where that had come from. He didn't want to think about Amy, but he couldn't get her out of his head: the moon in the desert sky, her face on the pillow, flushed and warm, the feel of her body under his hands.

Amy.

He had had his life all sorted out before she came on the scene; the relationships he embarked on always carried the seeds of their own ending, relationships with women who were married, or women who were leaving the Kingdom soon, relationships where no future could be planned or intended. He had been called heartless, he had been called a bastard, but the nature of the attachment had been on the table from the first. But with Amy . . . sometimes it felt as though they were both edging towards the precipice of a commitment that neither of them seemed to welcome.

He pushed his mind away from things he didn't want to think about, and let the events of the evening before run through his mind: his unsatisfactory talk with Joe Massey that had been cut short abruptly when Massey had left him to join his wife. *Haroun Patel is dead*, Massey had said. *That's the end of the story as far as I'm concerned.*

There would be no more sleep tonight.

He sat at the window watching the moon set. The light on the stone turned it silver like sand. He stayed at the window until the call for *Fajh*, the prayer between the beginning of dawn and sunrise, came from the minaret, and the night, one among the thousand and one, came to a close.

And then Aboulhusn the sleeper woke up.

18

Amy lived in one of the characterless apartment blocks crowded behind the wall of an ex-pat compound. Damien always thought that it must be like this to live under a witness-protection programme, a flat that had been occupied by a hundred transient inhabitants who had left no trace behind them. He wondered sometimes why she didn't move somewhere more attractive. She'd been in the Kingdom for over two years, long enough to have made some decent money, but she always shrugged the suggestion off. 'Why should I pay extra money for rent? This is good enough. What more do I want?'

He'd been surprised when she'd called him a couple of hours ago, asking him to come round and see her. 'I need to talk to you,' she'd said, but so far, talking hadn't come into it.

He lay back on the bed watching the sky through the dimness of the nets. Amy's hair was fanned out across his chest and he could feel the steady beating of her heart. The moments after sex were some of the best when the antagonism that sparked between them was satiated and quiescent. He remained there for a while, enjoying the silence, then he checked his watch. 'I'll need to go soon,' he said.

Amy sat up, stretching. She had been uncharacteristically subdued, and he could see the troubled expression come back to her face as she returned to reality. He felt her eyes on him as he came back from the shower and began pulling on his clothes. He didn't say anything. She would talk to him when she was ready. If she was ready.

'Damien, there's something I have to tell you.'

He looked at her, buttoning his shirt. 'I know. What is it?'

She wrapped the sheet round herself and got out of bed, then came and stood close to him by the window, letting the light that was diffused by the nets fall across her. 'I don't want to say this.'

'But you're going to.'

'Yes. This . . . thing we have, this . . .'

'Relationship,' he said. 'It's called a relationship, Amy.'

'Relationship, then. It can't go on. We have to finish it.'

Of all the things he had expected, it wasn't this. A stab of pain, shocking in its intensity, silenced him for a moment, then quick, angry responses jumped to his lips. He suppressed them and kept his voice even as he said, 'I see. Do I get to know why?'

'Because we're bad for each other. You know that.'

'I don't know anything of . . . Amy, if you want to end it, then do it. But tell me why. Don't play games.'

'But we *are* bad for each other. That's what I mean. I do this all the time – I get into destructive relationships and I let them take me over, then it all goes wrong. It's got to stop. It has to. I know where this will end, otherwise. We don't care about each other, not really. It's about sex. About . . . Christ, face it, Damien: it's all about fucking.'

'Is that what this was, Amy? Just fucking?'

It wasn't, and they both knew it. Her eyes moved away from his. 'I don't know. I just know we aren't going anywhere. When we aren't fucking, we fight.'

That was true. He and Amy were like opposite poles. As soon as they were together, the sparks, edgy and dangerous, started to flicker and arc. He met her gaze and held it. 'I thought that was foreplay.'

Her face flushed and softened. 'Stop it, Damien. Please. This is difficult for me. I don't want to do this, but I can't go on with it. I just can't.' It was the nearest thing to a plea he'd ever heard from her.

'It could be different.'

'It couldn't. Not here.'

He looked at her in frustration. He was angry

173

with himself for letting this happen, for not realizing soon enough what was in her mind. 'Does this have anything to do with seeing Roisin Massey?'

She shook her head. 'No. Yes . . . maybe. I don't know. It reminded me about things . . . There are things about my life I have to change. Maybe Roisin made me see that. I'm going on leave soon. I need to think some things through. I want to spend some time with my family. With my sister. I've let all of that go. I'm . . .'

She'd never talked about her family before, never mentioned a sister. 'It sounds like more than just a holiday.'

'It is. It's going to be a time to get things sorted out in my head. I need to decide what to do next. Don't you see, Damien? I don't know anything at the moment. It's all . . .' She shook her head and stopped speaking.

He didn't know if she was right or not. His thoughts about her were always tied to her physical presence – her touch, her smell, the feel of her body, and these were things he didn't want to lose. 'You have to choose, Amy,' he said. 'I don't want this.'

'I know.' Her eyes searched his face, but whatever she was looking for, she didn't find it. 'I had to say it, now, or I wouldn't have been able to.' A single track of moisture glittered on her cheek. A tear, from Amy?

He touched his fingers to the trace, then put

them to his lips. His eyes didn't leave hers. 'Then this is goodbye?' he said. . . . *my love, good night. My moment with you now is ended . . .*

She nodded.

There was nothing else to say. He could feel her eyes on him as he left the room, and when he reached his car, he looked up to see her watching from the window. He raised his hand in salutation, and after a moment she raised hers in return.

When Roisin woke, the sun was bright. The light stabbed through the blinds, making her eyes ache. Joe's side of the bed was empty. He had got up quietly and left without disturbing her, and she had no idea when he would be back.

They'd had – not exactly a row. Joe didn't row. He just withdrew behind a bleak, cold wall that she couldn't break down. He wouldn't tell her why he didn't want her to contact Amy. 'She sounds like bad news,' was all he'd say. And later, 'Christ, Roisin, leave it. Contact her if you want to. I need to get to bed.'

She'd spent the night in an exhausting half-sleep in which Joe and Amy were running together along the canal tow path, getting further and further away while she struggled to free Shadow from something that lurked in the darkness of the undergrowth. Then Amy was in the lock, calling out in words that Roisin couldn't hear as the gush of water dragged her under. *I can't hear you!* And Joe, beside her, said, *Sounds like bad news . . .*

She'd planned to do an extra day at work, but she felt so weary, she decided to stay at home. She made herself clear up the kitchen and clean the house, but these chores weren't absorbing enough to engage her mind.

Needing something to distract her, she went up to the study to download the assignments the students had been working on. She logged on to the university site, but instead of downloading the students' work, she went on to the discussion forum. Damien O'Neill had been quick with his questions when she'd asked him about a possible women's movement in the Kingdom. He'd been more relaxed when she'd told him that her interest had arisen from the online forum, which was partly true. One student at least was posting arguments in favour of reform for women in the Kingdom, a student who posted under the pseudonym Red Rose.

But when she logged on to the discussion boards, she saw that all the threads that had originated in postings from Red Rose had been tagged with a sealed letter sign: *This topic is now closed.* She tried the link, but she could no longer get access to them. So much for the new openness.

She posted an article about teenagers and junk food that she'd told her students to look out for, then began downloading the work for marking. Most of the students had completed the assignment, but not Najia, which was odd. Najia was usually meticulous about deadlines.

The marking took her over an hour, then she began to plan her classes for the following week. It was peaceful working in her study. The window looked out over the garden, and she found herself drifting away from work and watching the birds that came down for the crumbs she put out every morning.

Amy. She had to decide what to do about Amy. Or did she need to do anything? They'd seen each other at a party. She had no idea what Amy was doing out here, where she lived. Her name was Seymour now, which meant she must be married, maybe had children. It was sixteen years since they'd last seen each other. Did they even want to meet again?

The phone rang, interrupting her chain of thought. She picked it up. 'Roisin Massey.'

It was one of Joe's colleagues, wanting Joe's direct line at the hospital. Roisin could never remember it. She rummaged round in the desk drawer but she couldn't find her address book. 'I'll call you back,' she said, and pulled Joe's work folder out of the filing cabinet. Her fingers slipped, and the papers spilled across the desk and on to the floor.

She swore, and crouched down to pick them up, but they were hopelessly disordered. She scooped them up and was about to try sorting through them, when she heard the door bell. She wasn't expecting anyone.

Dumping the papers on the desk, she ran downstairs and opened the door. A tall woman stood there, her face shadowed by a wide-brimmed hat. She was wearing jeans and sandals. Her eyes were hidden behind dark glasses. 'Hi,' she said. Her voice sounded uncertain. She lowered her glasses, and for a dizzy moment, Roisin felt as though she had stepped back sixteen years.

It was Amy.

The silence seemed to go on for ever, then Roisin found her voice. 'Amy!' She stood back from the door. 'I hardly recognized you. Please, come in.'

'I didn't know if you'd want to see me.' And now this new Amy looked uncertain as she followed Roisin into the low-ceilinged living room. She ignored Roisin's invitation to sit, and walked slowly across the room to one of the photographs on the wall. Roisin had taken it in Newcastle years ago, the River Tyne from the iron bridge, a study in shades of grey, the heavy girders making dark lines across the mist that rose from the water. The only colour was the faint glimmer from a warehouse sign. Amy looked at her. 'I remember that.'

'So do I.' The warehouse had provided a venue for raves when they were both younger. 'It's a wine bar now.'

'No, I mean the photograph – I was there when you took it. That day on the high bridge – do you remember? That was when we decided to go to Europe together.'

'I remember.' For years after Amy had gone, Roisin had missed her with a painful intensity, first with puzzlement, then with anxiety, and later, much later, with a kind of bewildered anger that had no clear focus – towards the authorities for refusing to look for her, towards Amy for not being there. She had vanished completely.

Roisin realized she had been staring at Amy in silence. 'Coffee?' she said. Her voice sounded brittle.

'I thought . . .' Amy bit her lip then delved into the bag she was carrying. She brought out a bottle. Roisin was amazed to see it was champagne, genuine French champagne. 'I brought you this. If you threw me out, I was going to give it to you as a kind of sorry-welcome-goodbye present. If we're going to talk, maybe we could have a glass.' Before Roisin could say anything, Amy went on quickly, 'Of course, coffee would be fine, if that's what you . . . Roisin, listen. All I want to do is say sorry. I did a dreadful thing to you. I made all sorts of promises, and then I let you down. I've wanted to say that for years, but I was too ashamed of myself to get in touch.' Her voice died away and she watched Roisin anxiously.

Roisin felt a thousand responses in her mind. Among the confusion of emotions, the only one she could identify clearly was gladness – Amy was here, Amy was back. 'I just wish you had – got in touch, I mean – I didn't know what had happened to you. I thought you were . . .' She felt her throat thicken and shrugged angrily. Those emotions belonged to yesterday. They looked at each other in silence. Amy's eyes were suspiciously shiny. Roisin forced a smile. 'Champagne. I don't know when I'll taste that again. I'll get some glasses.'

'Good.' Amy placed the champagne bottle carefully on the table.

Roisin escaped to the kitchen, which gave her a moment to collect herself. This was Amy, on her doorstep after all these years. She told herself that she didn't know the elegant, sophisticated woman who was standing in her living room. Amy had been a teenager when she last saw her. They were both different people now.

When she came back into the room with glasses, Amy had picked up the small framed photograph that stood on the coffee table and was studying it. 'Is this your wedding?' she said.

'Yes. We got married just before we came out here.' She could remember looking up as the petals showered down, Joe's hand in hers as they stood there laughing. She could still feel the touch of his fingers as he gently disentangled a petal from her hair. She touched the wedding ring that hung slightly loose on her finger. It was engraved round the outside in a fine script: *Joe~Roisin*, and around the inside with a phrase from a poem that they had chosen to read at the ceremony: 'Western Wind' . . . It was a fragment of a love poem that dated back to the seventeenth century:

O western wind, when wilt thou blow?
The small rain down doth rain.
Christ, that my love were in my arms
And I in my bed again.

'Does he know . . . ?' Amy said.

Roisin nodded. 'We talked about it last night.'

Amy put the photograph down carefully. 'He looks like a nice guy.'

'He is.'

'That's good,' Amy said after slightly too long a pause. She looked at the photo again. 'I've met him at the hospital,' she said.

'I know. He told me.'

'I don't *know* him. He's just been around. It's so strange – there you were, and I didn't know. Where did you two meet?'

'In London. He'd just finished his first contract here. My dog tripped him up on the canal tow path.'

Amy grinned. 'Useful dog. And now you're married . . .' She looked from the photo to Roisin and back to the photo again. 'I couldn't believe it when I saw you. When I asked . . . I saw you leaving and I asked someone. I should have come straight over, but I was afraid . . . I thought, if she's going to tell me to piss off, I'd rather it wasn't in the middle of a party. What are you doing here? Are you working? You aren't just stuck at home, are you?'

'I've got some teaching at the university. English.'

Amy studied her glass, her finger tracing circles under its base. 'You trained as a teacher? That's what your father wanted, wasn't it?'

'I did a degree in Fine Arts.' Amy's departure had made her more determined to do what she wanted to do, rather than what her parents had planned for her. It was ironic that she had ended up teaching anyway.

'In London?'

'Goldsmith's.' One of the colleges they'd planned on going to together.

'I thought you'd study photography. You were a brilliant photographer.'

'All I do these days is take snapshots.' Roisin picked up the champagne bottle and loosened the wire. She eased out the cork, and the *pop* sounded celebratory in the silence. Amy picked up the glasses and held them to catch the wine as it frothed up over the lip of the bottle.

Roisin raised her glass to Amy. It suddenly struck her as completely appropriate that they should have a reunion over an illegal substance. As their eyes met, Amy raised an eyebrow as if she, too, was appreciating the irony of the situation.

'So what have you been doing?' Roisin said. 'Are you married?'

'I was. We broke up.'

'I'm sorry.'

'Oh, it was years ago. I was far too young. It was all part of the mess I was in. Roisin, listen . . .'

Roisin didn't want to hear apologies or reasons. She wanted to leave the past where it was and start again from here, but an explanation seemed important to Amy.

'I'm not trying to make excuses. But I was a mess. More of a mess than I realized. I told stories – lies, actually. Even to you. I told you that both my parents had been killed in a car accident, remember?'

Roisin nodded.

'That wasn't true. It was my mum who was killed. That's how I ended up in a home.'

'What happened to your father?'

'Oh, he'd left years before. I don't remember him.' For a moment, there was an edge to her voice. 'My mother married again, and she had another child. My sister. Jesamine. Jassy, for short. The marriage didn't last. My mum met someone else. I was furious with her. We'd had a good life with my stepfather. He was the only dad I'd ever known. And I loved Jassy. I was ten when she was born. I helped to bring her up. That's what it felt like, anyway. And then, when I was thirteen, my mum was killed. I thought we'd go back and live with my stepfather. He came . . . but he only wanted Jassy. He didn't want me . . .' She shrugged. 'I went into care. I thought I'd never see Jassy again.'

At thirteen years old, Amy had lost her mother,

her sister and her home. No wonder she hadn't been able to tell people the truth. 'I'm sorry,' Roisin said. It seemed so inadequate, she felt her face flush. 'I wish I'd known . . . I made up stories as well. I used to pretend we were sisters.' They had been closer than a lot of sisters she knew.

'Me too,' Amy said. Her face softened. 'Remember our plans?'

'Europe, then art school in London. Of course I do.' Roisin often wondered how her life would have turned out if they'd followed those plans, she and Amy. Her with the naïve recklessness of seventeen that sees itself as fully adult, Amy, unstable and unhappy. Maybe it would have worked. They'd never know.

'I left because I heard about my sister. I hadn't heard anything for four years, and then I got an address in London.' She looked at Roisin as if she was asking her to understand. 'I had to go.'

'Of course you did. I just wish . . .'

'That I'd told you? I thought you'd never forgive me when you found out I'd lied to you.'

'It wouldn't have mattered. And why didn't you come back? Or get in touch, at least?'

Amy shook her head. 'It all got very complicated. And not good. I got into some serious trouble. I was ashamed to come back after that.' She shivered, then shook her head. 'It was a long time ago.'

Roisin remembered the reckless bravado of the

seventeen-year-old Amy that had concealed all this unhappiness and uncertainty. 'Did you find her?'

'In the end. I found her in the end.'

'I wish I'd known what you were going through. I would have done anything . . .'

'I know, but it was probably best. You had your own life to sort out, you didn't need mine.'

Roisin shook her head again. She would rather have been involved in some way. 'But your sister. Where is she? What's she doing?'

'She's married.' Amy's face cleared, and she smiled. 'She's expecting her first baby. I've taken some leave so I can be with her. I don't trust some know-nothing midwife with my sister. Anyway, that's enough about me. What about you? Have you got any children?'

'Not yet.'

'But you want them?'

'We thought we might start a family when Joe's contract finishes. He's looking for work in Australia.' When they'd discussed it, back in England, the idea was that Roisin could take a year out and maybe start again looking at the viability of her own language school. They hadn't talked about it for weeks.

'Don't leave it too long. Australia would be a good place to bring up children. I'll come and visit, I promise. If you want me to.' Amy settled herself in the chair, her legs curled underneath her. Roisin had a sudden flash of Amy at college sitting like that in one of the sofas in the coffee-bar. 'Your parents. How are they?'

'My father died,' Roisin said. She felt the sharp pain that time hadn't really diminished when she thought that she'd never see him again.

'I'm sorry. He was a nice man. I always envied you him. He was so . . . I don't know – solid. A dad you could rely on.'

'We seemed to fight all the time then. He used to say, *You won't be told, will you?*'

Amy smiled. 'I remember. You never used to let anyone tell you anything. You drove the lecturers mad at college, do you remember? *I can do it, thank you.* No one was allowed to help you.'

'Well, I thought they were pretty lame.' For a moment, they were seventeen again, united in their contempt for the adult world around them. 'God, I was an arrogant little cow.'

'Your father liked you being independent,' Amy said. 'You weren't . . .'

'Like my mum? I know. He worried about her right to the end.'

They talked for hours. It seemed to Roisin that they barely scraped the surface of everything that had happened in the last sixteen years. Amy had been in the Kingdom for over two years, which practically made her a veteran these days. Remembering what Damien O'Neill had said the evening before, Roisin asked her about the women's movement in the Kingdom.

'It's pretty minimal, but it's there.' Amy bit her

lip, then said, 'I can tell you this because I know you don't gossip with the Stepford Wives. One of the things I do is work at a women's clinic that's been set up in one of the villages. A lot of women come to the hospital in Riyadh now, but there are some . . . The villages can be quite traditional. The men don't always let their women come in to the city. It was a pretty radical idea when it was set up. I think they thought we'd be helping women to have illicit sex. Oh, it happens,' she added, catching Roisin's surprised look.

'I was just thinking about the students I work with. I don't know where they'd find the opportunity.'

'Oh, they do, they always do,' Amy said. 'And it's a serious issue here. Even being seen with a man who isn't a close relative can ruin a girl's reputation. Fathers, brothers, uncles – they have more or less complete control of a woman's life. If a woman has a good husband, or good male relatives, then their lives are OK, but it all depends on that. Some of the men . . . They can do the most dreadful things to women who step out of line, but it all happens behind closed doors. Everything is rumour. The veils aren't just on the women's faces, you have to remember that. You must have heard the stories about the police in Mecca chasing girls back into a burning school because they weren't properly covered up, and some of them burned to death? That happened. Women are beaten for illicit sex. And we hear about other things . . .' She shuddered. 'You've heard about women being stoned to death for adultery in Iran? I'm told it happens here, too. It's the law, but I don't know if it's ever carried out. All we hear are rumours.'

It was hard to reconcile this portrait of medieval barbarism with the bright, intelligent faces of the students, and with Souad's brisk dismissal of criticisms about the state: . . . *what you thought you were looking at, it isn't there any more.* 'So what happens to a woman who gets pregnant when she isn't married?'

Amy shrugged. 'Who knows? We used to be able to deliver the babies and then let the women leave. We'd hand the kids over as abandoned. The state takes care of them, that's not a problem. But now, if a woman comes into a hospital or a clinic to give birth and she doesn't have a man with her, then we've got to inform the police.'

So what would a woman do under those circumstances? Run away? Where to? Throw herself on the mercy of her family – if such mercy existed?

As the light began to fade, a car pulled up outside and sounded its horn. 'My taxi,' Amy said. She stood up to go. 'I don't want us to lose touch again, not now. Let's meet again, soon. We could have coffee, go to the mall? Whatever you'd like to do.'

'Of course. Let's make it soon. Phone me.'

Amy looked at her. 'Roisin, you're just . . . I

wish . . .' Her voice broke and Roisin found herself wrapped in Amy's impulsive hug. She could feel Amy's hair brushing against her face, and smell the fragrance of a warm, spicy perfume.

She hugged her back. 'I'm so glad you came.'

When Joe got back, she didn't tell him about Amy's visit.

When Damien got home that evening, his house felt strangely empty. He knew Rai was in the kitchen, and he called a greeting, but he didn't want to talk to anyone. He went upstairs, keeping his mind focused on the moment.

His copy of *One Thousand and One Nights* was on the table by the bed. It lay open at 'The Lady and Her Five Suitors', the story of the married woman who was trying to free her lover from gaol. She used seduction and trickery to imprison those responsible – high-ranking officials and the king himself – in a specially manufactured cabinet before the pair fled. When he first read the story, he'd wondered what kind of life the young lover would lead with this resourceful but distinctly dangerous woman. He could remember thinking that, whatever the price, it would probably be worth it.

Amy.

He stood very still for a moment, then he let the book fall shut. It was dark outside now. He could see the lights of the city as a glimmer beyond the *mashrabiyaat*. He had to go out. He'd been invited to a dinner hosted by someone sufficiently influential for it to be politic that he at least put in an appearance.

Even before the events of the morning, he hadn't relished the prospect of an evening among the ex-pats. They came to the Middle East only to huddle in enclaves of Westernization, spreading it around them like a disease. There were very few who spoke any Arabic, and a vanishingly tiny number who were fluent.

They had no use for Middle Eastern culture and history. They thought they had the power, like the men in the story who did indeed have the power and who used it to try and force the favour of someone they thought was weaker. And the result? The king got his head pissed on by a carpenter.

Damien put on his jacket and went out.

19

Embassy of the United States of America
Riyadh, Saudi Arabia
WARDEN MESSAGE
December 2004

Avoid areas frequented by Westerners and avoid establishments at times when Westerners constitute the majority of the patrons.

Keep your colleagues and family aware of your daily plans and ensure that they know how to reach you.

In traffic, always try to leave space in which to manoeuvre. Do not get boxed in; always leave yourself an exit . . .

The next day, two months after she had started teaching, Roisin found a message from Professor Souad inviting her to a meeting after her classes ended for the day. She had seen very little of her head of department since she started work, and wondered what had prompted the communication. Perhaps it had something to do with her non-appearance the previous day.

Her classes went quickly, though she was disappointed that Yasmin, who normally assisted on Tuesdays, wasn't there, and Najia was absent too. She had started looking forward to their after-class conversations.

When she knocked on the door of the professor's office, Souad al-Munajjed greeted her affably enough and offered her tea and pastries. 'So,' she said, 'is all going well? How are you liking our university?'

'Very much,' Roisin said truthfully. She was enjoying the teaching and liked the students, who were hardworking and, now they had got to know her, friendly and welcoming. Even the austere Haifa had unbent a little and had said that she found the classes 'interesting'. Souad poured the tea and listened as Roisin outlined the progress that the students were making. 'So you are happy with the students? They are doing well?'

'Yes. Some of them have excellent English.'

'Yes. The ones who work hard. Haifa – she is good, is she not?'

'She's . . . making progress.' Roisin had a theory that Haifa expressed her dislike and suspicion of Western culture by resisting the language. She had acquired enough to communicate, but made no effort to correct her errors or improve from the standard she had reached.

'And Najia?'

This time, Roisin didn't need to be diplomatic. 'She's making excellent progress.'

'Good. The students report that they are enjoying the class. They have been doing a lot of reading and discussing.'

Roisin felt herself relaxing. It looked as though the professor just wanted a general progress report.

Then the other woman said, 'But now there will, of course, be changes.'

Roisin looked at her in surprise. 'Changes?'

'You will do more lectures. We have many students who want English – you can lecture to all of them.'

'Lectures?' She looked at Souad blankly. 'What can I lecture about?'

'What you have been employed for. You will teach them English.'

Roisin began to understand. She'd known that her teaching had been under surveillance. Souad had been happy enough for her to work in the way she was familiar with, but now she was being pulled back to more traditional methods. It would make the rapport she'd established with the students difficult to maintain, and would make her job a lot harder.

'I could lecture,' she said carefully, 'alongside the seminars. But the seminars are important. That's where they learn to use the language.'

'I hope you do not presume to tell me what is best for the students,' Souad said. Her voice was mild, but her eyes glittered.

'Not at all. I'm saying what works for me, as a teacher. I find that seminars work best.'

'But this is not for you, it is for the students. So, for now, you will lecture.' It had the force of an instruction. 'This is how you will do it.'

'Are the students unhappy with the way I've been teaching? I thought they were enjoying the course.'

'They are not here to enjoy. They are here to learn. It is not for them to decide. This is not,' she gave Roisin a cool smile, 'a democratic institute.'

Roisin realized that Souad knew exactly what she was thinking, and had no intention of changing her mind. 'If you're instructing me to do it this way, then I will, but I don't think it's the best way for me to work with the students. I'd like to make that clear,' she said.

'Certainly.' Souad watched her for a moment, as if she was checking for further signs of rebellion, then she settled her scarf carefully over her hair. 'You say that Najia's progress is excellent,' she said. 'Will she pass her exam?'

'I'd be very surprised if she doesn't.'

'Najia does not pay the attention she should to her other work. If her English is good, then I think she needs to put her effort into her thesis. I have talked to her brother.'

'I don't –'

'So Najia will not be attending your class any more.'

Roisin was speechless. Souad continued as if

she hadn't said anything unusual. 'You know, of course, that Najia is the one who has been posting on the web site as Red Rose?'

Roisin hadn't known. She suspected that Najia's exclusion from the English classes was a punishment for her expression of dissent. Souad was watching her closely. 'The articles she posted . . .' Roisin shrugged. 'They were harmless discussion, surely?'

'Najia is still young.' Souad's slight emphasis carried the implication *unlike you*. 'The young can be badly informed. And foolish.'

'In my experience,' Roisin said carefully, holding on to her temper, 'it's the older people who lose touch with their ideals. Young people are often very clear about their beliefs, and very well informed.'

'And they are unable to distinguish between what is good and valuable, and what is merely fashionable and transient, which is why young people must be guided by their elders. Islam does not bend its beliefs for compromise. You may go.'

Roisin had trouble containing her anger as she went along the corridor to the cloakroom. The professor had banned her from teaching the way she wanted to and had issued a clear warning. If Roisin put a foot wrong from now on, her job would be in jeopardy. Employment laws in the Kingdom were close to non-existent. Her contract allowed the university to sack her at any time. Joe was not automatically entitled to have his wife with him. They had made concessions and allowed him to bring her with him because they needed his skills, but her work permit was dependent on her job. If she lost it, she would have to spend the next nine months sitting at home in the compound, which she didn't think she could stand. It was possible she would lose her permission to stay in the country.

As far as she could see, she had no choice – either she did it Souad's way, or not at all. Souad had been unreasonable – unprofessional even, in Roisin's eyes. But it wasn't Roisin's opinion that counted here, as Souad had made very clear. She tried to work out what it was that she had done to cause this upset. She had run the classes as seminars – but that had been understood from the start. Seminars gave her access to the students, allowed the exchange of ideas and the expansion of discussion. Although she'd been careful to keep away from topics that would be controversial in this most closed of societies, she'd become friendly with Yasmin and Najia. Maybe that was where she had overstepped the mark.

She was still trying to work this out as she stood in the cloakroom adjusting her headscarf. It had to be something relating to the articles Najia had been posting on the web site, even though they were nothing to do with her. They were hardly inflammatory by Roisin's standards, but by the standards here – who could tell? Did Souad think she had been encouraging Najia?

The door of the cloakroom opened, and a woman came through. Roisin picked up her bag, then put it down again slowly as she realized that the woman was Yasmin. 'Yasmin . . .' she said.

Yasmin looked round. 'You have been to see the professor?' she said.

'Yes. She wants to stop the seminars.'

'I know. She talked to me as well. Don't worry, Roisin. We have learned a lot from you, and I'm sure we will enjoy your lectures.'

Roisin sighed. 'I wish I knew what had happened.'

'It is not you,' Yasmin said, shaking her head. 'These are difficult times. If things go wrong, the professor has to show people that she is doing something.'

Roisin made a rueful face. 'I didn't realize that anything *had* gone wrong.'

Yasmin didn't reply but concentrated on re-arranging the folds of her scarf. 'Truly, it is not you, Roisin,' she said. 'But I . . .'

She stopped abruptly, and Roisin looked at her in surprise, then saw the black-shrouded figure standing in the doorway. It was Haifa.

'Hello, Haifa,' she said, after too long a silence.

Haifa ignored her and spoke to Yasmin in Arabic.

Yasmin replied, then said in English, 'She says my driver is waiting. I have to go.' She moved past Roisin to the door.

Haifa stood there for a minute longer, then she left. Roisin fastened her bag. Her own driver would be here in a few minutes. She walked down the long, cool corridor where the darkness was punctuated by pools of light. As she came to the end, a voice spoke quietly from the shadows. 'Roisin.'

She stopped. Yasmin was standing there, almost invisible in her dark abaya, her face concealed. 'Roisin, would you meet me next weekend? Thursday? I am going to the al-Mamlaka mall then. I will be at Starbucks at three o'clock.'

'Yes. Yes, of course.'

Yasmin moved away down the corridor towards the exit. Roisin waited a moment, then followed. As she came into the bright sunlight, she saw Souad standing in the doorway of her office, watching. As Roisin's eyes met hers, she smiled and nodded.

20

It was like the quiet before the storm. Damien had been watching the clouds gather, and had been bracing himself for the onslaught – and suddenly, everything was quiet and still. The security clamp-down seemed to be having its effect. The attacks hadn't ended, but the police had started making arrests. Majid looked less stressed than he had for months when they met at one of the pavement cafés.

'You are well, my friend?' Majid said, after a greeting that was, for such a reserved man, close to ebullient. Unusually, he talked about his wife, or at least the impending birth of their child. 'I am very happy,' he said. 'You must marry, my friend, and have children. I want to see you happy as well. A man is nothing without children.'

'Maybe.' Damien thought about Amy, about him and Amy living together somewhere with a family of their own. If he'd offered her that, would it have made a difference? If he went to her now,

199

and made those promises, would it give them a new start? But the image had the thin, translucent quality of fantasy.

Later, he drove to the hospital where Amy worked. It was a world-renowned centre for excellence in obstetrics and neo-natal medicine. Many of those training as researchers and clinicians were women, but even though their education received active government support, the hospital was having trouble filling vacant posts.

Damien pulled up outside the hospital and swung himself out of the cool interior of his car into the heat of the late afternoon. The entrance doors slid open in front of him and he entered the cool of the air-conditioned lobby.

The atrium was high and airy with marble pillars. There was a drift of coffee in the air from stalls selling drinks and pastries. Across the open expanse of stone floor, there was a rock sculpture. Water glistened as it ran across the surface and trickled away bringing a fresh coolness to the air.

Through the doors, he could see a car drawing up outside. He recognized the driver as one of Arshak Nazarian's staff – the man who drove Nazarian himself. Nazarian, coming to this hospital? He stepped back into the shadow of one of the palms and watched.

A woman stepped out of the car and came through the main entrance. She was moving briskly towards the lifts. Her face was shadowed by her scarf, but Damien knew that quick, high-stepping walk.

Amy.

As she turned her head, the light fell on her face and he saw her eyes were bright with an emotion he couldn't quite interpret in that quick glance. He crossed the lobby towards her.

'Amy,' he said.

She spun round. 'Damien! What are you . . . Oh. You're here for a meeting.'

He nodded.

Her eyes went back to the entrance, where the car was just pulling away. 'If it's the staffing, it's about time. We're using – I hardly know the people on my ward, they come and go so quickly. I . . .'

'It's OK, Amy. You can do what you like. It isn't my business any more.'

The colour flooded her face. 'I didn't mean . . .' The lift doors opened and she stepped inside. He moved back, and her eyes met his as the door slid shut between them.

Amy and Nazarian. Where in hell had that come from?

Suddenly he was breathing in the scent of her body, could feel the warmth of her breath on his mouth. He forced the thoughts out of his mind. Maybe Amy had been right. Maybe there had been nothing beyond sex in his feelings for her.

But the thought of her with Nazarian was a gnawing ache.

*   *   *

201

Roisin called in to collect their post on the way back from work. Her mind was still going over the encounter with Souad as she let herself into the house. She dumped her bag in the kitchen and poured herself a glass of fruit juice, then she sat down to check the mail. There was a letter from her mother that she put on one side for later, a couple of things for Joe, including one from the university in Melbourne where he had applied for work once his contract in Riyadh was over. There was also an expensive-looking white envelope addressed to Dr and Mrs J. Massey. She opened it and slipped out a thick white card with dark lettering.

It was an invitation to a party the following weekend from one of the senior consultants at the hospital where Joe worked. The date of the party was 8 Thul Qedah. Roisin glanced quickly at the conversion calendar and realized with a jolt that it would soon be Christmas.

Here, Christmas would be just another working day. The Mutawa'ah had very definite ideas about overt celebration of this non-Islamic festival. A party at Christmas was what they needed. It would be their first Christmas together – if *together* described their life these days.

Putting the thought out of her mind before it could depress her too much, she pinned the invitation on the noticeboard and turned to her mother's letter, which was full of chatty news from home and barely concealed anxiety about the insecurity in which Roisin was living. *Please take care of your-self* was the theme of the letter. *I hope you have a good special day*, her mother signed off.

Roisin had posted a card ten days ago with the typical American *Happy Holiday* that seemed to be acceptable here, warning her not to send any Christmas greetings. Her mother had taken the warning literally, and even in the letter the forbidden word was not mentioned. Roisin smiled as she read it again. She could picture her mother sitting at the kitchen table as she wrote, frowning as she selected the code that would allow her to wish them a happy Christmas.

But the date made her wonder about the party. She looked at the invitation again. Maybe it was a pretext to celebrate without offending their Saudi hosts. The address, as befitted someone of the status of the consultant, was in one of the wealthier suburbs on the far side of the city. She'd heard that at some of these parties they served champagne, real champagne that had been smuggled into the Kingdom. The Mutawa'ah rarely interfered with ex-pat parties, as long as events remained firmly within the walls of the house.

She waved the invitation at Joe as he came through the door. He looked at it, frowning. 'I didn't expect us to be asked to this. Do you really want to go?'

'Are you crazy? Of course I do. It's in Millionaires' Row. I'd love to see it.'

'Billionaires, more like.'

'Do they pay their top consultants that well?'

'No chance. His wife's the one with the money. Most of the people who live out there are bastards – it's in the job description for being that rich.'

Roisin was tired of the moral ambiguities of the Kingdom, tired of the long hours spent on her own and tired of looking over her shoulder. 'So what? Joe, it'll be Christmas. Our first Christmas together. Let's go and drink their champagne.'

Joe smiled reluctantly. 'You've heard the rumours too?'

He was opening his letter from Melbourne as he was speaking. As he scanned it, his face changed and he let out a whoop of triumph. 'Yes! Sweetheart, they want me. They want me the moment my contract's over. They want me sooner if I can do it.' He put his arms round her waist and lifted her off the ground, waltzing her around the room. 'Australia. What do you think? Shall we cut our losses and go?'

He put her down and she looked up at him, breathless and surprised. 'Go? What do you mean, *go*?'

'I mean we can leave. We can get the hell out of here.'

Leave. For a moment, the words meant nothing, then she felt her whole mood start to lighten, as if a curtain had been pulled back, one she hadn't been aware of until it was gone. They could leave. They could go. They didn't have to spend another nine months in the stifling restrictions that

Riyadh imposed on its inhabitants. 'Can we do that?'

'My contract says a month's notice – I made sure of that before I signed. Yours will be even less. It'll take us a week or two to get exit permits, and we'll have to sort out accommodation over there. Visas. Permits – shit, all that paperwork. But yes. We can do that. A month, six weeks tops and we can be the hell out of here.' He looked at her. 'Christ, I'd forgotten how much I hated this place. You're right about the party – we've got something to celebrate.'

The strain she'd seen on his face had gone. He was smiling as he kissed her. 'This has been rough on you. Not the best start to a marriage. I sometimes think we might have done better somewhere else.'

Suddenly, he was the Joe of the London summer again. 'We're fine.' And she found she could say that with confidence.

'I love you,' he said. 'You know that, don't you?' She nodded. 'I've been thinking. If we go there, we'll be there for a few years.' His eyes were warm as he looked at her. 'You know that baby we were talking about . . . ?'

'Baby . . . ?'

'Mmm. Want to go for it? Do you fancy having a little Aussie?'

A baby. Her and Joe and . . . 'You know I do. Oh, Joe. When?'

'Well – now? We could make a start.'

So it wasn't until much later that she got round to telling him about her day. As they lay in bed together, tangled in the sheets, she told him about her meeting with Souad, but all the frustrations of the day had evaporated into a minor annoyance. She didn't want to spoil their evening by making him anxious, so she didn't mention the odd encounter she'd had with Yasmin as she was leaving.

21

The mall took Roisin's breath away. The retail section of the soaring needle that had drawn her eye that first day in Riyadh occupied three storeys of the building. The third floor, closed from the outside world, was reserved for women. It was a fantasy land of mirrors and glass and reflections with high ceilings and long walkways where the shop fronts displayed their wares.

Lights glittered off the polished metal and the reflective sheen of the walls and floor. A fountain splashed in the centre of the massive concourse, refreshing the air, and coloured lights glimmered from ornamental pools. Women strolled through, stylishly dressed in jeans and tight tops, immaculately made up. Roisin couldn't equate them with the dark triangles of the streets or the veiled faces she saw looking out from the back seats of cars.

They were surrounded by a luxury that amazed her, display window after display window crammed with designer clothes, jewellery, accessories, all, presumably, to be worn hidden away under the enveloping abaya. The women around her may live in cages, but they were cages gilded with wealth and comfort.

'Roisin.' The voice behind her made her jump. She turned and saw two women sitting at a table outside a café with the familiar Starbucks logo. For a moment, she didn't recognize them, then she realized that the one dressed in the uniform of fashionable youth – stylish blue jeans and a shirt – was Najia, and the other, more conservatively dressed, her head covered with a lacy scarf, was Yasmin.

A third woman was standing in the background. She was older than Yasmin and Najia, and was dressed in a drab shalwar kameez. She didn't look like a Saudi. She stood silently with her hands clasped in front of her.

'Hello, Yasmin,' she said. 'And Najia. I wasn't expecting you. And . . . ?' She looked at the third woman.

'This is Bakul,' Najia said. 'She is my mother's maid.'

'Hello.'

The maid looked at her unsmilingly and made no response to Roisin's greeting.

'Bakul, buy Roisin coffee,' Najia said.

'No. It's fine. I'll get my own.' Roisin reached into her bag.

'Please,' Yasmin said quickly. 'Bakul will get it.'

The two women sat silently as the maid moved

away. Roisin studied them. Najia looked younger, freed from her hijab. She also looked tense and unhappy.

Once Bakul had gone, Najia leaned forward. 'Roisin, I'm sorry we were not quite honest when we brought you here today. I asked Yasmin not to tell you I would be here because of the trouble.'

'Trouble about the articles on the web site?'

Najia nodded. 'The professor spoke to my brother. And now . . . my brother says I must leave university. He wants me to stay at home.'

Yasmin touched her wrist. 'He's upset. He will change his mind,' she said. Her worried frown suggested she wasn't convinced by her own words.

'He won't, because he's afraid. Everyone is afraid.' Najia's voice was agitated. 'I am the one who is angry, but what can I do?'

'We have been to Versace, but we still have all the other shops to visit,' Yasmin said.

Roisin looked at her in surprise and saw that Bakul had returned with her coffee. The maid put it carefully in front of Roisin. Roisin smiled at her. 'Thank you.' Bakul seemed surprised and quickly resumed her place behind Najia's chair. Roisin looked at her uncomfortably. 'I can't –' she began. She wasn't going to sit here while the maid stood, but Yasmin interrupted her.

She patted her stomach. 'I have to get things for after, you see.' She turned to the maid and spoke rapidly in Arabic. Bakul looked at Najia, then at the other women and nodded reluctantly.

Then she left. Yasmin looked at Roisin. 'I asked her to go to our next shop and arrange for them to have a chair for me.'

Najia stirred her coffee with angry vigour. 'My brother won't let me go out now unless I have Bakul to go with me. She tells them everything – who I talk to, where I go and what I do.'

'I'm sorry.' Roisin wanted to help Najia, but she didn't know what she could do. She recalled Damien O'Neill's warning: any intervention from her would only make matters worse. 'I thought that things were getting better here for women.'

'So we thought, for a small while,' Najia said. 'But then they refused us the vote. Roisin, the elections were a set-back, not progress. Those who want reform are being arrested and prevented from speaking out. The traditionalists have been made more strong than they were before.'

'And they are the ones who make people afraid,' Yasmin said. 'The government, the authority – they don't worry if some woman puts an article on a web site about the vote. They just get it removed. But the others – they will kill for this. And they will harm your family too. People are too afraid to see that the only way to win is to fight back.' Her eyes were constantly checking for the return of the silent maid.

'My mother . . .' Najia's voice had dropped, and Roisin had to strain to catch what she was saying. 'When I was eight, my mother took part in a protest. She drove, with other women, to show that the laws against us driving were wrong. She lost her job, and my father almost lost his. And all of us, the children, were threatened. It made my father afraid. He divorced my mother and wouldn't let me see her. My brothers grew up believing that what she did was wrong. It was dreadful what happened to her, to all of those women, but if they had done it now, I believe they would be killed, and their families with them.'

Roisin had a sudden flash of Joe in London, the first evening they spent together, when he'd talked a bit about the Kingdom. *It's like one of those optical illusions.* She had been seeing a society at a point of change – exciting, challenging, fraught with difficulties but moving forward. And suddenly the pattern had switched, and what was in front of her was a country clinging to its feudal past in which talented, vibrant young women like Yasmin and Najia were broken on the wheel of tradition and repression. And what had looked like a bit of student radicalism, the posting of mildly subversive articles on a web site, was actually a dangerous and revolutionary act.

'I'm sorry, Roisin,' Yasmin said. 'You come here and we tell you all our troubles.'

'You know I'll help you if I can.' Roisin thought about Damien O'Neill at the party. *I don't think it would help if a Westerner was to take up the cause – they'd lose a lot of credibility.*

The two women exchanged a quick glance, then Yasmin said, 'There is something you can do for

211

Najia, this is what we wanted to ask you. Her brother won't allow her to attend college. She won't be able to complete her degree. Could you go on teaching her English?' She checked quickly over Roisin's shoulder again.

'So I can get my Proficiency exam.' Najia looked at her with doubtful hope.

Roisin's impulse to laugh was prompted more by her dismay at her own fears than by amusement. She'd been afraid they would ask her to do something subversive, when all they wanted from her was her teaching skills. But she was looking at the problem from the wrong perspective. There were countries where the education of women was just that – an act of subversion. 'Of course I will. I'll be glad to.'

There was silence for a moment. Roisin picked up her coffee. She got the impression that Yasmin had something else she wanted to say. There was an air of tension about the two women that couldn't come from a simple request for English lessons. Or was she still looking at this through Western eyes? In taking lessons, Najia would be disobeying her brother.

'There is something else,' Yasmin said.

Roisin nodded. 'I thought there was.'

'It is just – very simple, but hard for us to do. There is a girl who is missing – we want to know where she is, but we haven't been able to find her.'

Once again, they'd surprised her. 'A missing girl . . .' Roisin wasn't sure where this was going.

'We thought that . . . maybe you would be able to help us?'

There was a guardedness in Yasmin's voice that made Roisin uneasy. Yasmin wasn't telling her everything. 'I'm not sure I'd know where to start. I don't have any access to . . .' She had access to the British Embassy. Was that what Yasmin was hinting at? 'Who is she?'

'She was a maid. She worked for one of the families here – she ran away. I would like to know what happened to her.'

Roisin frowned as she drank her coffee. This was tricky. She wanted to help, but she had to know what she was getting into. 'Yasmin, why do you want to find her? Why is this so important?'

She saw Yasmin and Najia exchange a quick glance. All of their lives their activities had been curtailed by people with the power to give or withhold their permission. 'It doesn't matter,' she said. 'But I can't do much. I can ask some questions.'

'I know. But you can ask people that we cannot.'

With the feeling that she had just stepped on to the top of a long and slippery slope, Roisin said, 'You'd better tell me about her. What's her name?'

'Jesal. Jesal Rajkhumar.'

Roisin jotted the name down quickly. 'How old is she?'

'Not old. Maybe twenty-two, twenty-three.'

Roisin looked at the name, frowning. 'Is she British?'

'No. She is Pakistani.'

Roisin looked at the two women, who were watching her with barely concealed anxiety. She was at a loss to understand why they had asked her. She had no way of looking for a missing Pakistani woman. *You can ask people that we cannot.*

There was the British Embassy – but why would they know anything about a Pakistani woman – and, if they did, why would they tell her? She suddenly thought of Damien O'Neill. If anyone would know where to start looking, he would. But would he be willing to give her the information? She could find a way of asking. 'OK. I'll try.'

Yasmin glanced across the mall, checking again to see if Bakul was returning. The words came even more reluctantly now. 'She . . . was hurt.' She gave Roisin a significant look. 'This is what she told . . . someone. And the police may have been looking for her.'

Roisin felt the ground under her feet start to give way. She gave Yasmin a level look. 'Why?'

'Before she ran away, her . . . employers, they said she stole. I don't know if she did, but this is what they told the police.'

Stole. The penalties for theft in the Kingdom were harsh. 'Is there anything else I need to know?'

Yasmin bit her lip. 'You understand, she had great difficulty. I was worried about her. I tried to help her, but then she disappeared and . . . no one seemed to know what had happened to her.'

Roisin thought quickly. 'If she went into

214

hiding . . .' The woman had been hurt. Did Yasmin mean she had been raped? It happened – the maids had little protection from their employers. Amy had talked about a clinic where women could be helped. Maybe this runaway maid could have gone there. Amy might know. Or she might know where to ask. She watched Yasmin scan the café again. 'If she was hurt, could she have gone to the hospital? My husband, Joe, he's in charge of the pathology department. I can get him to ask a few questions. I'm not sure if there's –' She jumped as Yasmin's coffee cup clattered to the floor.

There was the silence that follows a sudden noise, and then the voices around them started up again.

'I have a headache,' Yasmin said. 'I feel unwell.' And she looked unwell. The blood seemed to have drained from her face.

Najia looked at Roisin in alarm. 'Yasmin, I am calling your driver. You must go home. Where's Bakul?'

'Do you need help?' Roisin stood up.

Yasmin shook her head. 'I will be well again soon. It is just small thing. But I need to go home.'

Najia was talking quickly on her phone. She snapped it shut. 'They are send her car,' she said to Roisin. 'And Bakul is coming now,' she added.

Yasmin said something in Arabic and Najia helped her to her feet as Bakul began to collect their bags. Roisin could see the distinctive logo of Louis Vuitton.

'Let me help you,' she said again. 'I'll come with you to your car.'

'Thank you, but we will manage,' Najia said.

'It's no trouble.'

Yasmin wouldn't meet her eye. 'No, Roisin. I will be fine.'

Defeated, Roisin stood back and watched them as they left the café. She could see Najia talking agitatedly as they crossed the open space of the mall, and Yasmin's gesture of dismissal. Then they vanished into the crowd.

Damien was at home when the phone call came. Majid's voice, filled with suppressed excitement, came on the line. 'Damien, God bless you, how are you, my friend?'

'Majid. I'm well. How are you?'

'Very well. I have to tell you something. Soon I will be a father. My wife, she was just taken to the hospital and I thought I must tell my good friend my news.'

'Congratulations. You'll be a great father.' Damien was pleased and touched. The traditions of Arab hospitality made them generous in all walks of life. Majid wouldn't step across Damien's threshold without a gift, and when he had good news, he shared it with his friends to spread his happiness around.

But Majid's joy made his own life feel stark and empty. It was almost a week since he and Amy had said goodbye, and the raw edges of that parting still chafed like a wound. Why had he held back? He'd known from the start that Amy was different but he hadn't had the guts to go for it. And now? He could try – he could go to Amy, talk to her, persuade her that . . .

'We will celebrate,' Majid was saying. 'When my son is born, we will celebrate and you will join us.'

'It would be an honour.' Majid's voice had shaken as he said the word 'son'. Even now, a lot of Saudi men only wanted sons. Hell, a lot of Western men wanted sons – it wasn't just Arab misogyny that was the problem here.

A boy, born as the Kingdom struggled with its own rebirth. Damien wondered what the child's future would be.

22

Roisin ran over and over her encounter with Najia and Yasmin in her mind as she waited for Joe to come home. She went into the kitchen and pulled stuff out of the fridge. It was a motley assortment. She decided to make soup – they could have soup and salad. And she could make some bread.

She wondered how Yasmin was. She had no way of finding out – she didn't have home addresses or telephone numbers for any of her students. Yasmin had looked tense and weary from the start. It probably wasn't good for a woman in late pregnancy to get stressed. Maybe that was what had caused her sudden illness.

Hard as she tried to focus on what she was doing as she chopped onions and thawed out some chicken stock she'd made a few weeks ago, her mind wouldn't stay away from the events of the afternoon. They'd been talking about this woman Yasmin wanted to find, this maid called Jesal, a migrant worker alone and apparently guilty of theft in a country where such crimes were brutally punished.

And then . . . just before she became ill, Yasmin had glanced round the mall, looking out for Bakul's return. And something had made her drop her cup in shock, causing the colour to drain from her face. She hadn't seen Bakul – Najia had had to use her phone to summon the maid. She'd seen something else that had upset her. Roisin tried to picture the mall again, but she'd had her back to whatever it was Yasmin had been looking at. And after that, her attention had been focused on the two women and the importance of getting Yasmin home.

To stop her mind from fruitlessly going over and over the incident, she started thinking about the problem Yasmin had set her. She hadn't asked, but the question that was bothering her was, *why?* Why did Yasmin want to trace Jesal Rajkhumar?

Jesal had been in trouble – that much was clear from Yasmin's reluctant admission. Yasmin had tried to help her, and then Jesal had vanished . . .

A young woman escapes from her Saudi employers, claiming they are abusing her. She has stolen from them, and applies to another Saudi woman for help. Why Yasmin? Why would a runaway woman in trouble turn to Yasmin?

The 'cultural salons'. Yasmin had talked about the cultural salons that she and her friends had. Roisin had asked Damien O'Neill about the women's movement in Saudi Arabia. It looked as though she might have found it. If so, what Yasmin and Najia were doing was dangerous. There was a government department whose Arabic name translated as 'the rejecting evil and evoking right association'. She could remember joking about it with Joe, but to women like Yasmin and Najia it was deadly serious. 'Shit.' Roisin didn't realize she'd spoken aloud until her own voice broke the silence. If she was right, Yasmin's request meant trouble.

She tipped the chopped vegetables into the stock and began frying chicken. In her bag, she had the contact number for Damien O'Neill – he'd given it to her and Joe on that first day. She was certain that he had the means to get her the information she needed – either where Jesal was, or how she could find out – but he'd want to know why she was asking. She tried to think of a pretext that wouldn't involve any mention of Yasmin or Najia.

She put a tight lid on the pan and left the soup to cook over a low flame. On impulse, she picked up the phone and keyed in O'Neill's number. There was no point in being evasive with him, she decided. She would simply put the question with no explanation. Either he would tell her where to look, or he would refuse to help.

The phone rang seven times, then his voice came on the line: *I can't take your call at the moment. If you need to contact me urgently, call my mobile. Otherwise, leave a message and I'll get back to you.*

She hung up without leaving a message – this was something for a direct conversation.

Of course, there was Amy. Amy probably knew a lot more about the women's movement – she worked with women, and she had hinted, briefly, that she had given some assistance to women who were pregnant and single. Amy might be able to help. Roisin had been waiting for Amy to call her since that day she had visited, but there had been nothing. Maybe she felt awkward about pushing the connection. It was time for Roisin to take the initiative.

She tried the number Amy had given her, but once again all she got was the answering service. This time, she left a message. 'It's Roisin. How are you? Let's meet sometime soon.'

Then there was nothing else she could do.

23

Roisin hadn't been looking forward to her next session at the university, but she had too many things to think about now to let it worry her. Now that the end was in sight, Joe was relaxed and happy. He was home by four most days and they spent their spare time together, sometimes walking in the cool of the evening, sometimes sitting in the garden they'd barely used in the two months they'd been here. It didn't matter. They were just enjoying themselves. Roisin stopped doing the extra days at the university and spent her free time catching up with neglected correspondence. She wrote to old George back in London – guiltily aware that this was only the second letter she'd sent. And she started sorting their things out for the time they could leave. Once they left Saudi, they planned to take a month off so they could go back to the UK before they travelled to Melbourne.

'It's going the long way round,' Joe pointed out when she suggested it.

'I know, but I want to show you Newcastle. And Bamburgh, and Seahouses. And Druridge Sands.'

'OK, OK.' He was laughing at her.

'You wait. It'll surprise you.'

Coming back to the campus was like stepping back into a different world. She felt detached from it all, as though their new life in Melbourne had already begun. She knew it was far too soon to start wondering if she might be pregnant, but the prospect made her smile at people she didn't know as she walked along the corridors of the women's campus.

She'd expected to find instructions about the new regime in her pigeonhole when she went into the office, but nothing seemed to have changed. The seminar room was set up and the students were waiting for her. They worked hard and cheerfully, their voices rising in a buzz as they tried out the English Roisin had taught them. Even Haifa was as friendly as she seemed capable of being. The only sour note was the absence of Najia. No one remarked on the empty place. There was no sign of Yasmin either, but it was one of the days she was chauffeured to the villages outside Riyadh to teach English. Still, Roisin felt anxious, remembering that Yasmin had been unwell at the mall. None of the students seemed to know anything.

She didn't see Souad until the end of the morning when she was packing her bag to leave. The professor came into the seminar room and greeted her, sounding friendly enough. She looked at the notes on the whiteboard, and at the hand-outs Roisin had been working with. 'This is interesting,' she said. 'May I have a copy?'

'Of course. I put everything I use into the resource bank.'

'I know. This is all most helpful to us. I have come to tell you that I have booked the lecture theatre for you from next week. You will be ready by then?'

'Whenever you want me to start.' Roisin gave a mental shrug. Today had just been a brief hope of a reprieve. It didn't matter now anyway.

'We will record your lectures for other use, so please dress appropriately.' She spoke as if Roisin was in the habit of teaching in crop-tops and shorts.

'Will what I'm wearing today be suitable?'

'Perfectly acceptable,' the professor said. 'As long as you wear your scarf. You will lecture to all the students who are studying English,' she went on. 'We have beginners and intermediate as well as advanced. So you will do three lectures.'

Suddenly it was clear to Roisin what Souad had in mind. Roisin would lecture, they would film, and then Souad would have a teaching resource she could use for as long as she wanted without having to worry about employing another trouble-some foreigner. Roisin was being asked to co-operate in her own redundancy. In addition, the programme amounted to six times the work she'd been contracted for. 'I'll have to concentrate on the intermediate level this month. As you know, that's what I came here to teach.'

Souad's eyebrows lifted. 'But you have done the other levels. I don't see the problem.'

'Ah, but not as lectures. If you wanted me to do seminars and classes, then I could do it at once. Lectures will need some time to prepare.'

'I believed, when we employed you, that you were prepared at all levels,' Souad said coldly.

'I am. For seminars. As we agreed.' Roisin smiled helpfully. It was a small victory, but she was enjoying it. She'd still be busy most of next weekend as it was. Except the party. She was damned if she was going to miss the party because of Souad al-Munajjed. 'But I'll be ready to do the intermediate work next week.' She didn't want to get tangled in an argument so she said quickly, 'I haven't seen Yasmin today.'

'Yasmin has had her baby – a son.'

Roisin forgot about the lectures. Yasmin's illness at the mall must have been the onset of labour. 'A little boy? That's wonderful. Is Yasmin all right? And the baby?'

'Yasmin is well, but I believe the child is having some problems.'

'Is it serious?'

'The child was born healthy, but he seems to have become ill now. He was due to go home, but they are keeping him in the hospital. I have no more information. Yasmin should not have worked as long as she did. She was warned it could be dangerous.'

That was ridiculous. Yasmin was young and fit. 'Will you let me know how they both are? When you hear?'

'Yasmin is no longer my responsibility,' the professor said. 'It is a matter for her family.'

'Is she in the hospital?'

'Yasmin is home. The child is not.'

'But if you have any news, let me know. I'd like to see her. And the baby.' Before she left the mall, she'd bought a baby shawl, a drift of white cashmere, ridiculously expensive, that was now wrapped in tissue at the bottom of her wardrobe.

'It is a matter for the family.' Souad went to the door. 'Lecture. Next week,' she said.

Roisin watched her leave and turned back to her books. Souad wasn't going to tell her anything. It didn't matter. The students would let her know, or she could e-mail Najia.

She turned her mind to the problem of lectures.

'Damien. It's Amy.'

'Amy,' he said, keeping his voice level.

'How are you?' Her voice sounded thin and far away.

'I'm fine. How are you?'

'Fine. I just wanted to tell you, I'm leaving tonight.'

'Leaving?' He had no idea she'd been planning to leave. 'For good?'

'I'm not sure yet. I think so.'

'Why? You never told me.' But there was no reason why she should. He had no right to know about her plans, not any more.

'I did,' she said. 'More or less. I told you I was getting my life sorted out.'

Then that was it. 'I hope everything works out for you.'

'Thank you.' There was silence.

He couldn't leave it there. 'Amy, don't you think you should have told me about Nazarian? Didn't you owe me . . . didn't we owe each other that much honesty?'

She was quiet for so long that he thought she must have put the phone down, then she said, 'I was as honest as I could be. As honest as you've always been with me.'

As he'd always . . . 'Amy, I have never lied to you.'

'No. You didn't need to. You never told me anything.'

The truth of what she was saying silenced his objections. She was right. The habit of secrecy had always been strong in him. 'I thought that what we had was enough.'

He heard her sigh. 'That's what I thought, too. But it wasn't.'

'And now . . . ?'

'And now I'm going. I'm leaving tonight. I want to be with my sister when she has her baby. I've taken a month's leave, so there's no need for me to work out my notice.'

They'd already said goodbye in all the ways that mattered, but . . . 'What time's your plane? I'll come to the airport to see you off.'

The brittle edge of her voice broke. 'Will you? I'd . . . I'd like that.'

They'd say their final goodbyes in the chaos of the departures hall of Riyadh International Airport. Maybe it was the best place. In the meantime, there was work.

He had another meeting at the hospital. The management there seemed to think he could work miracles. He'd already told them: put up the incentives, or people won't come. He pulled into the car park and was picking up his laptop from the back seat when he saw Majid. He was by his car, the key in his hand, staring into space. He looked as though he had been there for a while.

Damien slammed his car door shut and went across. He wanted to congratulate Majid on his recent fatherhood, but his greeting died in his throat when he saw Majid's face. His jaw was clenched and tears were trickling down his cheeks.

'Majid,' he said.

Majid jumped and looked round as though he had forgotten where he was. Then he saw Damien. Damien put his arm round the other man's shoulder, and held him in a quick embrace. 'What's wrong?' he said, then, in Arabic, 'You have troubles, my friend?'

'I'm sorry. It's not your trouble,' Majid said.

'My friend's troubles are my troubles.' The

Arabic rituals of politeness were sincere and helped over difficult moments. Damien waited. It had to be Yasmin or the baby.

Majid stood in silence, trying to get his emotions under control, then he said, 'Yasmin's – *our* baby, he was born too soon. He is . . .' His hands cupped themselves as if he was holding something fragile. 'Perfect. Perfect.' His gaze met Damien's in baffled confusion. 'But now they are saying . . . they do some blood tests – just routine, and then everything changes. This is wrong, that is wrong, nothing is well. So why didn't they find it at once? Why did they wait? They moved him this morning to the ITU. They say, "This we will do, that we will do" . . . I am a policeman. I know when they are lying. They have done something wrong.' His face twisted in grief. 'I am afraid my son will die.'

Damien felt his throat tighten. 'Majid,' he said. 'I'm sorry.' He didn't try and hide his own emotion. That wasn't the way here.

Majid's expression was bleak. 'Yasmin . . . all these weeks she has been working.' He shook his head wearily. 'My mother says that our baby is ill because Yasmin didn't take enough care. She wouldn't go to the clinic. She went to work, she went to the mall, she saw her friends. My mother says it is Yasmin's fault.'

Damien could remember the night he had seen the beautiful young face looking out of the window. 'Majid, sometimes these things just happen. Sometimes it's no one's fault.'

'A good wife and a good mother will always put her husband and her children first. Yasmin did not do this.'

Damien had seen this in Saudi families before – the mother held sway over her daughter-in-law, and the husband often listened to his mother before he listened to his wife. If the two were antagonistic, the daughter-in-law's life could be hard. 'Your son's still here,' he said. 'He's alive, he's . . . perfect. You said he was perfect. Majid, he might be all right.'

Majid's mouth tightened and he shook his head. 'There is something wrong,' he said. 'I know it.'

24

Later that afternoon, Damien headed towards the hospital exit. He had been distracted through the meeting, his mind only half on what they had been discussing. He couldn't get his conversation with Majid out of his mind. Majid's insistence that there was something wrong, something odd or underhand going on, was making alarm bells ring in his head. He couldn't ignore it. Majid was a policeman, he had an instinct for these things.

He needed to make some discreet enquiries. For a moment, he thought about asking Amy, but she was a professional to the bone. Even though she was leaving, she wouldn't discuss details of a hospital case with him. He hesitated, thinking, then he followed the signs to the pathology department where he found one of the junior technicians, a man he knew, filling in report forms. Everything was quiet and orderly. This place had been chaos a few weeks before. Joe Massey had done a good job.

Damien and the technician exchanged greetings and the usual small talk. Damien wasn't sure if this young man would do what he asked, but it was worth a try.

'I've got a query about one of the infants in the neo-natal ITU,' he said. 'He was born earlier this week. He was moved to the ITU – this morning, I think. Apparently the blood tests came back showing there were problems. Can you give me some idea . . . ?'

The technician looked puzzled. It was an odd thing for Damien to ask.

'There's just some potential for trouble. I'm covering my bases,' Damien said. This vague excuse seemed to work. The man's face cleared.

'What do you want to know?' he said.

'Just the reason for the concern – do they know what's wrong with the child?'

'Hang on.' The man went and checked through a pile of reports in a document tray and pulled one out. 'OK.' He read through it, frowning slightly. 'For some reason, the oxygen levels aren't right. That suggests problems with the lungs, or the heart.' He looked uncertain, and the alarm bells started ringing in Damien's head.

'Is something wrong?'

'No . . . I can't understand why they didn't put the kid in an incubator at once. Problems like this don't just . . .' He was leafing through the papers. 'The first set of results don't seem to be –' He stopped abruptly and put the report back into

232

the folder. 'Maybe you should talk to the consultant.'

'Maybe I should.' If someone had made a mistake, missed a serious health problem when the child was born, and as a result it died, then Majid would turn the hospital upside down in his search for the person who was responsible for the death of his son. He looked at the technician. 'The child – is it going to survive?'

The technician shook his head. 'I don't know. I can't answer that. I can call the senior pathologist for you. He could tell you better than I can.'

Joe Massey. 'It's OK. I'll get on to him later. Thanks.'

Damien left, still unsatisfied. Majid's story had disturbed him in more ways than simply his sadness for his friend's looming tragedy. All his unease had found its focus at the hospital. It was at the hospital that Haroun Patel had been arrested. It was here that Joe Massey – or someone – had started stirring up the Patel case. It was here that Amy had started asking questions about things that were perhaps best left alone. And now Majid and Yasmin's baby was seriously ill, and there was some indication that all wasn't well in the laboratory. Damien had been able to complete the sentence the technician had started. The early reports on Majid's baby, the ones that should have detected the problem immediately, were missing. Someone had made a mistake – a mistake that could have serious consequences – and the evidence had gone.

The problem filled his mind as he drove to the airport, and acted as some distraction when he put his arms round Amy for the last time. Her eyes were shiny with tears. 'Goodbye, Damien. I'll . . . miss you.'

He managed a smile. 'I'll miss you too.'

There was no sign of Nazarian. Whatever farewells she'd planned with him, they had already happened.

It was the weekend of the party. Roisin spent the whole of Thursday writing her lectures. She resented the task because Joe was at home – one of the first weekends he'd been able to take off. He didn't seem to mind that they couldn't do anything together. She could hear his music playing as he worked round the house. He brought her tea and fruit juice at regular intervals, and stayed to talk. 'How are you doing?' He leaned over her shoulder to have a look.

'I'm nowhere. I'll be at it for hours yet.'

'Why bother? We're leaving anyway.'

'I know.' But it was a matter of pride. She was a professional, and she was going to behave like one until she left. Joe understood. He was the same about his work. 'I just wish this hadn't come up.'

'She's protecting her turf.'

'Right. Doesn't mean I have to like it.'

The phone rang. 'I'll get it,' Joe said. She heard his feet on the stairs, and his voice, 'Joe Massey.' She smiled as she turned back to her work. He was so different – it was as if the news from Melbourne had woken him from some dark place the Kingdom had taken him to. Suddenly he was the Joe she knew, the man she loved and had married.

She heard him coming back up the stairs. His footsteps were slow. 'I've got to go into work,' he said. 'There's a PM they want me to check.' He made a reluctant face. 'Great stuff for the weekend. Do you want to come in with me? I'll be an hour. We could go for a walk round the market afterwards.'

'I've got to get this finished.' She stood up and stretched, and followed Joe into the bedroom where he was getting changed. He pulled off his shirt and threw it at the linen basket. It fell on to the floor. 'Changed your mind?' he said when he saw her standing there.

'No. I just needed a break.'

'Poor love. If I didn't have to do this . . . Wait. I've got something to make you feel better.' He rummaged in the wardrobe and came out with a small packet. 'Here. I was going to give you these tonight.'

It was the first present he'd bought her for ages. She looked at him, and then she carefully unwrapped the package. Inside, there was a box and, when she opened it, she saw a pair of gold earrings with long, delicate chains.

She swept her hair up and held one of them against her face. The chains sparkled and glittered. Joe stood behind her as she turned her head, admiring the effect in the mirror. 'Bling,' he murmured into her hair. 'I got them at the gold market. For tonight. It kind of felt right, you know?' He looked at his watch. 'Shit. I'd better go.'

She heard the door close and the sound of the car starting up and fading into the distance. She could hear the sounds of the weekend afternoon around her: children playing in the gardens, voices calling, laughter, the *snip, snip* of secateurs. She could smell the first smoke of the day's barbecues.

She could be in her mother's house on a Sunday in Newcastle listening to the neighbours. The TV would be on downstairs, and her mother would be clattering pots around in the kitchen and keeping up a vague, unfocused barrage of chat: *Can I get you some tea, pet? Have you seen what they've done to the house on the corner? Did I tell you about . . . ? You'll never guess what . . .*

Her fingers slowed on the keyboard and she let her mind drift. She was looking forward to showing Newcastle to Joe. He had never been there. It would be grey winter, but it didn't matter. They could walk along the Tyne under the seven bridges. They could cross the gossamer arc of steel that was the Millennium Bridge to Gateshead. They could go to North Shields and watch the fishing boats bringing in the catch in the icy wind, then walk back along the river to the ferry eating fish and chips . . .

She'd lost her place again. She read through the notes she had been writing, and found she had no idea what she was doing. What had seemed like a good idea a couple of hours ago had faded into an irretrievable memory.

The phone rang. She picked it up, glad of the distraction. 'Roisin Massey.'

'Roisin, it's Amy.'

'Amy!' She had been expecting this call since she'd left the message a few days before. 'How are you?'

'Fine. I'm sorry it's taken me so long to get back to you. I got your message.'

'That's OK. I wondered if you wanted to get together. There was something I was going to . . .'

'That would be great, but listen, I'm not in Riyadh. I'm calling from Paris.'

'Paris?' *A railway station, and Amy, hanging out of the train window as it pulled away, calling and calling* . . . No wonder she hadn't been able to make contact. 'Is it your sister?' She tried to remember the name. 'Jassy?'

'Yes. I left in a rush. The baby's due any day. I wondered if – is Joe there? I wanted to ask him something.'

'Joe? Is everything all right?'

'Everything's fine. It isn't about Jassy. There was something at the hospital before I left. I just thought he might be able to . . .'

'He's at work. Do you want him to call you?'

'No, it's OK. I'll try and get him at the hospital. Tell him I called.'

'I will. When will you be back?'

There was silence for a moment. 'I'm not sure,' Amy said slowly. 'I've got things to sort out. I'll see after the baby's born.'

'You'll be an aunt. Amy, I'm so glad for you. E-mail me lots of pictures. And we'll celebrate when you get back.'

There was that same silence, then Amy said, 'I'll do that. Listen, Roisin, I've got to go.'

'OK. Keep in touch. Let me know how you get on – and don't forget the photos.'

'I won't.'

The phone clicked into silence, leaving Roisin feeling unaccountably alone. She felt almost as if her only ally in the Kingdom had gone, which was crazy. And she hadn't had a chance to ask Amy about Jesal, about where a runaway migrant worker might go if the police were looking for her. Maybe it didn't matter now. Yasmin would have other things on her mind. She had her baby to worry about. But Roisin couldn't forget the tension on Yasmin's face as she had asked about the missing woman.

Unable to face doing any more work, she put her notes back in the proper files and the books on the shelves. There were papers piled up on the window sill gathering dust. She picked them up and flicked through them. They were the papers from Joe's work file that she'd tipped out by accident the day Amy had turned up on the doorstep and had never got round to clearing up.

She tried to stack them so she could put them into a folder out of the way, bumping the edge of the pile against the desk to make the papers line up, but they were different sizes and refused to slip neatly into order.

Taking a few at a time, she started putting them away. She picked one up that had fallen on to the desk, her eye going over it automatically. She'd put it in the file before her brain registered what she had seen. She took it out again and looked at it more closely.

It was a photograph of Joe and another man. They were standing together by a car in a dusty landscape – somewhere on the edge of the desert by the looks of things – grinning triumphantly at the camera. The car bonnet was raised and Joe was holding up a piece of machinery – part of a car engine, maybe – in the manner of a hunter holding up a trophy.

It was a good photo, but that wasn't what had caught her attention. The man with Joe, a small, dark man, looked very familiar. She stared at the photo for a moment, then went to the filing cabinet where Joe kept his papers. After a quick search, she found what she wanted: the newspaper cutting that had been in the case she'd unpacked, weeks ago.

Supporters of a man who was executed in Saudi Arabia last week, today accused the government of failing to intervene. Haroun Patel, a Pakistani national who was a student in the UK in 2003, was convicted of smuggling heroin in Riyadh, Saudi Arabia. A spokesperson said, 'Her Majesty's government is unable to intervene in cases involving nationals from other countries.'

She could still remember their conversation that evening when she first began to realize that there was something wrong. She'd asked him:

Was it someone you knew?

And he'd shaken his head. *I told you, I don't know why I kept it.*

Looking at her from the newsprint, faded along the lines where it had been folded, was the smiling face of the young man who had died. It was the same man who was laughing with Joe in the photograph from . . . She turned the picture over. Scribbled on the back was the date: *October 2003.*

Haroun Patel, five months before his death.

Riyadh Central Hospital, Neo-natal ITU

It was night time and the lights were dimmed. The room was filled with the low hum of machines, the beep of heart monitors, the rhythmic pulse of the respirators. The cots were lined up down the centre of the ward, each one an enclosed environment in which children who had been born too early began their struggle to survive.

The infants themselves seemed strangely out of place among the clear plastic and the gleaming steel. They were messy, human, flesh and bone. Someone had made an attempt to soften the atmosphere, placing colourful pictures above the cots, but the infants couldn't see them, or interpret them if they could. They were there to comfort the families.

It was the start of the evening shift. The nurse, coming on duty, checked through her list of charges. There had been a new admission earlier in the day, a boy just a few days old whose condition had deteriorated unexpectedly. She read through the notes: the child had been healthy when he was born but had suddenly, inexplicably, become ill. He'd been taken for a scan just before the shifts had changed over.

She looked at the notes again, checking the time the child had been taken. They must have run into problems – the scan was taking a long time. There would be someone from the ITU down there with him – someone who was having to do overtime now. She ticked the child off on her notes to indicate that she was aware of his current location and condition, and moved on to the next cot.

25

Roisin sat quietly in the car as Joe negotiated his way through the city traffic. She listened with half an ear as he explained the reason he'd been called out. 'They wanted me to review a death,' he said. 'A baby died – he was very premature, born a few days ago. The family asked for a post mortem. That's unusual here.'

A sick baby. 'Joe, my friend at the university – Yasmin. Her baby was ill.'

He glanced at her quickly. 'I didn't think of that. Was it premature?'

'Not by much.'

'OK. Do you know the family name?'

She shook her head. 'She's just Yasmin.'

'OK. I'll check, tomorrow. Don't worry. This baby was definitely premature. And that hospital takes sick babies from across the Nadj – there's no reason to think it was your friend's.'

'I know.' She thought about the way Souad had

seemed almost pleased that Yasmin's baby wasn't well. 'Why did it die, this baby?'

'From being born too soon. Some are strong enough to make it and some aren't.' Like life, Roisin thought. Some of us are strong enough and some of us aren't. Joe was saying something else, and she pulled her attention back: ' . . . there's something that I should . . . Oh, shit. This fucking country. I don't know what to do.'

'What?'

'Nothing. Don't worry,' Joe said again.

There was silence in the car, then he said, in a clear attempt to change the subject, 'We ought to feel pretty good about being asked to this do.' He switched lanes to avoid a swerving truck. 'Apparently, these are the real Riyadh A-list.'

'That's good.' She was aware of his quick glance. 'Sorry, I was thinking about something else.'

He squeezed her hand. 'I thought you were looking forward to this. We don't have to go if you don't want to.'

'I know.' She stared out of the window. The streets were brightly lit but the road was strangely empty. There was a car ahead and a car behind, but nothing else in sight. She watched as the car behind them pulled out to pass. It drew alongside then kept pace with them. She could see the driver's face turned towards her. She realized that another car was closing behind, and the car ahead was slowing down.

Boxed in. They were boxed in. . . . *In traffic, always try to leave space in which to manoeuvre. Do not get boxed in; always leave yourself an exit . . .*

It was on journeys like this that people had been pulled from their cars and butchered.

'Shit!' Joe had seen it as well and was braking hard. Her stomach lurched in panic, and then the road cleared and the vehicle behind them pulled out and overtook with an impatient blast on the horn. She could feel her heart hammering in retrospective fright. The threat had arisen so suddenly, and receded just as quickly.

'Stupid bastards!' Joe's anger was a mark of the shock they had both had. His face was white. 'Jesus! You can't tell the difference between terrorism and bad driving.' He shook his head. 'This place is making me paranoid.' He kept his eyes on the road as he spoke, watching to make sure that the traffic had cleared around them. The road was busy again, the moment of quiet over. Cars shot past in a maze of weaving lights. They were an anonymous vehicle on a busy freeway. 'Are you all right?'

'Yes. I'm fine – but God, that was scary.'

'We'll be out of here soon.'

She wasn't sure if he meant the road, or the Kingdom itself.

'I know.' There was silence for a moment, then she said, without thinking or planning, 'Joe, who was Haroun Patel?'

She felt the car swerve as he reacted to her

question. He straightened the wheel, swearing as the horns sounded around him. 'Christ, Roisin, what kind of time is it to ask me that?'

'I didn't know it was that kind of question,' she said.

'Why do you want to know? Who's been talking to you?'

'No one. I read about him in that cutting I found, remember?'

He checked in the rear-view mirror. 'I can't talk about this while I'm driving.' He took the car across a couple of lanes, ignoring the outraged horns, and began to slow. They were passing one of the strip malls that lay on the outskirts of the city, and he pulled off the road into the car park. It was busy with families packing goods into the boots of cars, or heading in disorganized groups towards the entrances of the market. The light from the store fronts reflected in green and red and gold, the richness of the old ornamentation transformed into commercialized razzmatazz.

Anycity, Anyplace.

Joe turned to her. A flashing light from one of the shop fronts illuminated the inside of the car: red, blue, yellow, and then darkness. She studied his face, but the changing lights made it impossible to read his expression.

'I found a photograph – you and Haroun Patel. Joe, you told me you didn't know him.'

He looked away across the car park. The muscles in his jaw tightened. 'I didn't want you involved in this, Roisin. Yes, I knew Haroun. I'd known him for about eighteen months before I came out here. That photograph – I was working out in the villages, and my car broke down. Haroun fixed it. He was a genius with engines.' In the turning lights, his face looked sad. 'He's dead now.'

'I know. I saw the article.'

'He worked as a technician, and he moonlighted as a hospital driver. He did the deliveries round the clinics. I was working in the villages then, and he'd turn up two or three times a week with supplies. The trouble started a couple of months before my last contract ended. I was working in the hospital here by then. The police did a drugs check – they came at short notice. There'd been some pilfering going on. We knew about it; it was no big deal, just antibiotics and minor painkillers. We had a pretty good idea where the stuff was going. Only this time, something serious had gone missing. Some morphine. A lot of morphine. The police went berserk. They were going to drag the hospital administrator off and put him through the third degree. He had friends, otherwise he would have been in serious trouble.

'They questioned me. It was frightening. They were looking for someone to blame and they're not fussy about how they get their information. I could have ended up in jail so easily, and once they get you there . . . Anyway, we knew the stuff must have been taken in the last twenty-four hours, because we'd done our own inventory before the visit. But then it was as if they'd been given a tip-off. They decided to search the hospital.'

'Wouldn't the person who'd taken it get it out of there at once?'

'Knowing there was a police check coming? Of course they would. In fact, they wouldn't have touched anything until after. It was crazy. The whole thing was crazy. Unless that person didn't know. Anyway, they searched, and they found the missing stuff. It was in the hostel where the hospital drivers lived, in Haroun's locker. It was such an obvious plant, but they didn't see it that way. They said that the drivers wouldn't have known about the drugs check because they weren't told directly. But everyone knew. And I know that Haroun did because I'd told him myself.'

He looked at her. 'He was a good friend. I first met him in London – he was a student in London at the School of Pharmacy. I was working at Barts and I got to know Haroun when I did some teaching. He was one of those people everyone knew. But he got thrown out for a visa violation; it was nothing, but they were having one of their illegal immigrants scares, and Haroun got caught up in the middle of it all. It was a disaster for him and his family. I tried to help – shit, we all did – but the papers were screaming their heads off about immigration, the government was in trouble over Iraq, so Haroun had to go. I kept in touch with him, and when I came out here, I told the hospital pharmacy about him – he wasn't qualified, but they were short-staffed and he knew his stuff. I contacted him, told him to bung in an application. He'd make some money, maybe get a chance to finish his qualifications. I gave him the professional reference he needed to work at the hospital, and it all worked out fine. He kept saying thank you to me – his good friend Joe Massey who had helped him out.' In the changing light, his face was bleak.

'When I heard he'd been arrested, I thought maybe he'd taken a stupid chance. He was desperate to get enough money to cover his university fees. He was married by then, with a child on the way. But, when I thought about it, I knew it wasn't him. Haroun wasn't stupid, he wouldn't have made a mistake like that. But they took him away and three days later, we heard he'd confessed.'

Three days . . . 'And then they executed him?'

Joe nodded. 'These things happen fast here, but in Haroun's case, it was really quick. We tried to do something, the people who knew him. We tried to get the Foreign Office to take up his case, but they didn't want to know. I went there. The day they . . . It was the only thing left I could do for him. We all knew about as-Sa'ah Square. O'Neill was right – it's like a Roman circus. Word gets round when there's going to be an execution, and people go. You visit the fort, you drive through the desert, you watch a beheading, and you've done Saudi. I'd never been near it. But I wanted

Haroun to have one friend in the crowd. Sometimes I wish . . .'

She remembered his reaction when she'd got lost that first day in Riyadh, when she'd found her way to the blue-tiled square. 'Joe, why didn't you tell me?'

'I didn't want you to have this thing in your head. I see it all the time. First there was the empty square. Then there was a van, a prison van. It drove into the square so slowly.

'It seemed to take for ever before they brought him out. He was blindfolded, and I think he was drugged. I said his name – when they took him out of the van, I said his name. Maybe he heard. Maybe it helped. I'll never know.' His face looked haunted. 'Roisin, what I can't stop thinking about is – I'm a doctor. I know how the human body works. I know that the brain, that consciousness, can survive for minutes without oxygen. It doesn't shut down at once. I tell myself that the shock would do the trick, but I don't know. I keep thinking, what would it have been like, those last few seconds, after . . . ?'

Images she didn't want invaded her mind. 'Oh God. Joe . . .' She took his hand.

'I'm sorry.'

She shook her head. 'After all that . . . why did you come back?'

'When they arrested Haroun, I thought they were just going for the easiest target. That's how crimes get solved here: grab a likely-looking suspect and make it stick. But then I began to wonder . . .' The sound of his pager interrupted them. 'Shit. Not again. I'm off *duty*, for fuck's sake.'

He checked the number, and picked up his cell phone. 'Joe Massey. Yeah, I . . . Look, I'm not on duty now, you'll have to . . . Oh hell. Can't you get . . . ? Well, who . . . ? Where? . . . ? OK, I'll be there . . . When I get there, all right?' He slammed the phone on to the dashboard. 'Fucking hell . . .' He looked at her. 'I'm sorry, sweetheart, there's an emergency at the hospital and they need me in.'

'It's OK. I don't feel much like a party now anyway.'

He gave her a mirthless smile. 'Me neither, but I haven't got time to take you home. Look, we're almost there. I'll drop you off at the house, and I'll get back to you as soon as I can – I don't think it's going to take long. They just need someone in there to get them organized.'

'Kick ass, you mean?'

'Exactly. Kick ass is exactly what I'm going to do.'

'OK. Drop me off. I'll keep the side up with this lot. We don't want to lose our A-list status.'

His smile was grim. 'Fuck our A-list status.'

She laughed. 'I'm with you on that one.'

Joe edged the car out into the traffic and ten minutes later they were driving through an affluent suburb. Joe stopped at the gates of a compound that looked far larger than the one where Roisin and Joe lived. She could see the high concrete walls and the razor-wire along the perimeter.

The security checks took longer than usual as the guards went through their documentation, checked their numbered invitation and phoned through to verify their credentials. They asked for photo ID and studied it minutely. Finally, the gates opened and they were inside the compound.

They drove through wide streets. The houses were invisible from the road, set back behind high white walls over which oleander and hibiscus tumbled. Cameras followed them as the car crept towards a high metal gate, which swung silently open to admit them. A uniformed man opened the car door. Before she got out, Roisin leaned across to Joe. He put his arms round her. 'Don't be long,' she said.

'I won't.' He released her and the man helped Roisin out, and spoke quickly into a hand-held radio. She looked back at Joe. 'I'll see you later,' he mouthed.

She watched him drive away.

26

Damien didn't know what had made him accept the invitation to the party. Ever since he'd said goodbye to Amy at the airport, he had felt restless and unsettled. He'd made several attempts to contact Majid, but his calls had gone unanswered. And everything had gone quiet – ominously quiet – on the Haroun Patel front.

He cast a quick, professional eye over his surroundings. The house was a temple to the gods of conspicuous consumption. The room in which the party was held was vast, two storeys opening up to a glass roof with a gallery running round above. Picture windows opened on to the garden where the swimming pool was already in use.

The noise was rising as the guests took advantage of the availability of champagne. The consultant's wife – he checked his mental inventory and retrieved her name: Cordelia – greeted him effusively. Damien returned her kiss, reflecting that

252

his avoidance of much ex-pat socializing and his integration with the Saudis gave him novelty value. Cordelia Bradshaw clearly saw his presence as some kind of coup and kept him with her for a while, introducing him to various guests. 'Damien has been here longer than any of us. If you want to know what's really going on, he's the man to ask,' she said.

Damien turned down the offer of champagne and politely disengaged himself. He moved through the room, greeting people, checking out the groups, getting the feel of the place. The party looked sedate enough, which was a relief.

In the days when ex-pats could party with impunity, young, rootless people with more money than they had ever dreamed of indulged themselves with a contemptuous disregard for the mores of their hosts. And, to be fair, the wealthy among the hosts partied too. The parties, fuelled by drugs and alcohol, spiralled into excess until death brought everything to a sudden halt.

A young woman had died in, it was claimed, a drunken fall from a balcony, but darker stories of rape, murder and cover-up had circulated, and even now, a quarter of a century later, the scandal lingered. The dead woman remained unburied, her cadaver stored in a morgue in the UK, as her father searched fruitlessly and hopelessly for the truth of what had happened.

Then Damien saw someone he hadn't expected to see: Arshak Nazarian. He was deep in conversation. Damien moved round to see who he was talking to.

Roisin Massey. There was no sign of her husband.

The house amazed Roisin. She had thought their own house was large, but now she realized that she and Joe had been slumming it by Saudi standards. The front door led on to an atrium with a high glass ceiling and an expanse of wooden floor. There was an open staircase with wrought-iron balustrades. Carefully tended houseplants tumbled over the railing. At the far side of the atrium, double doors opened on to a huge room with a floor-to-ceiling window that looked out on to the garden where the pool reflected the evening sky.

The room was already full of guests and the hum of conversation filled the air. She could hear music, and some couples were dancing, but the lights were dim and she couldn't make out the faces. This was very different from the ex-pat parties she was familiar with. She could smell spices in the air and the fragrance of incense.

A Filipina in a maid's uniform was waiting to greet her. She glanced quickly at Roisin's invitation and said, 'Mrs Massey. Welcome. May I take your coat?'

Roisin handed over her abaya, and the maid ushered her across the room to where a skeletally thin, impeccably dressed woman was holding court. 'Mrs Massey,' she said.

The woman's smile was perfectly tuned to the appropriate wattage for the wife of a junior consultant as she greeted Roisin. 'Cordelia Bradshaw. So pleased to see you.'

'Thank you for inviting us. I'm afraid my husband got held up at work. He's on his way.'

'Oh, men,' Cordelia Bradshaw said. 'Always working. Sunanda!' She summoned one of the maids. 'Find Mrs Massey a drink.' Roisin was gently eased out of the central group.

Amused, she turned to the Filipina maid, who was holding out a tray of drinks, and took a glass. 'Thank you.' The rumours were true. It was real champagne. She thought about drinking champagne with Amy – and now Amy had gone again. It would have been fun if she'd been here – they could have talked about Cordelia Bradshaw, about the extravagant luxury of the house. She suspected Amy had an entertaining take on the ex-pat wives: *the Stepford Wives*, she'd called them . . .

'Mrs Massey?'

She turned round. A dark, heavy-set man with shrewd eyes in a strong, intelligent face was smiling down at her. He held out his hand, which engulfed Roisin's when she clasped it lightly with hers. 'Yes?'

'My name is Arshak Nazarian. I am Yasmin's father.'

'Yasmin's . . . How is she? How's her baby?'

His face was serious. 'The baby is not well, not well at all.'

'What's wrong?'

He shook his head. 'The doctors – they seem to be baffled. He was well, then suddenly he was ill. I saw him after he was born – a beautiful boy. Now I am not allowed near.'

'I'm so sorry. Tell her . . . Give her my love.'

'Of course. Yasmin has spoken very warmly of you.' He looked round the room. 'I should not be here, I suppose, but I have colleagues who expect me to – what is the phrase? – put in the appearance. Is your husband not with you tonight?'

'He's been called out to an emergency. He's coming later.'

Nazarian nodded. 'Good. That's good. I would like to meet him.'

'Of course.' Joe's department would have done any lab tests. The last thing Joe would want tonight would be an interrogation by an anxious grandfather.

He smiled, a rather bleak smile that she could understand in the circumstances. 'We may talk later.' He excused himself and vanished into the crowd.

Another man appeared beside her. 'Hello. I don't think we've met. I'm David Morley.' He was young and attractive, and was studying her with approval that he didn't try to conceal. Before her conversation with Nazarian, she would have enjoyed a mildly flirtatious chat with a good-looking stranger, but her party mood, already at a low ebb, had evaporated.

'Roisin Massey,' she said.

'What brings you to the magic kingdom?'

She told him a bit about her work at the university. 'And you?' she finished. 'What do you do?'

He worked for one of the major oil companies and she listened politely as he told her stories about the entanglements that awaited the unwary visitor to the Kingdom, checking her watch discreetly while making interested noises. Half an hour. It was too early to expect Joe. Gradually she began to get involved in his stories, and found herself laughing at some of the bureaucratic mix-ups he described. The champagne was starting to kick in. Some fifties rock started on the sound system and her feet wanted to move to the music. David took her hand and whirled her out on to the dance floor among the jiving couples.

She could see the lights in the garden, a warm orange glow over banks of flowers and, in the centre, the pool lights reflected from below the water. As she watched, the surface shattered into a thousand dancing images as a man dived in. She could see his body snaking through the water.

'Have a dip later, if you want,' David said. His arm tightened round her waist as he swung her through a complicated step then released her again.

When the music ended, she excused herself. 'Would you mind if I phone my husband? I want to find out what's happening.'

A door off the main room opened on to a quiet

corridor. She went through and pulled it closed behind her to make the call, but she got Joe's messaging service. A door at the end of the corridor opened into the garden, and she went out, the air suddenly warm on her arms after the chill of the air-con. The fragrance of the flowers mixed uneasily with the smell of incense. She thought she could see people moving in the shadows beyond the lights, but decided that her eyes must be playing tricks.

She went back in and leaned against the wall. There was no sign of David. She listened to the voices around her, the chatter of the women, the deeper voices of the men, sudden bursts of laughter. She'd probably had enough champagne. She was out of practice with alcohol.

A man stopped in front of her. His eyes were slightly unfocused. 'Hey, Blondie, why haven't I seen you before? Come on out into the garden. The fun's just starting.'

'Sorry, got to go.' She moved away from him. The room was more crowded now and she had to push through a group of men who were talking with the loud voices of people on the edge of drunkenness. She tried not to listen to what they were saying as she made her way through them: ' . . . used to go for R and R in Bangkok. Bang-cock. Good name.' The sound of male laughter drowned him out for a moment.

'Listen. First time I went, there was this group of them standing outside one of the bars. And this little one, she was just wearing a thong, and when our truck went past she waved at us and turned round, and she had the sweetest little ass like . . . And she'd written "fuck me" on one cheek, and "American soldiers" on the other . . . So we stopped the truck, right . . .'

The exchange vanished into the general noise of other voices. The crowd was denser now, and she kept snagging on the people she passed. The unfamiliar faces swirled round her.

She felt her phone buzz in her bag. She retreated to the side of the room where it was quieter and took it out. 'Joe?'

'Roisin? Listen, sweetheart, there's a problem here. I've got to sort out some stuff. I'm going to be a bit of time. I'm sorry.'

'That's OK. I'm feeling a bit tired. I think I might get a car and just go home. Do you mind?'

His voice sharpened with anxiety. 'Are you all right? Roisin?'

'I'm fine. I just don't feel like a party any more.'

His voice was grim. 'Me neither,' he said.

'What's happened?'

'It's complicated. I'll tell you later.'

'OK. I'll see you at home.'

'Can't be too soon for me. Take care, sweetheart.'

'I will.' She moved away from the crowds to a quiet corner near the door, scooping up another drink as she passed the bar. There was a settee and she sank down in its cream leather softness, and called the number she always used for taxis. *Thirty minute*, the voice said abruptly, and hung up. She lifted her glass to her lips, and dumped it on the side table after one swallow. It wasn't champagne, it was the ubiquitous home-distilled spirit, *rat*.

She leaned her head back against the cushions, looking at the ceiling. She could almost be in London on a summer's night, sitting outside a bar in Soho with Joe as people pushed past along the narrow streets, music blaring out of bars, shouting, laughter . . . A pang of homesickness went through her, so sharp it was almost like a physical pain.

'Roisin.' The voice from behind her made her jump.

She tipped her head back and saw Damien O'Neill. 'Damien. Hello.'

He came and sat next to her on the arm of the couch. 'I wouldn't have expected to see you here,' he said. 'Where's your husband?'

'He got called back to the hospital – some kind of emergency.'

His eyebrow lifted. 'It wasn't a . . .' He stopped what he was about to say and looked at her glass. 'You don't have to drink that muck.' He lifted his hand and a waiter appeared with a tray. He swapped the glass for another. 'Here.'

Roisin took it. This time, it was champagne. 'Thank you. It wasn't what?'

'Forget it,' he said. 'It's no big deal. What are you doing here?'

'I'm just waiting for my taxi – then I'm leaving. I'm not really in a party mood.'

She could see David, the man she'd been dancing with, watching her from across the room. She smiled and waved, and after a moment, he waved back.

'A friend of yours?' O'Neill asked.

'I was dancing with him earlier.' The noise was getting louder. 'I think I'll go and wait outside,' she said. 'It's quieter out there.'

'I'll come with you,' he said. 'I could do with some air. Then I think I'll get off myself.'

'Not your kind of party?' she said.

'Please.' He walked with her to the door, clearing a way through for her. 'Have you got a jacket? And your abaya?'

'Someone took it.'

'Wait there. I'll go and find it.'

After the noise of the party, the space and silence of the atrium felt wonderful. At first she thought she was alone, then she saw a couple half obscured by one of the hanging vines. A man was talking in low, urgent tones to a woman. He was holding her arms and thrusting his head forward. She was pulling back, but the man was too drunk – or too thick-skinned – to pay any heed to the clear signals of rejection he was getting. As Roisin watched, he grabbed her shoulder and started shaking her backwards and forwards.

Roisin's reaction was instinctive. She grabbed his arm. 'Stop that! Leave her alone!'

261

His bleary eyes focused on her. 'Blondie . . .' he said. She recognized him as the man who had spoken to her earlier. He looked even more drunk now.

The girl had freed herself and was clutching her bag close to her as if it offered some kind of protection. She looked terrified. 'Are you all right?' Roisin touched her shoulder, but the girl moved away quickly. 'It's OK . . .'

The drunken man grabbed Roisin's wrist and jerked her back. 'Keep out of this. This is between her and me.'

Christ, where was everybody? 'I said, leave her alone.' She yanked her wrist free, staggering back as she broke his grip. She almost fell, but someone caught her and moved her to one side. Suddenly Damien O'Neill was in front of the man, turning him firmly back towards the party, talking in a quiet voice, his hands on the man's shoulders as he propelled him forward. The man seemed to protest, cast a dark look at Roisin, then straightened his jacket and stalked away.

Roisin blew out the breath she didn't realize she had been holding. O'Neill looked round for the girl, but she must have taken advantage of the distraction to make her escape. 'Are you OK?'

'Yes. What about . . . ?' She looked round, but there was no sign of the girl. 'Is she going to be all right?'

'I think she must be one of the maids. She's probably worried about getting into trouble – I'll have a word with the Bradshaws. Let's get out of here.'

Outside, the air was warm. The night was soft velvet and the palms were cartwheels against the sky. She breathed in the clean air. 'Oh, God,' she said.

'Are you sure you're OK?'

Roisin nodded, her eyes closed. 'I saw a whole crowd of them getting drunk.'

'That's the ex-pat A-list for you. It's not just the cream that floats.' He offered her a cigarette.

She accepted it gratefully. 'Thank you.' She checked her watch. It was almost twenty minutes since she'd called the taxi. It would be here soon. 'You don't need to wait with me. You'll make sure that girl's all right?'

'Don't worry,' he said again. 'I'll see you into your car, then I'll go back and get it sorted as soon as you're on your way.' She was aware of someone else waiting and looked round. Arshak Nazarian was standing in the doorway, staring down the drive. She remembered that he'd wanted to talk to Joe.

'I think he's hoping to see my husband. I told him Joe was meeting me here, but he isn't now. I don't want another conversation with him about . . .'

'I'll ride shotgun. You just get in the car and go, OK?' His phone rang as he was speaking. He took it out and checked the number, frowning as he saw who was calling him. 'I've got to take this,' he said, turning away.

She was aware of him speaking as she watched the gates begin to swing open, and a car moving between. Her taxi? It was early. 'It's . . . what?' She was aware of Damien's exclamation of shock and turned to look at him. 'From the ward? Someone took him from the ward?' She could see incredulity and alarm on his face. Then his gaze moved beyond her and his face froze.

She swung round. The car was a black hump in the darkness, showing no lights as though the driver was relying on the street lighting to find his way. It wasn't moving. Everything seemed to happen in slow motion. Nazarian had stepped back from the doorway, and the girl from the earlier altercation was standing behind him, blocking his return to the house. She had a phone in her hand.

'That's –' Suddenly everything was wrong. The car was wrong. She couldn't see a driver behind the wheel. 'I don't think . . .' she said, and she was flying backwards as O'Neill threw himself against her, pushing them down. She was falling and felt his hand behind her head as she hit the ground, then she was rolling as he twisted round so he was above her. She felt him press her face hard against his shirt as the night lit up with a white flash and there was a *crack!* that seemed to go on for ever but was over before she realized she'd heard it, and something heavy punched all the air out of her lungs.

Silence. Blue after-images blinded her as she struggled to breathe. Her ears were ringing and

264

she was lying on the hard ground. She didn't know how much time had passed. Her face felt warm and sticky, and she was pinned down by something heavy that lay on top of her. Now she could hear things, far away as though she was listening through thick felt. The clink of hot stone rapidly cooling, a creaking sound that became a rush then stopped abruptly. Something dripping.

And someone was screaming.

27

The pale light of the dawn washed over the desert, over the sands and dry, stony surfaces baked by the relentless sun, casting hard-edged shadows from the rocks and the strewn rubble across a moonscape wasteland. The road shimmered in the first heat of the day, vanishing across the plains. Nothing moved.

A vehicle had been through not long before. The smell of exhaust fumes still hung in the air. The tracks veered off the road and made furrows across the sand. They ended where the sand was churned up, then they returned to the road and vanished on the metalled surface.

The dawn light crept across the rocks, making the shadows lie long and low. Dew formed briefly and vanished as the sun rose higher. The light glinted off the crystals in the sand, off the rock surfaces polished by centuries of abrasion, off the edge of the knife that had been discarded by the road.

The man lay on his left side. He was very still,

but his hands reached out as though he was frozen in the moment of trying to dig himself into the ground, to hide himself below the surface of the desert. Or maybe he was trying to find some grip so that he could crawl back towards the road. But now he lay still.

The light moved across him, across hair that was matted with something sticky, something that attracted the desert flies in a dark, buzzing cloud, moved across the tanned face where the laughter lines had started to etch into the corners of the eyes.

His mouth, frozen in a grimace, was filled with blood. His eyes, half open, attracting the attention of the flies, were blue. He was dressed in a white shirt and light trousers.

The sand was stained a dark red that was already baking black in the early sun. The blood had spurted far away in thick gouts from where the man was lying, and some was still seeping, thin and watery, from the wounds across his neck. Whoever had cut him had done the job well, opening the larynx, severing the tongue, rendering him speechless before he died, cutting through the major vessels that carry the blood to and from the brain. He had been cut to the bone.

A gold ring on one of the out-flung hands caught the light, the shadows etching the pattern deeper for a moment, two words engraved in a fine script: *Joe~Roisin*.

The blood soaked into the sand and vanished.

PART THREE

28

Snapshots.

A couple stand in the middle of a celebratory group. The woman is small, with fair hair and the man, tall and dark-haired, has his arm round her. They are laughing. Fragments of bright colour are scattered on the ground around them and some have caught in the woman's hair.

The same couple against an anonymous, scrubby background. The man's face is obscured as the woman, clowning, holds her scarf up against it. Her face, and her head, are uncovered.

Water sprays against the sun in rainbow arcs as children play in a lush green garden oblivious to the man in a light-coloured garment hunkered down on the grass, working the soil with a machete as the sun beats down on him.

The desert. The sun is a brilliant sphere, bright enough to burn through closed eyelids. The sand

271

curves and crests in high dunes and the shadows lie in black pools. The bones of a desert creature protrude from the sand which is stained with black, heavy smears.

A garden at night, lit by flames in an eerie silence.

She walks down a path towards a flower bed, where a creeper, heavy with flowers, grows up the wall.

The light flickers as the flames climb up, a sickly orange against the shadows. There is no sound. She can see the girl's face, a pale glimmer in the darkness of the foliage. The face is serene, the eyes closed, the mouth curved in a faint smile.

Only her face is visible. The jumping shadows must conceal her body completely. The orange light reflects off the leaves, and now she can hear the sound of the flames, muffled and far away. She reaches out to touch the face . . .

. . . and it falls forward as her touch frees it from the vines, then the girl's head drops, disembodied, into her hands.

Roisin jerked upright, wiping her hands frantically against the sheets. Her heart was hammering and she was breathing fast. Gradually the sound of the flames became the noise of rain beating against her window, the light became the glow of the floor lamp she had left burning all night. The relief of being out of the nightmare was replaced by the leaden awareness of the day.

She lay back down, her hand reaching out to the empty space on the other side of the bed. Her dreams were always about the dead girl, the girl she had last seen in the doorway with Nazarian, the girl whose body had been ripped apart by the explosion.

She had been back in the UK for a week, a week of sleepless nights interrupted by vivid, violent dreams and long, grey days when she lay on the settee, too weary to get up, just watching the time drag past.

She had been in hospital for a week after the bomb, shocked and concussed, aware that she had lived and Joe was dead. She could remember police officers by her bed, asking her about Joe, about the time he'd left her, the time he'd phoned, about what he had been doing, what they had both been doing in the day leading up to the party. Where had they been? What time? How well did she know Yasmin? When had she last seen her? Her confused mind had struggled to understand. 'Yasmin wasn't there,' she said, watching as their faces remained impassive.

The Embassy had arranged for her to be flown out of the Kingdom as soon as the doctors said she was well enough to travel. A representative had turned up by her bedside one confusing morning and rushed her to the airport with an urgency she had been too dazed to understand. He'd answered the few questions she had been able to formulate: Joe hadn't died in the explosion, he'd been the victim of a random attack, possibly a robbery; Damien O'Neill was in hospital, where surgeons were fighting to save his hand. She'd scrabbled in her bag and found a photograph she'd taken in Riyadh weeks ago. She scribbled on the back: *Thank you. Roisin.* He promised he would deliver it.

And then she was being rushed through passport control, the man from the Embassy still by her side, still there as her flight was called. Then she was stepping on to the plane, a BA flight direct to London. He didn't leave her until the last minute, until the plane was about to leave the stand. And then they were in the air and she could see the lights of Riyadh below her.

Somewhere down there, Joe was lying dead and alone in a foreign morgue.

The flight was a blank, and then she could remember walking through the cold air of the winter night at Heathrow, could remember seeing her mother's face in the arrivals hall with the relief that she wasn't to endure this homecoming alone.

'We'll go back to your flat tonight, pet.' Her mother's hand touched hers, fluttered away, touched her again. 'Then we can go home tomorrow. I've got your room ready. In the new house. I said, remember, that that was your room, yours and . . .' She fell silent.

'Joe. Joe's dead.'

'I know, pet. I know.'

The taxi driver had dumped them with her cases

at the block of flats behind King's Cross, and driven off. The street lights wavered yellow through a wintry mist. The concrete stairwell was dank and uninviting. 'Such a place . . .' her mother muttered as Roisin fumbled for her keys. But Roisin hadn't heard her. She was watching the door of the flat swing open, and she waited for the sudden flood of light, for the waft of coffee and for music drifting from the box room where Joe was working at the desk.

'I'm back!' she whispered into the dusty silence.

'Hey, babes,' and the sound of his chair being pushed back echoed in her memory.

But memories were all she had.

Joe was dead.

She climbed wearily out of bed and released the blind to look out at the London day. The sky was heavy with clouds that the pale winter light had barely penetrated. At this time of year, the daylight arrived late and began to fade by four. She stood for a moment watching the rooftops and the pavements shining with the wet.

Her mother was moving around in the small kitchen. When Roisin had refused to go back to Newcastle, she had stayed, cleaning, tidying, doing the shopping, cooking meals that Roisin could barely eat.

She pulled on a pair of jeans and a sweater and went through to the living room. It was impeccable, unrecognizable from the casual disorder that she and Joe had maintained. The bed-settee where her mother had been sleeping was put away, the bedding neatly folded. The bookshelves had been tidied so that the books stood in disciplined rows instead of leaning against each other in untidy piles. The furniture was carefully placed, the settee was lined up with the wall, and the chair positioned at a suitable angle, the plumped cushions neatly aligned. A vase that Roisin didn't recognize – her mother must have gone out and bought it – was dead-centre on the coffee table. Early daffodils stood to attention.

Her mother, building her familiar ramparts to keep her daughter safe. Roisin's throat ached.

'Rosie? Is that you? I was going to bring you tea in bed. You should be resting.' Her mother came bustling through.

'I'm fine. I'm rested.' Roisin kissed the soft cheek and took the proffered cup of tea. In the short time she'd been away, her mother had aged. When she was younger, Maggie Gardner's eyes had been the same clear green as Roisin's, and her hair had been a rich gold. Sometimes, to her secret delight, people had commented on the resemblance between mother and daughter. Now, the gold hair had faded to white and the creamy skin was dull and shadowed. 'Are you keeping an eye on the time? You mustn't miss your train.'

Her mother was going back to Newcastle where she had a long-awaited hospital appointment and Roisin wasn't going to let her miss it.

'I don't like leaving you, pet.' Her mother frowned with worry. 'I really don't need to . . .'

'Yes, you do. It's important. I'll be all right. I'm not far away. Not any more.'

'I wish you'd come home with me.'

Why wouldn't she? It would make her mother happy. What was there for her in London? She just knew she couldn't leave, not yet. 'I can't. I was going to bring Joe to Newcastle in February. We were planning to come home . . .' She couldn't talk about it.

'That place. Animals. They're animals.' Her mother's grief for her expressed itself in a virulent hatred of the Saudis.

'They aren't,' Roisin said wearily. Najia, Fozia, Haifa – even Souad – they were people she thought of with warmth, some with affection. And Yasmin. She wondered what the news was about Yasmin's baby.

'But still . . .'

'Still, nothing. I will come home for a visit. Soon. I promise.' Focusing on her mother kept her mind away from the things she didn't want to think about. She finished her tea. 'Have you packed?'

'I've got everything. I didn't bring much. I could come back . . .'

'Have a break. Come back in a couple of weeks.' She was physically better now, and she needed to be alone for a while. A wave of tiredness washed over her, and for a moment, all she wanted to do was lie down and sleep. She turned away so her mother wouldn't see her face. 'I'll get myself some breakfast,' she said.

'Sit down. I'll get it.' Her mother was delighted at the sudden evidence of appetite.

An hour later, Roisin walked with her mother to King's Cross. She made sure she had magazines for the journey, and saw her on to the train. Just before she climbed into the carriage, Maggie Gardner hugged her hard. 'Rosie, pet, if you need anything, anything at all, call me.'

'I will. I promise.'

She walked slowly back. Even though it wasn't noon yet, the day had a heavy dreariness to it as though the sun had barely risen and would shortly sink defeated into the long evening and night. She let herself back into her flat, and stood for a while with her back to the door. Then she pushed open the door to the small bedroom, the one Joe had used as a study, where she had dumped the remaining cases that had come back from Riyadh. The table light came on when she pressed the switch, casting a warm glow over the desk. The chair was pushed slightly away, as though the person sitting there had just that moment left the room.

Joe?

Hey, babes.

She knelt down by the cases that had been dumped against the far wall. She opened the first one and pulled the clothes out – skirts, trousers, scarves, all in light colours. Something jangled among the fabric, and a cluster of silver bangles fell to the floor. She picked them up and held them.

Something for you . . .

They're beautiful. Thank you.

One of Joe's shirts was tangled up among the clothes. It was crumpled and slightly stained. Slowly, she unfolded it.

And she was breathing in his smell, and he was there, all around her. She knew he was just in the next room, he was going to come through the door. *Hey, sweetheart, where did you put . . .*

Joe.

She'd made them tell her what had happened to him. 'He's dead,' the consul had said. 'They killed him.'

'How?' she'd insisted. 'How did they kill him? Tell me what they did.'

He hadn't wanted to, but in the end, he told her. They'd cut Joe's throat and left him to bleed to death by the side of the road. Alone. Afraid and alone. He'd died afraid and alone.

She crouched by the case with Joe's shirt crushed against her face. The pain was so intense she could hardly breathe. She had no idea how she was going to survive.

29

It was a fortnight before Damien was discharged from the hospital. For the first few days, he drifted in and out of consciousness, surfacing to headaches so intense he was glad when the feeble grasp he had on reality loosened and spiralled him away to a world of nightmares and more pain.

The room was banked with flowers. He was at a funeral. In his dream-state, he saw his ex-wife by his bed, looking down at him. 'Yes, that's my husband,' she said. 'That's Damien. Bury him.' Her face was cold.

'Catherine, please . . .' Then he was standing by a crib, looking down. The bedding was rumpled, a soft toy was discarded on the floor. The crib was empty, and somewhere, he could hear a woman crying. 'Catherine?' he said. But he and Catherine had never had children.

A face, beautiful, and shockingly unveiled, watched him from an upstairs window. As he stared back at her, he saw a tear trickle down her cheek. 'I'm sorry,' he said. 'I can't help you. I can't do anything.' He woke up with a start and the nurse who was adjusting his drip looked at him in surprise.

'We thought we were going to lose you,' one of the doctors told him cheerfully as he began to come round, as the world solidified into the reality of the hospital room, the routine of doctors' visits, therapists' visits, boredom and mundanity.

'You're a hero,' a nurse explained later, when he asked about the flowers.

They had come from all over the city, sent by ex-pats, by people he barely knew and didn't much want to know. As soon as he could take control, he asked for them to be taken away. 'Give them to someone who hasn't got any,' he said. There was only one card he kept. It was from Roisin Massey and said simply, *Thank you.*

He was a hero because he had saved Roisin Massey's life. He couldn't remember the moment when his brain had put the images it had seen together – the open gate, the car that had stopped in the middle of the drive, the girl standing behind Nazarian, her phone in her hand – but he could remember the moment when he knew that the low wall by the door where they were standing was the only protection within reach, and he could remember the crack as his head had hit the ground. After that, there was nothing.

Murder had walked the streets of Riyadh that night. In a separate incident, Joe Massey had been dumped by the side of the road in the desert, his throat cut. The aftermath of the two attacks was still causing waves in the ex-pat community, sending the security services on high-profile exercises as they worked to reassure people that all was safe, all was well.

And that same evening, or sometime during that same day, Majid and Yasmin's baby had been stolen from the hospital ITU, and had vanished, so far without trace. Given the child's precarious health, it was probably dead by now. If the kidnapper – whoever he was – had made it out of Riyadh, then the child's body could be anywhere in the vast desert that was the Kingdom. It might never be found.

As soon as he could, he asked for a phone and called Majid. There was no reply. He left a message – it was hard to find the words: *I'm sorry . . . anything, anything at all, that I can do . . .* But he was helpless, isolated in his hospital bed. All he could do was think.

And his brain felt slow and sluggish. He knew there had to be a connection, but he couldn't find it. The bomb, the murder and the kidnapping – they had to be linked. A sign kept flashing in his head, a big neon sign with candy colours and exploding fireworks: *Night life in Riyadh!*

But why use a bomb when Joe Massey was already bleeding to death in the desert sand? Why kidnap Majid's child? His mind turned the images over and over, but nothing would come into focus.

He knew there was more, but he couldn't see it. And for now, there was nothing he could do. He just had to wait as his shattered system recovered, and hope that, gradually, he would be able to work out the whole story.

He picked up Roisin Massey's card again. *Thank you. Roisin.* He'd tried to call her as soon as he was alert enough to understand what had happened, but by that time she had gone. She'd come to Riyadh with a new marriage, a new job and a new future stretching out in front of her. She'd left with her life in pieces.

And he was in for months of hard work before his recovery was complete, if it ever was. His doctor, an English consultant, had been blandly evasive in response to Damien's questions. Damien got one of the Saudi consultants to come and talk to him. This man was honest. The Saudi rules of courtesy might make social interaction a mine-field, but they saw no necessity in wrapping up the truths of life and death for their patients. The news was better than he expected. 'You are making a full recovery from the head injury. You are lucky. It could have been more serious. Your hand and arm are less certain. We think we have saved the hand, but the injury was very severe.'

'Will I get anything back?' Damien was more and more aware of the numbness, the immobility of his fingers, the feeling of something dead at the end of his arm.

The doctor assessed him with a speculative eye.

'It'll never be what it was,' he said. 'Do you want my prognosis?'

Damien was glad the man was prepared to be honest.

'If you don't give yourself a chance to heal, you'll lose the hand. We've done what we can, but the nerves were damaged. The best outcome you can expect is that you'll get some limited use back.' He inspected the room. 'Your flowers have gone.'

'I didn't want them,' Damien said. 'They were sent – on a misunderstanding.'

'You saved your friend's life. People admire that bravery.'

But Roisin Massey wasn't a friend. He barely knew her. Damien had no illusions about his courage. He'd pulled Roisin behind the wall because she was the only person he could reach in time. *Sauve qui peut.*

The tributes he didn't want kept pouring in from the ex-pats, but there was no word from Amy. Maybe it was stupid, maybe it was a mark of weakness, but he'd expected her to contact him when she heard that he'd been hurt. But there was nothing.

And there was no news of his Saudi friends. He thought about Majid, wondered how he was, how he was coping with the loss of his child, with the nightmare of uncertainty and the cruelty of hope. If the child wasn't found, Majid and Yasmin would live all their lives in the unreasonable, impossible expectation that one day their child might be restored to them.

He didn't tell anyone when the day came for him to leave the hospital. He didn't want other people to see his weakness until he'd tested his limits out himself. His taxi left him at the entrance to the narrow lane where his house opened on to the street. As he pushed open the door, he expected the musty smell of abandonment to meet him.

Instead, the air felt cool and carried the fragrance of spices. The shadows of the ground floor were welcome after the recycled air and relentless brightness of the hospital. The house was silent. He went through to the kitchen where everything was in order, everything clean and put away. There was a net on the table, and under it, bread and fresh dates. There was coffee in the cupboard, milk in the fridge. Somehow, Rai had found out the day of his release and had worked to ensure his return would be welcoming and comfortable.

Slowly, he climbed the stairs and saw that the cushions had been placed where they would have been sheltered from the day's sun, and his chair was by the window, the shutters closed so that the light dappled the stone floor. The book he'd been reading lay on the table. He picked it up. *One Thousand and One Nights*, open at 'The Sleeper and the Waker', the man who thought that his reality was a dream.

He sat down in the chair and tried to read, but the print blurred as his eyes filled with tears. He didn't do anything to stop them from falling.

Roisin told herself every day that she'd go down the stairs and knock on the door of old George's flat. She dreaded having to tell him what had happened – each telling was a reliving of the moment she realized that Joe was dead – but she couldn't put it off any longer.

When she had told George back in October that she was leaving, he had grunted an acknowledgement. All he had said was, 'What you want to go out there for?' Then he'd turned away so that she wouldn't see his face, and shuffled back into his flat, Shadow looking back at her as the front door closed. She'd written to the old man twice from Riyadh, but he hadn't replied. She hadn't expected him to.

When she woke up that morning, she decided she couldn't put it off any longer. After she'd had coffee, she pulled on her coat and went down the stairway. The familiar route down the steps and along the walkway brought back that morning just a few months before. It had been a day like this when she had first met Joe. If she closed her eyes, she could conjure it up in sharp, stark detail, the leaden grey of the canal, the icy wind channelled by the high walls, Shadow tugging at his lead or dancing in and out of the undergrowth and Joe, just a figure in the distance, running,

running, coming closer and closer to the moment when . . .

If she hadn't gone running on the tow path that day, if Shadow hadn't made him fall, if he'd decided against phoning her, would those simple changes have altered what had happened? Maybe if they hadn't met, he would never have considered going back to the Gulf state that had killed him. And if he were alive now, somewhere on the face of the planet, then one day, one ordinary day when she was going about her business, a tall man with an easy smile would come up to her. 'I'll take the opportunity to introduce myself,' he'd say. 'I'm Joe.'

She dug her nails into the palm of her hand and forced her mind to stop. If she wanted to survive, she had to stop thinking like this. She had to stop trying to turn the world into a place where Joe still walked the earth somewhere.

She knocked on George's door. It was thrown open at once by a young woman with a thin, pale face and hair that was bleached almost white. As she opened the door she said, 'It's about time . . . Oh.' Her expression changed when she saw Roisin. 'Yeah?' she looked doubtful.

'I was looking for George.'

The girl's face became wary. 'Who?'

'The old man who lives . . . who lived here. I'm from upstairs, number 31,' Roisin explained. 'I used to walk his dog for him. I've just come back from . . . I've just come back.'

Comprehension dawned on the girl's face. 'Oh,' she said. 'The old guy. Yeah. He went into a home. I've just moved in.'

'Into a home?' Roisin could see George turning away as he pulled the door closed behind him. 'Where?'

'Up Bromley way,' the girl said. Past her shoulder, the hallway ran back into the familiar old flat, but the way through was blocked by a pram. Unfamiliar coats hung on the pegs. She could see boxes piled up in the room beyond, all the indications of a recent move. 'I think he must have been senile. You should have seen this place.' She shuddered.

The flat had been dingy, but clean enough, apart from the constant, faint smell of dog. She could hardly bear to ask the next question. 'Shadow? His dog?'

'No idea,' the girl said.

'Did he leave an address?'

The girl looked round vaguely. 'Somewhere.'

'I'm Roisin, by the way.'

The woman gave the remark the same quick assessment for hostile intent, then smiled for the first time. Her thin, rather sharp face was suddenly pretty. Roisin wondered how old she was – sixteen? Seventeen? She looked very young. 'I'm Mari.' There was the sound of a baby's cry, then silence, then it started again in earnest. She sighed. 'If you don't mind, I'm a bit . . .'

'Of course. If you could find me that address . . . ?'

'Yeah, yeah, I'll dig it out.' The door swung shut.

30

Damien went back to work the day after he left hospital. He knew he hadn't fully recovered – he was aware all the time of an unaccustomed stiffness in his movements, and a weariness in his bones that he had never felt before. This must be the harbinger of old age. Worse, there was a reluctance, a wariness in his mind, as if something had erected a barrier between him and the people he'd lived and worked among for so many years.

The director of the agency was surprised to see him back. 'Are you sure you're ready for this?'

Damien wasn't sure at all, but he wasn't going to admit it. He knew he was needed. They wouldn't argue for too long. 'I'm sure.'

He spent the morning at his desk, working his way through the routine tasks that had built up, letting his mind go over everything he'd discovered since he'd left hospital. Rai had been his eyes and ears, but what he'd found out had only confused the picture more.

The first theory about the kidnapped child – that it had been stolen from the hospital by some bereaved mother whose desperation for a child had driven her insane – had now been dismissed. The kidnapping had been too carefully planned, and there was evidence of something dark and malicious at work. The baby had been taken for a scan late that afternoon. All the papers had been correctly completed and signed, and a nurse had handed the child over to a porter at the ward entrance. Somewhere between the ward and the X-ray suite, the child had vanished. The porter claimed he had handed the child over to a nurse at the entrance to the suite. He was unable to identify the nurse, who had been fully veiled. On questioning, he hadn't been able to confirm his initial assumption that the veiled figure had, in fact, been a woman. They hadn't spoken. The nurse had checked the paperwork, signed the forms and the porter had left. The child had never arrived at the scanner, and had not been expected. The forms were simple forgeries, easy enough to do for anyone with a knowledge of hospital proce-dures. The incubator in which the child was being transported was found in a service corridor near an exit.

And here there was evidence of a co-conspirator. The incubator had been sabotaged – the life-support systems were disabled. The extra oxygen that should have assisted the child's struggling lungs had never been switched on. The tank was full. The drip that had been set up to deliver fluids to help the compromised blood supply had seeped uselessly into the bedding on which the child had been lying. Of the baby itself, there was no sign.

Damien hadn't attempted to contact Majid since he'd left the message. He didn't want to intrude on whatever Majid was going through. But now he needed his professional help. Joe Massey, an ex-pat recruited by the agency had died, and Damien had a duty to find out what had happened. Massey had been called to a meeting at the hospital when the child's disappearance had been discovered. He had arrived at the hospital – the CCTV had picked him up leaving his car in the car park – but somewhere between the car park and the meeting, he had disappeared, until his body was found by the roadside the following day.

Damien wasn't sure if Majid would be working, but when he dialled the direct line, a familiar voice answered.

'Majid, it's Damien. How are you?'

There was a moment of silence, then Majid said, 'I am well. And you?'

'I left hospital yesterday. I'm very sorry . . .'

Majid cut in before Damien could finish. 'I am pleased you are recovering.' His voice was formal and distant. Taking his lead, Damien kept the talk to business, and made an appointment to see Majid in his office later that day. This was something he'd done often enough before when ex-pats had become entangled in the coils of Saudi law, but this time, Majid seemed reluctant and Damien had to apply some pressure to get the appointment.

He waited until the time for noon prayers had come and gone before he set off for the meeting. The police headquarters where Majid worked was in the centre of the city, in the An Nasriyah district. The building had been badly damaged in a suicide attack the previous year, and the damage was still visible as Damien drove towards the gates, aware of the eyes of the security guards, aware of the way their weapons were aimed directly at him. He knew that if he aroused the slightest suspicion, they would shoot.

He handed over his papers and gained admittance through the first gate, where he had his identity checked again and went through a pat-down search before he was allowed through the entrance. All the time, guns were trained on him. Electronic barriers kept him in the small reception lobby where a man behind security glass took his name. He was directed to a waiting room where he sat under the suspicious eyes of the guards and the ever-vigilant cameras. Men in light khaki uniforms moved purposefully in and out, phones rang, the staccato sound of Arab voices filled the air. Time dragged on. He waited forty-five minutes before a uniformed officer gestured to him. 'You come.'

He led Damien to Majid's office and ushered him in. Majid was at his desk, his attention focused on the papers in front of him. At first, Damien thought that Majid was going to keep him standing, was going to use the dismissive Arab technique of refusing to acknowledge a visitor for minutes, or sometimes longer. Damien had often had to soothe the ruffled feathers of ex-pats who had been kept standing in front of the desks of officials who established the power relationship by ignoring them.

'Majid,' he said.

He saw Majid's body stiffen, and then he looked up. 'Welcome.' His face showed a flash of concern as he looked at Damien, and then went blank. 'Please,' he said. 'Sit.'

Damien took the chair Majid offered him, trying to conceal the relief he felt as he sank into it. But the barrier was still there. He waited in silence for the other man to speak.

'I am pleased to see you are recovering,' Majid said formally. 'Many people offered prayers for you.'

'Thank you. I'm doing fine. And you, Majid? How are you?'

Majid's expression didn't change. 'You have business to discuss, I believe?'

Damien watched the other man's face. Majid met his gaze impassively. 'I need to know what happened,' Damien said when Majid remained silent. 'All I know right now is that someone got a car bomb through the security at that compound, and that Joe Massey was murdered.' He didn't name the third crime. Majid needed no reminding of that.

'You are a victim here.' Majid's voice was cool. 'These things are for the police.'

'I know. But people in my charge were hurt – died – as well.' He looked at Majid, trying to see through the mask of officialdom to find the man who had been his friend for so many years. 'I have information you need. I know these people. I know what they've been doing, who they've been seeing. It's my job, Majid. Let me help you. And I want to know for myself. Someone tried to kill me. Tell me what happened.'

Majid's gaze didn't waver. The silence stretched out uncomfortably, then he nodded. 'Very well,' he said.

Damien felt the tension inside him ease. He waited.

'We believe that the attack may have been connected with a breach of security relating to one of the guests.'

There was only one person he could mean. 'Arshak Nazarian,' Damien said. Majid's father-in-law.

Majid inclined his head. 'The breach of security happened at his offices. Someone attacked his computer system. I understand you knew about this.'

'Yes.' Damien didn't elaborate. He hadn't mentioned it to Majid – it hadn't been his role. And he was pretty sure he knew who the hacker had been. He had seen Joe Massey in the internet café the day before Nazarian told him about the first breach. 'Do you know who it was?'

Majid studied him for a long moment. 'We have some thoughts.'

The internet cafés. The police would have gone to those as soon as they realized there had been a hacker at work, and Joe Massey's identity would have been spotted quickly enough.

Could it all be coincidence? Could the murder be simple robbery, the bomb a terror attack, and the kidnapping a separate event altogether? But Massey had breached Nazarian's security, and Nazarian had nearly died. A bomb in the middle of that party – when Damien thought about what the carnage could have been, he felt cold. As it was, only one person, the girl who seemed to have some link to the bombers, had died. 'We were lucky,' he said. 'Do you know who it was?'

'No one has claimed responsibility,' Majid said. 'We cannot be sure why this has happened.'

Damien looked at him in surprise. Majid was implying that he believed the bomb was not a terrorist attack. In the past the Saudi authorities had turned a blind eye to the obvious evidence and blamed outsiders and gang rivalries for atrocities committed in their midst, until this position became untenable. 'What does Nazarian say?'

Majid's face was expressionless. 'I do not know. He left the country immediately after the bombing. He went to Damascus, and then on to Europe. I have no knowledge of his current whereabouts.'

Nazarian's daughter was bereaved and ill, and her father had fled the country. Why? Because he was afraid that whoever had done this would try again, or because there were things he couldn't afford to have uncovered? He looked at Majid. 'Why has he left?'

'I do not know.'

He clearly wasn't prepared to say more, and seemed about to end the meeting. Damien said quickly, 'And Joe Massey?'

'The matter is under investigation.'

'What happened? His wife said he was called away to an emergency at the hospital.'

'He was. After the . . .' Majid's voice faltered, but when he started speaking again, his voice was cool and steady. 'After the loss was discovered, the medical team met to disclose what treatment the child would have to have – they thought that it might be possible to locate the kidnapper through the drugs and equipment that would be needed. But Joe Massey never arrived at the meeting. By the time they thought to check the pathology department, all the records and samples relating to . . . the child were gone.' Majid's face was a frozen mask as he flicked through some papers on his desk. 'His wife told the men investigating the case that he called her from the hospital to say he was held up there. We have no way of verifying this. His phone and his pager are missing.'

Majid had not only suffered the loss, but now

had to sit on the sidelines while others investigated the kidnapping of his son.

'She decided to leave the party after he phoned. We went to the entrance together to wait for her taxi.'

'You heard the phone call?'

'No. She told me.'

Majid said nothing.

'She – Roisin Massey – she's left the Kingdom?' Damien wanted to be certain she was safe.

'She was interviewed the morning after the attack. She was too unwell to be interviewed fully. She gave them her statement. They thought that they were dealing with a terrorist kidnapping. She had lost her husband. They allowed her to leave. They did not have . . . the other information, at the time.'

Thank God she'd managed to get out before the Saudi preference for the simple solution had asserted itself. Damien closed his eyes, trying to picture the sequence of events. Joe Massey had been called to an emergency. He'd dropped Roisin at the party shortly after nine and had driven off, ostensibly to attend a meeting at the hospital. He'd arrived at the hospital, but he hadn't turned up at the meeting. He'd phoned Roisin to say he was going to be longer than he'd expected – where had he been when he called her?

'Where was he found?'

Majid pointed to the map where a road ran west out of the city towards the Tuwayq escarpment.

'Here. They killed him where we found him. They must have followed him. Then they forced him to stop, cut his throat, threw him out of the car and left him to die.'

Damien studied the map. The road was a quiet one, especially at night, and there was no obvious location that Massey could have been heading for when he was stopped.

'They knew what they were doing?'

Majid nodded. His face was grim. 'Two cuts. One got the artery, the other severed the trachea.'

'And the car?'

'We found it at the airport.'

So the killer had gone.

But Damien couldn't concentrate any more. He could feel the strength leaching out of him. He made a last attempt to break through Majid's reserve. 'Please give my best wishes to your family.'

He saw the flicker of pain in Majid's eyes then his face was blank. 'Thank you. And now, I have . . .'

'You're busy, I understand. Thank you for your time.'

When he got back to his car, he sank back in the seat. Exhaustion had drained him and he felt dizzy with fatigue. His face in the car mirror was grey, with dark shadows under his eyes. He let the weariness wash over him.

The information he'd got from Majid had only confused the picture more – now he had no idea whether he and Roisin Massey had been the victims of a terror attack, or of an attempt on Nazarian's life. And Joe Massey's death formed a dark shadow in the middle.

The world around him seemed oddly sharp and distant as his mind worked at the problem. The only victims of the bomb had been the girl who had died, himself and Roisin Massey. He and Roisin would have died too if he hadn't seen the low wall and moved in time. Maybe he had been the bomb's intended target – but how would they have known he was going to be at the party? He hadn't decided himself until the last minute. He could have become a target of one of the more fanatical groups who believed in complete separatism. His integration into the community was a living offence in their eyes. But he would have known. He would have heard a whisper. And there were far easier and more effective places to assassinate him than at a party he had never planned to attend.

He felt the edge of uneasiness as the picture he was trying to put together shifted and reformulated. Suppose that Joe Massey's death hadn't been an unlucky coincidence. What if the bomb at the party was part of the same elaborate plan?

And suppose the target hadn't been Nazarian, hadn't been Damien, hadn't been Western decadence – suppose it had been Roisin Massey . . .

31

Roisin tried to impose a structure on her life, but sometimes even the task of getting out of bed in the morning came close to defeating her. She had to fight against a weariness that made her want to sink into her chair and blot the world out behind the mindless babble of daytime TV.

Today, she had somewhere to go. It was a week since her mother had left – three weeks since her return. The day before, her new neighbour, the monosyllabic Mari, had surprised her by coming up the stairs. She'd borrowed some cigarettes, and handed over George's new address by way of exchange. She'd seemed more willing to chat this time, leaning in the doorway of the flat, lighting one of the cigarettes with the avid haste of the true addict and blowing the smoke over the railing as Roisin cradled the sleeping baby, enjoying the feel of his weight in her arms. He was a boy, and his name was Adam, Mari told her. She looked pale and tired. 'Bring him up here some time,'

Roisin had said, 'if you need a break. I'm not working just now.'

Mari had brightened at that. 'Yeah, OK. Thanks,' but Roisin hadn't seen her since.

She was aware of a heavy reluctance as she got ready to go out. She had memories of care homes from her school years when she had done her work experience in an old people's home. She could still remember the smell of urine, the bleak sitting room where the old people sat mumbling to themselves, the fear and anxiety she had seen in the eyes of the few who were struggling to hold on to their mental faculties. She dreaded seeing that fear on George's face.

She pulled on her coat and looked out of the window to check the weather. The prospect of heading out into the cold wasn't inviting, but at least the rain had stopped. The street below was empty, and the pavement looked muddy and wet. It had become little more than a cul-de-sac that gave the workers access to the building site, and taxis access to the station. As she watched, a truck lumbered past, weighed down with rubble, and a small white van negotiated its way into a space in front of a now disused gate.

She stood for a while longer watching the van, wondering what it was doing in the no-man's land of redevelopment. She could see the driver's hands as he tapped a cigarette out of a packet. They vanished for a moment then came back into view, the tip of the cigarette a red glow in the mono-chrome day.

It was time she set out. As she hurried to the tube, she noticed how ubiquitous Middle Eastern dress had become: the burka, the abaya and the niqaab covering the anonymous shapes walking the streets of London. Any one of them could be someone she knew – Yasmin, Najia, Souad, Haifa – and she would only recognize them if they chose to greet her, otherwise they could pass unrecognized, anonymous, and silent. She headed down the steps to her train.

As it turned out, her fears about the care home were unfounded. The place where George had moved to wasn't a home at all but a small flat in a block of sheltered accommodation. 'He's a lovely old man,' the warden said with the cheerful optimism of one who could attribute the vagaries of old age to an endearing second childhood.

She could hear Shadow barking as she rang the bell, and the irascible *Geddown* that took her back at once to the days before she had left, the days before she had met Joe.

She was almost knocked off her feet by Shadow's ecstatic greeting. He leapt up and licked her face, dashed round in little circles, ran away and came back, ran away again and came back carrying his lead. In the middle of all the chaos, it was easier to greet George, who had immediately quashed the delight she had surprised on to his face with a gruff, 'Oh, it's you. You'd better come in. Dog! *Geddown!*'

She climbed through Shadow's manic dance of joy into a small, neatly appointed flat. Her first impression was of warmth, and then of clutter. It looked as though George had moved his entire stock of possessions from his flat into this tiny studio apartment.

They stared at each other for a moment. 'How are you?' she said.

He ignored this. 'Been having a rough time, girl?'

She felt tears come into her eyes as she nodded. He indicated a chair, and she sat down. Shadow pressed his chin into her lap and looked up at her with troubled eyes as she stroked the soft ears. The two of them, the old man and his dog, were conspiring to make her cry.

George looked better than she remembered him. Before, he always looked unkempt, a bit too thin, not quite clean. Now, he had put on weight, he was clean-shaven and he was wearing a neatly pressed pair of trousers and a big sweater. Before, he'd always sat in his overcoat and a pair of gloves because he couldn't afford to run the heating, or was afraid he couldn't. Now he looked like someone who was eating regularly, who was living in warmth and comfort. 'You look very well,' she said. 'Do you like it here?'

He grunted a dour assent, adding, 'Could do without all the busybody women. Now then, Rosie, you'd better tell me about it.'

And she found that she could. She told him in

clear, spare detail about the party, about the bomb and about Joe. She kept her fingers buried in the silky hair around Shadow's neck as she spoke.

George just sat and listened. When she'd finished, he sighed. 'There's bad places in this world and that's a fact. Come on, let's have a cuppa.' He heaved himself to his feet and went through to the kitchen. She followed him, noticing the brand new electric kettle unused on the worktop, and the blackened kettle from his flat on the hob. 'Did he find you then, that chap?'

'Who?' She moved across to pour the boiling water into the pot. She knew he must do it for himself all the time, but it made her nervous to see his unsteady hand so close to the scalding liquid.

'That chap who came looking for you. Just the day before I left. I've been keeping an eye on the place for you, don't you worry. Saw him hanging around your door. Shadow gave him what for, didn't you? Good boy.' He thumped the dog's head and Shadow, who had crowded into the kitchen behind them, panted eagerly up at him.

'Someone came looking for me?'

'*Is she coming back?* he says. *Not my business*, I told him. *And not yours, neither*. Couldn't have told him if I'd wanted to.' He looked at Roisin expectantly.

'I did write,' she said, aware that she'd only managed two letters in the welter of new experiences. 'I don't know who it was. Did they leave a message?'

'Not with me. You don't want nothing to do with him, Rosie. Nasty piece of work, if you ask me.' Roisin didn't take this comment too seriously. Every stranger was a nasty piece of work to George.

He turned on the TV and they watched an afternoon quiz show in companionable silence. When it was time for her to leave, she said, 'Do you have someone to walk Shadow?'

'With all the busybody women round here? We don't get a minute, right, dog?' He looked at her. 'If you want to take him for a run, any time, Rosie . . .'

'I will,' she said. 'I'll be back.'

She kissed his cheek and let herself out, leaving him watching TV. She went along the front of the flats until she found the warden's office. The woman looked up. 'You off? He's doing nicely, isn't he?'

'Yes. He looks a lot better. Listen, could you tell me how long he's been here? I mean, what was the actual date he arrived?'

The warden hesitated for a moment, then decided the request was harmless. 'He came here on the 27th,' she said.

'December?'

'Yes. We don't usually move people during the holiday, but there was a tenant who needed his old flat urgently, so we made an exception.'

So the person who'd come looking for her had called just a few days after the party, a few days after Joe . . . after Joe had died. Someone who knew she might be returning. She puzzled over it on the way home, but couldn't make any sense of it.

The light was fading as she headed back. The street lights reflected orange on the wet flagstones and she made herself hurry, juggling her handbag, her shopping and her umbrella. She thought about the evenings in Riyadh, the sudden darkness, the way the hot air cooled and it became possible to move around outside in comfort, the smell from the evening barbecues, the night sky in the desert . . .

When she got back to the flat, the street was silent and empty, the twilight making grey shadows of the space where the van had been parked. She fumbled with her keys as she opened the outer door that let her on to the stairway, suddenly uneasy.

The door shut behind her with a reassuring clunk. She had never been nervous in the dark, or worried about who might be behind her. She had always walked the streets confidently, knowing her way around, knowing how to take care of herself. Now, she expected danger around every corner. Her security was another thing that Riyadh had taken from her.

She climbed the dim and poorly maintained stairway to the top level and let herself into the flat. The light from the street lamps shone through the window and she went to close the blinds, taking a last look at the street outside. She could see from here that the van was still in its impromptu parking bay, a dark shape among the shadows. She wondered if it belonged to someone who lived in the flats.

As she watched, she thought she saw a spark of red in the darkness, the glow of a cigarette, rapidly fading and gone.

32

Damien left Riyadh early one February morning. The sky was already clear blue, a blue that would intensify to white as the sun rose fully and the baking heat of the day began. He'd known at some level since the first day he'd left the hospital that his time in the Kingdom was coming to an end, but he'd been postponing the decision to go. Part of him still didn't want to leave the place that had been his home for so long, even though it had changed, or he had changed beyond restoration. Officially, he was on sick leave. He'd gone to see his boss to hand in his resignation, and had been persuaded to take a few weeks off, to leave the Kingdom for a while and postpone any decision until after that.

Two days before, he had gone to visit Majid. He didn't want their last encounter to be that interview at police headquarters. He hoped that, within the privacy of his home, Majid might become, once more, the friend he knew. But there had been no news of the missing child, and the trail must be growing colder each day. The loss of his son had turned Majid in on himself, driven him behind the mask that his job allowed him to wear, and into the certainties and securities of his family. His welcome to Damien was cool. Damien sat in the familiar room as coffee was served, and Majid and his brothers watched him in silence. They accepted coffee as the servant brought it to them, but none of them drank.

'You are leaving?' Faisal said. He spoke in English. In the past, he had always addressed Damien in Arabic.

'Yes. This may be my last real time in Riyadh.' Damien let his gaze move to Majid, who dropped his eyes. He looked stressed and tired.

Silence fell as Damien lifted his cup. He had two choices. He could take his leave quickly and accept that he was now excluded from this house, or he could stay and try to re-establish some contact with the man who had been his friend for over ten years. He wanted to give Majid his sympathy, and his support. 'These have been sad times,' he said.

'Sad times come and go,' Faisal said. The other men remained silent as Damien put his cup on the low table.

They were speaking English. Perhaps it was time for some English directness. He addressed Faisal but he was aware of Majid in his peripheral vision. 'I came to take my leave from people who have become good friends. And who will remain good friends in my mind always. If there is anything I can do for you now, or at any time, remember that I will.'

Faisal bowed his head. 'I hear your words,' he said. He didn't lower his guard of formality, but this time he spoke in Arabic. Damien stood and the three brothers rose to their feet. The farewells were stiff and formal.

The next day, Rai drove him to the airport. The two men embraced as Damien took his bag from the car.

'A few weeks,' Damien said. 'Then we're in business again.'

'In business.' Rai gave him the thumbs-up and grinned. There were tears in his eyes.

He listened to the sound of Arabic around him, to the men at work greeting each other with the blessings of God, to the calls of the water-sellers on the streets, and he wondered if he would ever hear it again.

He'd sent Majid a note telling him the time of his leaving and giving him a forwarding address. He had hoped, against all expectation, that Majid would come and say goodbye, but he didn't.

Me and my brother against my cousin.

Me and my cousin against the stranger.

And Damien was the stranger now.

33

It was late afternoon when Damien stepped off the plane at Heathrow and set foot in the UK for the first time in ten years. He hadn't expected any jolt of familiarity, any moment of nostalgia, and he didn't get one. An airport was an airport. In his mind, he'd severed all ties with the UK when he'd gone to work overseas. The only things that had bound him to the place were gone. His brief marriage was over and Catherine was dead. He'd left with no intention of coming back.

His eventual return was low key. He went through Customs unimpeded and found himself once again under skies that were heavy with grey clouds, the chill air wet with recent rain and threatening more. England was much as he remembered it.

The first thing he intended doing was contacting Roisin Massey. He joined the queue for taxis, then called her number. She answered at once.

'Roisin, it's Damien O'Neill.'

'Damien!' Her voice sounded distant and oddly faded.

'Have I called at a bad time?'

'No, it's . . . No, of course not. How are you?'

'I'm . . . *fine*,' he said, choosing the word deliberately. She laughed, sounding more the way he remembered her. 'And you?'

'I'm OK. More or less. Damien, where are you?'

'Right now? I'm second in line in the queue for taxis at Heathrow.'

'Heathrow? You're here?'

'Yes. Just for a couple of weeks.'

There was silence, then she said, 'That's so . . . Look, we can't talk like this. Will you come and see me?'

'Of course. It's one of the reasons I'm here.'

'Why don't you get settled in, then come straight over. Where are you staying?'

'I've taken a flat in Camden Town.' He opened the taxi door and threw in his case.

'That's not far from me. Call me when you're on your way.'

'I will.' He rang off and looked at the phone. 'Roisin . . .' he said.

He didn't realize he'd spoken out loud until the taxi driver said, '*Where*, mate?'

When Damien O'Neill's call came, Roisin had been trying to put some order into her life. A job would be a starting point. She didn't need the money, or not yet. Joe's salary was still coming through

313

from the company. This was for her own recovery. Her mother phoned regularly, and in her weekly letter she had started putting cuttings with job opportunities. Roisin was touched to see that none of these would take her to the North East. It was as if her mother were saying, *I'm not trying to force you home. I want this for you.*

She'd gone out that afternoon to pick up the *Times Educational Supplement*, and had just settled down with a cup of coffee and the jobs pages spread out across the table when the phone rang and the voice at the other end of the line took her straight back to Riyadh.

Damien O'Neill. She barely knew him, and yet the events at the party had formed a link between them that made it feel as though an old and welcome friend was coming home. As she whipped round the flat, tidying up, she remembered the rather distant man who had shown them the ad-Dirah souk that first day, the day she had found her way to as-Sa'ah Square. She thought about the man at that first party who had stonewalled her with conventional politeness until she had started making fun of him, then he had laughed and become more approachable. And then she remembered the man at the Bradshaws' who had been concerned for her, watched out for her welfare, and in the end had saved her life, nearly losing his own in the process.

A couple of hours after he'd called, the entry phone buzzed. 'Roisin? It's Damien.' As she pressed

314

the button to release the lock, she was suddenly afraid that, now he was away from Riyadh, she would find he had become another stranger, that he would be just another once-familiar face in the massive darkness that was London. But when she opened the door, he was the way she remembered him: a slim man with light hair and grey eyes, who carried himself with an air of watchful caution.

'Roisin.' His smile was warm. She kissed him and he put his arms round her and held her close. He gave her a bunch of flowers, early daffodils. 'I think the spring flowers are the only thing I missed about England,' he said. Their pale yellow brightened up the gloom of the day and filled the dark hallway with the promise of better days to come.

'Thank you,' she said. As she took the flowers, she realized that the daffodils would be blooming along the canalside in a few weeks.

They talked in a desultory way as she made them both coffee, about his flight and about the flat he was renting in London. It wasn't until she was sitting down opposite him that she began to see the toll that the bomb had taken. Under his tan, he looked pale and she could see the lines around his eyes and mouth that had been etched by pain and exhaustion. He was observing her with the same closeness and she wondered what he saw.

'How are you?' he said.

She didn't find it necessary to prevaricate with

him. 'I'm keeping myself busy. Looking for work.'

'What are you going to do next?'

He'd understood at once that this life was just temporary. This was crawling into the hole to heal. 'I don't know. Yet. You?'

He shook his head. 'I don't know either.'

She suspected that he knew perfectly well, but she didn't push it. The fact that they were both here, that they had both survived this far, was a cause for celebration. 'We should have a drink.' She went and got some wine from the fridge and poured them each a generous glass. 'Here's to . . .'

He thought for a moment. 'A meeting? Wherever we are, whatever we're doing, this time next year, we'll meet.'

She met his gaze as she lifted her glass. 'That's a promise. This time next year.' They drank.

He leaned back in the chair. 'Has anyone from the consulate been in touch with you?'

'They told me that someone's been arrested for robbery and might be charged with murder. It didn't . . .' She could remember the sense of distance and unreality when they told her. Closure. Her friends had said this would mean closure, but it hadn't meant anything.

'Do you believe that?' He was watching her closely.

'I . . .' She shook her head. 'No, I don't.'

'Neither do I. Listen, Roisin, I'm sorry to talk

about things that are going to distress you, but I'm trying to find out what happened that night.'

That night. She could remember standing by the door at the Bradshaws', watching out for the car. She could remember falling and hitting the ground, feeling the impact knocking the breath out of her, but not remembering the pain. She could remember Damien's hand pressing her face hard against his shirt. Then there was nothing. That was the point where the dreams took over. 'What do you want to know?'

'Joe – when he called you at the party, what did he say?'

'That it was going to take longer than he thought – he was going to go over something with someone.'

'How did he sound?'

She thought about it, calling Joe's voice into her head. She could hear him speaking as if he was standing beside her: *Listen, sweetheart, there's a problem here. I've got to sort out some stuff. I'm going to be a bit of time.* 'He sounded . . . serious. As though it was serious.'

'Did he say anything about the missing child?'

She looked at him blankly. 'Missing child?'

'You don't know about . . . Christ, I'm sorry. It's more bad news. A baby was taken from the hospital that day – that's why they called Joe in.'

'A missing baby?' She could see there was something he wasn't telling her. 'Whose baby?'

'A Saudi family.'

317

She knew he was being evasive so she supplied the name. 'Yasmin. Yasmin's baby.'

He nodded, watching her closely.

Her eyes stung and she blinked rapidly to clear them. 'But he was ill. The baby was ill.'

'Yes.' He didn't elaborate.

'Joe didn't say anything when he got the call. We'd been talking about Yasmin just before.' Because a baby had died. There'd been a post mortem.

'They won't have told him something like that over the phone.'

She was back in the car. They were in the car park in front of the strip mall and Joe had been talking, telling her about his friend Haroun Patel. *Haroun is dead* . . . And then . . . She shook her head. 'No. It was a call on his pager. Then he called them back.'

'And it was the hospital?'

'Yes. But no one said it was anything serious. He was pissed off because he wasn't supposed to be on duty. Why would they call him in for that? What could he have done to help track a kidnapped child?'

'He'd have had the information they'd need to identify the child if they found him.'

'The blood tests?'

He nodded. 'What happened then?'

'He dropped me off at the party. He said he'd phone me . . .' He'd put his arms round her, and she'd said, *Don't be long.* He'd said, *I won't.*

'Did he?'

'I called him. Well, I tried, but I couldn't get through.'

'Was his phone busy, or was it switched off?'

'Switched off.'

Damien was staring into the distance, calculating. 'He never made it to the meeting.' His voice was absent. 'It sounds as though he was calling you from the hospital. The police never found his phone or his pager. A thief would take the phone, but the pager . . . ? Maybe. But it means the police can't check on any calls. The hospital paged him – that's on record. But where he was calling from . . .' He looked at her for a long moment. 'If he'd gone somewhere else, would he have told you? Did he always tell you what he was doing?'

She wanted to say yes, but that wasn't true. 'No. Not always.'

He wasn't looking at her. His left hand was resting on his thigh and she could see him moving it, trying to make a fist with fingers that were stiff and crooked. 'Does the name Haroun Patel mean anything to you?' he said.

She felt her glass start to slip through her fingers and grabbed at it quickly. She was back with Joe on the road out of Riyadh, the traffic weaving around them.

Joe, who's Haroun Patel?

Christ, Roisin, what kind of time is it to ask me that?

The last time she'd seen him.

Damien was watching her reaction. He didn't

319

say anything, just waited until she was ready to speak. 'Why are you asking me that?'

'I'm not sure. Maybe I'm just clutching at straws.'

'OK. Well, yes, it does. He was a friend of Joe's. Joe told me about him, that last evening . . . We were driving to the party, and we stopped and he told me.'

'You know what happened to him?'

She nodded. 'Joe was there. When they . . . when they did it.'

'I knew he was asking questions about Patel. I never knew why. You said that he told you that last evening. Why did he tell you then? Why not before?'

'He told me because I asked him. I found some stuff among his papers, on his desk. I wanted to know what it was all about.'

'What did you find?'

It was like an interrogation. 'Damien, you need to tell me what's going on. Why are you asking?'

He sighed. 'I don't know much. That's the truth, Roisin. I've been cut out of the loop as well, so this is all guesswork. I don't know the police officer in charge of your husband's case, but I understand he's going along with the robbery story. I suspect they aren't as convinced as they say they are, but they're coming under pressure to solve it in a way that won't embarrass the government. No one will talk to me about it. There's something I need to ask you. Do you think that Joe kept quiet about what he was doing because he thought it was dangerous?'

Dangerous . . . Joe had been tense for most of the time they'd been in Riyadh. He'd been preoccupied and stressed. He'd said it was work. And then that last weekend he'd seemed . . . different. More relaxed. And glad that they were going to leave. She stalled. 'Dangerous, how?'

'How do you think, Roisin? He kept what he was doing a secret. He didn't want you to know what he knew. But then, the night he died, you were almost killed as well. What kind of coincidence is that?'

She had a sudden, farcical picture of Souad tracking her through the streets of Riyadh with murder on her mind because she didn't like Roisin's seminars, but it wasn't a farce. It wasn't funny. Whatever it was, it had killed Joe. And it had almost killed Damien, and almost killed her.

'I need to know what it was that Joe was looking for,' he said. 'Roisin?'

But she didn't know. That was the thing. Even now, she didn't know. 'All I know is what he told me that night. He told me that this man was his friend. He told me that he went there, the day he was executed. And he said that he thought Haroun Patel was innocent. That's all.'

But it hadn't been all. She could still hear Joe's voice, still see his face as he said, *I know that the brain, that consciousness, can survive for minutes without oxygen. It doesn't shut down at once.* Joe, his head half-severed, bleeding to death by the side of the road. She turned her face away.

'I'm sorry,' Damien said. 'I shouldn't have come here to talk about things that upset you.'

She shook her head. 'Talking about it makes no difference. It's there all the time. I'm glad you're doing this. I'm glad you're asking questions. You're the only one who is.' Or the only one who was asking the right questions.

'I may not get very far,' he said. 'It's all speculation. I just don't see why asking questions about Haroun Patel would be such a big deal.'

'If Joe was right, if there had been a miscarriage of justice . . .'

'No one would care – and Joe would have known that. They might have thrown him out if he'd started kicking up a big stink in the overseas press – but, be honest, Roisin, who would have listened? Organizations like Amnesty give the Saudis a hard time on a regular basis, but no one else is worried. Whatever happened, I can't see that the Patel case is anything to do with it.'

They both fell silent. There didn't seem to be anything else to say. After a while, she forced her mind back into action. 'Have you eaten?'

'No. I don't know what they served on the plane, but I don't think it was food.'

She managed to laugh. 'I'll make us something, OK?'

'That would be great. Thank you.'

She went into the kitchen, glad of something

to do to distract herself. She put a heavy pan on the burner and turned the flame up high, then she cut some tomatoes and put them in to roast with a drizzle of oil and a sprinkling of dried herbs. When she and Joe lived here, she always had fresh herbs growing in pots along the window sill and spices waiting to be ground into whatever she was making. There was always good cheese from the deli, fresh bread, fresh fruit. Now, the shelves were empty.

She dug around in the cupboard, looking for some pasta, keeping her mind focused on what she was doing. While she was waiting for the water to come to the boil, she made a salad with the rest of the tomatoes and some oil and basil. The fragrance of the herbs filled the kitchen with the smell of summer.

When the tomatoes were done, she crushed them into a thick sauce and spooned it over the drained pasta. She put the salad into a dish, put everything on to a tray and took it through to the other room. He jumped to his feet to help her set the table, then produced a bottle of red wine from his bag and poured them both a glass, though she noticed he hadn't finished the glass of wine she'd given him earlier.

They talked about casual, easy topics while they ate. 'This is good,' he said. 'I'm out of touch with European food.'

'I enjoy cooking.' It was something else she missed. She'd always taken trouble to cook, even when it was just for herself, but since she'd come back, she'd lived on bread, cheese, fruit – things she could just grab and eat. Cooking had seemed like too much trouble.

'Are you going to stay in the UK?' she asked. 'Do you have family here?'

He shook his head. 'I'm just here to sort out some business. I'm going to France tomorrow for a few days, then I'll be back to finish some things off. I need to think about what I'm going to do.'

'Are you going back?' To her, it seemed inconceivable.

He shook his head. 'I don't know. Maybe not to Saudi.'

He told her a bit about the other Gulf states: about Kuwait, that still bore some of the scars of invasion and war; about the glittering opulence of Dubai, which he dismissed as Blackpool in the desert; about how much he liked Oman – the only Gulf state, in his view, that hadn't been damaged either by Westernization or by excessive wealth. He wanted to live in an Arab country. 'A lot of the ex-pats think that the Arabs are cold and distant. They aren't. They're among the most friendly and hospitable people in the world. The Saudis aren't so easy, I'll grant you that. I like them fine, but they do have . . . I don't know what you would call it – a superiority complex, I suppose.'

Roisin thought about her meetings with Souad, the barely disguised contempt with which she reacted to both Roisin and her views. But Yasmin hadn't been like that. Nor had Najia. 'Not all,' she said.

He shook his head. 'No, not all.'

She didn't want to talk about Riyadh, so she turned the conversation back to him. The level of wine in her glass was barely falling, but she was starting to feel more relaxed. 'Where were you born?'

'In Lancashire – in a village that's probably part of Greater Manchester by now.'

'Your family – are they still there?'

He shook his head. 'My parents are dead.'

'Brothers? Sisters?'

'No.'

'Do you have any children?' She knew she was pushing. 'I don't know you at all, and I feel as though I should.'

'There's no great mystery about me. I grew up in England. I went to Oxford to do my degree and then I worked for the diplomatic service in France and Germany. I left Europe when I was twenty-seven, and I've worked overseas ever since. I've been married, but it didn't last. I have no children. I'm just another ex-civil servant carving out a living.'

'I'm sorry. I didn't mean to pry.'

He grinned. 'Really, this is all there is. What you see is what you get. OK, my turn. Tell me about yourself. Where do you come from?'

She found herself being more forthcoming than

325

he had been, telling him about her family, her adoption, her lack of memories of her early life, her worries about her mother, the way she missed her father.

He listened quietly, topping up her wine glass from time to time. 'And do you have brothers? Or sisters?'

She shook her head. 'No.' She thought about the gap that had always been there in her life. 'I had a sister, but she died when my parents were killed. I don't remember her. I had a friend, once, who was almost like a sister.' She realized that all these weeks, she had been waiting for Amy to get in touch, but there had been nothing but silence. It had been the same all those years ago when Amy had gone to London and never come back.

It was as if he'd read her thoughts. 'Amy?'

She looked at him in surprise. 'How did you know? You know Amy?'

He smiled. 'I know just about every ex-pat in Riyadh. Yes, I know Amy, and she told me she knew you.' He topped up her glass again.

'She was my best friend.' She stared into the deep red of the wine. She told him about how she and Amy had met, the plans they had shared. 'She told me she'd lost her family, like I had. I used to pretend we were sisters – we were close enough, or so I thought. Then . . . I didn't know at the time, but Amy really *did* have a sister – a half-sister, and her stepfather took her away.' She looked into the distance, remembering Amy sitting on the settee, talking about what had happened to her. She told him about Amy leaving, about the brief trip to London that had swallowed her up for fifteen years. 'I don't know what happened. Except that she found her sister. That's why she left Riyadh. Her sister was going to have a baby, in Paris. Amy trained as a nurse in Paris. She told me.'

'And her sister's there?'

She looked at him. She was having trouble gathering her thoughts. Her glass was still full, which was odd because she could have sworn she'd been drinking it. She took another swallow of wine. 'Paris. Amy was going to Paris to be an aunt.' If her sister had lived, maybe she would be an aunt by now.

'What's the sister's name?'

'Nell. She was . . . Oh, you mean Amy's sister. Jassy. She's called Jassy.'

'Jassy?'

'Jesamine for short. I mean – shit – Jesamine for long.' For some reason it struck her as funny and she started laughing.

He was smiling as he watched her.

'What?' she said.

'You look better. Better than you did before. More wine?'

'I think I've had enough. Jesamine for short . . .' She wanted to start laughing again.

'Have you heard from her since you left?'

'No.' And just like that, the laughter stopped. 'I

thought she'd get in touch, after . . . She must have heard. But it's like last time. She's gone. She was like my sister, and then she went away. I didn't see her again until she came knocking on my door in Riyadh.' Amy had said *I'm not going to lose touch again*. 'She said she'd keep in touch and then she didn't. And now I don't know where she is.'

She was having trouble enunciating her words and she could hear the wobble of self-pity that had come into her voice. The wine bottle was empty and so was her glass. If she wasn't careful, she'd end up on a crying jag. 'Oh, God, ignore me. I've had too much to drink. I'm sorry.'

'No,' he said. 'I'm the one who should be sorry. It's OK, Roisin. Listen, it's getting late and I'm a bit jet-lagged. I've got a trip to make tomorrow. Can I call you when I get back?'

'Of course.' They both stood up and she forced her eyes to focus.

'Will you be all right?'

She dismissed this with an airy gesture that sent her off balance.

He steadied her with one hand on her arm. 'Careful.'

'I'll be fine. I'm not as bad as I look. You go. Have a good trip.' This came out rather garbled, but he seemed to understand her.

'If you're sure.' He let go of her, watching her assessingly. She kept herself determinedly upright and gave him what she hoped was a reassuring smile.

'Call me when you get back,' she said.

'I will,' he agreed, brushing his lips against hers.

When the door had closed behind him, she went back to the living room. Unsteadily, she piled up the plates and carried them through to the kitchen, but she was too tired, and too drunk, to do any more.

As she wove her way into the bedroom, she reflected that she'd at least have a good night's sleep – she must have drunk enough to guarantee oblivion. But as she lay in bed trying to still the sway of the mattress, the orange light from the street glowed through the blinds, and her dreams were filled with visions of flames in the darkness, of a path leading to the creeper-hung wall where a pale face glimmered in the shadows, the face serene, the eyes closed.

But as she drew closer, the dead eyes snapped open. They were wide with terror and somewhere in the shadows the red glow of a cigarette burned, then faded.

Damien flagged down a taxi and headed back towards the flat he'd taken for the next month, uncertain how long his stay in the UK would be. He wasn't pleased with himself. He'd gone to see Roisin with an agenda – to find out more about the night when Joe Massey had died, and to get as much information as he could about Amy. And instead of just asking her, he'd pushed the conversation until he could introduce Amy's name, then he'd let her talk, nudging her with questions as he refilled her glass before the level sank too low so she wouldn't notice how much she was drinking.

He told himself it had been therapeutic for her to talk, that getting drunk might help to relax the edgy tension that had marked her every move and every action. But he knew himself too well for that trick to work. He had used all the skills he brought to his professional work, and he now knew a lot of things that Amy had never told him. Like where she might be.

And it might just be enough to help him find her.

34

Roisin sat up, squinting her eyes against the hard light that poured in through the window. The blinds were half open. No wonder the light had kept her awake. She crawled out of bed and stood looking out at the new day. She must have drunk the best part of the bottle of wine Damien had opened. She was just glad she hadn't made a complete fool of herself. Or she hoped she hadn't. Her memories of the last part of the evening were a bit hazy.

The living room was still a mess from the night before: glasses on the table, the smell of cooking in the air. She cleared up quickly, noting as she did that Damien's glass was barely touched. Not only had she got drunk, she'd got drunk in front of someone who was stone-cold sober.

She threw open the windows to freshen the air. The flowers he'd brought gleamed in a dark corner and she moved them into the light. The winter sun shone through the window, turning the petals gold. Dust danced in the sun, and the air from the open windows smelled clean and fresh.

Her door bell rang. She wasn't expecting anyone. She pressed the intercom button. 'Who is it?'

'Mrs Massey?'

'Yes.'

'Police.'

She felt a lurch of alarm as she pressed the buzzer to release the lock and waited in the doorway. Her mother? Had something happened to her mother? She'd sounded fine on the phone the previous day. After a few seconds, she saw a man and woman coming up the steps. They weren't wearing uniform. Detectives?

They produced ID before she could ask. The man introduced himself as DC Lovell, and the woman as DC Syed. 'Can we come in?' the woman said. She must only be in her early twenties, but she had an air of self-possession beyond her years.

Roisin led them through into the living room and faced them anxiously. 'What's wrong? It isn't my mother . . .'

'Nothing like that,' the woman said, and Roisin felt the tension inside her relax slightly. 'May we sit down?'

'Please.' She gestured to the armchairs.

The man remained standing, and she sat down slowly, feeling suddenly at a disadvantage. She could see his eyes make a quick sweep round the room, observing the empty bottle and the two glasses. Her head ached, making it hard to concentrate. 'How can I help you?'

'We're investigating a death that occurred last year,' the woman said. 'Last September. A young woman drowned in the Thames. Dr Massey was a witness.'

Roisin looked from one to the other, her sense of bewilderment growing. 'September?' In September, Joe had asked her to marry him. In September, they'd made their plans – ill-fated plans – to move to Saudi for a year. 'I don't know what you're talking about.'

'He gave evidence at the inquest,' the man said. 'Didn't he tell you about that?' His eyes weren't friendly.

Joe had never mentioned a drowned woman, or an inquest. 'I think you must have the wrong person,' she said. 'Whatever you want to know . . .'

'We're sorry about your husband, Mrs Massey.'

'Yes. Me too.' She heard the break in her voice, and could feel her eyes stinging. She sat very still, her head carefully erect to stop the tears spilling out. She didn't want them to see her cry. There was a moment of silence.

'Can I get you anything? Would you like a cup of tea?' The woman's sympathy had a detached professionalism that allowed Roisin to pull herself together. She excused herself to go and wash her face. When she came back, the two detectives were waiting for her. The man was studying the framed photograph of their wedding, the only thing she had retrieved from the cases that still remained unpacked in the box room . . .

'I'd rather you left that alone,' she said sharply. He put it down without comment.

It was the woman who spoke. 'I'd like to ask you some questions, if you wouldn't mind.' She paused briefly, then said, 'Dr Massey returned from Saudi Arabia in spring 2004, is that correct?'

'Yes.'

'And how long had you known him then?'

'I didn't. We met that April.' *A tall man with dark hair, running towards her on the tow path . . .*

'You got married a few months after you met?' This was the man with the unfriendly eyes.

'We had to be married for me to get my visa to Saudi,' she said. But it hadn't been like that. They'd been happy. Joe had brought champagne and forgotten to bring glasses. They'd drunk it out of the bottle, the wine foaming up out of the neck and spilling over them as they tilted it, laughing until they could barely swallow.

The woman took up the questioning. 'Do you know why he came back to the UK?'

'Because his contract had ended.'

'Yes, but why the UK?'

'Because he could get work here.' Joe had never said exactly why he'd come back – just that he didn't want to stay.

'His decision to go back to the Middle East was very sudden.'

Roisin looked at them both, wondering how they knew that. 'He'd applied for a job in Canada. He didn't get it, and they made him a good offer to go and work in Riyadh. It was just a year's contract.' She realized she was starting to sound defensive. 'Why are you asking?'

The woman flicked through some papers she was carrying. 'After Dr Massey gave us his statement, he told us that his plans would involve him leaving the country in the near future. He gave us a contact at McMaster University in Ontario in case we needed to talk to him again. We tried to contact him there . . .' She passed Roisin a letter.

Roisin looked at it. It was on headed paper from McMaster University, and it said that Dr Massey had been offered an appointment starting in October 2004, but he had turned it down as his commitments made it impossible for him to take up the post. She kept her head bent over the paper so that the two detectives wouldn't see her face. Her head was spinning with confusion. Joe had wanted that job. It had meant everything to him. 'I don't understand,' she said.

'It's quite clear.' The man had moved closer and was standing above her as he spoke. 'Your husband turned this job down in favour of one in Saudi Arabia.'

'Doug . . .' The woman said.

Roisin looked at him. 'What does it matter now?'

'He never mentioned it to you? That he saw a woman drown?'

335

'No.' But Joe knew about drowning in the river. He'd talked to her about the bodies brought to the mortuary at the hospital where he used to work. *She's dead if she does . . .* And she was by the river on a cold spring day, standing on the embankment with Joe watching a tour boat go past.

DC Syed consulted her notes. 'We don't know the woman's identity, but we do know she was working as a prostitute. We're working on the assumption she was an illegal immigrant.' Her gaze met Roisin's for a long moment. 'When Dr Massey gave us his statement,' she said, 'he told us he saw the woman standing on the wall by the river walk. He said he called out to her, and then she fell. Or jumped. The problem is, a witness has now come forward who says she saw Dr Massey walking along the river path with an Asian female whose description matches the woman who drowned. She said the woman looked upset, or possibly frightened. We'd very much like to know why Dr Massey didn't tell us that. Can you shed any light on it?'

Roisin felt as though all the air had been knocked out of her. There was nothing she could say.

DC Syed put a sheet of paper on the table in front of her. 'Do you recognize this?' It was a photograph of a ring. It was metal, and looked heavy. Underneath the photo, there was an inscription in Arabic, and beneath that, a translation: *Take what is here now, let go of a promise. The drumbeat is best from far away.*

336

Roisin looked down at the photograph, glad of the chance to hide her face. Her mind was spinning. She made herself focus on the inscription. It was tantalizingly familiar, and then she realized what it was. '*"Ah take the cash and let the credit go, nor heed the music of a distant drum."*' The two detectives looked at her, and the woman tilted her head in query. 'It's from the *Rubaiyat of Omar Khayyam*,' Roisin said. 'I only know the Fitzgerald poem – it was translated in the nineteenth century. But that text must be from the original.'

Roisin couldn't tell if the woman knew this already. 'And the ring – do you recognize that?'

'No. No, I don't.'

The man chipped in. 'It was part of a collection of jewellery that was stolen from a family in Riyadh, about eighteen months ago. Whoever stole it probably thought it was gold, but it isn't. It's just brass. Sentimental value. Your husband would have been on his first contract then, wouldn't he?'

'Yes.' It came out as a whisper. Her mouth felt stiff and frozen. *There is a girl who is missing – we want to know where she is, but we haven't been able to find her.* She couldn't trust her voice. She waited, dreading what he was going to say next.

But the woman stood up. 'Well, thank you for your time, Mrs Massey. And I'm very sorry about your husband.'

As he stepped through the door, the man turned

and looked at her. 'Did you know that Saudi Arabia doesn't have an extradition treaty with the UK?'

Before she could respond, he turned and followed his colleague along the walkway.

35

After the police had gone, Roisin sat at the table in the stillness of shock. The police had come looking for Joe because they had 'more information' about the woman who had drowned in the Thames. All these months later, they had come to talk to her about Joe's involvement, even though they knew he was dead.

Did you know that Saudi Arabia doesn't have an extradition treaty with the UK?

They were investigating a murder.

She went to the box room where their cases, still full, were stacked against the wall. Joe's shirt, the one she'd found the last time she tried to unpack, was draped over a chair. She hadn't been in here since that day.

The cases had been packed by someone from the Embassy. She'd told them not to bother, to get rid of everything, but instead they'd packed up all their belongings, hers and Joe's, and now she had cases full of books, boxes full of bric-a-brac – relics of a life she wanted to leave behind. The only thing she had wanted to keep from her life in Riyadh had been taken away from her. Nothing else mattered.

She started going through the cases, pulling out all the clothes and stuffing them into a bin liner. They could all go to a charity shop. She lifted out her abaya, light, silky and black. She could see the dark shapes of the women in the streets, hear Najia's voice saying, *The law forbids me an education if my brother withdraws his permission.* The men who wanted these laws, enforced these laws, had killed Joe. She was sure of it. She gripped the fabric and tried to rip it down the seams, but the garment was tough, and all she succeeded in doing was making herself breathless and angry. She screwed it up and pushed it down into the bin liner.

At the bottom of the second case, she found what she was looking for. There were two folders full of papers that had come from the desk and the small filing cabinet in the study. She took out the first folder and flicked through the contents: teaching materials she'd been putting together for Souad, that last weekend when she'd had to work instead of going out with Joe. She threw them away.

Then she opened the second folder, slipped out the papers and began to go through them. The photo jumped out at her. It was the one she'd found that last day, Joe and a man she now knew was Haroun Patel. Joe smiled at her out of the picture, lost and gone. She looked at him, her fingers touching the surface, two men, friends, casual, carefree, sharing a joke. And now they were both dead.

Why?

She started going through the papers more carefully. They seemed to be notes relating to some kind of research Joe had been undertaking. She knew how he worked; he jotted down his ideas at random, then he started sorting them into groups, looking for connections and gaps that needed filling. She could picture him, sitting in the reclining chair in the evenings, a notepad on his lap, staring into the distance and then scribbling things down as they occurred to him. And she could remember his smile of triumph as the route through some intractable problem suddenly became clear.

But whatever problem Joe had been working on here, he hadn't got beyond his first ideas: *Ghatghat, Manfuha, Ad Diriyah.* She stared at them, frowning, trying to catch the fleeting familiarity. For a moment, the memory eluded her, then she realized they were names of small towns and villages on the outskirts of Riyadh. Places Joe had worked in? Intended to visit?

There was also a list of numbers that looked like times of day: *09.30, 11.30, 12.15, 13.00.* There were lists that looked like names of proprietary drugs – she recognized a few – and then some

random jotting: *Memo – Muharram 20? 21? – check.*
INSPECTION DATE???? She sat back on her heels,
staring into space. She couldn't make any sense
of it. She held the sheets of paper in her hands
for a few minutes, trying to picture Joe, his pen
moving quickly across the page, the irritation on
his face when he scratched the words *INSPECTION*
DATE in angry capitals, the pen digging into the
paper.

At the bottom of the pile, there were two
forms. They looked like photocopies of application forms – job applications, visa applications?
She couldn't tell. They were written in Arabic.
Each form had a photograph that had come out
dark and blotchy on the copies. She looked at
the first one. A young man with a carefree grin
looked back at her. She knew him now: Haroun
Patel. It was the same photograph that had
appeared with the newspaper article she'd found
in Joe's luggage.

Haroun is dead . . .

There was a second form, only this one was for
a woman – a girl. Her face, pretty despite a rather
tense expression, was framed by the tightly bound
hijab. Her eyes looked at the camera nervously.
Once again, the script was Arabic. Joe had been
able to read it without too much difficulty, but
Roisin was still barely able to distinguish the individual letters; full texts were just meaningless
scrawl to her.

She sat and studied the paper as if staring at it

for long enough would force it to give up its meaning. Eventually the photograph became no more than shapes in grey and white, a meaningless blur on the page in front of her.

36

The Parisian sky was a brilliant blue, but the winter cold cut through Damien as he walked briskly along the broad avenues. The trees, that had been in full leaf the last time he had walked these streets, were bare, their branches dark lines against the sky. The street was busy. The cafés were packed, couples wandered in and out of the shops, and roller-blading teenagers wove through the crowds.

He had last been here seventeen years ago. He'd come here with Catherine in a futile attempt to rescue their marriage from the pit of mistrust and anger it had fallen into. He had been young enough to be drawn to her fragility and her beauty, and to call that feeling love, but that hadn't been enough to make her feel safe and secure, and whatever love he felt for her – and he had felt some – had not lasted the course. He had left her shortly after they returned to England.

He pulled his mind away from a past that he

would rather forget. Now, he was here to find Amy. She'd told Roisin she was in Paris, and that much, at least, was true.

Visitors to France had to register at the hotels where they stayed. He assumed that Amy would be staying with her sister, but he decided to check. He still had contacts at the British Embassy, and after a few phone calls and some reminders of overdue favours, the first of his anxieties was removed. He was able to confirm that Amy had arrived safely in Paris. She had stayed in a small hotel off the Boulevard de Port Royal, close to the cemetery of Montparnasse.

He left the café and took the Métro to Les Gobelins. Amy's hotel was a short walk away. The streets were quieter here, more sheltered from the cutting wind that blew up the river. The hotel itself, as the location suggested, was a small budget establishment. Amy, with an underused Saudi salary under her belt, was still economizing. Maybe she was planning for leaner times ahead. Damien had a quick chat with the concierge and showed her a photograph of Amy. A folded note, for more Euros than the information was probably worth, confirmed the dates of Amy's stay: she'd arrived at the hotel a week after she'd left Riyadh and stayed for a few days. The concierge also told Damien that Madame had spent some time at L'Hôpital Cochin St Vincent de Paul. She'd left the hotel after a few days.

He took the Métro back across the river, where

he found a café. He sat down at a table, ordered some coffee and lit a cigarette while he let his mind wander over what he knew. His own knowledge of Amy's past was minuscule. She'd never talked about it, and he'd never asked her. All he knew was that she came from Newcastle.

Where do you think of when you dream about home?
The North East. I grew up in Newcastle.

But now, thanks to Roisin, he knew that her mother was dead, her father . . . he had no information about her father. She had a half-sister and a stepfather who had apparently abandoned her, as she had been left in care after her mother's death. The sister's name was Jassy. *Jesamine for short.* He smiled, remembering Roisin laughing helplessly as she tried to negotiate her way through the sentence.

He knew where she had been born and where she had grown up. He knew a bit about her family, about when she'd left her home city, and he knew that leaving had been fraught with some kind of difficulty.

She was away from the Kingdom now. Whatever the threat was, they'd left it behind them. Or had they?

The people who had planted the bomb were still free, as were the people who had murdered Joe Massey. He didn't buy the story of Joe Massey's murder being a robbery that had gone wrong. And after talking to Majid, he was no more convinced by the theory of a terrorist attack. Terror went for maximum targets. The people who had got a car bomb through the security at the party could have killed scores of people. Instead, it had exploded some distance from the house, claiming only three casualties.

Somewhere in that complex equation was Haroun Patel and the questions Joe Massey had been asking. Someone didn't want the details of that story known. Had that someone achieved what he wanted by driving them all out of the Kingdom, or was there more to come?

He decided to call Rai, who had promised to monitor developments in Riyadh. He sounded cheerful when he answered Damien's call. 'You are well?' he said.

There had been developments in the Massey case. The police investigating the case were able to confirm that Massey had made it to the hospital. The jacket his wife said he had been wearing was in his office in the pathology department. And they had a witness who had seen his car driving away from the hospital car park. It had been picked up later by a camera on the main road from Riyadh.

The map of Riyadh was still clear in Damien's head as Rai explained where the car had been spotted. Massey had been heading west, on the side of the city where the party had been held, but the route that Rai was describing wouldn't have taken him to the suburb where the Bradshaws lived. It would have taken him towards the city's outer limits.

'There is something else . . .' Rai was warming to his story. 'He has fellow traveller.'

'Fellow . . . ?'

'There is someone in car with him.'

Damien sat in thought for a while once he had put the phone down. Joe Massey had gone somewhere after he'd talked to his wife. The last known sighting of his car had been on the road out of Riyadh, the road that led to the desert where his body had been found. And there had been someone in the car with him. Joe Massey had driven his killer to the place of his death.

Suddenly he felt himself come alert. During his time in Riyadh, he had got used to the constant watchfulness that was necessary to survival. It had become second nature. He was used to monitoring the behaviour of people around him, to knowing who was there, who was changing places, who they were talking to and what they were doing. Something had aroused his subconscious watchman.

He picked his phone up again, and keyed in the number for rail enquiries. As the automated system ran him through a series of options, he spoke briefly, letting his gaze wander around the café. No one seemed to be paying any attention to him, no one was suddenly interested in the menu or their newspaper, no one turned their face away.

He smiled at the waitress, the phone still to his ear, and opened his hand slightly to show her the

348

bank note he was holding. She nodded. He tucked it under his plate in her sight, and stood up. He walked straight out of the door, his senses alert for someone getting hurriedly to their feet, and crossed the road. He went down the steps into the Métro, then placed himself where an information screen shielded him while still allowing him to see who was coming down from the street. He was being paranoid, he knew, but the habits of Riyadh were hard to break.

People streamed down the steps and past him through the ticket barriers. He waited for a while, then walked back up the steps. The feeling of unease had gone.

Paranoia.

He decided not to go back to his hotel but to stay with the crowds heading along the river towards the Louvre. The wind tugged at his scarf and cut into the exposed skin on his face.

The gallery itself was closed. The courtyard opened up around him, a few people wandering across the expanse, looking up at the walls that surrounded them. A small crowd had gathered around the pyramid entrance, talking and gesturing. Plane leaves skittered across the ground as the wind caught them then died away. The last time he'd been here, it had been a bright spring day, and the stone that now looked grey and forbidding had looked golden in the sun. For that short afternoon, he and Catherine had been able to pretend they were happy.

An intermittent sound echoed across the court-yard, and he looked round, trying to locate it. There was something familiar, something evocative about it. He scanned the courtyard trying to locate it, and then the walls, up and up.

High on the wall, impossibly balanced on a ledge below a balcony, a small child sat playing his drum. His serious eyes gazed into the distance, his neat, dark hair undisturbed by the breeze that carried the leaves across the ground. Damien moved closer, curious and alarmed by the almost surreal image of a child drumming high on the walls of the Louvre. Then, as he looked, he saw the repetitive movements of the tiny wrists as they wielded the drumsticks, saw the blank stare of the face, and realized that he was looking at an automaton.

'Realistic, isn't it?'

He turned round. A man was standing behind him, contemplating the drummer. He was wearing a heavy coat and a fedora hat. A scarf muffled his ears. Despite the cold, he looked debonair and jaunty.

Arshak Nazarian.

'Nazarian.' Damien felt a bleak satisfaction that he'd been right. Someone had been watching him. He hadn't been careful enough. 'Last I heard, you were in Damascus.'

Nazarian's eyes were on the automaton. 'It would be easy to mistake it for a real child,' he said. His gaze moved to Damien. 'No, Damascus was just a port of call. I felt the need to be out of the way for a while. I see you have made the same decision. That was probably wise.'

'What brings you to Paris?'

'Business,' Nazarian said shortly. 'You?'

'Nostalgia.'

Nazarian's eyebrows raised in polite incredulity, but he didn't pursue the topic. 'I heard you were looking up old friends.'

'Only the kind you find in places like this. Buildings, statues, memorials . . .' Damien looked up at the automaton again, and waited to see what Nazarian wanted.

'You're not the only one who needs to talk to Amy Seymour, O'Neill. If you find her before I do, tell her to contact me. Tell her it's important.' He slipped a card out of his wallet and handed it to Damien.

As Nazarian spoke, his eyes moved briefly to Damien's injured hand. Damien resisted the impulse to conceal it in his pocket. 'If I see her, I'll pass the message on.'

Nazarian registered the non-intent in his voice. 'I don't know if Amy has any plans to return to the Kingdom,' he said. 'She would be well advised to talk to me first.'

'If I see her, I'll pass the message on,' he said again. 'Are you staying in Paris?'

Nazarian's eyes travelled over the bleak court-yard. 'Not much longer. You?'

'The same.'

'Then I was lucky to run into you.' He nodded a curt farewell.

Damien watched Nazarian walk away. Luck had nothing to do with it. Nazarian had known he was in Paris all along. He had a bad feeling that the only outcome of his own search would be to lead Nazarian closer to Amy.

The cold had penetrated to his bones. After years of living in the Kingdom, his body had no defences against it. He took the Métro back to his hotel. His injured hand felt heavy and clumsy; when he looked at it, he could see the skin had a bluish tinge.

Once he was back in his room, he logged on to the internet and did a quick search for the hospital Amy had visited during her stay.

It was a world-renowned centre for maternity and neonatology. So maybe Amy had told Roisin the simple truth. She had left Riyadh to be with her sister who was about to give birth. He wondered why, in that case, she had chosen to stay in a hotel rather than with her sister. Family tensions? And then she'd signed out, leaving no forwarding address.

Arshak Nazarian was looking for her as well. Amy's dealings with Nazarian, whatever he might think of them, weren't his business, but he wasn't going to help Nazarian to find her.

Joe Massey had been cut, viciously cut. His death had been ugly. And the people who had killed him were still out there. Damien didn't like knives and he didn't like the people who wielded them. If he kept on digging around in Amy's life, he might do more harm than good. But he knew he wasn't going to stop.

37

Roisin couldn't get the visit from the police out of her mind. She could still see the detective standing in her doorway asking, *Did you know that Saudi Arabia doesn't have an extradition treaty with the UK?*

If they were investigating a murder, and if they thought that Joe was implicated, would they continue the investigation now that he was dead? She could remember reading about cases where the prime suspect had died, and the bland comment: *The police are not looking for anyone else.* It was tantamount to an accusation of murder, and one that the accused had no way of refuting.

She needed to know more about the death, more about the inquest where Joe had given evidence. It was several days before the obvious solution occurred to her and she took the tube out to Colindale in the bleak suburbs of North London to visit the British Library newspaper archive.

She presented herself at the desk and after a short wait was issued with a day pass. She'd made notes on her journey out there, and after a quick search through the catalogues, accessed back issues of the *Evening Standard* which were available electronically for the previous eight months. The *Standard* should have reported the incident in some detail. The nationals, she wasn't sure about.

The sheer volume of information was so vast, and the bit she was looking for so tiny, she felt daunted. The detectives had said the woman had died in September the year before. So . . . she tried searching using woman, drown, Thames and different combinations of the words, but she got no useful hits. Then she started on the sections recording the findings of the Coroners' Courts in September and October.

There were two records of people drowned in the Thames in September. One was recorded as suicide, the other was the death of an unknown woman in her early twenties. The verdict had been an open one.

Armed with a date, she began hunting for news reports, and at last she found them. There was the first report of the body being washed up, and then, a couple of days later, a much briefer report noted that a woman had died from drowning. Roisin kcpt going, now having to resort to a page-by-page search. She almost missed the story, though it had been given more prominence than either the discovery of the corpse or the cause of her death: DEAD WOMAN 'ILLEGAL IMMIGRANT' screamed the headline.

The opening two paragraphs were devoted to the dead woman in the river. She was probably from the Indian subcontinent. She carried the marks of a recent beating. She was wearing a distinctive ring. No one had reported her missing and no one had claimed her.

But most of the story was devoted to the number of illegal immigrants in the country, how they came here and the problems they caused. It went on to discuss the problem of trafficking, and the way that women from poor countries were lured to the UK by promises of work, only to find themselves forced into prostitution when they got here.

Roisin sat back in her seat, massaging her temples. The woman had died in the first week of September. The inquest had been towards the end of the month. The dates were etched in her mind. She had a memory for dates that could be her curse: a year ago today, we met. A year ago today, we first made love. A year ago . . . She didn't have to check the date of the inquest again to know it happened a few days before Joe had told her about his plans to return to the Gulf, and had asked her to marry him.

Did you know that Saudi Arabia doesn't have an extradition treaty with the UK . . . ?

She printed off the article. She didn't know where to go now with the information she had. All the way on the long tube journey back to the flat, she swayed to the movement of the train, hanging on to the overhead rail, oblivious to the people crowding on and off at each station. It was the rush hour. She could almost be back a year ago, heading home from work, looking forward to an evening with friends, a glass of wine, a shower – nothing too much on her mind.

She was pushed and jostled as she fought her way through the crowds at King's Cross and headed up the road towards the flats. 'Goddammit, Joe, I need to talk to you!' She was angry with him for being dead, for leaving her with all of this to plague her and no answers to be found. She didn't realize she'd spoken out loud until she heard a voice saying, 'What?'

It was Mari, the woman who had moved into George's flat, who must also just have fought her way out of King's Cross, hampered by a heavy pushchair. 'Nothing,' she said quickly. Then, because that seemed abrupt, she said, 'How are you? I haven't seen you lately.'

'Yeah.' Mari's voice sounded clogged. Her nose was red and as Roisin watched she fished a tissue out of her pocket and blew it resoundingly. 'I've got a cold,' she said unnecessarily. She joggled the pushchair by way of illustration. 'This one's been keeping me up.'

Roisin made a sympathetic face. She could remember when a friend of hers, talking about her own new baby, had said, *Happiness just means getting enough sleep.* 'He'll grow out of it.'

They started to walk up the road together. She could hear Mari's snuffling breath. 'Do you want me to push him for a while?'

'OK.' Mari handed over the pushchair with relief.

Roisin took the handle and smiled at the baby, who was awake. He was a beautiful child with a mass of fair hair. His eyes were dark blue. He still had the slightly crumpled look that babies have in their first weeks. 'Hey, Adam,' she said, smiling again and leaning towards him. This time he seemed to register her, and his eyes fixed on her face.

Mari was silent, so Roisin chatted to the tiny child as she pushed the buggy along the road, which sloped almost imperceptibly upwards. She tried not to puff too audibly. 'Thanks for finding that address for me,' she said to Mari. 'I went to see George. He's fine.'

'George? Oh, the old man. Yeah. Good.' She sneezed.

'He said someone came looking for me, just before he left. No one's been since you moved in, have they?'

Mari shook her head. 'There's not been anyone visiting at all,' she said.

Roisin studied her covertly as they walked up the road. She looked tired and ill. Adam was only a few weeks old. Mari must have barely recovered from the birth, and now she was living on her own with full responsibility for her baby. Roisin wondered how she would have coped at Mari's age.

When they reached the flats, Mari opened the security gate and stood back as Roisin manoeuvred the heavy pram over the threshold.

'If you come along to mine for a minute,' she said, 'there's a letter for you. It got put through my door by mistake. I've been meaning to bring it up.' She led the way as Roisin followed with the pram.

'Home,' she said to the baby as Mari unlocked the door. She unbuckled the straps and lifted him out, carefully supporting his head. 'Hello, Adam,' she said, holding him up to her face. He gazed at her with unblinking eyes. 'Shall I take his bonnet off?'

'It's a hat,' Mari said. 'He's a boy.'

'His hat,' Roisin corrected herself, carefully loosening the ties and easing it off the child's head. She freed him from the tight wrappings, and looked round for somewhere to put him.

'I'll take him,' Mari said, carefully cradling him. 'He might go to sleep now. Here's the letter.' She handed Roisin a rather battered manila envelope.

Roisin took it. 'Thanks.' She remembered how she had got to know George through the postman's inability to tell the difference between 13 and 31. 'Listen, I meant it about baby sitting,' she said. 'Here –' She scribbled her number on a piece of paper.

Mari studied it. 'It doesn't seem right to leave him,' she said.

359

'If you need to catch up on your sleep, or if you decide you want to go out, just call. Any time.'

'OK,' Mari said. 'Thanks.'

Roisin stuffed the envelope into her bag as she went up the stairs. Mari's flat, from her brief glimpse of it, looked spartan and comfortless, but there didn't seem to be anything else she could do. She'd made friendly overtures, and she'd offered to baby sit. Anything else would be intrusive.

Besides, she had other things to think about.

Damien called her two days later to say he was back. She felt uncertain with him, remembering, but only half-remembering, her drunken confidences. His voice sounded cautious as they talked, as if he was wary of what she was going to say. Maybe he thought she regularly drank herself into oblivion to cope with Joe's death, not knowing that, before the oblivion, the dreams came, and they were far worse than anything she endured sober.

'Something happened the day after we met,' she said. 'The police came looking for Joe.'

'The police? What did they want?'

She told him about the interview, and the disturbing remark that the man had made as they left. 'I looked the case up in the newspaper archives. There was an inquest – they said the woman had drowned.'

'I'll come over,' he said. 'OK?'

Half an hour later, he was at the flat, shaking the rain off his mac as he came through the door.

'You're soaked.' She offered him a towel.

'I walked,' he admitted, rubbing the worst of the wet off his hair. 'You forget . . . in Riyadh, when it rains, it's warm. Here . . .' He gave her back the towel. He was dressed more casually than she had seen him, in jeans and an open-necked shirt. His hair was tousled where he'd rubbed it dry. He touched his fingers to the radiator, and gave a rueful smile when he realized she'd seen him. 'I can't seem to get warm.'

'You're what my grandfather would have called *nesh.*'

'Nesh?'

'It's a Yorkshire word. It means you feel the cold.' But what he was feeling was more than that, she knew. He was still recovering from his injuries, and he had not long since come from one of the hottest places in the world. 'I'll make us some coffee.'

He followed her through to the kitchen and leaned in the doorway, watching her as she filled the kettle and spooned coffee into a jug. 'I'm sorry about the other night,' she said.

He raised an enquiring eyebrow.

'I drank too much. I hope I didn't . . .'

'You were fine. It probably did you good.'

The kettle was boiling. She made the coffee Arab style, crushing some cardamom seeds into the jug before she poured in the water. The

361

fragrance of the spice filled the room and, for a moment, she was back in the house in Riyadh. Her hand shook as she poured the coffee.

They went into the living room and he sank down into one of the armchairs. He looked drained – worse than he had done when she'd seen him before, when he was straight off the plane.

'OK,' he said. 'Tell me about this police business.'

She told him about the two detectives, about the woman Joe had seen fall into the river, about what the detective had said. She told him about the ring that had been on the dead woman's finger, and the connection with Riyadh, but she didn't tell him about Yasmin's disturbing request. He listened without commenting, a line appearing between his eyes.

'I went to the library and copied the newspaper articles,' she said. 'And I went through Joe's papers.'

She held out the sheaf of papers she'd found in the suitcases the morning the police came. 'These . . . These are the papers Joe was working on.'

Damien took them and flicked through, frowning. She saw him stop when he saw Haroun Patel's photo, and again when he saw the one with the photo of the girl. 'I'll need a bit of time with these,' he said.

'I'll make some more coffee.'

She left him reading as she put the kettle on

and tidied up the kitchen. When she came back, Damien was sitting at the table with the papers spread out in front of him. He looked up, his face serious.

'What have you found?'

'I'm trying to put this together,' he said. 'You were right about what your husband was doing. All this stuff – it's from around the time of the drugs theft, the one that got Patel into trouble. He put together a timeline. I've been trying to follow it. Look –' He moved his chair and she came and sat next to him and looked at the papers spread out in front of her. 'This is a driver's schedule.' He pointed to the top of the page. 'That's Patel's itinerary. He took the hospital van out the day before the drugs went missing to take deliveries to the clinics in the villages, OK?'

She nodded.

'It looks as though your husband spent some time making sure those deliveries actually took place – he's confirmed them all. Judging from the time of the last delivery, Patel would have got back to Riyadh around ten that night, at the earliest.' He looked at her to make sure she was following what he was saying. 'Here, we've got the inventory of the drugs stock. They completed it at eight thirty that evening, the day before the check was due. All present and correct. But by eight the next morning, the morphine has gone.' He looked into the distance, his eyes narrowed in thought. 'So unless the thief was a key holder – and Haroun

Patel certainly wasn't – the morphine vanished sometime after eight thirty but before the pharmacy was closed for the night, which would have been about nine, nine thirty – more or less immediately after the late drugs round. So it can't have been Patel who stole the drugs.'

'But . . . the police would have looked at this, wouldn't they?'

'I doubt it. They found the drugs in his locker and they got their confession. They'd just say that Haroun stole the security codes or had an accomplice. It could have happened like that, I suppose, but it's unlikely. It had all the signs of an impulse theft. If it had been that well planned, the thieves wouldn't have left the stuff lying around. Besides, why touch anything the day before an audit? Everyone knew it was going to happen. You don't mess around with the Saudi police.'

'So they executed an innocent man?'

He shrugged. 'Any country that has the death penalty executes innocent men. It's par for the course. That's not what this is about. The authorities wouldn't have been worried about this. As far as they were concerned, Patel got due process. What I don't understand is why . . .'

'You're saying Joe was killed for this? Someone killed him because of this?'

He rubbed the back of his head. 'That's what I don't see. Why would they? If Joe had taken this to the authorities, no one would have been interested. They lost some drugs. They had a culprit.

End of story. Another thing I don't understand is why he was chasing it. He must have known it was pointless. There was no way the authorities were going to reopen the case. No way they'd even look at it. The Saudi courts don't make mistakes.'

'Haroun was his friend,' Roisin said. 'I think Joe felt responsible for him. He knew Haroun in London when he was a student here. It was Joe who suggested he look for work in Saudi.' Joe had cared. He'd cared enough to go back, to go over all the evidence, to . . . what? 'What about these?' She pushed forward the two forms. She hadn't been able to decipher them because they were written in Arabic.

'They're applications for visas to Saudi. I know what the first one is. It's Haroun Patel's.' He picked it up and skimmed it. 'I'd forgotten that . . .' He shook his head. 'It doesn't matter. There's nothing there that's secret. His age, his sponsor, where he came from . . .' He looked at the photo of the smiling young man. 'Haroun,' he said. 'I knew him. He was one of those people who gets to know everybody. He was a good guy. He didn't deserve what happened to him.'

He picked up the second form. 'This is just the same. And from the same source, I suspect. Was Joe into computers?'

Roisin nodded. 'He was pretty good. He liked to play around with them, and he took computing as an extra course at uni.'

Damien nodded, as if this had confirmed something he already suspected. 'But it's just the same kind of information – name, date of birth . . .' There was a moment's silence. 'Oh, Christ.'

'What?'

'Her name's Patel. She gives Haroun as – she's his sister.'

Just for a moment, relief flooded over her. It wasn't Jesal Rajkhumar. Whatever Joe had been doing, it was nothing to do with the woman Yasmin had been looking for.

And then Damien spoke again and she was pushing her chair away from the table, jumping to her feet as the cold lump formed in her stomach.

'Her name's Jesal,' he said. 'Jesal Rajkhumar Patel.'

38

There is a girl who is missing – we want to know where she is, but we haven't been able to find her.

Did you know that Saudi Arabia doesn't have an extradition treaty with the UK?

Damien's voice seemed to come from miles away. 'Roisin!'

She blinked and she was back in the flat. Damien was on his feet, looking at her in alarm. 'OK, come and sit down. You've gone white.' He steered her across to the settee and sat her down. 'What is it? What's wrong?'

'Yasmin. She asked me . . . just before she had her baby, she asked me to look for this woman.'

She felt his hand on her arm tense. 'You're sure? Yasmin asked you to look for Jesal Patel?'

She nodded. 'Yes. No . . . not quite. She asked me to find Jesal Rajkhumar.'

'Rajkhumar isn't a family name. A lot of Gujratis take their father's name as a second name. Or women take their husband's. What did

367

Yasmin say, Roisin? As closely as you can remember.'

She closed her eyes. She was back there, sitting in the incongruously familiar Starbucks in the middle of the glittering opulence of the mall. 'Yasmin said . . . there was a girl who was missing. She had been a maid, I think. She'd been accused of stealing from her employer before she ran away. Yasmin hinted that there had been something going on, some kind of abuse. The dead woman – I think this is her. Jesal Rajkhumar.'

'Oh, Christ.' His voice was calm, but she could hear the underlying tension. 'Did Yasmin say who this woman was working for?'

She shook her head. 'No.'

'Was it her family?'

'I don't remember. I don't think so. What's this about, Damien?' If she'd said something to Joe, would everything be different?

He didn't reply at first, then he said, 'How much do you know about the immigrant labour system in Saudi?'

'Not much.'

'The first thing you need to know is that Saudi is a country that hasn't long revoked its slavery laws. And the Saudis – the urban ones, the middle-class ones, the wealthy ones – they think they're a chosen people. As if the world hasn't got enough of those.' His smile contained no humour. 'Non-Saudis count for nothing. They employ a lot of domestic staff from the third world and they don't look after them well. The life of a domestic employee is hard. They work long hours, they get treated badly, their employers sometimes abuse them. Saudi is a very repressed society – it isn't uncommon for the women to be raped. Often, the employers hold their documents so the women are pretty much trapped.'

'Slaves,' she said.

'More or less. Yasmin's father makes his money by bringing women like this into Saudi. If this girl wanted to get away, if she was being abused, it would have been difficult. She wouldn't have her passport, she wouldn't have an exit permit. To get that, she'd have had to pay back everything she owed, which would have been a lot of money – that may be why she stole in the first place. Once she'd been convicted of theft – and if her accuser was a Saudi, she would have been convicted – she would have faced jail and a flogging.'

'They'd have flogged her? But she wasn't even a Saudi!'

He shrugged. 'Nationality doesn't come into it if you're a third-worlder. They're a bit more circumspect when the government has more power, but they've flogged Westerners too. They just haven't executed any – yet.'

She looked at him. 'Civilized of them.'

'That's the way it's done, Roisin. Don't pretend you didn't know. If you take the money, you subscribe to the system.'

She couldn't answer that. 'Why didn't she go

to her brother? If she was being abused – Christ, if she was being raped – he was there. He could have helped her.'

He frowned. 'Sex . . . it's hard for us to understand the kinds of attitudes that exist around it in other cultures. In Pakistan, in the rural communities . . . I came across a case a few years ago. A man thought his wife had been unfaithful, so he strung her up from the ceiling, beat her, cut off her nose and ears and gouged out her eyes with a piece of wire. He scraped his fingers round the inside of the sockets to make sure there was nothing left. No one in the village took any action against him. She was the one who became a pariah. The only reason it ever came to trial was because a government minister, a woman, took up the case.'

Roisin swallowed her nausea. 'And you think that Haroun . . . ?' She had never met him, but he had been Joe's friend. She couldn't equate that level of cruelty and barbarism with the smiling face she had seen in the photograph.

'No. Haroun was an educated man, a reformer. He would have tried to help his sister. But it would explain why she couldn't go back.' He was frowning as he looked at the papers. 'You've just given him the most believable motive I've seen so far for taking the drugs, but these papers show that he didn't.' He put his face in his hands, then looked at her. His eyes were weary. 'There's something else. The Haroun Patel case – it was investigated by Yasmin's husband.'

'Her husband's a police officer?'

'She never told you?'

'It never came up.' They'd never discussed their homes or their families. They'd talked about work, about politics, about the status of women.

Damien was studying the papers again. She could tell by his slight tension that there was something else he wanted to say. She waited.

'Roisin, do you think . . . Shit, I hate to ask you this, but I've got to. Do you think that Joe could have been involved in the kidnapping of Majid's baby? Some kind of revenge thing because his friend had been killed? Or . . .' He shrugged as he met her gaze. 'There has to be a connection.'

She shook her head at once. Not Joe. 'No. Never.'

'I'm sorry,' he said. 'I had to ask.'

The Saudi police had thought Joe might be involved as well. And so had the consulate. She understood, now, the reason for the haste when she was rushed out of the country. 'You're not the only one,' she said. Her voice sounded dull in her ears. Joe the killer, Joe the kidnapper – how easy it would be to pin it all on one dead man.

'I'm sorry,' Damien said again.

'You didn't know him.' They sat in silence for a while, then she said with an effort, 'Is there any news about Yasmin's baby?'

He shook his head.

'I should contact her. She was a good friend to me.'

'Maybe you'd better leave it. For the moment.'

She looked at him, but his expression gave nothing away. 'I bought the baby a present. A cashmere shawl. It's probably here, somewhere.'

He gestured at the papers in front of him. 'Did Yasmin say why she wanted to find this woman?'

Yasmin had looked tired and stressed that day. 'I don't know. She said she was worried about her, that's all. I'm trying to remember.' All that was clear in her mind was the way the colour had drained out of Yasmin's face. 'She said she'd vanished "last year", but she wasn't any more specific than that.'

'Haroun died in April 2004. That would have been . . .' he closed his eyes as he worked it out '. . . Safar or Rabi Al-Awaal.' He saw her incomprehension. 'The Hegira year has twelve months like the Gregorian calendar, but it starts in Muharram, which is around February, and ends in Thw al-Hijjah which is January–February. So "last year", . . . depending which calendar she meant . . .'

'Could be either before or after Haroun was executed.'

'Right. Or even arrested. That may have been the trigger that made her run. But, whatever happened, it happened long before Yasmin approached you. Why did she come to you then?'

'I didn't ask.' And she should have done. She could see that now. Now she could see all the questions she should have asked Yasmin.

372

'I can't get a clear picture. I need to get some distance from it.' He sighed. 'I don't have a lot of time. I didn't find what I was looking for in Paris.'

'Amy,' she said. 'You were looking for Amy.'

'That was the plan. She'd been there, but I have no idea where she is now. Amy and I had a bust-up before she left. I think she might be lying low.'

'If she doesn't want to see you, then why . . . ?'

'I'm worried about her.' His eyes met hers. 'Amy was asking questions about Haroun Patel too.'

'Oh, Christ.' She sat down on the settee. She could remember Joe, that night after the party when she'd told him about Amy, and he'd said, *Why stir it up? If I were you, I'd leave it.* He'd known what he was doing was dangerous. He'd tried to keep her away from it. She felt her eyes sting, and kept her face down as she spoke. 'When Amy called me to tell me she was in Paris, she sounded . . .' In her recollection, Amy's voice had been high and . . . what? Excited? Edgy? The words had seemed to spill out and she hadn't seemed fully in control of her breathing. She looked up at Damien. 'Frightened,' she said.

He was silent. The lamplight cast shadows across his face. She could see the hollow in his throat, his skin brown against the white shirt. 'Then I still need to find her. I'm pretty sure she's left Paris.'

'If she came to the UK,' Roisin said slowly, 'she might go back to Newcastle.' Amy, leaning out of the carriage window, calling out, over and over.

What had happened on that trip to London to make her stay away all those years, and what had happened now to make her vanish again? She felt as though her world was crumbling away around her, turning to dust in her fingers as she tried to hold on to it. Her parents were dead, her sister was dead. They didn't even live on in her memory, just as a moment of laughter and someone pushing her as she sat on a pile of leaves in a wheelbarrow, just a hand in hers as a camera clicked, and a line from a song *Between the salt water and the sea sand* . . . Her father, her adopted father, was dead. Joe was gone. And now Amy had faded away into silence.

'What is it?' Damien had moved beside her and was brushing her hair off her face.

She shook her head. There weren't any words. The orange lights were starting to flicker in her mind, trying to take her to a place where she didn't want to go. She was too tired to fight. 'I just can't make it stop,' she said.

He kissed her gently, then put his arms round her and drew her in closer as he kissed her again. He smelled warm and male and his closeness was healing against the wounds of the past few weeks.

'Stay,' she said. 'Tonight. Stay with me.'

He drew back slightly. 'Are you sure? Is that what you want?'

'It's what I want. I need to know that I survived.'

'You survived, Roisin.'

She shook her head. 'I don't know,' she said. 'I don't know.'

'You do. You know.' He ran his fingers down her neck, then ducked his head to kiss her throat. He unbuttoned her blouse and slipped it down off her shoulders. His hands felt warm on her skin. He pushed the sleeves down her arms, freeing her breasts from the fabric. His fingers stroked her nipples, then pinched them gently as they stood erect. 'See? Do you believe me now?' His hands were still caressing her as he spoke.

'No. No, I don't. I need you to show me more.'

He kissed her again. When he spoke, his mouth was close to hers. 'Roisin, you know that I'm leaving soon. I've only got this to give you.'

'I know. This is what I want.'

The past stepped back into a distant place that it would return from later, but now, here and now, it was giving her respite. The future was nothing, just a blank, but it didn't matter. What mattered was the moment.

When she woke up, the room was dark. The green light from the radio told her it was six. She could remember Damien waking her an hour before, his mouth pressing down on hers and his voice whispering, 'Roisin, I have to go.' Then she had sunk back into a dreamless sleep.

She could just make out the shapes of the rumpled sheets, the indentation in the pillow where his head had been. She slid across the bed and put her face against it. It had to be her imagination, but it felt warm, as though the occupant had left the bed just the moment before. She closed her eyes.

Roisin? Hey, babes . . .

She was sitting bolt upright, her hand groping for the light switch. In the sudden brightness, the window was a black square of night. The room was empty. There was just her, sitting up in the rumpled bed.

'Joe?' she whispered.

But there was only silence.

39

Damien left Roisin in the early morning. He tried not to think about her, her face warm and sleepy on the pillow as she roused herself to kiss him goodbye, but she lingered in his mind. For Roisin, it had been a break from the exhausting struggle out of the depths of grief and chaos; for him, a sweet and memorable interlude in the emptiness that seemed to be his life these days.

He and Amy had always clashed against the emotional barriers they both hid behind. It was as if they could only make contact when those barriers were ablaze with their need, and afterwards they had to negotiate their way through the ashes.

Roisin had no barriers, or maybe she hadn't needed them. She had opened herself to him without any restraints, to his hands, his mouth, his tongue – to all of him. When he had left her, her face on the pillow was relaxed in sleep as if their night together had swept away the demons that were haunting her. He had woken her with a kiss to tell her he had to leave, and she had kissed him back, warmly. He had had to fight the impulse to stay.

He took a taxi back to his flat. There was information he wanted to check. One thing he had forgotten until Roisin had talked about it was that Patel had completed almost two years of study at the University of London, in the School of Pharmacy, before he had been made to leave because of visa violations. This had been just two years before his death.

And Massey's connection with Haroun Patel was of longer standing than he had realized. Patel had been not just Massey's friend but his protégé. He let his mind wander over the possibility that he had broached to Roisin, and that she had so emphatically dismissed. Something had been wrong at the hospital. The diagnosis of the infant's serious condition had been delayed, and then the blood tests and the lab results had vanished with the child. Had Massey taken a terrible revenge for Patel's death? But he had found Roisin's dismissal of that idea convincing. He hadn't much liked Massey, but he couldn't see the man he had met, the man who had conducted that meticulous investigation into Haroun Patel's death, engineering the murder of an innocent child.

But he was now convinced that Majid's child was dead.

University colleges and schools were vast places,

and tutors probably had little recollection of their students, two years down the line. But events had made Haroun memorable. He had been getting good grades when his course had been abruptly terminated, and the manner of his death could hardly have been missed by the people who had known him.

Later that morning, he headed back towards King's Cross. He walked away from the chaos of the station, down Gray's Inn Road towards Brunswick Square where the School of Pharmacy was based. Barts Hospital was nearby.

The School of Pharmacy edged on to an area of parkland where grass fought with mud in the damp ground. The trees were bare now, but in summer, the place would be leafy and attractive.

He'd phoned beforehand, so when he gave his name at the reception desk it wasn't long before a brisk-looking man in a white coat appeared and began shaking his hand with enthusiasm. He introduced himself as Paul Halloran. 'It was a dreadful business,' he said, without preamble. 'I'm glad that people are starting to do something about it. Far too late, of course.'

'How well did you know Haroun when he was a student?'

'Oh, quite well. He was in my labs sessions. He wasn't one of the brilliant ones. To be honest, most of those go for the courses that will lead to research. Haroun was bright, and he was a hard worker. That's the big secret. Hard work will get you a lot further than genius. He was thinking of switching to a medical degree, if he could afford it.'

'He knew one of the doctors at Barts, right?'

Halloran looked taken aback. 'Amazing you knowing that. Yes, one of the visiting lecturers – not someone I knew. He was the one who persuaded Haroun to switch to medicine – thought he had the ability. Haroun was keen, but there were cost implications. I was going to look into grants for him.'

'It was a waste that he couldn't finish.'

Halloran made a sound of disgust. 'It was a disgrace. They should just have given him a rap on the knuckles. All he was doing was working longer hours than his visa allowed. OK, he shouldn't have done it, but plenty do. They need the money. Where's the harm? And Haroun was in love, God help him.'

'In love?' Damien kept his voice casual, but suddenly he was alert. Haroun Patel came from a traditional family – his marriage arrangements would have been in the hands of his parents. He'd married not long after he'd returned to Pakistan. 'He had a girlfriend? A local woman?'

'No. She was a student who was over here from Europe to improve her English. But she wasn't European. Her family were from Saudi Arabia, I think.'

Saudi. Damien could see the glimmer of his quarry, far in the distance, as the light caught, just for a second, something that was supposed to be hidden. 'Saudi Arabia?'

Halloran cast him a quick look. 'Yes. Her father whisked her off PDQ, once he knew what was going on. Next thing we heard, Haroun had lost his visa. There was some speculation afterwards. Dirty work at the crossroads and all that. But I'm afraid I can't help you any more than that. I don't *know* anything.'

'It was two years ago. Students who studied with him must still be here. Would any of them know?'

'I'll ask. Is there somewhere I can contact you?'

Damien left his e-mail and his mobile number. He wasn't sure how long he'd be staying in London. But the timing was clear in his mind. Two years ago, Nazarian had brought his daughter Yasmin home. Not long after that, she had married Majid. Just over a year later, the man who had been in an illicit flirtation in London with a Saudi girl had died at the instigation of the man Yasmin had married.

40

In the days that followed, Roisin found that something had changed. When she opened her eyes in the morning, she wasn't escaping any more from the flickering light of the fire. The days no longer seemed like a void she had to fill to stop her mind from falling into it. She started walking by the river again, and even went jogging by the canal, shocked by the way her fitness had deteriorated.

Joe's absence was a sharp, deep pain, but it felt like a clean pain, as though a wound that had been infected was no longer festering and was beginning the long, hard process of healing. She missed him with an aching regret. He was the first thing she thought about when she woke up and the last thing before she fell asleep at night. She still felt the lurch of recognition when a tall, dark-haired man came into view, still watched with irrational hope until the familiar figure became a stranger who looked at her with puzzled unease. But the dreams had changed.

Now, she dreamed about him, dreamed about their life together, dreamed about the life they would never have, and often woke up with the glad realization that he was still alive, only to face the bleak reality once more. But the flickering flames and the pale face glimmering in the night had gone to wherever it was that nightmares went.

Damien phoned to tell her he would be away from London for a few days. 'How are you?' he said.

'Surviving.'

Someone had survived. She just wasn't sure who it was.

A week after Damien had left, Roisin was sitting at the small breakfast bar in her flat. She was drinking coffee and talking to Joe, a conversation that had started when she came back to London, and ran through her head in a constant flow.

Do you mind? That he stayed? I love you.

And I can't be here.

I know. And I've got to keep going. Somehow.

She went through to the living room and turned on her computer, intending to do an internet search for teaching work overseas. Instead, she found herself typing in the URL of the King Saud University web site. She'd had no contact from the university, and had made no attempt to contact any of the people she had got to know. The thought of Yasmin, still without her baby, tugged at her.

She explored the familiar pages, the photos of buildings she knew, the road her taxi used to follow to take her to the women's college, the map of the campus, the names of the staff. She saw that Souad was about to have another book published on the problems of translation, and was due to speak at a conference in Dubai. But there was a name missing. Yasmin's name was no longer on the list of staff in the English Language Department.

She hesitated, then entered her password. She logged on to the discussion forum. Yasmin might have posted something there. And she wanted to know if Najia now had any contact with the university at all, or if she was condemned, like her mother, to become a woman whose life was confined to the home and the false freedom of the shopping malls under the watchful eyes of her guardians.

The topics flashed up on to the screen: *Help with essay writing; English idioms.* The thread she'd started herself, *Life in the UK,* was still attracting visitors. She moved on to the *Social interaction and discussion* site. The topics seemed to range from the devout to the banal: *Hey, it's my birthday; I need the advise; Blessings on our great ruler.* There was nothing posted by Red Rose, and the threads that had been there were gone. There was nothing to show that political discussion had ever occurred on the site.

She scrolled through her address book until she found Yasmin's home e-mail. She thought for a minute, then wrote: *Dear Yasmin, I have been thinking about you a lot since I left the Kingdom. I heard the terrible news about your baby. I'm so very sorry. With much love, Roisin.*

She couldn't ask about the missing girl, Jesal. Not now. She clicked *send*, then remembered that she still had Najia's e-mail address as well. She could ask Najia. She wasn't sure how private it would be, so she kept the content anodyne:

Dear Najia, I hope you are well. I am back in the UK. I'm not sure what I am going to do next. I heard the news about Yasmin's baby. If there's anything I can do, let me know. Are you still concerned about the person we discussed that day at the mall? With much love, Roisin.

Then she went back to the university site. For some reason, her log-on had expired. She tried to log on again. A message flashed up on the screen: *Incorrect login and password.* She tried again, in case she had mistyped it, but the response was the same.

Her visit to the site had been observed, and in the brief time since she had left it, someone had revoked her password.

The computer chimed to tell her that she had new mail. She looked in her inbox. *Undeliverable.* Her e-mail to Yasmin had been returned.

The recipient's name is not recognized.

Damien was leaving for Newcastle later that day. Before he set off, he decided it was time to check in with Rai. He looked at his watch. It would be late morning in Riyadh. He keyed in the number

385

and stood by the window watching the people walking past in the street as he waited.

'Damien?' Rai sounded anxious. 'I expect to hear from you.'

'Yes, I'm sorry. I've been busy. Is there any news?'

Rai's voice sounded grim. 'There is news. After you go, I look at everything, you understand?'

'Yes.' This was Damien's own method of dealing with intractable problems: go back to the beginning. He listened as Rai went over it again. Joe Massey had not arrived at the meeting to which he had been summoned, but he must have made it to the hospital. His jacket had been found in the laboratory where he customarily worked. Massey must have arrived at the hospital and gone to the lab to collect his notes for the meeting. Or maybe he'd never had any intention of attending that meeting. Maybe there was something in those notes that had to be kept secret. Whatever had happened, they had vanished. Then . . .

Massey had been seen leaving the hospital. The security camera had picked him up in the car park. And then one of the traffic cameras had filmed his car travelling west out of the city, and there had been a passenger travelling with him. Whoever that person had been, he had not come forward. So far, nothing Rai had told him was 'news' – certainly not the kind of news that Rai's dark tone had intimated. He waited.

'But now there is something else. The missing

386

reports – they find one on Joe Massey's desk. And he was doing some work on it they don't understand. But what the report tells them – the blood group. Your friend Majid, he cannot be the father of that child.'

Damien felt everything freeze inside him. *Cannot be the father* . . . Jesus Christ! He thought about Majid's phone call the night the baby was born, and about the way happiness could burn away to ashes. And Yasmin . . . In the Kingdom, adultery was considered a serious crime, on a par with murder. 'Where's Yasmin? Where's Majid's wife?'

Rai's voice was sombre. 'No one has seen her.'

Nazarian. His influence might protect her for a while. But Majid was not a political man, he was a man of convictions. If he thought that his wife had committed adultery, and then had planned to pass off another man's child as his . . . He wouldn't wait for the courts, and no court in the country would convict him for that. Why wasn't Nazarian there to protect his daughter?

He rested his head against the cool of the glass. Majid was his friend. And yet Majid would do this thing – he had no doubts about that. He thought about the face he had seen in the window that day. That face had haunted him from the moment he had first glimpsed her at the window.

Yasmin.

He wondered if she had known even then that she was going to die.

41

The main road into Newcastle swept over the river on a high iron bridge. Damien almost missed his turning, a small road that took him down to the level of the river, across a low swing bridge that stood in the shadow of the Victorian behemoths that carried the road and the railway.

He had booked into a small hotel on the riverside. It was on a narrow cobbled street, one of a row of buildings that had probably been offices and warehouses once, old with warped timbers and small, low-ceilinged rooms, converted now into bars and restaurants.

This was the city where Amy had grown up. She'd talked about it to him, not so very long ago. *Sometimes I can't wait to go home. But the trouble is I don't know where home is any more . . . The place I dream about? It doesn't exist, not now.*

If she wanted to get away, this was where she would come. Roisin had talked with a wistful nostalgia about the days that she and Amy had spent here together, and even allowing for the large quantity of red wine she had drunk that evening, there had been the ring of authenticity to her story. Damien thought that maybe Amy had been happy here. He wasn't sure she had been happy anywhere else.

He checked in to his hotel, then walked along the quayside to look at the restoration of one of the glories of industrial England.

As he came out of the shelter of the bridge, the wind battered him. High above, sea birds screamed. The river flowed past, glittering in the winter light. The heavy stone stanchions of the iron bridge loomed over him. Down the river, he could see the new bridge, a thread of steel arcing across the water to the far side where a square, four-towered building stood. It was bleak and beautiful.

But he wouldn't locate Amy here. He left the river, and walked up a steep hill into the city centre. The road wound round under the high arches of one of the bridges, unexpected passageways and flights of steps leading away, a city of narrow alleyways and dark passages, the forbidding northern version of the old cities of the Gulf.

He was here to track down Amy's sister, the elusive Jassy – Jesamine for short. The recollection made him smile. He had a feeling that, wherever Jassy was, Amy would be close by, but in order to find her, he needed to know her name. His first port of call was the Register Office. He could have done this by phone, but he only had one starting point: Amy's name and her date of birth. Anything else would depend on what he found. It was quicker to come here himself than to play the game of telephone to-and-fro that would use up the little time he had.

He'd known her by her married name, Seymour, but she'd been born Amy Fenwick – something else he had found out from Roisin. He knew her birthday, so it was easy enough to get a copy of her birth certificate.

The information didn't get him much further. Amy's mother was Marguerite Fenwick, née Johnson. Her father was Martin Fenwick. It wasn't hard to track down the marriage certificate. Marguerite Johnson had married Martin Fenwick when she was eighteen and he was twenty. They'd married three months before the birth of their daughter.

The marriage had ended when Amy was still a small child. As for Marguerite's second marriage, he had no time for a painstaking trawl through the records based on what little information he had. But he did know that Amy had been ten when Jesamine was born, which gave him a twelve-month period in which to look for Jesamine's birth records.

He waited until one of the clerks was free, then went and gave her the details he had. 'I'm trying to find a distant relative,' he said. 'Family history.'

The woman smiled her comprehension. Tracing family history had become a popular hobby for large numbers of people; it was as if a realization had dawned that everyone's family went back ultimately to one absolute root, and people were trying, in an insecure world, to anchor themselves as closely as they could to that one sure point.

'I don't have much information,' he said. 'She was born in 1981. Her mother was called Marguerite. I don't have the father's surname. Her given name is Jesamine. Any chance of finding her in the records?'

The woman leaned over the paper he'd given her. 'Do you have the mother's maiden name?'

'It's Johnson, and she was married to a man called Martin Fenwick before she married Jesamine's father.'

'You don't know which area?'

He shook his head.

The woman bit her lip as she thought. 'We could do a search, but it's going to take us a bit of time. We're very busy. And we might not find anything.'

'I'd be grateful for any help you could give me.' He smiled at her, and she smiled back.

'I'll find it,' she said. 'If it's here.'

He filled in the application form she gave him and paid the required fee. He remembered the ease with which Nazarian had tracked him through the streets of Paris, and left the name 'David Johnson'. The clerk wanted postal details, but he explained he was a visitor who would be moving around. 'I'll be back in a week,' he said. 'I'll call in then.'

'If we don't find it,' she said, 'you could try the Family Records Centre. They would do a search for you. I'm not saying they'll have more success, but . . .'

'Thank you. You've been very helpful.' He made a note to do that when he got back to London, and left the building. He walked briskly towards the main shopping area, aware of the chill cutting into him. His arm was aching and his hand was starting to throb with pain. He needed to get out of the cold. He found a café – one of the ubiquitous chains that had sprung up all over the country – and ordered the smallest cup of coffee he could. It came in a huge, heavy mug, a bucket of indifferent grey fluid. He sat down by a window, looking out at the street. The window was partly obscured by condensation, and every time someone came in to the café, a blast of cold air cut through the dank humidity. The British had no talent for comfort.

The café was quiet enough. He took out his phone and checked his messaging service. There was one message for him from Rai, an impene-trably cryptic reference to 'revolver doors going round and round', and something about 'more people than you see'. He tried returning the call, but there was no reply. He'd have to try later.

Roisin had asked him a good question: *If she doesn't want to see you, then why . . . ?* Why was he looking for Amy? Because she had left Riyadh so suddenly, because Roisin had said she sounded frightened, because Nazarian was looking for her – and because he had things he needed to say to her. He wanted to tell her that he was sorry for the way things had been, and he wanted to tell her that, if what she had said was true, if she had really wanted it to work, then that was what he wanted too. They could go somewhere else, somewhere they could make a life together. They could give it a chance.

And if she said *No*? Then at least he would have tried. For once in his life he wouldn't have walked away from something that could have been valuable.

But in the meantime, he had to make sure she was safe. She had got herself involved with Nazarian. She knew something or she had found something out, something that had driven her out of Riyadh, shortly before an attempt was made on the lives of the other people involved in the Patel case. And whatever it was, it was keeping her away not just from the Kingdom, but from her friends and her work.

He stared out through the misted window, letting his mind work through the problem. But in all his calculations, he had forgotten the one crucial thing about the northern cities. You could lose yourself for ever in London, in Paris, in New York, if that was what you chose to do. But Newcastle was a village by comparison. As he pushed aside his unfinished coffee and stood up, he could see the street outside more clearly. And there, looking into a shop window, veiled in scarves against the cold, her bright hair a beacon in the grey day, was Amy.

42

'Amy.'

She spun round. The bag she was holding dropped to the ground. Her face was white with shock, and she stepped backwards, her hands held up as if she was warding him off.

'Steady.' He put his hand against her arm and she stared at him in disbelief.

'Damien! I thought it was . . . Oh, God, you gave me a fright.' He could feel her shaking.

'Thought it was who?'

'No one! It was just . . . I didn't expect. Oh, God.' The blankness of shock was gradually leaving her face as she looked at him. 'Damien. It's really you. I was so . . . when I heard. I thought you were going to die.'

'I've got a thick skull. I'm not easy to kill. Look, we can't talk here. Do you want to get some coffee?' Her eyes followed his to the steamed-up window of the café. That was no place for the conversation they had to have. 'I'm staying in a hotel about five minutes down the hill. We'll be better there.'

She made an attempt to smile. 'You always were a fast mover. Five minutes and you're asking me back to your hotel. I . . .' She looked at his face and the brittle smile faded. 'Yes, OK, your hotel.'

They didn't speak as they walked down the hill. Damien had to resist the impulse to grip her arm to stop her from disappearing again. 'This way,' he said. 'It's just opposite the bridge, on the water-front.'

She stopped and looked up at the iron girders far above them. 'I used to come here all the time when I was younger. With Roisin. You see up there?' She pointed. 'We used to go up on the bridge and sketch the view down the river. This was all so different then . . .' She turned away. 'Come on.'

The hotel had a small coffee lounge that was unoccupied at this time of day. He took Amy there and put her in a seat by the fire. Then he ordered coffee from the receptionist.

When he came back, the pinched, frightened look had gone from her face, but she kept glancing nervously round the room as they began to talk. 'So, what brings you to Newcastle?'

'I could ask you the same question.'

'Me? I live here. I told you I might not come back to Riyadh. I've got a job, now I'm looking for a house.'

So simple. 'And I'm here because you're here.

I was looking for you.' The warmth of the fire was bringing the delicate flush to her skin that he remembered so well. Drops of water from the misty day sparkled in her hair like jewels.

'But . . . How did you know where to find me?'

'You talked about it – remember? You said it was the place you dreamed about.'

She studied his face. 'You remembered that?'

'I remembered. And I talked to Roisin.'

'Roisin . . . But why? Why were you looking for me?'

'You know why. They killed Joe Massey. They tried to kill me and Roisin. And if you'd been at that party, they might have succeeded in killing you.'

'It was a terrorist attack, wasn't it? That's why I haven't gone back. I don't want to get blown up. It wasn't . . . personal.'

He wondered if she really believed that. 'Maybe. But everyone who was asking questions about Haroun Patel is either dead or gone from Riyadh.'

He watched her face closely. He could see her start to say something, then she stopped. Her eyes moved away from his face. 'That's just coincidence. No one liked what happened to Haroun. Lots of people said things.'

'That's not what Arshak Nazarian thinks.'

'Nazar . . .' Her voice faded away.

'I saw him in Paris. He gave me a message for you. He wants you to contact him. He said it was important.'

She swallowed. 'Nazarian? I thought . . . Why were you in Paris?'

'I went to look for you.'

'Christ, Damien! What the hell did you think you were doing?'

It was like being back in Riyadh. A quiet interlude had become a battlefield.

'I told you, Amy. I was worried about you.'

She was quiet for a minute. 'It's just . . . I have some issues with my family. I don't want anyone upsetting them.'

'I didn't meet your family. I have no idea where they are.'

She chewed her lip, but didn't say anything.

'Maybe if you tell me about it, I'll understand what's going on here. You told me that you were leaving, but you didn't say it was final.' He spoke quickly as she drew a breath to interrupt him. 'You said *maybe*. Amy, you don't just walk out on the kind of position you had in Riyadh. It isn't just the work, it's . . .' He didn't need to finish the sentence. It was her professional reputation that was at stake.

She shrugged. 'Sometimes you have to make these decisions.'

'OK. But it isn't too late.' The hospital would be accommodating. They didn't want to lose someone with Amy's skills.

'I can't. I don't like letting people down, but . . . my sister needs me closer to home. That's more important.' She was quiet for a moment, choosing her words. 'I feel bad about the clinics – the women's clinics. I didn't tell them I might be leaving for good. When you go back . . .'

'If,' he said. '*If* I go back.'

'You might not? I can't believe you won't go back.'

He gave her her own words. 'Sometimes you have to make these decisions.'

Her gaze dropped. 'I'm sorry. If it's anything to do with me. I'm sorry.'

'No.' He touched her hand. 'It wasn't you. What is it you want me to do?'

'If . . . if it seems like the right thing . . . go to the clinic in al-Bakri and tell them I've gone. That I'm sorry.'

'If it seems like the right thing? Amy, how in hell should I know that? That's your decision, not mine.' He waited, but she didn't say anything. 'OK. If I go back, I'll do that. Your sister – is she here?'

She shook her head, and reached into her bag for a packet of cigarettes. She offered him one, but he shook his head. 'She's in Paris.'

'And she's had the baby?'

'Yes.' She smiled suddenly. 'I'm an aunt.'

'And it's all right?'

'Fine. So is Jassy.'

'Good.'

Amy was playing with her cigarette, pinching the end and turning it round and round in her fingers. 'My mother . . . I never told you about her, did I?'

'You never told me much about anything.'

'I hated her when she died. Or I thought I did. I blamed her. But I still miss her. She was lovely. Her hair . . . it was the colour of honey, you know? And she was fun, she used to play with us – me and Jassy. She must have been very young when she had me. She liked going out, she liked dancing, but he used to stop her doing that.'

'He?'

'My stepfather. I never knew my real father. She married my stepfather when I was eight. We moved to London – I never told you that, did I? Our lives changed just like that. We had a house, and I went to this private school, and . . . He was . . .' she shook her head '. . . different, I suppose. I was used to my friends' dads back in Newcastle, they liked a drink, they watched football, they didn't have much to do with their kids. But my stepfather . . . He was very generous, he used to buy me stuff. I had all the clothes I wanted. But he had to know who my friends were, he had to know exactly where I was. It pissed me off, but it made me feel as though he cared.' She laughed without humour. 'Or that's what I thought at the time.'

Damien didn't say anything, just waited.

'Then my mum left him. I don't know why. I think it was because he wanted to live abroad and she didn't. She went back to Newcastle and moved in with someone else, and she took me and Jassy with her. And then her new boyfriend left and Mum just went to pieces. All the things that made our home just fell apart. Mum was drinking too much and it was just row after row. Then she died in a car crash. I thought that we'd be OK, then. I thought my stepdad would come for us.' She looked at Damien and shrugged. 'He did, but he didn't want me. He took Jassy, and left me behind. So I ended up in care.'

Damien leaned forward to take her hand. 'That was rough.'

'Yeah. It was. But I wasn't his child.'

'Roisin said that you left Newcastle to find them.'

'Four years on.' She shook her head and picked up her coffee, tasted it and put it down again. Her face was averted.

'You found them? You must have done. You're in touch with your sister now.'

'When I was seventeen, I found an address for them. In London. My mother had left us a bit of money, and it was due to come to me when I was eighteen. The solicitor wrote to me, and there was an address for my stepfather as well. So I went to see him. I wanted to tell him, you know, I'm an adult now, I'm not going to ask you for anything, I just want to see Jassy. After Mum left him, it was more or less me bringing Jassy up. I hadn't seen her for four years. I missed her.'

She looked at the cigarette in her hand. 'It seemed like he was pleased to see me. Of course I could see Jassy. She was away at school. I was lucky I'd called that day because he was just about to leave. He was going to collect her. They'd be back in a few days. He booked me into a hotel. "You don't want to be on your own in the flat," he said. Actually, I'd never stayed in a hotel. It terrified me. But he was doing me a favour – or that's what I thought. He paid the bill up front and everything. And a week later, the day he said they were due back, I went to see them. I got all dressed up – I was just a scruffy kid from Newcastle, and Jassy had been living this different life, I wanted her to be proud of me. And . . .'

She sat tensely for a few seconds, her eyes focused on her hands. 'When I got to the flat, the security guy wouldn't let me in. My stepfather had gone. He'd sold the flat and left the country. Jassy had never even been there. There'd never been a child at that flat – it was just a place he used when he was in London. I think he felt sorry for me, the security guy, and that made me so angry. *I'm fine*, I said and walked out. Only I wasn't fine. I didn't have anywhere to stay, and I'd spent all my money. And I couldn't come back here. I just couldn't . . . The people I knew, once they found out what . . . How could I face them? So . . .'

'Amy.' Damien didn't know if he was more shocked or angry at the story she had told. 'I'm sorry,' he said inadequately.

She smiled, a bleak, bitter smile. 'Why? You didn't do anything.'

'I'm sorry that it happened to you.'

'It was a long time ago. I survived. You do.'

At the moment, she didn't look like a survivor. 'Why didn't you tell me before?'

'It was all in the past by the time I met you. It didn't matter, not any more.'

'Of course it mattered.'

'It's not something I want to remember. I had to do some pretty dodgy things to survive. That first night, I had nowhere to go. This guy picked me up and took me back to his place. In the morning, he gave me money.' She shook her head. 'I was lucky it wasn't worse.'

'You were seventeen, Amy. Someone who was supposed to have responsibility for you left you with nothing. OK, you did something stupid. So did I when I was seventeen. And after.'

She smiled with genuine humour. 'Christ, Damien, don't tell me you sold your arse on the streets.'

And he found he could laugh. 'No. Nobody made me an offer. But I've done other things. One day, I'll tell you.'

'OK. One day. I'll hold you to that.' She touched his injured hand. 'Something hurt you,' she said. 'I didn't think anything could hurt you.'

'Does that make you like me better?'

'It makes you more real.' She ran her fingers over his and he registered the spreading numbness in his hand. 'After all of this, do you still . . . ?'

'Love you? Of course.'

Her eyes were shiny and he saw the colour flood her face. 'You never told me that.'

'Didn't I? I thought I told you every time I saw you.'

'Maybe. But not in a way I could understand. It's too late now.' Her tone was final.

'Is it?' There was a moment of silence, then he quickly moved them away from the dangerous ground. 'Did I tell you I've seen Roisin?'

'How is she?' Her voice was oddly incurious.

'Not too good, but she's getting there.' He planned to call her later, bring her up to date with what was happening. 'I think she'd like to hear from you.'

'I know.' Amy studied the carpet. 'I have a track record of letting Roisin down. I'll call her. I will.'

He knew her well enough to know that she'd told him everything she was going to. 'I wish you'd trust me. I wish you'd tell me what you're so frightened of.'

Her response was instant. 'I'm not frightened. Get out of my head, Damien.'

He didn't say anything, just watched her in silence as her eyes moved away from his and back. She flushed. 'I decided not to go back because I'm afraid I'll get killed. Is that clear enough?'

He smiled faintly and shook his head. It was a good enough reason, but it didn't explain the fear he'd seen in her eyes when he'd first spoken to her.

43

Roisin wandered restlessly round the flat, checking her e-mail periodically. Each time something arrived, she checked it eagerly, but each time it was spam. It was almost nine before the chime from her computer signalled the reply she was waiting for. Najia had e-mailed back.

Dear Roisin
I am glad you are getting in touch, and I am very
sorry about your husband. I hope you be better
soon. The person you ask about, it doesn't matter.
But she went in Shawwal. I don't know when that
is your month.
*   I have no news about Yasmin. She doesn't*
contact anyone. I am coming to classes again, but I
cannot study English no more. My brother say I
have enough English because I will not be working
anywhere but maybe small things in KSA so
perhaps he is right. I don't know.

Thank you for being good friend to me. May God bless you.
Najia

Roisin sat staring at the screen, then sent back, *Please send me Yasmin's new e-mail address.* She couldn't believe these two women had retreated into silence. They had been so different that day at the mall. Najia had been angry at the restrictions that were being imposed on her. Roisin could remember her voice, low and tense, as she argued her case. Yasmin's eyes had been scanning the floor behind Roisin, looking out for the returning Bakul.

Then suddenly, the colour had drained from Yasmin's face. There had been a panic to get her things together, then she, Najia and Bakul had left. Later that week, she had gone into labour, and then her baby had been abducted.

What had Yasmin seen that had upset her so much? Roisin sat for a while with her eyes shut, letting the scene reconstruct itself, but all she could see were the faces of the two women and the glitter of the coffee machine and the shelves behind the counter. There was nothing. She had been sitting with her back to whatever it was.

She waited by her computer, willing Najia to reply instantly, but nothing came back. She wandered restlessly round the flat, then decided she may as well go out. She would drive herself mad waiting here. She looked out of the window.

The winter had settled into a dull greyness, but at least it wasn't raining.

As she came out of her front door, she noticed with irritation that someone had discarded cigarette ends on the landing. The cleaning of the common areas was sketchy, to say the least, and a constant source of friction between the managing agents and the tenants. Roisin had never really got involved with it, but she did object to someone using her doorway as an ashtray.

The street was crowded, and she was being jostled on the pavement, so she turned off and walked through the backstreets of Bloomsbury, past the green enclosures of the squares, gardens confined behind railings that struggled to thrive in the shadows of the tall buildings. She remembered the hard light of Riyadh, the etched shadows, Joe slipping the silver bangles round her wrist, Damien, a stranger then, urging them through the streets until she had taken a wrong turning and ended up in as-Sa'ah Square.

Damien who had touched her life lightly, who had made love to her for one long night and had then gone. She heard his voice from the first day: *After 9/11, a bad joke went round Riyadh that they used it to train the hijackers . . .* She could see the gleaming towers above her. The Kingdom Centre, where she had gone that day to meet Yasmin and Najia. And they'd talked about Jesal – Jesal whom Najia no longer wanted her to search for. *The person you ask about, it doesn't matter*. Shawwal. Jesal had disappeared in the month of Shawwal.

Which was . . . she reached for her phone and began to key in Damien's number, then decided that she didn't want to disturb him. Instead, she turned back on to the main streets and walked briskly down to Charing Cross Road where the bookshops were. She went into Foyles and found the books on Arabic culture. She flicked through them until she found one with the Hegira calendar.

Shawwal. That fell between November and December. When Yasmin had said *last year* she was referring to the Gregorian calendar. She and Damien had assumed what had happened to Haroun Patel had triggered Jesal's disappearance, but in fact she had gone long before the drugs incident that had led to her brother's arrest.

What had Yasmin said about Jesal? That she had run away, and she had stolen some jewellery.

The police had shown her a heavy ring engraved in Arabic that had been on a dead woman's finger . . .

It was coming back to her now. Yasmin had said: *I tried to help her, but then she disappeared and . . . no one . . . seemed to know what had happened to her.*

Roisin felt the book drop from her hands and grabbed for it before it fell to the floor. She had always used her maiden name at the university – it was the one on all her teaching documents. And she, Yasmin and Najia hadn't talked about their home lives, their families, their husbands. She could remember her own surprise when Damien had told her that Yasmin's husband was a high-ranking police officer. And that day at the mall she had told Yasmin: *I can ask a few discreet questions at the hospital. My husband, Joe, he's a pathologist, he works there. I'm not sure if there's . . .*

That was when Yasmin had dropped her cup, her face going white with shock. It hadn't been because of something she had seen. What had caused the colour to drain out of her face was the realization that she had just confided her secret to Joe Massey's wife.

Did you know that Saudi Arabia doesn't have an extradition treaty with the UK?

44

After Amy had gone, Damien stayed by the fire in the hotel lounge. It was late afternoon, and the hotel was getting busier. He let the noise and bustle of the arrivals distract him from his thoughts as he sat staring into the fire. Amy's story had left him with a feeling of weary disgust at the way she had been treated, and he was trying to lose the image of a vulnerable seventeen-year-old left to fend for herself on the streets of London.

He still had no idea what was happening, or if there was any link between Amy's disappearance and the events in Riyadh. Roisin had described Amy as 'frightened' when she'd called to say she was leaving, and everything he'd seen told him that she was still afraid.

He went up to his room. The place depressed him – the pale walls and floors, the production-line bland art, the standard minimalism of the design. He was willing to bet that a thousand hotel rooms like this existed across the country and that he could move from one to the other, barely aware of the transition. He'd preferred the shabby, run-down interior of Roisin's flat – it was a home where a person lived, a person with individual tastes and a life to lead. This place was dead.

Amy had scribbled down her address before she left. She'd taken a flat on the Byker Wall, a temporary rental while she looked for somewhere to buy. 'It's central, and you can always get a flat in Byker,' she said. 'I had one there when I came out of care. It's a nostalgia thing.'

He'd achieved everything he'd come up north for. He'd hoped to find a route to track Amy down; instead, he'd found her. And though he still wasn't convinced by her story, it was no longer up to him to pursue it. If she needed his help, she would ask him. And if she needed him . . . He would talk to her again, once.

He felt weary beyond belief. His hand ached, sending hot wires of pain up his arm. He had a sudden longing to be back in his house in Riyadh, sitting in the spice-scented shadows of the upstairs room, watching the patterns from the blind moving across the floor.

Outside, he heard the sound of the wind rising.

By the time Roisin got back to the flat, it was already dark. Her mind was going over and over what she had just realized.

Yasmin had known something about Joe, and whatever it was, it had terrified her. And then her

411

baby had been taken. Now Yasmin was in trouble – excluded from work, separated from her friends, her e-mail contact apparently cut off. Why?

Joe had been called into work that day, that last day. He'd talked about it in the car afterwards. *They wanted me to review a death. A baby died a few days ago.* He'd done a post mortem, and he'd said that the baby had died because it was premature. And then he'd said . . . *there's something I should . . . This fucking country. I don't know what to do.* Maybe Joe had known something about Yasmin . . . And Yasmin's baby had been stolen, and still hadn't been found.

She looked at her computer, and saw that the *new messages* icon was showing. Najia. At last.

But the e-mail wasn't from Najia. It was from Souad:

Roisin, I have information from Najia's brother that he does not wish you to contact her. There has been enough trouble at the university from bad influences as you well know. I must ask you to make no further communication with any of the students.

Roisin hit the *reply* button:

I have no idea what you are talking about. If you don't wish me to contact Najia again, you must give me your reasons.

412

This time, the reply came within five minutes.

If you contact Najia, you will only cause her trouble. There is talk. They are saying that Yasmin's husband was not the father of her child.

Damien was jerked out of a deep sleep by the sound of the phone. He sat up, reaching for the light switch. He was sitting in a chair in an anonymous room. Rain was battering against his window, and in the orange light of the street lamps, he could see the water running down the glass. The window rattled as the wind blew, and in the background, he could hear the low roar of a river running full.

For a dizzying moment he had no idea where he was. Then the ladder of memory lifted him out of his confusion and the events of the day came flooding back. The phone was still ringing. He checked his watch. It was only half past seven. He picked it up. 'O'Neill.'

'I have found something that is wrong.'

For a moment, he couldn't make sense of what the speaker on the other end of the line was saying. There was an echo, and the voice sounded distorted, then he realized it was Rai, calling from the Kingdom. 'Rai! What? What's wrong?' He realized he hadn't called Rai about the odd message he'd left – he'd shelved it. He hadn't been thinking straight.

'Wait.' He put the phone down and went and splashed water on his face to wake himself up. Then he picked the phone up. 'Sorry. I was asleep. Tell me. What is it?' It had to be urgent for Rai to have called.

'I have checked at the hospital, because I hear there is trouble. They make a mistake. They look at the results more closely, the missing baby, and they find that this blood, the blood of the baby who is so unexpectedly ill, comes from a different child altogether. Not Majid's child, not Yasmin's child. But from one who die the day before Majid's child was taken.'

It took Damien a moment to understand the implications of this. Somehow, in the hospital system, there had been a terrible mistake. The hospital had mixed up the blood samples and diagnosed a healthy child as gravely ill.

Yasmin's child had been healthy when he was born, then there had been a blood test and the child had been whisked away to the ITU for sick and premature babies. He could remember Majid's face when they talked in the car park, his grief and his dawning suspicion that there was something wrong at the hospital. And Damien's own visit and the technician's puzzlement as he looked at the report.

He wondered how long it had been before anyone had thought to check that the blood test that ruled Majid out as the father of the child also ruled out Yasmin as his mother. This wasn't just a mistake, it was a mistake that could have proven fatal.

Maybe it had. They would have treated Majid's child for an illness he didn't have, treatment that could have seriously damaged or killed him.

And then the child had vanished.

45

Not the father of Yasmin's child . . .

Roisin stood at the window watching the light starting to fade. The last cars were leaving the building site, and the street was quiet. The white van was back in its niche by the disused gate. She decided it must belong to one of the residents in the flats. She wished it was spring. She wanted the light evenings back. And summer. Maybe by summer she would know what she wanted to do. Maybe by summer she would be able to see beyond the next few days. Not the father of Yasmin's child . . . No wonder Yasmin had been so afraid – but she hadn't been frightened for herself. She'd been afraid for a woman she barely knew, a runaway maid called Jesal.

Roisin thought about the e-mail address that no longer worked, and wondered if Yasmin was still alive. She shook her head to clear the thoughts away and picked up the phone. She wanted to see if Damien had called while she had been out.

She wanted to talk to him. She wanted to talk to him about Yasmin, and tell him what Souad had said about Najia. There was no message, but one person had phoned. She checked the number – someone had called her from Newcastle.

With a tug of anxiety about her mother, she called back and waited as a phone rang at the other end. She was just about to hang up, when a voice said. 'Hello?' It was low and cautious.

'Hello. This is Roisin Massey. You called this number earlier.'

There was silence, then the voice came back more clearly. 'Roisin, it's Amy.'

For a moment, surprise took her voice away. 'Amy! My God.'

'I'm sorry I haven't been in touch before. And I'm so sorry about Joe.'

'Yes.' She felt her throat tighten and spoke quickly. 'You're in Newcastle! I told Damien that was where you'd be. Did he find you?'

'Yes. I saw him today. And I'm coming to see you.' Amy's voice was fast and breathy, the same as it had been when she made that last call from Riyadh. 'There's a train that leaves in forty-five minutes – it gets in just after ten thirty. I was calling to make sure you were there.'

'You're coming to London tonight?'

'Yes – is that OK? I can get a hotel room when I . . .'

'You don't need a hotel. You can stay here.'

'Are you sure?'

'Of course I am.'

'Roisin, I . . . OK. Thank you. I'll call you when I get to King's Cross.'

After Amy had rung off, Roisin forced her mind on to practical things. She went and got some clean sheets, and made up the sofa bed in the tiny study. Then she went into the kitchen to see if there was anything to eat. She knew she was using these domestic details to stop her from thinking about Amy's impending visit. What had Damien said to bring her racing down to London with such urgency?

Was it just concern about her welfare? She and Amy had been close friends in the past, but that had been a long time ago. Did she know more about Haroun Patel? Damien said she, like Joe, had been asking questions. Or was it something else? Roisin concentrated on slicing onions and putting them to soften in some warm oil.

The phone rang, jerking her out of her reverie. 'Hello?'

'Roisin?' It was a woman's voice, and she sounded strained and shaky. A baby was howling in the background. 'It's Mari. From downstairs. I've fallen. I think my leg . . .'

'Hang on. I'm on my way.' Roisin grabbed her keys and ran down two flights of stairs and along the walkway to number 13. Unlucky for some. She rattled the handle, and heard the sound of someone moving on the other side. She could hear Adam's howls reach screaming pitch, and Mari's

voice saying effortfully, 'It's all right. I'm coming
. . . Oh shit. Jesus.' And then the door opened and
Mari, white faced, was standing there supporting
herself against the doorframe.

Roisin caught her as she collapsed and eased
her back down to the floor. One foot was still
encased in a high-heeled sandal – presumably the
cause of her fall. Her ankle was swollen and
misshapen and her breath came in sharp gasps.
She was shivering. 'Have you called an ambulance?'

Mari shook her head. 'I can't go to hospital. I
can't leave . . .' Her normally pale face was
bleached of colour. Roisin ran through to the main
room and saw the screaming baby in a cot. OK,
Adam was safe. She found the phone and called
an ambulance, giving them the information as
quickly and concisely as she could.

She went into the bedroom and pulled the cover
off the bed. Then she went back to Mari. She put
the cover over her, holding it away from her
injured ankle, then pulled off her own sweater
and rolled it up into a makeshift pillow. Mari's
foot was swelling rapidly so she unbuckled the
strap of the shoe, eliciting a groan and a barrage
of swearing from Mari, but she didn't attempt to
do anything else. She didn't have first-aid training.

'Adam's fine,' she said. 'He's just had a fright.'

'See to . . .' The tears were streaming down
Mari's face. 'I can't go to hospital. I don't want
the social . . .' Roisin didn't know anything about

419

Mari's background, but she had the same brittle independence that Roisin could remember in Amy at that age. Was Mari another refugee from care, aware of the hovering system that might take her baby away from her?

'Adam's fine,' she said firmly. 'I'll see to him in a minute. Don't worry. I'll take care of him for now. Is there someone . . . ?'

'No one. There's no one. You're not to . . .'

'Don't worry,' Roisin said again. Her mind was working fast. If Mari's leg was broken, it would need setting. She would probably need a general anaesthetic which would mean at least an overnight stay in hospital. OK. Roisin didn't have anything better to do. 'I can take care of him.'

The ambulance was there in less than twenty minutes, but it felt like for ever. Mari's eyes were beginning to look glazed. Roisin, worried she was going into shock, sat with her, talking about anything that came into her mind, about the way Mari had decorated the flat, the poor state of the staircases and walkways in the block . . . anything to stop Mari drifting into unconsciousness. She watched as the paramedics strapped the injured girl into a chair and carried her out of the flat.

The baby's howls had barely abated, and Roisin found herself alone in the sparsely furnished rooms in sole charge of a baby who was less than two months old. Adam had had a bad fright and he wasn't easy to soothe. She jogged him gently in her arms, and sang to him. She found a feeding bottle and gave him some milk, and gradually his crying quietened to hiccups and then silence.

She had to decide what to do. Adam would be happier in familiar surroundings, but Roisin had things she needed to do, and Amy would be arriving in just over an hour. She hunted round the flat. It was very different from the days of shabby clutter when George lived here. There was little furniture, but the space was filled with baby equipment – a chair, a padded playpen, stuffed toys, baby clothes hanging over drying racks and over the radiators, a huge teddy bear that must have dwarfed Mari, never mind Adam.

Working one-handed, she found a bag and packed it up with nappies, baby milk and some toys. She looked at the pushchair, which was as beautifully upholstered and sprung as a top-line car, but decided not to use it. She could remember its weight. It would be a nightmare to drag it up the steps. There was a detachable carry-cot – that would do.

She pocketed Mari's keys and slung the bag across her shoulder. Adam was well wrapped up in a hooded sleeping suit, but it was freezing outside. She wrapped him in a blanket and tucked him into the carry-cot, then, almost impossibly burdened, she set off along the walkway. She noticed that the security door wasn't properly shut. The ambulance men must have forgotten to close it. She couldn't leave it like that – not round King's Cross.

She pushed it to shut it, but it seemed to be

jammed. There was a stone stuck under it and she had to step out into the street to free it. A vehicle switched on its lights catching her and the baby in the dazzle. Then they went out, leaving her in darkness. She blinked the afterimages away, feeling the door start to swing free. She stepped back and heard the lock click shut behind her.

When she got into her flat she dumped everything on the floor and lifted Adam out of the cot. He'd stopped crying. She sat on the settee, cradling him. His eyes were fixed on her face. The world must be an amazing place until familiarity turned its regular miracles into the commonplace. Roisin smiled at him and touched his nose with the tip of her finger. His eyes opened even wider and he kicked his legs.

'Pretty cool, hey?' Roisin said.

He made an *ah ah* sound and kicked his legs again.

They played like that for a while. She found he liked big, bright things that he could focus on and make an attempt to grasp with his hands. He seemed to like peek-a-boo games, and when she blew in the soft folds of his neck, it made him chuckle. She changed him, and put him back into the hooded sleeping suit. The night was cold, and she was suddenly aware of the chill draughts from the poorly fitting windows. He was becoming fretful and she had to walk up and down rocking him until he fell asleep.

She could hear the wind starting to blow,

rattling the windows and clattering the spilled rubbish around in the air well. But the flat felt secure against the stormy night, and the baby was a warm weight in her arms.

For the first time since that night in Riyadh, she felt happy.

Damien made himself go to the hotel bar and order something to eat. He sat in the fashionably minimalist expanse of polished floor, steel-topped tables, dim lighting, listening to the voices of the evening drinkers echoing round him, the sound perceptibly rising as the evening went on and more and more people piled in.

The past few weeks were catching up with him. He felt as though he'd reached the end of his resources. Fatigue was like an ache inside him, and his arm felt heavy and cold – or hot? He couldn't tell. He looked at his hand. The skin was white with a bluish tinge, except for his fingers which were swollen and painful.

The wrong blood. He wondered what treatments had been given to Majid's child before the error was spotted. Unnecessary drugs? Too much oxygen? More radical treatment? And what would the result have been? A hospital error that harmed – or proved fatal – to the child of a high-ranking police officer. The penalties would have been severe for all those implicated in the mistake. So severe that it was worth the risk of removing the child? Or the child's body . . .

He thought about the face he had seen in the window that day. That face had haunted him from the moment he had first glimpsed her looking down from the window. Yasmin. He wondered if she knew that her child was probably dead.

The waitress put a plate in front of him. He couldn't remember what he'd ordered; it looked like some kind of elaborate sandwich, garnished with an assortment of leaves. She fussed round him for a minute, offering him a choice of dressings, waving a pepper grinder at him, then hurried off. He had no appetite.

Something was nagging at him. Damien shook his head to clear it. He felt hot, and his mind wouldn't focus. Before . . . There had been something . . . Rai's message. Rai had left that odd message that had been pushed out his mind by the news about the mistake at the hospital.

He drank some water, grimacing at the slight bitterness of the lemon that was floating in the jug. He hadn't asked, and Rai hadn't said what it was that he had found. It was after eight. Rai would be asleep by now.

But Damien needed to know. He had half a picture – any bits that were available might help to complete it. He took out his phone, but the noise in the bar was rising. He paid his bill, leaving the sandwich untouched on the table, and went into the lobby where it was quieter. He keyed in Rai's number and waited as it rang.

'Damien?' Rai sounded bleary.

'Yes, I'm sorry to wake you. I . . .'

'You are OK?' Rai's voice sharpened with sudden anxiety.

'Yes, yes, I just needed to check . . .'

'You do not sound OK,' Rai said flatly.

'I'm tired. I'll be fine once I can get this sorted out and get some sleep. You left a message a few days ago, something about "revolver doors", something you were going to check. What was it?'

'I am not certain yet. I want to . . .'

'Yes. But I need to know what it is.'

Rai stopped arguing. 'I look at who leaves the country that day.'

Damien waited. The police had already done this. There can't have been a name on those flight schedules that rang any alarm bells.

'I look at flights, but I also talk to the drivers,' Rai said. 'And that night – the night of the bomb – one driver takes someone we know from Riyadh to Bahrain, someone who leaves the country by road across the causeway.'

The King Fahd causeway that linked Bahrain with the town of al-Khobar in the east of the Kingdom, a five-hour drive from Riyadh. *Someone we know*. 'Who was it?'

'This is why I want to check it. It has to be mistake, because this person has already left the Kingdom.'

'*Who*, Rai?'

'It is Amy Seymour.'

46

The storm caught Damien as soon as he stepped out of the hotel. The rain was bouncing up from the cobbles and the wind seized him as he moved away from the shelter of the bridge. He gritted his teeth and braced himself against it as he ran to the car park. His raincoat, a heavy riding mac that he'd bought in anticipation of the British weather, barely protected him. By the time he was behind the wheel, his hair was dripping and the bottoms of his trousers flapped wetly against his legs.

He put the car into gear and then hesitated. He remembered that day in Paris when Nazarian had found him. Was he leading the people Amy was afraid of straight to her? But she was making no effort to conceal her location. She'd been strolling about openly, making no attempt to hide. Besides, she had questions to answer. He had to talk to her. Now.

He kept his eyes on the road as he drove, watching the mirror, watching the cars around him. The traffic was light. The storm had kept a lot of people indoors. The road was wet and the water splashed up under his wheels. The light from the street lamps wavered and shattered. His headlights picked out the pillars of a flyover, blocks of flats looming darkly out of the night, and gone.

The Byker Wall presented a blank face to the city, a wall in reality, not just in name. Its massive presence was ominous and forbidding. He didn't want to risk his car in the estate so he left it outside a nearby supermarket. He crossed the wide road where heavy lorries threw the spray in great sheets as they ran their cargoes through the night, and went in through the wide entrance.

And the world around him was transformed. The noise of the traffic was silenced by the wall. He was in a wide basin where the flats tiered up around him. Lights illuminated paths and walkways, and he could see the shapes of trees, and the shadows of creepers tumbling from balconies. He had a feeling that in daylight, there would be bright colours. It was almost as if he'd left the dark city and stepped into a Mediterranean hill village, except the cutting edge of the wind and the sharp needles of the rain were there to disabuse him.

And there were other reminders that destroyed the fleeting illusion. Litter blew around on the ground. Discarded fast-food containers were tangled in the creepers. There was graffiti on the fences, and jagged gaps where the timber had been pulled away.

He followed the path through the estate, looking at the numbers. The housing consisted of apartment blocks, maisonettes and houses. Amy's flat was in one of the blocks, on the first floor, not far from the entry point he'd used. He found the door to the stairwell, noting as he went in that the security locks had been recently vandalized – he could see the fresh marks on the metal. The door swung open.

The steps were bare and functional. Here, the lights had all gone and he had to feel his way up in the darkness, his hand on the gritty brick of the walls. When he reached the first level, he found that the lights were also out along the walkway. The clouds must be thinning, because there was a glimmer of moonlight through the slatted timbers of the roof.

He became aware of the stillness around him. Music was playing from somewhere close by, a dull *thump* of bass that sounded insistently. Dogs barked in the distance and voices shouted, but here, there was no sign of life apart from the music that beat out almost below the threshold of hearing. As he moved along the walkway, he passed the front doors that were firmly shut, windows with the curtains pulled across and no glimmer of light showing, as though the inhabitants had decided to hide themselves away from the night.

Like animals who knew there was a predator abroad.

The music drew him on.

Amy's flat was at the far end of the walkway. He was moving carefully now, stepping quietly, his senses alert. The door of her flat was a dark shadow, closed like all the others. He reached out and pushed it gently.

It swung open and the heavy beat poured out into the night.

He hesitated on the threshold. He wanted to call for help, but he didn't know who might answer, or what secrets Amy was hiding. He stepped inside and pulled the door shut. There was no key, but there was a bolt. It wasn't damaged. He pulled it across. He didn't want anyone coming into the flat behind him.

He moved along the corridor, registering the doors and the layout. Room to his right, door open, check, empty. Room to his left, in, check, out. At the end of the corridor was the main living room. He could see the bulk of furniture against the faint light that came from the window. The music was louder.

He pressed the light switch, and the window became a black square. If anyone was watching in the night, they now knew he was here. He crossed the room and turned off the CD player that stood on a low table.

Silence.

He took in the room in one moment of perception: a closed door at the far side of the room, a settee, an armchair, a TV. A book lay open on the floor. There was a coffee table in the window. The drawers on the small sideboard were half open, and papers were scattered across its surface.

As his ears adjusted, he became aware of an electronic sound that glided between two notes, persistent and penetrating. The phone had been left off the hook. He picked up the handset and hung up, then out of curiosity checked the last caller. The number was familiar. He ran it through his mind and came up with a name.

Roisin. Roisin had called Amy earlier that evening.

He crossed the room to the sideboard. He wanted to check through the papers that had been scattered there. There were two framed photographs that he glanced at, then looked at again as what he had seen clamoured for his attention. He picked them up.

The first one he looked at was of two girls – the older one was in the leggy, awkward stage of early adolescence. He recognized her at once as a young Amy. The other girl was a child, small, plump, with dark chestnut hair. Even given the difference in ages, there was an uncanny similarity between the faces. Amy's sister, Jassy.

He looked at the second photograph. It was hard to tell where it had been taken – against an anonymous background of a modern street. Amy, the Amy he knew, looked back at him. The young woman with her was unmistakably the child of the earlier photograph, now grown up. She was wearing a long coat and the hijab. He'd only seen this face unveiled once before, but he had never forgotten it, looking out from an upstairs window, staring at him for a long moment as their eyes met.

Yasmin.

Yasmin was Amy's half-sister. Yasmin was Jassy, the sister Amy had lost and then found. That was what had haunted him about the face at the window. His subconscious had recognized the similarity that his conscious mind had missed. But Amy had left Riyadh for this woman, to be with her when she had her baby . . . He began to realize the significance of what Rai had told him.

He had seen Amy at the airport, but he hadn't seen her leave.

Amy had been in Riyadh the night of the party.

Arshak Nazarian was her stepfather.

Oh, Jesus.

And now, as a cold finger crept up his back, he became aware of the flat around him. It was freezing. Even with the door shut, there was no warmth building up. He touched the radiator. It was on. There was a faint smell – as if someone had been cooking and something had burned. And the silence wasn't absolute. There was a sound almost below the threshold of hearing, a low roar like the sound of a central heating boiler.

His eyes moved to the closed door at the far side of the room. The kitchen.

Slowly, unwillingly, but irresistibly drawn, he went towards it and pushed it open.

The sound immediately became louder. It was the noise of a kitchen fan, turned up to full blast. The window was wide open, the cold air pouring in. He could see water on the floor from the rain. His eye was drawn to the old-fashioned hob where a metal coil glowed, the dull red fading in places to a grey, ashy bloom. There were bits caught on the metal, charred black by the red hot iron. A pan lay on its side by the stove.

He took another step into the room, his foot losing traction as he stepped on something that had been spilled on the floor. He put his hand against the wall to keep his balance. The smell was stronger here.

And then he saw the figure crumpled on the floor. He could see the frill from a sleeve, the drape of a long skirt. And the blaze of red hair.

Amy.

'Amy!' He was across the room and kneeling down beside her almost before he was aware of what he had seen. 'Amy!'

Her hand, curled up against her body, had been burned almost to the bone. The flesh was blistered, red and oozing in places, blackened in others, clenched by the burning into a claw. 'Amy. Jesus . . .' He brushed the hair back from her face and swallowed the bubble of nausea that rose in his throat. Her face was a battered, contused mass, her visible eye swollen shut, her lip torn and crusted with dried blood.

He could see Amy standing by the shutters in

432

his house in Riyadh, could see the line of her jaw, the fine, delicate skin gleaming as the light and shadows moved across her. 'It's Damien. It's OK, love. I'm here now.' He was barely aware of what he was saying as he let his hand touch her shoulder, gently, but firmly enough that she would feel it. As he spoke, he was keying the number of the emergency services into his phone. 'Ambulance. Fast.'

He looked at her, his mind trying to fight its way through the priorities that were clamouring for his attention. Her arm was cold, and the flesh had that same dusky tinge that he saw on his hand, the tinge that said that the blood wasn't flowing properly.

He couldn't find her pulse. That didn't mean anything – it must be so faint with shock that he couldn't detect it. He held his hand over the mess that was her mouth. Nothing. Her airway must be blocked. CPR. CPR would keep her alive until help got here. He knew how to do that. Two breaths and thirty chest compressions, two breaths and thirty chest compressions.

Clear fluid seeped from her hand. There was a smell in the air that drew him back to summer evenings, to people calling to each other, laughter, music, the fragrance of cooking . . .

. . . and the hiss of raw flesh as it was pressed down over the red hot coals.

Amy.

He needed to clear her airway first. She might

be able to breathe on her own. Compressions and breaths, compressions and breaths. CPR saved lives. He moved her carefully on to her back and kept the optimistic litany running in his head as the ache of what had happened to her twisted in his stomach and gripped at his throat. But as he moved her, he saw what hadn't been clear before, the angle at which her head was twisted, the impossible angle that told him everything he needed to know.

Amy's neck was broken. She was dead.

47

Roisin had settled Adam to sleep. She tried to get on with what she had been doing, but kept stopping to check on him. It must be like this bringing a new baby home for the first time, the sudden awareness that she was the sole carer for this child, overwhelmed by his vulnerability and fragility. She realized that all the jokes about new parents hanging over their babies' cribs to see if the child was still breathing were simply true.

She could hear the faint snuffle of his breath. His face was serene and his tiny fists were close to his face. She resisted the temptation to pick him up again. It wouldn't be fair to disturb him just to satisfy a need in her that was deep and growing.

You know that baby we were talking about . . . ? Want to go for it? Do you fancy having a little Aussie?

I'm sorry, sweetheart.

She and Joe should be in Newcastle now. She should be showing him all the places she wanted him to see, spending their days exploring the city, enjoying the elegant lines of Grey Street sweeping up towards the monument where she and Amy used to meet on Saturdays, crossing the Millennium Bridge to Gateshead, driving along the coast where the castles of old Northumbria lined the shore.

And they should be waiting for the first signs of their baby.

Maudlin, useless, pointless. None of that was going to happen.

She checked the time. It was almost eleven. Amy's train must be delayed. She'd meant to call Damien, to bring him up to date with the things she had found, tell him about Yasmin, but it was too late now.

She looked at the pile of post that had arrived that morning. She'd dumped it on the table without looking at it. She flicked through it – a credit-card offer, a charity. Junk mail . . .

The letter, Roisin.

The letter?

And suddenly she remembered the letter that Mari had given her. She'd forgotten about it – distracted by everything that was happening. She hunted through her things, trying to remember what she'd been wearing that day. She'd been carrying her large bag, the one she used when she went shopping. And the letter was there, shoved to the bottom. It was hardly surprising that the postman had made a mistake – it was a mess. The envelope had been reused, the original address had been hastily scribbled out and the new one scrawled in. It was addressed to Joe.

And it had been posted in Saudi Arabia.

She stared at it blankly. It was Joe's writing. She knew it so well. And it was postmarked for . . . A terrible hope began to grip her as she studied the envelope. She squinted her eyes as she tried to read it, knowing that what she saw must be a mistake. It was postmarked for three days after he had died.

And then the hope faded. She knew what had happened. He must have put it in the hospital mailing rather than post it from their usual mail centre, and it had made its slow way through the system, ignored and unnoticed. And days after Joe had written it, it had been despatched.

She didn't want to open it. This was the last of him. She'd thought that the moment in the car when they said goodbye outside the party was the last, but here was something else, another communication. Once she had opened it, that would be that.

She looked at it again. The writing was an untidy scrawl – she had teased him often enough about his doctor's handwriting. *Careful! I can almost read that!* It looked as though he'd made a sudden decision to send this, and he hadn't remembered to put on an airmail sticker – or he hadn't had one, because it had made its way slowly by surface mail. And then it had been delayed further by being delivered to the wrong flat.

For a while she sat, holding the envelope, listening to the silence in her head where Joe had been a moment before, then she slipped her finger under the flap and opened it. A sheaf of papers fell out, and a small notebook.

She went through everything carefully, but there was no letter, no note. She'd hoped that maybe there would be one last message, but there was nothing.

As soon as she started looking through the papers, she recognized them. They were the papers that she and Damien had gone through to piece together the story of Haroun Patel, but these were neatly typed up, carefully headed, with explanatory notes added. The timetable of the drugs inventory was there, a list of all the ways in which Haroun Patel would have known about this, the timetable of his last delivery run with the clearly marked return time of 22.30, checked against the records of the van he'd been driving. Joe had even referenced the records of the garage where the hospital vans were kept.

It was the kind of meticulous investigation into someone's movements that the police should have carried out, but, according to Damien, they probably hadn't. They'd relied, instead, on the location of the drugs and the confession that they had obtained from Patel.

This was Joe's final write-up of what he had been doing. She remembered that day when he'd come back from work, suddenly the old Joe, the

438

Joe she knew. He'd been relaxed and happy, and eager to get them both out of the Kingdom as soon as possible. This was why he'd been happy – he'd done what he'd set out to do. This copy, mailed to himself, was probably just a failsafe in case his originals went missing.

He'd also written a report that would go with the tabulated and meticulously compiled evidence. Damien had identified what Joe was doing – demonstrating that Haroun Patel's conviction was wrong. But Damien had had no idea why Joe was doing this when there was no possibility of the conviction being overturned, no question of an admission of error.

And that wasn't what Joe had been after. As she read what he had written, she realized that Joe was putting together a case that would allow Haroun Patel's family to claim compensation – if not from the Saudi government, then from their own. One thing that hadn't been in the papers she and Damien had looked through was the fact that Patel had been a father: he had an infant daughter in Pakistan.

Incontrovertible proof of his innocence would give his family some chance of claiming any outstanding money owed on his wage, of claiming compensation for the fact that his government had not pursued his case sufficiently. It was as simple as that. Nothing strange, nothing sinister. No reference to drowned women or missing babies, nothing that would have caused anyone much concern.

When she'd finished reading, she sat there with the papers spread out in front of her. Was everything else coincidence? Had Joe been an unlucky bystander, as he had claimed, when the woman fell into the river? And in the end, had Joe been simply the victim of a robbery that she and Damien had turned into a conspiracy because their own needs had made it impossible to accept what had really happened?

She picked up the small notebook and flicked through the pages. There were lists ticked off or crossed out, jottings that looked random and isolated, and then, towards the back of the book, were four pages filled with Joe's loose, untidy scrawl.

What follows is speculation. I can't offer proof of it. When I began this investigation, I had assumed that the original thief had panicked and placed the stolen drugs in Haroun Patel's locker. However, having looked into this more closely, I don't believe it is the case. These lockers are in an obscure location in the hospital. Anyone leaving material in a locker would have had to know where they were, and go out of his way to reach them. Also, they are locked with security codes, and it is unlikely anyone would have been able to leave the drugs there by chance. They can only have been left there by someone who knew they were there and who had access to the door codes.

This suggests strongly that the locker was not the place chosen by a panicking thief but was deliberately targeted. This puts the drug theft in a new light.

It is possible that the drugs were stolen specifically on this date because of the impending police inspection.

In this case, the entire theft may have been an attempt, successful as it turned out, to implicate Haroun Patel. Given the known penalties for drug crimes in the Kingdom, this would be tantamount to murder.

Murder.

Joe had been right, more right than he knew. There was a killer walking the streets of Riyadh, and Joe had been on his trail. Now, Joe was dead.

She turned back to the beginning of the notebook and tried to make sense of what Joe had written there:

Refugee and Asylum-seeker Support

And then a list of cities, with names and addresses:

Cambridge, Portsmouth, Liverpool, Manchester, Sheffield, Bristol, Newport . . . RAM project . . . One by one, they were ticked off and crossed out. Then the list changed into London boroughs: *Hillingdon, Stockwell, Hackney, Marylebone, Westminster . . .* There were names and addresses, telephone numbers, times, locations. And next to some were cryptic notes:

Maybe? Edgy, doesn't want to discuss. Meet?

Sumira, KFC, Oxford St, 10.30.

And then: *Oriental escorts: speciality: Omega Health, Penthouse Sauna, Venus Sauna, Handy Sauna . . .* The list of dubious venues filled the page.

As she read, Roisin noticed that the entries were dated between April 2004 and the end of August. All the time they had been together, Joe had been conducting a search of refugee organizations across the country, then he had narrowed his search to London and the brothels that operated as massage and sauna parlours, offering 'exotic' girls to men who didn't know – and possibly didn't care – that the woman who entertained them was there by coercion.

And at the end of August, a dead woman had been pulled out of the river, a woman who had been seen walking with Joe shortly before her death.

Joe had started a letter to Haroun's parents, a scrawl of crossings out and places where the pen had dug into the paper, before the draft petered out. She wondered if he had ever completed it and sent it.

It began with Joe introducing himself, giving an account of his friendship with their son, and his deep regret at Haroun's death. It continued: *I am sorry to be the one to tell you this, but your daughter Jesal is also dead.* After all this time, Roisin thought, they must know this. But a letter would permit them to give up that last, destructive hope.

The story Joe told was a sanitized version of the search outlined in the notebook:

She had gone to work in London. I went to the address that I had been given to tell her the sad news about her brother. We were walking by the river when I told her. ~~The shock was too much for her and she stumbled and fell into the water.~~ She told me she liked to walk by the river, ~~and she must have had an accident, because~~

She was working in London, and she fell into the river. I saw this happen. It was an accident. ~~The police who death with her death can be contacted~~

~~She was walking~~

~~You can contact~~

She could work out the story now. Jesal Rajkhumar Patel had been taken out of Saudi – had probably paid the people-smugglers to bring her to England, the country where her brother had contacts and where he had been happy. But the plan for Jesal was not a new beginning, or not as far as the traffickers were concerned. She represented an investment and they expected a high return.

It wouldn't have been hard to coerce a woman as vulnerable as Jesal into prostitution. Any threat to turn her over to the authorities would imply a return to Saudi for flogging and imprisonment, or a return to disgrace at home. The casual rape and brutality that marked the breaking in of a prostitute would have been enough to confirm her fate. After that, all her choices were gone.

And then Joe had come and taken away her last hope.

Roisin thought about the newspaper cutting

she'd found, the one that identified the dead woman as 'probably' an illegal immigrant, and speculated about prostitution. How could Joe tell her deeply traditional parents that their daughter had been working as a prostitute and had committed suicide in the icy waters of the Thames? She looked at the crossings out in the letter as he tried to tell them what they had to know, without telling them the rest. She could understand now why he had never told the police that he knew who she was. Maybe Jesal's parents would be better off with the cruelty of hope.

Joe.

She carefully gathered the papers together and put them on the sideboard desk. She would show them to Damien when she saw him again.

Damien's eyes burned with fatigue as he drove up the M1. The rain was relentless, the spray thrown up by the wheels of the HGVs he passed obscuring the windscreen for heart-stopping moments before the wipers cleared it. Their rapid *scrape scrape* became the music that carried him through the night.

Once he'd realized that Amy was dead he'd moved fast. She was beyond whatever help he might have been able to give her, but there were other people who were still alive. With his senses alert for the sound of the ambulance arriving – and he had a feeling that ambulances took their time before they came on to the Byker estate – he'd moved through the flat, wiping anything his fingers might have touched. Then he'd searched it, taking anything that looked as though it might be relevant. Someone had been there before him, but there were things they had left.

He'd taken the photographs, scooped up the papers that lay scattered across the sideboard. He'd pocketed the mobile phone that lay on the table. He'd hesitated for a moment when he found Amy's passport, then left it, after checking the pages carefully. They confirmed Rai's story. Amy had left the Kingdom via Bahrain, the night of the bomb, the night that Joe Massey had died.

Amy.

Do you still . . . ?

Love you? Of course. Always, Amy.

He kept his emotions firmly shut away. Whatever he felt had to wait. His hand was throbbing unbearably and was clumsy and unwieldy on the gear stick. Everything around him had an odd distance and clarity. He knew that he needed to get to a doctor, but he had things to finish first.

The speedometer was flickering around the 120 mark. He eased off. He couldn't afford to get caught on a speed camera. He couldn't afford to get picked up by the police, and he couldn't afford to kill himself driving at ludicrous speeds in the icy rain. Three lives hung in the balance, and he had to get there in time to do something about it.

48

It was gone midnight. Roisin realized she had been sitting there for over an hour, the papers clutched in her hand. And still there was no sign of Amy. She should be here by now. She checked the phone in case she'd missed a call, but there was nothing. Just for a moment, she thought she smelled cigarette smoke, and wrinkled up her nose in distaste. The window was slightly open at the top, and she got up from the settee and closed it. Someone must have been smoking in the street.

She hadn't eaten since lunch time. She wasn't hungry, but she felt strangely light-headed. She went into the kitchen and hunted through the fridge for something she could eat quickly. She was just spreading butter on a slice of bread when she heard a sound. She listened again. It was a soft knock on the door of the flat. Amy. At last. She went quickly down the corridor before Amy could knock more loudly and disturb Adam. 'Amy?'

The voice was muffled at the other side of the door. If she hadn't been so tired, she wouldn't have released the lock. She realized her mistake at once. Her fingers fumbled with the security chain, trying to slot it in, but the opening door knocked it out of her hand. She jammed her shoulder hard against the wood and, for a moment, she thought it was closing, then she staggered back as the door was shoved open, hard.

There were two of them, pushing her back into the flat before she could shout out, grabbing her wrists and spinning her round, squashing her face against the wall.

'You're expecting Amy?' The voice was an angry whisper.

She didn't answer. She could hear footsteps move along the passageway and she struggled against the hands that were holding her. Adam was in there, sleeping peacefully.

'She isn't coming.' The man who was holding her turned her round, not releasing his grip. His face was hard and his mouth was tight with anger. 'We finish this,' he said. 'Tonight.'

The face was etched in her mind, though she'd only met him once, the night of the party, the night that Joe died. Arshak Nazarian.

She heard a triumphant shout, quickly suppressed, from the other man, and the uncertain wail of a baby. She wrenched herself away from Nazarian and tried to run down the corridor, but he grabbed her arm and pulled her back. His

447

hand swung and caught her across the face, and her head snapped back, hitting the wall with a crack. 'You're responsible for this,' he said, his voice low and hard. He looked at her, making sure that she was subdued, then pulled her along the corridor to where the other man was.

She recognized him at once – the driver of the van, the man who had been sitting there, the light of his cigarette glowing in the darkness. He was holding Adam up like some kind of trophy. Adam's eyes were wide open. Shock and surprise seemed to have silenced him, but she could see his face starting to collapse into misery.

'He's frightened,' she said. 'You're frightening him.'

Nazarian was watching her, his eyes narrowed in calculation. 'Give her the child,' he said, after a moment. The other man looked uncertain but then reluctantly handed Adam to her. Adam started crying in earnest as she took him, and she held him close, rocking him, trying to steady her breathing so he wouldn't feel her own terror. Her head was ringing and there was a dull ache in her cheek where Nazarian had hit her.

The other man looked at Nazarian. 'What now?'

'Nothing. We have the child. We go.'

'Her? We can't risk leaving her.'

Nazarian looked at her. 'What can she say? Without putting herself behind bars?'

One phrase was lodged in Roisin's mind: *We have the child*. For some reason, somehow, Nazarian wanted Mari's baby. She held the small body close. He was rigid with fear, and his cries were stopping her from thinking clearly. She had to get help.

Nazarian was still watching her with that slightly uncertain calculation. Then he seemed to come to a decision, and spoke to her directly. 'Roisin, if you want no harm to come to . . . anyone here, then you will do what I say. You will make the child ready, and then you will let us leave. It will be done quietly so there will be no more upset.'

'I'm not . . .' Roisin shut her mouth on the words. Verbal defiance would do her no good. She had to get them off their guard, find some way of making contact, some way of getting help.

'Can't you shut him up?' The other man had been checking the kitchen and he looked at Adam in irritation as he came out. She could remember the way he'd snatched Adam up out of his cot like a hunter brandishing a trophy, not a living, breathing child.

'What did you expect him to do?' she said. 'He's frightened and he's hungry. He won't quieten down until he's fed.'

'We haven't got time for that. It'll have to wait.' The man looked at Nazarian for confirmation, but Nazarian was still watching her with that slightly puzzled frown. He took out his phone and started speaking into it rapidly and urgently. He was speaking in Arabic, and she couldn't understand what he was saying.

She carried Adam into the kitchen, not waiting to see what the response would be. She was aware of the man's gaze following her. Once she was in the kitchen, she closed the door and leant against it, her eyes closed. She had no phone in here, the window was tiny and looked out into the air well – there was no chance of escaping and no chance of attracting anyone's attention. But she needed to be on her own to think. Away from the men, Adam's cries began to quieten. She rocked him gently, making soothing noises in his ear as she tried to work out what she could do.

They were going to take him. For some reason, some purpose she didn't understand, they were going to take Mari's baby. Her hand was shaking as she tried to open the packet of baby milk she'd brought up with her from the flat. Brave resolutions were fine – but she had nothing to fight with. If they took Adam and left her, she could phone the police at once, she could run into the road and get the number of their car, try and see which way they went – but they would know she could do that – *would* do that. So they weren't going to give her that option. 'Oh, baby,' she breathed.

Adam stirred against her shoulder and made a noise of complaint. He could feel her fear. She forced herself back into control. No panicking. Panicking wouldn't help. Her gaze leapt round the kitchen: the window – too small. The door. It led nowhere, just back into the main room. The knife block . . . The knife block.

450

The pictures jumped through her mind in a series of snapshots: her, slipping a knife – the thin, sharp one with the slightly curved blade – into the sleeve of her blouse. Her, carrying Adam into the main room, holding the bottle. Her, putting Adam on the settee, settling him so his face was away from the room, so he wouldn't see what was going to happen. Her, turning quickly and stabbing the knife deep into Nazarian's throat as he talked on the phone. Nazarian, falling, as the blood spurted out . . .

. . . like Joe.

She couldn't think about Joe now.

The other man would be prepared, but she'd have a moment when he was taken by surprise. She saw herself pulling the knife out of Nazarian, turning towards the other man, moving forwards as he came to her. And the knife . . .

Going into him. She'd have to push it into him as hard as she could. Into his stomach. The blade was only six inches long, but six inches was enough.

She closed her eyes and breathed deeply, trying to calm herself. She had to take the knife, go through the door, put the baby down, and . . . kill them both.

And she knew she couldn't do it. If she had had a knife in her hand when Nazarian hit her, if she'd thought he was about to hit her again, she might have been able to. If she saw them trying to harm Adam, then the move would be

instinctive, but to go out there in cold blood . . .
She couldn't.

She tucked the knife into her sleeve – she needed a weapon for protection if it came to that, and went back into the other room. Nazarian was still talking on the phone. The other man was pacing up and down, checking his watch, casting anxious glances at his boss. Roisin could feel him watching her as she sat down and offered Adam the bottle. He wasn't hungry – she knew he wasn't. He was too aware of the tension around him. Once they noticed him turning his face away, then . . . Nazarian had said it: *We have the child. We go.*

Nazarian put the phone down. He could see what she was doing. Before he could say anything, she put Adam down on the settee and started unbuttoning the all-in-one sleeper he was wearing. She ignored the men as she unwrapped a clean nappy, moving as slowly as she dared. She could feel the cold touch of the knife blade against her arm. It felt huge and conspicuous, and it also felt small and useless. Her mind went round and round in futile circles. She was running out of time and she had no idea of what to do.

She heard Nazarian's grunt of interest and looked round. He'd found the papers she'd been reading, the ones that Joe had sent. 'Those are private,' she said.

He ignored her and scanned them quickly, then glanced across at her. 'He was an intelligent man, your husband,' he said. 'Please believe that I . . .'

452

'Sir. It's getting late.' The other's man's tone was deferential, but urgent.

'Yeah, yeah, yeah. I know. Don't worry. Get him organized and we can go.' He picked up the papers again. 'What I don't understand is . . .'

He was talking to her. She allowed her hands to stop moving as she listened.

'Come on!' The other man's voice was rough and impatient. 'Get that kid sorted out. Now.'

'I'm changing him,' she said. 'I'm being as quick as I can.'

'There's no more time.'

He leaned over and was about to scoop Adam up, when Nazarian said, 'Wait!' His gaze had focused on Adam, had frozen as he saw the fair curls that had been released from the hooded garment, and his expression frightened her more than anything that had happened this evening.

49

Silence filled the room. Nazarian's gaze moved from Adam to her, then across the room to the other man. 'Did you know they . . . concluded the matter in Newcastle?' he said. 'Is everyone I employ incompetent?'

The man shook his head. He looked pale.

Adam, picking up the sudden tension in the air, began to cry. Nazarian's gaze moved back to him. His mouth was set in a thin, angry line. 'How long have you been caring for this child?' There was a coldness in his voice now that hadn't been there before. 'And keep him quiet.' It wasn't a request.

'You've terrified him,' Roisin said. 'That's why he's crying.'

'And you will make him stop. *How long have you been caring for this child?*'

For the first time, she knew that Nazarian was capable of hurting Adam. It was as if Adam had suddenly changed from something valuable to something that Nazarian no longer had any use for.

She shrank back into the sofa, as if she had been cowed by his voice. It was barely a pretence. She could feel herself shaking. The knife was still tucked up her sleeve, but it felt minuscule in the face of the threat. And if she got it wrong . . . Before, she'd thought that, if she attacked them and failed, she would die, but Adam would be safe. They would take him, but they wouldn't hurt him. Now . . .

She picked up the discarded bottle, remembering a trick the women who lived on the estate where she grew up used to use. She dipped the teat of the bottle into the sugar basin that was standing on the table and pushed it into Adam's mouth. His face contorted as he took a breath to cry more loudly, then he tasted the sweetness. She waited for a tense moment, but the strange new sensation had diverted him, and there was silence.

'Not long,' she said in response to Nazarian's question. 'He belongs to the girl downstairs, Mari. Mari had a fall. She broke her leg. I'm looking after him for tonight.'

'She's lying,' the other man said. 'The Seymour woman was coming here. That's what she told them. This one went to get the kid. She was expecting her.'

'Don't be a fool.' Nazarian's voice was level, but his tone was icy, and the other man's face paled. 'Have you looked at this child? This is not my grandson! What that bitch told them must be true.

And now they've . . .' He was breathing deeply, trying to control his fury.

Roisin forced herself to sit calmly and sent up a silent prayer that Adam would stay silent. When Nazarian lost it, he would lash out at the first thing that enraged him. She had seen anger like his before.

Joe . . .

Hang on, sweetheart.

Adam turned his head away and, before she could do anything, he began to howl in earnest. She saw Nazarian's arm draw back and she crouched down, curling herself round the screaming baby, trying to shield him with her body. She had a sudden memory of a picture she'd seen, a Palestinian man huddled against a wall, pushing his terrified son behind him as the bullets sprayed past, the soldiers firing indifferent to the fate of a child they saw as less than human.

And the child lying dead.

Her free hand fumbled for the knife.

Then someone spoke from the doorway. 'Enough. That's enough.'

It was Damien. His face was grey and he looked as though he could barely stand. His eyes were fixed on Nazarian.

The scene in front of Damien seemed a long way away, but at the same time clear-edged and bright: Roisin crouched in the chair, putting herself between the baby in her arms and Nazarian's raised fist. Behind her, balanced to move on the instant, a man he recognized as one of Nazarian's people. A professional fighter. Roisin and the baby she was holding would be dead in a second if that man got his hands on them.

Like Amy.

He watched the faces turn towards him.

'O'Neill.' Nazarian's rage was concealed in an instant. The baby's crying cut the air, a sharp, compulsive sound.

Damien didn't have a weapon – there was no point. He couldn't win a fight. But he didn't need one. He held up his phone. 'I've texted in names and dates,' he said. He didn't need to say more. Nazarian would understand. The numbers were coded in, the message was in the outbox – all he had to do was press one button and the message would go to the Newcastle police, the Met, Interpol and the UK and Saudi embassies. 'No one knows anything – yet.'

'Why should we believe that?' The other man was moving towards Damien.

Nazarian uttered a brusque order, and the man stopped. 'Because it's the only way to stop people getting hurt, right, O'Neill?'

'Amy. Have you forgotten about Amy?'

Nazarian's eyes moved to Roisin, and back to Damien. His gaze was level. 'You're judging me, O'Neill? If she'd been caught in Riyadh, that's what she would have got.'

'For what?'

Nazarian's voice was a whiplash. 'For kidnapping! My grandchild. My *grandson*. No one hurts my family.'

'And Yasmin? Your daughter?'

'She'll understand.'

Damien's gaze was fixed on Nazarian's face. He wanted to find . . . regret? Guilt? Some recognition of what had happened to Amy. There was nothing. 'She may not learn what you want her to from this.'

'All I wanted was the information. I knew Amy had something to do with it. One of my people saw her at the hospital that evening. She was veiled, but the veil slipped and he saw her face. He was curious – why was a Western woman wearing a veil? Why was *that* Western woman wearing a veil? He knew I had a connection with Amy, so he came to me with it. Once I realized she was still in Riyadh, that she hadn't left, then I knew. OK, they went too far. But it's the justice of the Kingdom. You kidnap a child, you die. I was just looking out for my own.'

'Who was there to look out for Amy?'

'That was never my responsibility.'

Damien stayed in the doorway. He didn't trust himself to stand without its support. The painful throbbing in his hand had faded to numbness. He hadn't taken his glove off to look at it since he left Newcastle. There was no point, there wasn't anything he could do until this was over. Black specks threatened at the corners of his vision. He wanted to kill Nazarian. He wanted to strangle him with his bare hands and feel the life draining out of him. Instead . . . 'If you go, now, I'm not going to stop you. After you've left, the authorities will get your name. You won't be able to touch Roisin. And you won't be able to come back to Europe.'

'And my grandson?'

'Do you think he's still alive? I don't. Whatever Amy knew . . .' He shrugged. 'It's gone.'

The silence stretched out. Damien waited for Nazarian to call his bluff. He was by no means as sure of his facts as he pretended. A lot of it was still guesswork. He held Nazarian's gaze until the other man spoke. 'Not entirely,' he said. His voice was thoughtful. He gave Roisin a small bow. 'I'm sorry to have inconvenienced you, Mrs Massey.' His manner was cool and courteous, but Damien could see the anger in his eyes. Nazarian gestured with his head towards the other man, and then they were gone.

Damien made himself stand until the door clicked shut behind them, then he managed to walk as far as the settee where he slumped down. The black specks threatened again, and he missed the first part of what Roisin was saying as she jumped to her feet.

' . . . their car? Quick! The police might be able . . .'

He reached out and managed to grip her wrist. 'Let him go. He's more dangerous here. They won't keep him locked up – he's too well connected. Amy's dead because of him. Let him go.'

She was looking at him in shocked disbelief from some distant point at the end of a dark tunnel. 'Amy? He killed her? And Joe. He killed Joe. I'm not letting him leave.' The baby's crying went on and on. As if he was watching her from a great distance, he saw her make a visible effort to calm down as she tried to soothe the frightened child. He wasn't sure if she would hear what he was saying. He was too far away from her now. 'He didn't kill your husband.'

And then the tunnel swallowed him up.

50

Snapshots.

Two girls, both in their late teens, outside a club. They are excruciatingly dressed in Goth style – pale faces, dark lipstick, black dresses. One, the smaller one, has ornamented her fair hair with beads and feathers, the other, tall and thin, has a blaze of red hair that hangs around her shoulders. Something has shattered their hard-won cool, and they are both laughing, their arms round each other.

A girl leaning out of a train that is pulling away. She is waving and calling to another girl who stands alone, her hand raised in a forlorn farewell.

A view from a high bridge, a study in shades of grey, the heavy girders making dark lines across the mist that rises from the water. The only colour is the faint glimmer from a warehouse sign.

I remember that . . .

A couple stand in the middle of a celebratory group. The woman is small, with fair hair, and

461

the man, tall and dark-haired, has his arm round her. They are laughing. Fragments of bright colour are scattered on the ground around them and some have caught in the woman's hair.

Is this your wedding? He looks like a nice guy.

A garden at night, lit by flames in an eerie silence.

The light flickers as the flames climb up, a sickly orange against the shadows. There is no sound. Only the girl's eyes are visible. Her face is veiled. The orange light reflects off the leaves. She reaches out to lift the veil . . .

. . . Amy's face looks back at her from the darkness.

And Roisin was awake. It was daylight. She'd fallen asleep in her chair, and the TV was hectoring her with the morning news. Her head was fuzzy with confusion as the impossibly bright faces of the presenters turned serious, as if someone had pressed a button, and a photograph appeared on the screen. It was a portrait of a woman. Her head and shoulders were draped with the hijab, but even without the distinctive red hair, Roisin could recognize her. Amy.

. . . the woman found last night in her flat in Newcastle's Byker estate has been identified as Amy Seymour, a nurse who has recently returned from working in the Middle East . . .

She turned up the sound, and the TV suddenly blared out. *Police were shocked by the brutality of the attack . . .*

Amy. Her dream came back to her, a girl leaning dangerously out of the window of a train, waving, calling out as the train pulled out of the station and faded into the distance.

Gone.

Damien was in hospital. She'd driven him there the night before through a ghost London of empty streets where the night people moved in the shadows, as he tried to talk to her, his voice rambling incoherently through some narrative that was haunting him, but that she couldn't understand. . . . *burned her . . . I had to let him go . . . for now . . . She didn't . . .*

She'd waited anxiously in the A & E which, in the small hours, was relatively quiet. Just her, Adam, asleep at last in the snug warmth of his carry-cot, and the few remaining drunks of the night. Damien had been admitted suffering from exhaustion, with an infection in his injured hand. It had been after three when she got back.

She got wearily to her feet and went to check Adam. He was still sleeping, but as she stood over him the blue eyes opened and he looked at her. She lifted him out of the cot. Her phone rang and she fumbled for it one-handedly. It was Mari. 'I'll be home in a couple of hours,' she said. 'I'm just waiting for the doctor.'

'Are you all right?'

'Yeah. It's just a bad sprain. I can walk on it in a day or two. Is he OK? Was he any bother?'

Roisin opened the curtains. The sky was clear

463

and the sun was shining. It was as if the night before had never happened. She looked out on to the street. The white van had gone.

'No,' she said. 'No bother at all.'

51

Damien's legs felt leaden as he dressed himself in the clothes he'd worn the night before. They were crumpled and stained. He wondered if the police investigating Amy's death would track him back from Newcastle. He was probably safe. The precautions he'd taken against Nazarian's people may have failed, but they should still protect him from the police investigation.

His name might be among Amy's papers, but he doubted it. She'd left her past behind. Someone might discover that a hunt had been done for Amy's birth details the day of her death, but among all the people who used those records, would anyone remember him?

He suspected that the police would come to Roisin though, and he needed to get to her first. Amy's body, crumpled on the kitchen floor, was suddenly in front of him.

Do you still . . .

Love you? Of course.

Always.

' . . . feeling all right?'

A nurse was looking at him with professional concern and disapproval. Damien was discharging himself against medical advice. He made an effort and smiled at her. 'I'm tired,' he said. 'I'm going home to rest. I'll look after myself.'

'You do that. I don't want to see you back in here.'

'You won't,' Damien promised. She'd brought his discharge notes and his medication. He was to take an antibiotic for the next ten days to quell the infection that had started in his hand.

'I don't think you understand how lucky you've been,' she said. 'These things can be killers.'

He smiled at her. 'I was born lucky.'

Outside, the day had dawned into early spring. The air was warm with a gentle breeze that brought some freshness to the streets. He found a coffee bar and called Rai. He wanted the rest of the story in place before he went to see Roisin.

Rai greeted him with anxious queries about his health. 'I've been to the hospital,' Damien reassured him.

Still dubious, Rai outlined what had happened since the call of the night before. Nazarian had arrived back in the Kingdom early that morning. He had spent a long time at the compound where Majid lived with his family, and had then returned to his own house.

'Yasmin?' Damien wanted to know that Yasmin was safe.

'She has gone with her father.'

'And the investigation, the missing child?'

'They are saying the child is dead.'

After he'd rung off, Damien ran his hands over his face. He felt as though he'd just run a marathon and still had miles to go. It wasn't over. He had a promise to keep, one he'd made to Amy. He took a phone out of his pocket, the one he'd picked up at Amy's flat, and scrolled through the names in the address book. Amy had to have a secure way of contacting her sister, and it was there in the list of names: *Jassy*. Before anything else, he had to make a call. He knew enough, now, to make Yasmin tell him the truth.

'I know about my sister,' Yasmin spoke in Arabic, a language that must have been alien to her when she first arrived in Saudi as a child. 'My father called my husband. They say it was the right thing to happen to someone who would kidnap a child.'

'And you?'

'Me? I have to sit quietly and be a good Saudi daughter and a good Saudi wife. This is what Amy would have wanted. Otherwise, she died for nothing, Mr O'Neill.' It was the low, quiet voice of the submissive Saudi woman, but underneath, he could hear the steel. She was warning him off.

'I know enough to guess some of it, but not enough to work it all out. If you can't tell me, I'll go on looking. Roisin deserves to know.'

There was silence as she thought about it. 'How is Roisin?'

'If she's going to survive this, she has to understand why her husband died.'

'And so you will endanger what my sister fought for? She told me that she loved you.'

'And I loved her. Yasmin, I saw her the day she died. She knew you owed Roisin. Will it help if I tell you what I know? It starts with Haroun Patel, doesn't it?'

There was silence again, then he heard the breath of a sigh. 'All right. But it starts earlier than that. It started when my mother took me away from my father. I had been Yasmin, and I lived with my family. Then suddenly I was Jesamine and we were living in the middle of a housing estate in the north with a man I didn't know and didn't like, where I didn't understand the way people talked and the way people lived. Then my mother died and my father brought me here. I was Yasmin again, but not the real Yasmin. He left me with strangers and they told me everything I did and everything I knew was wrong. I wanted my mother and I wanted my sister, but they told me they were *haram*, evil, because they rejected the faith my father showed them. It was as if the desert had stolen everything I wanted or cared about. I didn't see England again until I was twenty. My father had left Europe by then, but he wanted his child to attend a European university. I studied in Paris, and in my last year, I took a semester in London. In Paris, my sister found me. And in London I found . . . Those years brought me the greatest happiness of my life, and the worst sorrow.'

'So Amy came to Riyadh.' Damien thought of the other people who had been drawn, fatally, to the city: Haroun Patel, Joe Massey – and Amy. Amy had surely found her death in Riyadh.

'Yes. She always believed I would leave Majid, and I would need her help. I don't know. I didn't know how to be independent like Amy, not then. That's why I did what my father told me. But I loved Haroun, Mr O'Neill. You know that, don't you?'

He could remember his own first experience of love, the conflagration whose brilliance outshone all rational counsel. He had been caught in it when he had first taken up with Catherine. And the fire had burned out, leaving something grey and dead where love had been, as dead as Catherine herself was now dead. 'Yes. I know.'

He could hear the faint breath that was Yasmin's sigh. 'I thought I would never see him again. But then he wrote to me. It was a long time later. He said he was sorry if he'd caused me trouble, but his sister needed help and I was the only person he knew who had contacts with people of influence. He meant my father, of course. She had run away from her Saudi employers, and she'd stolen from them. She needed to get away. I was so glad to have his letter; just to hold it, something he had written, made me feel alive again. There was no hope, I knew that. I was married. He was married. I didn't want to think about that. But I tried to help him. I told my father, said the girl was a friend of my maid, and he said he would do something.' She laughed, a short, bitter sound. 'It was like my wanting a doll when I was small or a new dress when I was a teenager – anything like that, I could always have, but the people I loved? I was not allowed those. But he did it and I felt good because I had helped Haroun.'

A road to hell that had been paved with so many good intentions. 'Jesal Patel?' he said.

'Jesal. And then Haroun wrote again. I can remember when my mother-in-law gave me the letter. *A lot of letters* she said, and her eyes were hard. *Just students*, I told her. *They ask for help.* I was frightened because I thought she would insist on seeing the letter, but I was happy as well, just to see his writing. But it was bad news. His sister had vanished. He thought she had gone to London, but he had heard nothing from her. I asked my father, but he got angry so I tried to find out in other ways. I asked who I could, I asked the women in our groups, and I asked Amy. I think Amy may have guessed what had happened, but she didn't tell me. What could I have done? Anyway, one day I was feeling unhappy so I went to her flat to see her. Majid didn't know she was my sister, but he knew we were friends and I was allowed to visit her. But Amy wasn't there. Instead

– I can still remember how I felt. I walked into her flat, and he was there, Haroun was there, like a dream. He was just the way he used to look, the way I always saw him in my mind.

'Amy had given him her key so he could use her phone and her computer. He didn't have anything like that. He started getting his things together, he said he had to go, but he . . . We . . . He hadn't forgotten. We met there, times when Amy was working. We were happy, just for that short time we could be together.'

Damien could work out the rest, or most of it. 'The baby – it's Haroun's, isn't it?'

He could hear that same faint breath. 'I didn't know . . . then. Part of me prayed it was Majid's, but so much of me wanted it to be Haroun's. I was happy. I was terrified. I didn't know what to do. I even thought – Haroun and I, we can be together. He won't leave me. He'll leave this wife he has in his own country, and we'll go to Europe and . . . But that could never have happened. And then . . . Haroun was dead. The desert kingdom took him away from me. Then, when my baby was born, I looked at him and I saw Haroun looking back.'

'Did Amy know?'

'I didn't tell her, not until the end. I kept hoping Majid would let me go to Europe, let me get away, but he wouldn't. I didn't tell her until the baby was close to being born and I knew I couldn't escape.'

'And she took the baby. Yasmin, I don't understand why. Why not wait until you could just leave?'

'Because when they took the baby's blood – they do that to test for diseases – Majid asked them for our son's blood group. He likes to have all this kind of thing on record and he knew we would need it for the baby's passport.' Damien heard the short, hard laugh. 'I had asked so often to go to Europe. He did it to please me.'

The trap had closed on Yasmin suddenly. Amy had had to improvise, and to move fast. And she had done it. She had succeeded. But it had cost her her life.

'She had to keep my son in hospital, and she needed him to be in the ward where she worked – she could get him away from there. She took the samples from the lab and destroyed them. Then she took the blood of another child, one who was very ill. She labelled it with my son's name and took it to the laboratory. As soon as they saw the results, they moved him into the ITU. I was so afraid. I was afraid they would find out, or that they would give him treatment he shouldn't have, treatment that would harm him, but Amy said she'd take care of it.'

Damien remembered the incubator that had been found with the oxygen switched off and the drip detached. Amy had done what she had promised. 'And now? Where did she . . . ?'

'Please don't ask me. I can't tell you. He is safe.'

There was a moment of silence, then she said, 'Now I have to tell you what Roisin has to know . . .'

Damien listened as she told him the story he'd already worked out, but had hoped, up to this moment, was wrong.

52

When she opened the door to him, Roisin saw that Damien still looked drained and exhausted. The only improvement his visit to the hospital had made was that the hectic flush had gone from his face and his eyes were clear. 'You should be resting,' she said.

He grimaced as if he'd heard this already. 'I'll be all right,' he said.

'Amy – she called me, last night. Damien, what happened?'

He closed his eyes and seemed to be marshalling his resources. When he spoke again, his voice was stronger. 'Nazarian sent his men after her. He wanted answers to questions that Amy wasn't prepared to give. But they got one bit of information out of her – that she was coming here.'

She looked out of the window to the place where the white van had been. 'They were watching the flat,' she said. 'They saw me with the baby.'

'They were watching me, as well. They were waiting for Amy to get in touch.' He shook his head. 'I was stupid. Careless.'

'What were they looking for?' She knew the answer, but she didn't understand the way it had happened.

'Yasmin's baby. Nazarian knew that Amy had taken Yasmin's baby.' He told her the story as Yasmin had told it to him. 'Once Amy had got the baby safely hidden away, she left Saudi via the Bahrain causeway and flew to Europe. Everyone thought she'd already left – even me. It was vital that no one suspected her, because that would put the focus back on Yasmin. She had to find a job, get a house, somewhere Yasmin could bring the baby once she managed to get out. Only she reckoned without Nazarian. One of his people saw her at the hospital the day the baby vanished.'

'Where is the baby? Where did Amy take him?'

He shook his head. 'Yasmin wouldn't tell me. To be honest, I don't want to know. He'll be somewhere Yasmin can get him, when she leaves.'

'How can she have him with her? Her father would find out – and her husband. Even if she leaves . . .' Nazarian had had Amy followed from Riyadh to Newcastle to carry out his revenge.

'She's with Nazarian now. Of her limited choices, he's the best. She's going to divorce Majid; after this, her father won't be in a position to stop her. Once she's divorced, she can get her father's permission to leave the country. I don't know how she'll get the baby out. But Amy must have thought of a way.'

'And Joe? How did Joe . . . ?' She could hardly bear to ask the question. This was the bit she dreaded hearing, and the bit that she had to hear.

'He knew there was something wrong. He spotted an anomaly in the blood tests. I've seen his report – someone e-mailed me a copy. According to the test results, the sick child was rhesus negative. Yasmin was rhesus positive. It should have been flagged up – rhesus positive mother, rhesus negative father – potential for trouble. But it wasn't. So he checked again, and that's when he saw that Majid was rhesus positive as well. He couldn't have been the father of that child. Joe had no way of knowing that the blood samples had been switched. They showed him the truth, but for the wrong reasons. I asked at the hospital that afternoon, and the pathology technician indicated that there was something missing from the medical records. I think your husband must have taken something out until he had a chance to think about it. But once the child went missing, then all the information had to go back.'

She could remember Joe in the car, looking worried, saying, *there's something I should . . .* and then, *This fucking country. I don't know what to do.* He had been worried that he'd be forced to reveal something that would convict a Saudi woman of adultery and place her in the hands of the Mutawa'ah. 'And Nazarian killed him? For that?'

Damien, watching her face, wished he could give different answers. 'It wasn't Nazarian, Roisin. And it wasn't for that. Majid should never have been at the hospital that night. He wasn't allowed to investigate the kidnapping of his own child. But he went there anyway. He couldn't stay away. He was already suspicious that the hospital had got something wrong. He thought they'd made a fatal error and were trying to cover it up. He went to the labs to ask some questions about the tests and he found your husband, apparently altering the records, destroying the evidence – as far as Majid was concerned – of a mistake that had killed his son.'

Yasmin had told him that Majid had come back late the night of Joe Massey's death. He had told her that their son was dead, but the killer had been brought to justice. And then he had refused to tell her any more and had forbidden her to leave the house or to contact anyone. He had paid no attention to the rumours that were starting to circulate about the child's paternity. He knew those records were nothing to do with the child he thought was his. Yasmin had been under virtual house arrest until her father's return. All she had was the mobile phone Amy had given her in secret. She had hardly dared to use it.

'Majid assumed his son had died, and your husband was responsible. He thought the "abduction" was part of a cover-up and he knew that a Westerner would never pay what he saw as the appropriate price for the fatal error. He took Joe to the desert. I don't know what story he used, or how he persuaded him. I don't know why he went there. It may just have been a suitably isolated place, or he may have wanted to question him, to get the story out of him. Then he killed him.'

Her voice shook as she spoke. 'Mad. He must have been mad. Crazy. And all Joe was doing was trying to protect Yasmin. We were so close to leaving. We were going to go in a few weeks. Oh, God. There was no *need*.' The tears were streaming down her face. He hadn't seen her cry for her dead husband before. He touched her hair, and when she didn't resist, he pulled her against him and held her. He was praying to the gods he didn't believe in that she wouldn't ask him the questions he didn't want to answer.

He didn't want to share his last piece of knowledge with her. Yasmin hadn't challenged or accused her husband, and would never give evidence against him. By killing Joe Massey, he had removed the last witness to a story that would be fatal to her if it got out while she was still in Saudi. He didn't blame her. She had her child to protect.

And Majid hadn't been crazy. He hadn't killed in a fit of rage or insanity. He had executed Joe Massey with clinical precision, with two deliberate cuts to the throat. The first one had disabled him, a cut that had opened the artery that carries the blood to the head. The second cut had opened the larynx and severed the tongue, leaving him speechless and choking as his lungs flooded with his own blood.

And then he had left Joe Massey to die.

53

Roisin said goodbye to Damien at the station. He'd decided to go back. He was taking the Heathrow Express and catching the afternoon flight to Riyadh.

Outside, the day had the freshness of early spring. She walked through the backstreets of Marylebone and through the shabby grandeur of Bloomsbury, following the route that she and Joe had always used when they walked back to the flat together. She knew she would never see him again, that the part of her life that belonged to him was over, but she felt as though he was walking beside her.

Riyadh, March 2005

Damien slipped back into the Kingdom quietly. He didn't tell anyone he was coming, but the house greeted him like an old friend, the cool shade welcoming him home. Rai was waiting with his calm smile. 'Welcome back,' he said.

Damien wandered through rooms veiled behind

the *mashrabiyaat* to the cool dimness of the hallway. He stood on the stone flags, remembering the day that Amy had called here, slipping through the door and into his arms, the blue of her dress and the vividness of her hair brilliant against the monochrome shadows.

And later, her hair had splashed across his pillow like blood.

Then he went back upstairs and waited for the visitor he knew would shortly arrive. Just after eight, the bell jangled. He heard the sound of the door opening and checked to make sure he had what was needed to hand.

He heard feet moving heavily on the stairs. The door swung open. Arshak Nazarian stood there.

'Nazarian,' Damien said.

The other man's gaze travelled round the room. After a moment's hesitation, he came through the door and sat down in the chair opposite Damien's. 'You might have been wiser to stay away,' he said without ceremony.

Damien shrugged. 'So might you. They tried to kill you, remember?' The car bomb, indiscriminate though it might have been, had been targeted at Nazarian.

Nazarian dismissed this irritably. 'It was just a warning. A business misunderstanding.'

'They thought you were reneging,' Damien said. 'They'd taken a woman out of the country for you on a no-questions-asked basis, and suddenly there was your daughter stirring things up.'

481

'As I said, a misunderstanding.'

A stab of anger pushed Damien into speaking. 'Did you know that she died, the girl you gave them? She drowned herself in the Thames.'

'I'm not responsible for what people choose to do, O'Neill. You of all people should realize that.' He waited for a moment to see if Damien would respond. 'Your wife. She committed suicide after you left her, am I right?'

It was the threat Catherine had held over him for the duration of their marriage, the threat she had carried out once he had gone. 'Yes. She did.'

'So you understand.' He met Damien's gaze. 'I had no plans for Amy Seymour to be killed. I just wanted my grandson back.'

'But she didn't have him.'

Nazarian's face darkened. 'No.'

'Do you plan to stay?' The bomb had been the second attempt on Nazarian's life.

'I thought I might move to Dubai,' Nazarian said after a pause. 'I have some business interests there.'

'And your daughter?'

'She will come with me. She has left her husband. They're getting a divorce.' Once the divorce was through, Majid would no longer have control over Yasmin's movements. That would pass to her father.

Damien could see the calculation in Nazarian's eyes, the expression that said he was coming to a decision. He rested his fingers on the book in his lap and saw Nazarian's gaze follow his hand.

'I have no desire to do anything that might harm your daughter,' he said.

There was a beat of silence, then Nazarian stood up. 'In that case I'll show myself out,' he said abruptly.

Damien remained seated and waited as the footsteps went down the stairs. He listened for the sound of the door opening, then swinging shut. He heard someone whistling from the kitchen. Rai. Nazarian had left. He let out the breath he hadn't been aware that he was holding, and took his hand off the gun that was hidden under his book.

There was still an account outstanding for Amy, but neither of them was due to pay it today.

He waited a fortnight before he packed his car for a night's camping in the desert. He drove west out of the city towards the Tuwayq escarpment, past the place where Joe Massey had been left to bleed to death beside the road. He pitched his tent close to the rocks that were etched darkly against the night sky, and sat in the entrance to his tent, watching the stars that blazed above him in indifferent glory.

It made me think about that night in the desert. Do you remember?

Amy, why would I forget?

After all of this, do you still . . . ?

Love you? Of course.

Always.

The next morning, he packed his things away before the sun rose. No one had passed him in the night, no one had come near him. He drove along the unmade track, and took the main road through Duruma. Then he turned south towards the small town of al-Bakri.

If it seems the right thing to do, Amy had said. She had worked with the women of these villages, run the clinics, helped them with their health problems and their children's health problems, and possibly given them more discreet help when she could, as it was needed, as it was asked for. Maybe the women would help him.

The clinic was housed in a small concrete building on the edge of the town. It was staffed by a heavily veiled woman. 'I came to tell you about Amy Seymour,' he said.

'We have been informed,' the woman replied with the brusqueness that was often mistaken for impoliteness by Westerners.

'May I ask who . . . ?'

'By the English teacher,' the woman said.

The conversation was over. Damien left the building and went back to his car. *The English teacher.* There was a small school attached to the clinic where women could gain skills in basic literacy and numeracy, and for some, there were lessons in other languages as well. The English teacher . . . she could be anyone. An ex-pat. A local. A trainee from the university. Once or twice a week, the drivers brought women from the city to teach the women of the villages.

The English teacher.

Yasmin? Now she was with Nazarian, she would be able to work again.

He sat behind the wheel of his car, wondering if there was anything else he needed to do. Amy's request had been cryptic, and may have meant no more than she said.

As he sat there, watching the sharp-edged shadows move with the sun's progress, he saw the woman he had spoken to come to the door of the clinic. She stood, half in the entrance, her veiled figure merging with the blackness. In her arms, she held a baby. As Damien watched, she lifted the baby, holding him up as if she was showing him the silent square.

Damien saw the mop of chestnut hair and the dark eyes.

I looked at him and I saw Haroun looking back at me.

One day soon, Yasmin would be able to reclaim her son and take him out of the country. There was no future for them together here. He wondered how she would do it – across the causeway into Bahrain? Across the vast and barely patrolled borders where the traffickers operate? Risk the hazards of false papers and fly out? He had offered her his help, if she needed it. But she was Amy's sister. She was more resourceful than she knew.

He nodded his thanks to the woman, and put the car in gear.

54

Manly, Sydney, Australia, February 2006

The Australian summer was warm, but caused no difficulty to someone used to the extremes of Riyadh. Damien strolled along the Corso that linked the cove with the beach. The street was wide and bright, with vivid colours and signs advertising juice bars and ice cream. The people strolling past were lithe, tanned and lightly dressed.

He could see the café ahead of him. White tables filled the centre of the street, the sea with its breaking surf forming a backdrop. He could see the bright colours of the surfers as they broke through the waves.

And she was there. They'd met in one kingdom, come together briefly in another, and now they were meeting again in the far south. It was just for a few days, the fulfilment of an old promise. Their lives had gone in different directions since the last time he'd seen her in the grey of a London morning.

She was sitting at a table, turned away from him. One hand was stretched out towards . . . His feet slowed as realization grew. She was rocking a pram gently, looking out to sea, her chin resting on one hand.

Roisin.

He could see the child as he came closer. A baby with fair hair was staring at her with an unswerving gaze. As he watched, Roisin's head turned and she smiled down at the child who waved its hands and laughed in response.

To his inexpert eye, the baby looked about four or five months old. He began to do the sums, then stopped himself. If Roisin had anything to tell him, then she would. He came up behind her, interrupting her reverie. 'Roisin,' he said, leaning over to kiss her.

For a moment, the blue sea was the sea off the coast of Jeddah, and the sand was the endless desert where he and Amy had been together. It was as if he could see her, waving to him from a distant shore, as if she was telling him that somewhere in the world, there was a future.

And still the desert kingdom called him.